THE BLOOD QUEEN

A 'BHANRIGH FUIL

DAVID H. MILLAR

TITLES BY DAVID H. MILLAR

CELTIC HISTORICAL FANTASY/FICTION

Conall: The Place of Blood: Rinn-Iru

Conall II: The Raven's Flight: Eitilt an Fhiaigh Dhuibh

Conall III: The Sisters: Na Deirfiúracha

Conall IV: A Brace of Eagles: Snaidhm Iolar

Conall V: Retribution: Díoltas

The Dog Roses: Na Feirdhriseacha

The Blood Queen: A 'Bhanrìgh Fuil

The Blood Queen:
A 'Bhanrìgh Fuil
DAVID H. MILLAR

A Wee Publishing Company, LLC
HOUSTON, TX, USA
http://www.aweepublishingco.com/

Paperback ISBN: 979-8-9865756-2-9
eBook ISBN: 979-8-9865756-3-6
Library of Congress Control Number: 2023900692

A Wee Publishing Company, LLC, Houston, TX

*To Team Millar, without whom this book could
not have been written and published.*

ACKNOWLEDGEMENTS

The process of writing, publishing, and marketing novels is a team sport. It is often arduous, especially when faced with a blank page for days or weeks, and sometimes it is inspired. At all times, a good sense of humour and a bottle of Irish whiskey within reach are essential.

I am, as always, very appreciative of the international cast that comprises Team Millar. Thanks to my editors (Kahina Necaise and Naomi Munts from The History Quill/Fabled Planet), my cover designer and internal formatter, Ida Jansson, Amygdala Design, and my map illustrator, Chaim Holtjer, Stardust Book Services.

A big thank you to my beta readers: Authors Judith Fullerton, Jolie A. Reynolds, and Brendan Sullivan, and Lauren Millar. And finally, thanks to the characters who stubbornly want to tell their story, not mine.

CONTENTS

Titles by David H. Millar   *iii*

Acknowledgements   *vii*

Pronunciations   *xi*

Chapter 1   1

Chapter 2   5

Chapter 3   12

Chapter 4   21

Chapter 5   29

Chapter 6   33

Chapter 7   40

Chapter 8   51

Chapter 9   59

Chapter 10   69

Chapter 11   78

Chapter 12   83

Chapter 13   90

Chapter 14   101

Chapter 15   110

Chapter 16   118

Chapter 17   123

Chapter 19   142
Chapter 20   150
Chapter 21   159
Chapter 22   167
Chapter 23   179
Chapter 24   192
Chapter 25   202
Chapter 26   212
Chapter 27   221
Chapter 28   231
Chapter 29   243
Chapter 30   253
Chapter 31   260
Chapter 32   269
Chapter 33   288
Chapter 34   299
Chapter 35   314
Chapter 36   316
Chapter 37   319
Chapter 38   321

Background   323
Glossary   326
Dramatis Personnæ   329
Locations   331
About the Author   332
Keep in Touch   333

PRONUNCIATIONS

The world over, everyone wants to be Irish or Scottish or claim Irish or Scottish heritage. After the initial glow, probably from Guinness or whiskey (whisky in Scotland!), they are faced with the obstacle of an unpronounceable language—Gaelic, whether Irish or Scottish!

I have long maintained that Gaelic only ever sounds wonderful when sung. To my ear, normal spoken Gaelic sounds quite harsh and guttural. To increase my readers' misery, I have tended, whenever possible, to use ancient Irish/Scottish Gaelic. Also, there are inevitable regional variations of words and phrases. I have attempted in this tale to have the Irish characters use Irish Gaelic, and the Scottish characters use Scottish Gaelic. However, I hope I have limited these to add flavour to the story rather than confusion.

To ease your pain, I have provided a guide to the most frequently used character names used in the novel. I have included most family names, and if you stay with the "**bold**" first names, you will be safe!

I hope this adds to your enjoyment of the tale. One of these days, I promise to post a comprehensive pronunciation guide on my website and Facebook page. Until then, pronounce the names in the way that gives you the most pleasure. That is what I do!

One general comment on the language used. The story is written in British English.

IRISH GAELIC

Áine Ni Dedad (**AW-nya** NEE DAY-da)
Beacán Ó Cathasaigh (**B'YAG-awn** O KAS-akh)
Brighid Ni Conall (**BREED** nee-KON-ul)
Brion Ó Cathasaigh (**BREE-un** O KAS-akh)
Cassán Mac Brion (**KAS-awn** MAK BREE-un)
Conall Mac Gabhann (**KON-ul** MAK GAWN)
Cearbhall Ó Domhnaill (**KYAR-ull** O DON-al)
Danu Ni Conall (**DAH-noo** NEE KON-ul)
Fearghal Ruadh (**FER-ul** ROO-uh)
Íar Mac Dedad (**EER** MAK DAY-da)
Mongfhionn (**MUNN-yung**)
Mórrígan Ni Cathasaigh (**Moe-rig-gAHn** NEE KAS-akh)
Neamhain Ni Fearghal (**NYAV-in** NEE FER-ul)
Nuadha Ó Dubhghaill (**NOO-a** O DOO-l)
Sorchae Ni Íar (**SUR-a-ka** NEE EER)
Torcán Ó Dubhghaill (**TURK-awn** O DOO-l)
Uallachán Ó Dubhghaill (**OOL-akh-awn** O DOO-l)

SCOTTISH GAELIC

Blàr Mac Artair (**BLAWR** MAK ASH-ter)
Brandubh Mac Artair (**BRAN-doow** MAK ASH-ter)
Brianag Ni Brion (**BREE-uh-NAK** NEE BREE-un)
Carmag Mac an t-Sionnaich (**KAR-ah-mak** MAK an-CHUN-ich)
Ceana Nic Sèitheach (**KEMA** NAK SHAY-ke)
Crum Dubh (**CROM** doow)
Diadhaidh (**JE-ah-ee**)
Drostan Ruadh (**DROST-an** ROO-ag)
Dùghlas (**DOO-lus**)
Eachdonn Breac (**ISH-down** BREK)
Ealasaid Nic Finnean (**YAHL-uh-sek** NAK FIN-yan)
Eimhir Nic Finnean (**AE-veer** NAK FIN-yan)

Failbhe (**FAL-uh-vuh**)

Finnean Mac Sèitheach (**FIN-yan** MAK SHAY-ke)

Gòrdan (**GOR-dun**)

Gormal Mac Eachdonn (**GAU-rum-ul** MAK BREK)

Gràinne Ni Fearghal (**GRAN-yuh** NEE FER-ul)

Iasg (**EE-ask**)

Madadh (**MA-dugh**)

Malmhìn (**MAL-uh**-veen)

Mòrag Nic Artair (**MOR-ak** NAK ASH-ter)

Ròidh Mac Eachdonn (**ROY** mak ISH-down)

Seirbhiseach (**SHIV-er-shok**)

Seonag Nic Drostan (**SHO-nahk** NAK DROST-an)

Sidheag (**SHEE-ak**)

Sionn (**SHOONN**)

Teàrlag Nic an t-Sionnaich (**CHAR-lak** NAK an-CHUN-ich)

<u>OTHER</u>

Amodocus (Thracian)

Ares (God)

Kartimandu

Heilasa (Thracian)

Pytheas (Greek)

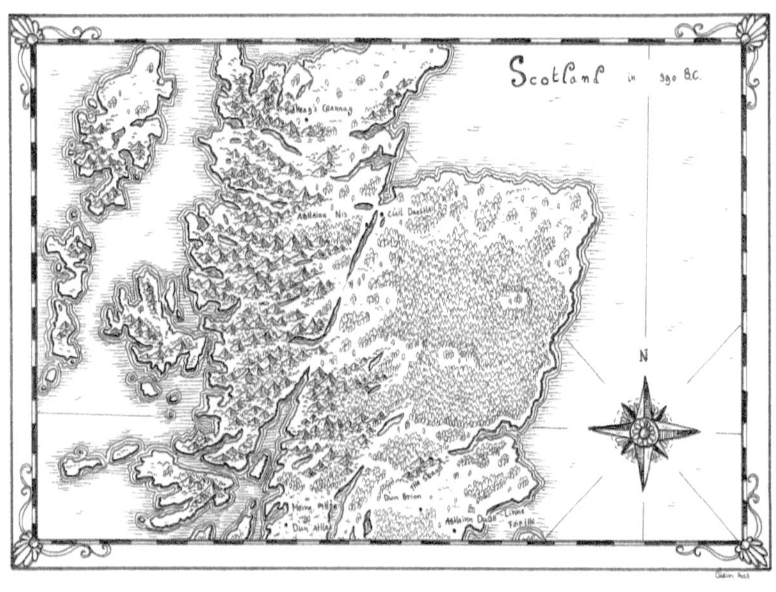

Scotland in 390 B.C.
Sulbheag's Crannag
Abhainn Nis
Cùil Dubhlair
Dun Brian
The Sheagh
Maine mhòr
Dun Atha
Abhainn Dubh
Linne
Torlith
N

CHAPTER 1

394 B.C.—Autumn

Spluttering, pitch-soaked torches spoilt the blackness of the autumn night. Splashes of red and yellow flames combined with the fragrance of pine to create a pleasant, if false, festive ambience. Across the loch's rippling waters, the sinister chanting of the Tuireadh—the Death Song of the Na Daoine Tùrsach—rang out. Such invocations had not been heard abroad in a score of summers.

The young girl looked into the eyes of the gaunt-faced man who stood before her. Her expression spoke of unconditional trust—much as a daughter looks into her father's face. He was a striking man, tall with a shock of snow-white hair and eyes that appeared violet and red in the torchlight. Yet her faith was born, not of parental love, but the blend of plants and fungi fed to her. Like her companions, she was naked, her feet were bound, and her hands were tied behind her back. She shivered uncontrollably in the chill of the autumn night.

He cupped her chin and tilted her head backwards. The act was deceptively gentle, as if he wished to let the silver moonlight bathe her face. Yet his desires were vile. Having abused her virginal body earlier, he needed to savour her terror. Her eyes widened at the sting of the blade's cold edge, drawn from one side of her neck to the other. Soft flesh parted. Helpless, she felt the throb of her lifeblood spurt from slashed arteries and warmth as the blood flowed over her adolescent breasts.

The priest turned the child slightly, allowing the surging blood to splash his nakedness. He sighed in orgasmic delight before pushing her backwards to tumble off the jetty and into the loch's icy waters. In total, the lives of nine young girls ended that night. Their eyes condemned the priests before, amid swirls of blood, their bodies slipped below the surface. Yet the thoughts of the ecclesiastics were not of guilt or regret but of anticipation of their next victims.

The High Priest smiled. The blood sacrifices began many moon cycles ago with the random slayings of young females. This night saw the beginning of a new, more deliberate phase and heralded the arrival of the promised one.

In one sense, he was right. Yet, in another, he was terribly mistaken.

* * *

On the deck of the trireme, Gràinne Ni Fearghal awoke screaming and fighting those who tried to calm and hold her down. It was an old vision, which had become more vivid with each passing night and the closer she got to her homeland in the highlands of Northern Albu.

She rubbed a hand across her neck and exhaled, relieved that only sweat wet her palm and soaked her clothes. Yet Gràinne could feel the sharp edge of the sacrificial knife wielded by her grandmother, Diadhaidh, and the satisfied look on her face as she drew it across her granddaughter's throat.

Recently, the old nightmare had changed. A new abomination stood behind Diadhaidh. Its mouth opened, revealing rows of needle-pointed teeth as it spoke: "Come, child, it is time to fulfil Diadhaidh's promise to me and take your place as *my 'Bhanrìgh Fuil—my* Blood Queen."

Brianag Ni Brion, wise beyond her years, smoothed her mother's long auburn tresses and mopped up rivulets of perspiration with a cold, damp cloth. "Hold me, Ma. You'll be all right. We'll be all right. You're safe."

Only after her mother slipped into a mercifully untroubled sleep did Brianag let the tears flow down her young cheeks.

✶✶✶

A score of summers past, lust for unlimited power drove Diadhaidh, the Blood Queen and High Priestess of the Na Daoine Tùrsach tribe, insane. Two black-shafted arrows and flames stopped Diadhaidh from sacrificing her granddaughter to the evil that lurked in the loch's depths. The missiles had been loosed by Mórrígan Ni Cathasaigh, *An Fiagaí Dorcha*—the Dark Huntress. The fire was provided by Mórrígan's hand-fast partner Conall Mac Gabhann, *Rí*—king—of the newly founded Clann Ui Flaithimh.

Ironically, Mórrígan's arrows pinned Diadhaidh to the same sacrificial post to which she had bound Gràinne. Fire devoured the Blood Queen and the royal *crannag*, burning the wooden edifice down to its pilings. The wind had scattered the building's ashes across the loch's surface by the next sunrise.

Among the people of the north-eastern highlands, the fiery glow in the night skies prompted heartfelt sighs of relief and an outpouring of thanks to the Goddess. Those of the Na Daoine Tùrsach's priests and acolytes who survived the final battle fled into the high mountains. They were hunted down and executed with a grim resolution by Drostan Ruadh, the one-eyed *rìgh*—king—of the Forest People, and Blàr Mac Artair, Rìgh of the Ravens.

Yet true evil is a persistent and tenacious beast, and its desire for existence is eternal and insatiable. It needs to infect but one mind for its insidious philosophy to take root and spread. By all accounts, Blàr and Drostan did an excellent job. Yet a handful of priests survived, which proved enough to restart the cycle.

In the eddies of the sacrificed's blood, an amorphous shape began to take corporeal form. At the mercy of the loch's currents, it drifted without direction. With blood came sentience, rage, and an all-consuming desire for the crimson liquid that sustained life. Its mind gradually re-formed; the evil ceased its dependence on being fed and began to rely on native cunning and an instinct for survival. It began to hunt.

A plan formed that did not distinguish between animal and human or age and sex. The latter was a human obsession. It would feed on all living creatures until strong enough to enjoy a more discriminating palate. As for the waste of young females, that would change.

CHAPTER 2

A lone and lonely man paced the stone ramparts of Dùn Brion. He looked up at the full moon and sighed. Instinctively, he attempted to scratch his left arm and then swore—quite loudly. The limb had been severed a long time ago after a chariot accident. Yet the memory and pain of the vehicle's wheel crushing flesh and bone remained seared into his thoughts. Over and over, he saw Gràinne's longsword flash in the moonlight and felt her tears splash his face as she cleaved the useless appendage.

Brion Ó Cathasaigh, Rìgh of Dùn Brion, held no rancour for Gràinne. She had saved his life, if not his arm. Both had been young and rash. At the time, he had assigned no blame for the tragedy, and nothing had changed that perspective. Brion tugged at his short beard and again pondered the reports that he was the father of Gràinne's daughter. *Why am I thinking about this now?* It was old news delivered by Drostan a decade of summers ago.

That he had a daughter was barely believable. He and Gràinne had rutted just once. She had straddled and rode him to a climax in a bout of remorse over the accident. Brion smiled crookedly. Gràinne had always been generous with her favours. By the time he had recovered, she had chosen to join Conall's quest, and he had accepted Drostan's proposal to lead the Na Mèadaidh.

He wondered if they would ever meet again. What was his daughter like? Why had he never visited her? There were many opportunities to accompany Drostan on his regular visits to meet Conall in Gaul? Brion's thoughts abruptly turned to his wastrel son, Cassán. His jaw tightened, and he spat over the wall. The answer stared him in the face. *I'm an awful father.*

The sound of drunken revelry drifted up from the yard and was quickly followed by cries of female protest—some faux, some genuine. Brion spat again in disgust. The antics of Cassán and the band of hangers-on who trailed in his path angered him.

As a child, Cassán had been coddled by his beautiful but flawed mother, Áine. In the aftermath of the tragic demise of the murderous *bitseach*, when Brion looked at Cassán, he saw Áine. Apart from fatherhood, which proved insufficient, he had shared little in common with Cassán as a child. As the boy grew into manhood, Brion lacked the motivation, and perhaps the compassion, to find mutual ground. Father and son retreated into bitterness.

Brion tolerated his son's boorish behaviour, taking the path of least resistance. For his part, Cassán took his father's disinterest and lack of rebuke as tacit approval. Brion had persuaded himself that, as a rìgh, he had more important matters that required his attention. It was procrastination, and, in periods of honesty, Brion knew it. He deeply regretted his lack of action, yet the time for discipline and correction had long passed.

"Shite!" muttered Brion and walked to the steps that lead down to the courtyard.

A tall figure emerged from her observation place and followed a discreet distance behind him. Advisor, battle commander, and protector, Seonag never strayed far from Brion's side. Seonag sighed, mirroring the king. He was a good man and rìgh and loved his adopted people. Yet he was weak in several areas. She shrugged. *Is any man or woman perfect?*

***

"You must do something about *him*. His behaviour cannot be allowed to continue." Seonag paced the small chamber. Her face flushed red in anger as she looked at the pregnant girl. Not more than fifteen summers, the young woman sat, head bowed. Alternately, she caressed her belly as if seeking comfort from the baby she carried or twisted her fingers in anguish. Tears flowed from eyes that had obviously been blackened. The kick marks and bruising on her arms and legs likely spread under her torn, knee-length *léine*.

"Just because she's only a serving girl doesn't mean she has no value and can be used and thrown aside." Seonag glared at Brion. "Are you hoping that, after Cassán's night of drinking and whoring, a brother or father will seek justice and, in a dark corner, slip a knife between his ribs? Then you can mourn and be free of the burden of fatherhood."

Anger flared in Brion's eyes but quickly subsided with a shrug of resignation. "That's unfair. What can I do? He's my son and is easily led by his friends. He's not totally bad." Brion knew his response was feeble, embarrassing, and overused.

"No!" snapped Seonag. "*He* is the leader of his friends. *He* chose them. *He* is responsible for their actions." Seonag looked at the girl. "She did not and does not demand recognition for the baby. All she asks is for a little support for the wee'un. All she wants is food for the child and her."

"Do we know who actually assaulted her?"

"Besides Cassán? They obviously tore her clothes off and took turns violating the girl. Nothing different from the many times they've done this before. Even her being obviously pregnant didn't stop them." Sobs from the girl reminded Seonag of her presence. "I'm sorry."

Seonag exhaled in disappointment. Most acknowledged that Brion ruled with a strong and just hand. None considered him a parental role model. Any sympathy the people may have had for Brion or Cassán following the tragedy of Áine had long since dissipated. Cassán had grown from a child spoilt by his mother into one ignored by his father.

"If she confirms it was Cassán, I'll punish him." Seonag rolled her eyes. "I promise."

"You know she won't. The girl is terrified of what Cassán and his friends will do to her. She knows she'll end up in the fort's ditch with her throat cut—if she's lucky. The lass is braver than most of Cassán's victims for sitting before you."

"What do you want me to do?"

"Be a king. Dispense justice to *all* your subjects—and that includes her."

Brion growled. Few dared to speak to him like Seonag. Yet his garrison commander held a special place in his heart, and there was none better at leading his warriors or guarding his back. He cursed the oath sworn to her father to provide sanctuary and protect her and the bargain agreed upon. Seonag had been just thirteen summers, and he almost thirty. She had been a daughter to him, and he loved her.

When Seonag blossomed into a beautiful, young woman and a fierce warrior, it became impossible to ignore the increase in his heartbeat when she passed by, or the desire in his loins. Brion repeatedly cursed the oath that honour would not allow him to break and the man who demanded it. He wondered if Seonag knew of his desire and, if she did, whether he would be rejected. Brion snorted. *I'm too old for her.* Then he shrugged. *Just more excuses.*

"Well?"

The irritation in Seonag's voice drew Brion from his reflections. "Choose two of Cassán's followers, preferably those closest to him. Detain, flog, and question them. Threaten them with banishment. If they agree with the girl's story, I'll take action against Cassán."

Brion turned to face the young girl, who was little more than a child. She flinched under his stern gaze. "I am sorry for what has befallen you. However, you were raped by many, and it will be difficult to determine who might be the father. Even when the child is born, looks may not give a definitive answer."

The girl started to sob again, and her chest convulsed. Brion placed his hand gently on her head, and the cries became snuffles. "I will not see you destitute. Seonag will take you to the druids with orders that you should be cared for. You will not want for clothes, food, or shelter. Come to me when the child is born, and we shall discuss the future."

Seonag pushed several strands of blonde hair from her face as the girl left the chamber. She looked at Brion and shook her head. Most acknowledged that, on balance, Brion was a better king than most. Yet often, his head fought against his heart, and that weakness could get him killed.

∗∗∗

Cassán Mac Brion rose at *máen-lae*—midday. His head thumped from too much wine and beer, and his nose wrinkled at the smell of stale drink, vomit, and urine from an overturned pot. As he pushed the furs aside from his cot, he shivered. *Why hasn't anyone lit my fire?* He grunted as he sat up, grimaced at the piss-sodden straw, and cursed the additional bruises on his torso.

Someone had given him a severe beating. He should make a report, but what would be the point? He and his friends preferred the dark alleys and shadows to provide entertainment and victims, which came with risks. No one in Dùn Brion or the outlying communities sympathised with him. Most would have applauded, if not helped, his assailants. *Why do they hate me?*

He felt the back of his head and flinched at the egg-sized lump. It would have been easy for his attackers to kill him. Why didn't they? Likely it was out of fear of his father's retribution. Cassán ground his teeth. None feared him or his friends, but they were afraid of his father. "Father! When have you ever been a father to me? I am not my mother. Yet when you look at me, you only see her."

What have you done to change his mind, to make him respect you?

The uncomfortable thought startled Cassán, and he tried to push it out of his head, but it persisted. It would linger until he was full of beer. He reached for a half-drunk jug of stale beer, raised it to his lips, took a gulp, and spat the liquid out. With a snarl, he threw the vessel across the room, where it smashed into pieces against the stone wall. Gripping the rim of the basin on the side table, Cassán dunked his head into the cold water. He needed time to think and to change. He longed for a real father.

Maybe it's not too late.

Cassán gruffly brushed past the guards outside his room and barked, "Have the servants clean my room and light the bloody fire."

The sentries rolled their eyes at his receding back, and one mumbled, "That one will never change until the worms are feasting on his corpse."

Exiting his quarters in the Great Hall, Cassán shielded his eyes from the bright autumn sun. He hoped for solitude but found a score of his friends waiting, eager to begin the day's mischief and debauchery. Most did not like Cassán but tolerated him. Being part of the *prionnsa's*—prince's—retinue gave them a license for deplorable behaviour. Arms around his shoulder, they dragged him across the square.

A bellow from Gòrdan, Seonag's captain and Cassán's shield-man, boomed out. "Cassán Mac Brion, you have duties to perform. Saddle your horse. The warband is waiting."

✳✳✳

Seonag watched as a reluctant Cassán was dragged away by Gòrdan and made to mount his horse. She smiled. The grizzled captain took no nonsense from Brion's son and faithfully tried to make him into a warrior. He was the closest thing the young man had to a father.

Seonag's memory of her father was nebulous. She imagined a giant, one-eyed warrior kneeling before her at the gates of Dùn Brion. She felt his embrace and heard him tell her she would be safe. She still saw the great tears rolling down his ruddy cheek as she turned her back and walked into Brion's embrace.

Yet the relationship between father and daughter was already weak. At the age of eight, she and her brother were put into the care of her father's brother, the druid leader, Crum Dubh. The druid explained that she was in great danger from her father's and mother's enemies. That she needed protection.

Yet Crum could not protect her from an unexpected adversary. Seonag chuckled as the memory became clearer. With the connivance of the Goddess, Serendipity allowed her to be captured by Conall. Later she was used to forge peace between the Forest People and Clann Ui Flaithimh. Alongside Conall had stood a much younger Brion.

She doubted that Brion remembered her from that time. Since then, Seonag's father and mother had become dim memories interspersed with moments of clarity. Brion had become a father to her—until recently. She had observed her father when he attended meetings in Dùn Brion. Still, there was little eye contact between the two, only glimmers of wistful regret.

CHAPTER 3

Under the watchful eye of the senior helmsman, three triremes glided past the headland fort guarding the estuary's upper reaches. It was not a notable achievement. The river mouth was vast; the water depth and the absence of sandbanks meant his fleet could safely navigate a midstream path. The sailor, his face weather-beaten by sea and sun, was well-acquainted with the currents and coastline from years of trading with its many fishing communities and hillforts.

He shook his head and sighed as he watched tiny figures emerge from *brochs*—stone towers—and the smaller *dùin*—forts. Likely they would track the ships to determine their destination. The territory had a long history of raiders, brigands, and slavers. The helmsman grunted as he rubbed a thin layer of early frost from the ship's cable. The same could be said for most of this cold, wet land of painted barbarians.

A cough made him turn around, and he looked into a face of swirling dark-blue sigils on a pale-green canvas. The sailor smiled, causing deep crevices to appear in the leathered skin. *She's a formidable warrior but never a sailor.* "We'll be at our destination shortly," he said, anticipating Gràinne's question.

The undisguised relief in Gràinne's expression once again turned up the corners of the helmsman's mouth, exposing uneven teeth. Not long after, he watched the triremes disgorge their passengers and cargo onto a rickety, wooden jetty. He mused that any misguided outlaw or warband chieftain seeking an easy prey to steal from or the weak to enslave was in for a shock.

"Serve the bastards right," he muttered.

***

Sheltered under the canopy of the ancient forest, Brianag shivered and wondered if her clothes would ever be dry again. She looked from the wall of rain to her ma and repeated the process a handful of times. At fourteen summers of age, she did it with an air of martyrdom that comes naturally to adolescents of all races and tribes. "You uprooted me from my friends and Southern Gaul's sun and blue skies for *this*. The Hag! Is that hail?"

With barely a pause for breath, Brianag looked pointedly at her ma's belly and then at the wet nurse who held her happily suckling sister, Heilasa. "And they say my generation is irresponsible. When will you learn to keep your knees together?" Gathering steam, she added with a practised roll of her eyes, "Or at least use common sense when choosing a rutting partner."

Gràinne looked upwards. Only the Goddess knew whether she prayed for divine intervention or forgiveness should she strangle her offspring. Whatever happened to the charming, thoughtful child who favoured her father's temperament? "It seems my daughter loves sea journeys as much as I do," she said. Gràinne's chariot driver chuckled and played with the reins to keep the vehicle steady. Like wind chimes, the musical clinking of the horses' tack soothed Gràinne.

Still, Gràinne had to admit that Brianag had a point. In Northern Albu, autumn was little more than the harbinger of winter. Rain, sometimes fortified with ice, had greeted them on their arrival and had been a constant companion since they disembarked. Thus, Gràinne found it hard to disagree with her daughter's judgment on the inclement weather.

Yet Brianag needed to respect her ma, so Gràinne growled, "Get used to it. Remember, it was *you* who wanted to visit your da. One more word, and I'll tie a rock around your neck and throw you into the nearest loch." This time it was the wet nurse who rolled her eyes. That said, Gràinne found her words unconvincing. Had she used Brianag's natural curiosity to meet her da as a ruse to find answers to the awful portents in her visions?

"Cearbhall's scouts report that a *dùn* is less than a sunset's walk from here. There we'll find dry accommodation and welcoming fires," said Gràinne in what she hoped was a calm and reassuring motherly tone.

"How do you know it's my da's fort? You haven't seen him for fifteen summers, and I've never seen him. *Rithe*—kings—are rarely long-lived." This time a tremble of potential disappointment slipped into Brianag's voice. Gràinne placed her hands on Brianag's slender shoulders, squeezed gently, and looked into her eyes.

"Your da is a brave and clever man. I'm sure he lives. Plus, he has the support of Drostan Ruadh, the most powerful rí in Northern Albu and an extremely hard man to kill. You saw Drostan a few times when we visited Massalia. He certainly would have mentioned if your father had passed beyond the veil."

Brianag thought for a moment before speaking. "But how do you know *we'll* be welcome? Didn't my da lose an arm because of you?"

Gràinne grimaced at a memory dredged up. "I felt guilty about the accident for a long time, but Brion refused to allow me to accept all the blame. We were young and stupid." Gràinne paused. "Your da's a good man, Brianag." At that, Gràinne fell silent.

✳✳✳

The warband leader was young, no more than a score of summers, tall, well-muscled, and passably handsome. He had tracked his prey since the last sunrise and had a decision to make. Should he attack or disappear back into the forest? He well knew the risks. His band were outnumbered four to one, and their target looked well organised.

Could his warriors snatch a few wagons and cut out a portion of the horses? The mounts were fine animals. In fact, they were the best he had ever seen and would fetch a high price. Perhaps he should just focus on them. His band's inevitable retreat would be slowed by the wagons but not the ponies.

The young man sighed in resignation. His warriors would not be happy if they returned to his father's dùn with no plunder, and he would be mocked mercilessly by his older brothers. He nodded to his shield-man, and the warband spread out and moved towards the camp.

✷✷✷

"You know we're being watched?" Cearbhall, the more senior of Gràinne's two *ceannairí céad*—leaders of one hundred—spoke. Two ceannairí céad accompanied Gràinne: one for the shield warriors and the other for the cavalry. "It will be a pity to kill them. Their leader shows more promise than most."

"Do we have to kill them?" It saddened Gràinne that her first act in her homeland would be to bring death.

"They know the risks, and we can't afford to lose warriors this early in our stay." Cearbhall sighed. "On another day with a different quarry, they might have been successful."

"How do you want us?"

"The chariots are useless in a close forest skirmish. Circle them with drivers and warriors armed and standing in the *creta*—baskets. Your daughter, the wee'un, and the wet nurse should stand in the centre. I'll take care of the rest." Before striding over to his men, Cearbhall chuckled and pointed to Brianag. "I don't envy you trying to restrain her from the fight."

✷✷✷

The young chieftain cursed. How could he be expected to think of everything? Shrieks of pain rang out as his men were snared by simple traps. Forearm-deep holes planted with short, sharpened stakes snapped ankles and lower legs. Having breathed easy at surviving the first line, they found the second two paces later. *What bastard plants two perimeter rings of snares?*

Cearbhall shouted, "Javelins!" The traps had done their job of slowing the attack and reducing the enemy's fighting numbers. The volley of one hundred *sleaghan*—spears—ensured there would be no other assault. In the forest clearing, the shrieking soon subsided to the moans and whimpering

15

of the soon-to-die.

"Deliver the wounded to Mag Mell. Strip the bodies of any valuables and behead them. The forest can feed on their flesh," ordered Cearbhall.

Moans on Cearbhall's right caught his attention, and he walked to stand over the warband's leader. A javelin pinned the young man's thigh to a fallen tree. A finger's breadth doomed the young man. Had the throwing spear's arm's-length iron spike not sliced through an artery, the wound would not have been mortal. Gore pumped out rhythmically, seeping into the forest floor.

"Blood loss would have killed you," said Cearbhall as his blade rose high and chopped down. It took another slash to cleave the chieftain's head from the torso, but the young warrior did not care. He was already feasting in Mag Mell.

***

"This is not a task fit for a *prionnsa*—prince—and the son of Dùn Brion's *rí*," whined Cassán. The assertion was aimed at no one in particular. Rather, its purpose was to engender sympathy from the pack of sycophants who accompanied him. As judged by the inevitable round of arse-licking comments, Cassán achieved a measure of success.

"It is precisely because you are the son of Brion that your father has commanded you to undertake this duty." Cassán's shield-man, the veteran named Gòrdan, considered his next words carefully. "One day, you may be Rìgh of Dùn Brion and have to defend the kingdom." The expected explosion of fury to Gòrdan's slight was predictable.

"*May* be? *May* be?"

Cassán's face flushed purple. For a moment, Gòrdan thought he may have pushed the prince too far. "I *will* be rìgh, and my first order will be your execution."

The veteran turned his back so Cassán could not see his frustration. He wondered if he should provoke the prionnsa more but shook his head. What was the point? He always hoped for fire and steel, but Cassán never failed to disappoint. What would it take for the boy to fight?

As if by a whimsy of the Goddess, Gòrdan's thoughts of clashing steel became a reality, although not from Cassán. From the forest, beyond the open ground, came the clank of iron and shrieks of men about to die. "Shite!" he muttered. His command was not prepared for a battle.

"Order them to surrender or die," said Cassán as the forest fell silent.

Gòrdan, appointed as Cassán's protector by his father, raised an eyebrow at the imperious command and gave Cassán a look that said, *Are you serious?* Infuriated at what he deemed a lack of respect, Cassán spat, *"Do it!"*

"Do you have any idea of what life is like outside of Dùn Brion? There are hundreds of dùin and brochs, many of which are inhabited by members of the same clann. An army can be raised with the blast of a horn. We don't know how many are in the forest—fifty, five hundred, or five thousand. Do you really want to poke the bear in its den?"

"Just do it," snapped Cassán, correctly assuming his mettle had been questioned.

With a shrug, Gòrdan turned to another carrying a war horn. "Announce us." A deep *barr-ewww* sounded across the clearing that edged the forest beyond.

"I said to order them to surrender, not warn them of our presence," yelled Cassán.

"We have one hundred warriors on foot and, for the most part, lightly armed." Gòrdan looked at the dozen hangers-on and said, "Certainly, your companions will be no use. As your father commanded, this is a reconnaissance patrol, not a warband for fighting. I will do all in my power to protect you—even from yourself."

"Coward!" said Cassán and walked his horse forward several paces. In a voice that barely carried to the forest and cracked midway through his rhetoric, Cassán spluttered, "Reveal yourselves and surrender. This is the domain of Rìgh Brion Ó Cathasaigh. I am his son and speak with his authority."

* * *

Brianag tugged on her ma's arm. "Is that…"

Gràinne nodded. "It's not exactly how I envisaged our first meeting, but yes, that appears to be your half-brother."

Thankful that the rain had finally paused, Brianag walked her mount closer to the forest edge and peered at the figure sitting astride a dapple grey.

"You mean that fat arsehole is my da's son? I hope I take after you."

Barely able to contain the grin that threatened to overwhelm her sober mask, Gràinne dipped her head and then turned to Cearbhall. "We, of course, will not surrender." The veteran smiled at Gràinne's next words. "However, I would prefer not to announce my presence in the rí's lands by slaughtering his men… or his son. Impress on the young man that his demand is foolish."

Gràinne turned to Brianag and the wet nurse. "Go to the rear. Stay in the forest until I summon you." As Brianag's lips parted, a stern Gràinne said, "I will not tolerate disobedience."

✶✶✶

Cassán turned to Gòrdan and smirked haughtily. His mien shouted, *"I told you!"* Both men watched three gaily coloured chariots, banners flapping in the wind, emerge from the forest line and stop one hundred paces away. About to triumphantly march his force forward, Cassán was abruptly stopped by the firm grip on his arm and shake of the veteran's head.

A horn sounded in the forest, and they watched one hundred heavily armed and armoured warriors march from the woods. They halted in a relaxed formation five paces behind the chariots. Each carried an oblong, waisted, red *sgiath* with a swooping black raven, and each hefted a javelin. To Gòrdan, the warning could not have been more unambiguous.

"We match their numbers," said Cassán and added, to the applause of his friends, "And we are better warriors." The shield-man's shake of his head only increased his charge's anger.

"Watch and learn," snapped Gòrdan.

Hunting horns sounded deep in the forest, and one hundred horses exited the treeline at a fast canter. Dividing into two, the mounted force came to a halt with fifty mounts guarding each flank of the shield-warriors. Each rider carried a small oblong shield and a javelin. The purpose of the cavalry and shield warriors was plain. Cassán's force would be decimated by missiles before they got close, and none could outrun a horse or chariot.

Aghast, beads of sweat formed on Cassán's brow and the blood drained from his face. Gòrdan thought he would faint and tumble from the grey's back. "Take a look at the chariots' wheels," hissed Gòrdan. "They are prepared for battle. Do you still think we outnumber them or are superior warriors?" More colour drained from Cassán's visage at the sight of the long, bronze knives attached to each wheel. He felt his *dil-lat* wet, and the pungent smell of piss entered his nostrils. Humiliated, he scowled at Gòrdan.

"Perhaps you will allow me to negotiate terms," said Gòrdan. He added, "Or *our* surrender." Without waiting for a response, Gòrdan walked his horse forward.

✶✶✶

"I am Gòrdan of the Na Mèadaidh, shield-man to Cassán Mac Brion. I apologise for our welcome. We were not expecting visitors, and there has recently been an upturn in warband raids. By the bloodstains, I see you have experienced this already." Gòrdan dipped his head and nodded to Cassán. Smiling, he said, "Thus, my prionnsa erred on the side of caution.

"Perhaps you would identify yourself and tell me why such a well-armed and disciplined force journeys through my rìgh's lands." As he spoke, Gòrdan's eyes unapologetically inspected the force before him. Something scratched at his mind. The red-and-black shields and the banners flapping on the chariots seemed familiar.

Gràinne smiled graciously, for she liked Gòrdan's demeanour. "Congratulations on the diplomatic retreat. For my part, announcing my presence with a fight would be folly. Especially since it would not have turned out well—*for you.*" A grin perched on Gràinne's lips. "Perhaps you would indulge me for a moment."

As Gràinne spoke, Gòrdan tried to put a place to the young woman's accent and curling designs. He dipped his head, and Gràinne turned around in the chariot, put two fingers to her mouth, and whistled loudly.

From the forest, a tall, golden-tan dun with black points and tail trotted forward and came to a halt slightly to the rear of the chariot. "Did we really need the blades, Ma?" scolded Brianag, before giving Gòrdan a disarming smile. He took in the girl before him, judging that she could be no more than fourteen or fifteen summers. Yet what took him aback was that she and her mount were as heavily armoured as the rest of the riders. That and she reminded him of someone.

"My daughter lacks some of the social niceties. I'm hoping that her father can educate her on that."

"Her father?" asked Gòrdan with an increasing sense of unease.

"Yes, may I present Brianag Ni Brion, the daughter of Brion Ó Cathasaigh, Rìgh of Na Mèadaidh? I am her mother, Gràinne Ni Fearghal of Clann Ui Flaithimh. I am also the Bhanrìgh of the Na Daoine Tùrsach." To Gràinne, her last words sounded like an admission of guilt rather than pride. She used the title with great reluctance.

"Shite!"

Gòrdan turned around on his dillat. For once, he was grateful that Cassán, having tired of the tableau, had taken his cronies, and departed.

CHAPTER 4

The mist briefly cleared, encouraging a timid sun to peek out from under its soft blanket of clouds. Perhaps the Goddess connived with nature to show the stronghold of Dùn Brion in a favourable light. Only a fool would deny Dùn Brion's strategic position. Perched on a rocky crag, which sat atop a high hill, the fort had steep bluffs to its northern, eastern, and western sides.

Dùn Brion dominated the Abhainn Dubh river valley and plain where the high- and lowlands met and cast its shadow over the downstream river crossing. Even the dense pine and oak forests swathing most of Northern Albu stepped back from the escarpment. Hence, the fort's sightlines were long, and its killing grounds gave scant cover to would-be attackers.

As they climbed the gentle incline of the long southern slope, Gràinne turned to Brianag. "I told you your da was clever. This is a much better location than the old Dùn Na Mèadaidh."

The party finally arrived at the gates of the austere stone hillfort, having crossed three lines of high earthen ramparts fronted with deep ditches. Brianag nudged her ma. "They must do a lot of fighting here to need such defences."

Trotting alongside Gràinne's war chariot, the scythes having been removed, Gòrdan laughed. "Your daughter is observant and, unfortunately, correct. Our location means that attacks come from tribes in the north and south and from a multitude of warbands led by ambitious young chieftains seeking wealth, lands, and power. Peace across Northern Albu is a future hope."

Hidden from the travellers, behind the gateway's walls, brawny men grunted and strained to slide heavy wooden locking bars from recesses in the rock and open the fort's great oak gates. Dùn Brion lacked curves to soften its appearance, and perhaps that was deliberate. Yet the stronghold was elegant in its angular simplicity.

Gràinne looked up at utilitarian, towering walls, all the thickness of two throwing spears. Dùn Brion presented a daunting challenge to would-be besiegers. Two-storey, square guard posts jutted from each corner, and two more were placed on either side of the main entranceway. In each tower, squads of hard-faced men and women stared down at the visitors.

Inside its walls, a huge, two-storey rectangular broch with a steeply sloping thatched roof dominated the spacious dirt yard. The building had one primary entrance. Its exterior walls were broken by strategically po-sitioned narrow slots to survey the courtyard. Gràinne's mien spoke of disappointment that her homeland had not progressed from when she had departed with Conall. She shrugged her shoulders, dismissing her musings. No matter the age, clanns and tribes would always fight for dominance. "A great place for a last stand," she muttered.

"Thank the Goddess, it has not come to that," said Gòrdan. His arm swept in a semicircle to describe the yard. "Apart from quarters for the garrison and their families, plus essential trades, the civilian population lives outside the fort in small neighbouring villages and farmsteads. In an attack, they can be moved inside the walls quickly. Most sons and daughters over thirteen summers are given basic weapons training." He chuckled. "It's a nasty shock for raiders looking for easy prey."

Gòrdan rubbed a stubbled chin. In this, he was an oddity. Most men in Dùn Brion sported long hair, bushy beards, and great whiskers. "Together with your personal guard, you will be accommodated in the broch. The rest of your party will lodge in the garrison's quarters." The veteran laughed.

"I'd be surprised if any will be short of company, male or female, for long. New faces are always welcomed with open arms… and thighs."

Gòrdan glanced at a smirking Brianag, said, "Sorry," to Gràinne, then scratched a mop of short, curly, red hair. "The challenge will be the several hundred horses that travel with you. We only have a small stable in the fort." The veteran shrugged. "Leave it with me. There is no shortage of timber and muscles to erect suitable shelters."

Gràinne was of above-average height and well-muscled, if lithe. That said, even a cursory glance would reveal the ample endowment of her upper torso. Yet the warrior who appeared at Gòrdan's side was a head taller than Gràinne. Long, lustrous blonde tresses, which held copper tones, were woven into three thick plaits. She whispered in Gòrdan's ear, and he nodded.

"It appears that the rìgh would like to meet you on the ramparts," Gòrdan chuckled. "Probably to show off his kingdom." He nodded to the female warrior. "This is Seonag. Ignore her perpetually fierce mien. As the rìgh's protector and commander of his army, she thinks her duty includes intimidating everyone."

Gràinne's gold-flecked eyes narrowed, and she smiled at Seonag. "Fortunately, I'm not easily intimidated." A tug on her hand caused Gràinne to turn to Brianag.

"Please, ma. No fighting. We're guests," whispered Brianag.

The growl from deep within her ma did not settle Brianag's concerns but did raise a glimmer of a smile from Seonag.

★★★

A disconcerted Cassán watched the quartet walk across the yard and muttered, "Bastard! Traitor!" The object of his ire was Gòrdan, who had walked away from the small group. Belatedly, Cassán realised his premature departure from the forest confrontation had put him at a disadvantage.

"This changes things in Dùn Brion and possibly the kingdom." The speaker was the eldest of Cassán's retinue, who saw himself as the prionnsa's counsellor. Like the others in Cassán's entourage, he was neither a friend nor loyal, viewing the prince as a means to garner wealth and lands. At twenty-five summers old and having been cloistered in the fort for most of his life, his experience was as limited as Cassán's. Hence, he lived by a silk tongue and whispering in ears primed to hear gossip and rumour.

"What do you mean?" asked Cassán.

The man pointed to Brianag. "*She* is Brion's daughter. Her ma is the Bhanrìgh of the Na Daoine Tùrsach and is rumoured to be his lover. Hence both mother and daughter have royal bloodlines."

Cassán shook his head. Patience and assimilating information quickly had never been his strength. "Get to the point."

"The mother would make a suitable and beautiful queen of the Na Mèadaidh. Fort gossip has it that she is also a fierce warrior. Consolidating the two kingdoms would make your father much more powerful. Furthermore, Drostan would see the union as a means of controlling the dark beliefs of the Na Daoine Tùrsach."

The man paused and held Cassán's gaze before speaking again. "According to the law, a rìgh can name his successor, and it doesn't need to be a male or even the eldest. Thus, mother and daughter are an attractive package as queen and heiress." The man stood in front of Cassán. "*You* need to tread a careful path. Don't do anything foolish. Uncertain times lie ahead." It was the first time the young man had given good counsel.

As Brianag mounted the first step to the ramparts, she turned and saw Cassán watching her. Not one to hold a grudge or rely too much on first impressions, she smiled broadly and waved. For Brianag, it was merely a friendly gesture. Cassán scowled, interpreting the greeting as the *bitseach*— bitch—taunting him.

✶✶✶

With his right hand, Brion grasped the stone of the waist-high wall that edged Dùn Brion's ramparts. The surface felt rough but comforting against the calloused palm of his hand. He straightened his shoulders and adjusted the thick wolf fur draped across them. No matter the season, it was always windy and cold on the parapet. "At least it's not raining," he muttered. As

Brion gazed eastward, seeking comfort in the green landscape, his mind roiled with conflicting emotions of fear and joy.

He had never seen Brianag and only knew of her from reports carried by Drostan on his return from trips to Conall's kingdom in Gaul. Brion smiled. The two, once enemies, were an odd couple but, along with the Greek merchant, Pytheas, had nurtured a successful business partnership. That their kingdoms were oceans apart avoided the covetousness and rivalry that often plagued powerful rìghrean.

It was Brion's fault that he had never met Brianag. Drostan had long tried to persuade Brion to join the trading partnership. *After this visit, I should enquire if the offer still stands.* He missed his sister, Mórrígan, his brothers, and old friends like Conall. Brion grieved for missed conversations with those who had passed beyond the veil. Absence did not increase affection but did make the pain ache more. He scratched the long scar on his left cheek. To any who knew him, the stark, white ridge was the surest sign of the rìgh's turmoil.

Brion had never ceased wanting to meet his daughter. Yet this was an ominous time for a visit. Northern Albu was a tinderbox, needing only a little kindling to start a raging fire. Typical of Gràinne's impulsive nature, there had been no warning of her visit. Yet she and Brianag lived a world away, so attributing blame was undeserved. Perhaps, like deciding to take a hand-fast partner or have children, the perfect time did not exist.

The perpetual raiding and mischief-making of Gormal, Rìgh of Dùn Athad, needed resolution, likely by war. Worse, reports of savage blood sacrifices in the north-eastern highlands were growing. All were centred on the Na Daoine Tùrsach, a tribe whose history was stained with blood. Brion wondered how Drostan would view the appearance of the tribe's rightful bhanrigh. *I doubt Drostan will be happy.* Brion groaned and exhaled a great sigh.

"I had hoped our visit would bring laughter and tears of joy—not groans and sad sighs?"

Brion turned and smiled. Gràinne's soft burr prompted a flood of long-forgotten memories. That it seemed to have acquired highlights of other accents only added to its richness. Blessed by the sun of the Great Sea, her skin glowed. Gràinne looked more beautiful than his dreams remembered.

Brion faced his former… what? One rutting a long time ago hardly made them lovers, despite the gossip. Suddenly uncertain what to do or say, he stood open-mouthed. His dilemma was resolved as Gràinne hurled herself at him, kissed him, and held him in an embrace, the strength of which belied her slim body. "There, I've made it easy for you. Your daughter awaits and is much more nervous than you."

Released from Gràinne's hug, Brion looked uncertainly at Brianag and gave what he hoped was a fatherly smile. Then he shook his head, dropped to one knee, held out his hand, and said, "Brianag."

The heartfelt cry of "Da!" was heard by all in the dùn. The sober greyness of Dùn Brion was overwhelmed by the smiles and tears of joy of a father united with his daughter. The cry of an infant demanding to be fed interrupted the reunion. Still holding his daughter, Brion stood and looked at Gràinne, a single eyebrow lifted questioningly. At a tug on his hand, he looked at Brianag. "That's my baby sister, Heilasa. It's a Thracian name." She looked to Gràinne, an impish smile on her face, and said, "Ma will explain."

"Dùn Brion? You're a bit full of yourself," said Gràinne hoping to divert the conversation.

Brion raised his hand and grinned crookedly. "It was neither my idea nor my fault. Dùn Brion was the working name while the fort was built, and it stuck. Simple and no-frills, it suits the people of the area and doesn't have the connotations or history associated with Dùn Na Mèadaidh."

"What of the old fort?"

"We burned it, broke its walls, and scattered the rubble across the Sleagh mountain range. Nothing of it was used in the construction of Dùn Brion. Too much of Finnean Mac Sèitheach's evil was associated with that fort. I couldn't take the risk." Brion shook his head. "That whole family—Finnean, his sister Ceana, and her son, Ròidh—were twisted and evil. They deserved their fate at the hands of Conall and Mórrígan."

Brion rubbed his chin. "Then there's Gormal. Ceana was his mother. Thus, Sèitheach blood flows through his veins, and that's part of his animosity towards Dùn Brion and me."

Gràinne frowned. "Evil is always with us. By now, your nieces, Brighid and Danu, will have landed in southern Ériu to put down a rebellion by Uallachán and his brother, Nuadha."

"The Hag's arse! Does it never end?" Brion shook his head in disbelief.

Gràinne felt the spider's web of fine scars from Diadhaidh's scourgings and the swirling dark tribal sigils covering her body suddenly writhe. She inhaled sharply to assert some control. Gràinne knew its cause was a sudden flash of the face of the new abomination that haunted her dreams. This time, its appearance seemed less blurred.

She glanced at Brion and Brianag, who had begun an animated conversation, and smiled. *Will she be secure here? I have to go where it started, and she cannot follow.* Resignation made Gràinne's shoulders slump. For a long time, she had been loath to admit she needed to understand A 'Bhanrìgh Fuil to exorcise her demons. Brianag's future safety and Gràinne's sanity depended on journeying to Cùil Daothail and, beyond that, to the land of the Na Daione Tùrsach. She shuddered again.

Brion observed the trembling and put it down to the breezes on the walls. "I apologise. I should have escorted you to a warmer room." Brion glanced at Seonag, who stood awkwardly on the periphery of the conversation. "Please escort Gràinne and my daughter to their quarters. Have the servants make sure there's a good fire in the hearth and food and drink." Then he looked at Gràinne and Brianag. "I will join you shortly, and we will celebrate as a family after sunset."

Lines furrowed Brion's brow as he said, "After that, you and I need to talk, and not all will be of pleasant matters." Gràinne shrugged. She knew her arrival would not be well-received by Drostan or Blàr. No Bhanrìgh of the Na Daoine Tùrsach had ever been a welcome guest at their tables.

Gràinne looked from Brion to Seonag several times, pursed her lips, and then smirked mischievously. The expression showed who Brianag took after. "Yet, perhaps, the discussion will not be without levity and scandal."

CHAPTER 5

The intent was a family meal with a select group of Brion's friends. Old and new acquaintances could get to know each other, but most of all, a proud father wanted to show off his daughter. That plan had a short duration when Cassán arrived with a dozen uninvited guests. From their unsteady gait and loud, slurred speech, it was obvious they had been drinking well before the feast.

The room quickly divided into two camps, with son pitted against father. Cassán repeatedly rebuffed Gòrdan's efforts at mediation. Exasperated and his face flushed in anger, Brion stood and roared, "Enough!"

Brianag, Gràinne, and Seonag started in surprise. Gràinne could count the times when Brion had lost his temper or raised his voice on the fingers of one hand. Among the chieftains, bushy eyebrows were raised and whiskers tugged. As quiet as someone walking in fresh snow, Seonag stood and moved to the rìgh's side.

She, and other friends of Brion, glared warnings at Cassán and his friends. It was to no avail. Believing himself immune to the consequences of his actions, Cassán's response was to drink more wine and aim vulgar slights at Gràinne and Brianag. Seeing his father's furious looks, Cassán's older counsellor tried to temper his friend's behaviour. Even the other sycophants fell quiet at the angry stares from the High Table. Still, too much wine had driven Cassán beyond propriety, common sense, and self-preservation.

Gràinne stood, and her hand went to where a sheath on her back usually held her longsword. Frustrated at its absence, she growled like a *lince*. The feral look on her face, combined with her curling symbols, succeeded in muting Cassán's offending mouth.

"I'm impressed. He fears you and not me," said Seonag, dipping her head in acknowledgement.

"It's only because I'm new. He doesn't know me."

"That, I very much doubt. You and I need a long conversation." This time Gràinne inclined her head.

Thinking the situation was resolved, both women retook their seats. Thus, they were surprised when Brion, still standing, pointed to Cassán's self-appointed advisor. "Guards, escort this ill-mannered and uninvited lout to the cells. He has plainly forgotten our traditions of hospitality. In the morning, bind him to the whipping post and strip the flesh from his back. Perhaps that will refresh his memory."

Brion's arbitrary choice seemed unfortunate unless the young man's past behaviour was considered. Indeed, Cassán's advisor had tried, albeit with no success, to dampen Cassán's and the group's loutish behaviour. "No!" shouted Cassán, rising unsteadily to defend his counsellor. "He is my friend and will sit with me." Cassán's voice slurred as his befuddled brain failed to synchronise with his speech.

"If he remains, you will take his place. Make your choice," snarled Brion. Much to his friend's angst, a shocked Cassán sat down.

"I thought not." Brion's disgust and disappointment were evident to all. He turned to Gòrdan and said, "When my son's arse-licking companion has endured his punishment, see that he has enough food for five sunsets. Then cast him out from Dùn Brion. He will be executed if he sets foot in Na Mèadaidh lands again." Pleading for mercy, the now snivelling man was dragged from the room.

As the entrance doors slammed shut, Cassán belatedly rose to protest, but a fierce glare from Brion halted him. "You provoked an attack on *my* daughter and her mother. Instead of offering regret and apology, you come to this celebration with the grace and manners of a pig. Perhaps Gòrdan should have allowed Gràinne and her warriors to slaughter you. You owe him thanks for staying your meeting with the *bean-sidhe*."

A hand touched Brion's thigh. "Thank you for defending my honour, but maybe you have gone a bit far," said Gràinne.

"I haven't finished!" said Brion. Gràinne flinched at the abruptness and tone. "Gòrdan, you have faithfully tried to counsel and serve my insolent son. I apologise for his intemperate and churlish behaviour. From this moment, you are relieved of that duty."

Those at Cassán's table stared at Brion, dumbfounded. Each knew that not only would Gòrdan yield his duties as Cassán's shield-man, but the guard of veteran warriors who accompanied the prince everywhere would also be withdrawn. It was the rìgh's way of saying, "I've had enough. You're on your own."

Yet Brion had not finished. "While Brianag remains in Northern Albu, and with her mother's consent, Gòrdan will be at her side and, if needed, protect her with his life." Brion made to sit down but stopped midway. Looking at Cassán's group, he said, "You are not welcome at this celebration. Leave!" Just half of the number, showing more prudence than Cassán and their remaining companions, bowed and slunk from the chamber.

A firm hand on her shoulder made Gràinne turn, and she looked into Seonag's deep-blue eyes. "This is not your fault. There was an incident before your arrival. This boil has needed lancing for a long time. On Brion's behalf, I apologise for the unfortunate timing."

More wine and beer amplified Cassán's anger and humiliation at his father's public favouring of Brianag. Yet Cassán—understandably, given his past experience—held to the opinion that his father, bound by blood and guilt, would never expel him from the room, let alone Dùn Brion. Hence, in a sulk, he made little attempt to dissuade his remaining followers from their boorish behaviour or their crude and disrespectful slurs.

That Cassán misread the stony faces of Gràinne, Brianag, Seonag, and his father as theatre proved to be a dangerous miscalculation. It was a toss-up as to who would explode first. Brianag, as impetuous and fiery as her ma, won. The fire that smouldered in emerald-green eyes burst into flames as she stood, her palms planted firmly on the oak table.

"*You* dare to call *my* mother a bitseach and *striapach*. Look to your own house. Your mother was an insane whore who murdered at least three of the men she rutted." Gràinne shook her head and, about to rise, stopped when the fiercest look she had ever seen from Brianag kept her on her seat. "Deranged and riddled with disease from her rutting victims, *your* mother was convicted of her crimes and beheaded by her brother, Íar Mac Dedad, Rí of Curraghatoor."

Brianag paused, but only to pluck another arrow dagger from her belt. "The only good thing ever to come from your mother's loins is your sister, Sorchae Ni Íar, who, thank the Goddess, is the most pleasant child on this earth." The shock on Cassán's face testified that he had never heard of his sister, and he looked furiously at Brion. Now, mocked by and the butt of his sycophantic friends' jests, even a wine-sodden Cassán knew he only had one recourse.

"Take your lying words back or face me on the battlefield, bitseach."

The smile on Brianag's face should have been a warning. Belatedly, Cassán realised his half-sister had deliberately backed him into a corner. Yet, how could a girl her age hope to triumph over him? His answer came all too soon.

"Knives, long or short swords, maces, bows, horses, spears, or fists. Choose your weapons. I'm ready… are you?"

"Oh shite!" Gràinne groaned, and she smiled weakly at the wary look on Brion's face.

CHAPTER 6

Few expected Cassán to show up for the duel. Indeed, Gràinne prayed to the Goddess that he would not. Yet at *meadhan-latha*—midday—the prionnsa of Dùn Brion strode into the yard accompanied by his friends. Gràinne turned to Brianag and gripped her shoulders firmly. Brianag was growing and only a finger's breadth shorter than her mother. Hence, the two had little problem holding each other's gaze as Gràinne spoke.

"Do *not* kill him. Show mercy. Try not to humiliate him—too much."

Gràinne looked at a perplexed Brion and shrugged. "Cassán is overweight and outmatched. Brianag has been trained since childhood by me and the best warriors of our clann, many of whom you know." Gràinne looked across to where Heilasa suckled happily and sighed. "And by those from other nations."

"I hoped that the presence of a sister would temper Cassán's character. Yet bad parenting and sly gossip has turned his head." Brion paused. "I have failed to be a good father to Cassán. That is on me, and, in my disappointment, my judgment may have been hasty. Now it is in the Goddess's hands, and I trust she is wiser than me."

To those gathered to watch, Brianag's appearance shouted *Warrior!* A boiled leather cuirass, sculpted to her upper body, rested on slim hips. Under it was a sleeveless shirt of chainmail which, in turn, sat on a soft woollen léine. Both shirts hung a hands-length over plaid, red and black *triubhas*, which were tucked into soft hide *bròg-éille*—boots. A broad leather belt, clasped at the waist, awaited Brianag's decision on her choice of weapons. The finishing touches were strips of sheepskin lapped and tied around each shin and ankle.

In contrast, Cassán's dress, bed hair, and armour shouted that he had overslept and had to scramble to keep his appointment. The smell of sweat and stale beer radiated from him. Yet, his demeanour spoke of dismissive arrogance. How could a girl stand against him? Cassán's boiled leather armour was ill-fitting but, like most of Brion's warriors, had iron scales sewn between its layers. Brianag smirked. She glanced at her mother, who hissed a single word: "Pride."

"You may choose the weapons," called out Brianag.

The confident tone raised a frown of concern on Cassán's face. He thought for a moment as the babble from his friends grew louder and their suggestions multiplied. Finally, he grinned and shouted, "Clubs!" Surely with his build and weight advantage, it had to be his best option.

"Oh shite!" murmured Gràinne. Her lover, Amodocus, a Thracian prince and father of Heilasa, favoured the mace, and Brianag had been his ardent student. Brianag fought back a smile as she walked to the rough wooden table on which her weapons and shields were laid. She settled an oblong, waisted sgiath on her arm. At about two-thirds the height of a traditional neck-to-knee shield, its weight suited Brianag.

Then Brianag stretched out her right hand, grasped a mace, and felt the smoothness of its blackthorn shaft. Significantly shorter than her opponent's bludgeon, its weight felt comfortable, which was unsurprising since it had been custom-built for her. Its heavy iron head was teardrop-shaped and flanged at the top. Brianag smiled at her mother and slipped its twin into a loop on the back of her belt.

Brianag's style, whether dress or armour, tended to the practical. Hence, she preferred an unembellished helmet of bronze and iron. It was, however, crowned with short red and black horsehair plumes, which erupted from an acorn-shaped nub. She nodded to Gòrdan, and he settled the helmet over her auburn braids and fastened its straps.

"The Goddess go with you," said Gòrdan.

"Thanks." Brianag dipped her head to Brion and Gràinne and strode towards the centre of the fighting circle. Her confident mien as she approached Cassán made him wary. Yet Brianag's thoughts were not of the fight but whether her ma had placed a wager on the outcome. From the clamour of those surrounding the arena, a lot of gold was changing hands. As she got closer to Cassán, her nose wrinkled in disgust.

"You stink!" The battle had begun.

Truthfully, Cassán's speed took Brianag unawares. His first blow would have been a crushing and crippling strike had Brianag not already been retreating. As the iron studs of Cassán's club scraped down her shield, she saw the look of glee on his face.

The haughtiness infuriated Brianag, and gripping her weapon firmly, she quickly closed the gap and attacked. A flurry of coordinated blows and sgiath bashes forced Cassán backwards until he could retreat no more. With the next burst, the mace's flanges stripped long slivers of hide and oak from his shield. More than this, it silenced his supporters.

Cassán gasped for breath and bemoaned the heaviness of the club and shield. He had counted on his first charge and strike to settle the fight. Yet it had accomplished little other than to expend his energy. His attempts to manoeuvre around his foe were matched and countered. He was a ponderous bear, and she a fleet-footed wolf. Brianag stalked her opponent relentlessly, dancing quickly beyond the range of his swinging club and instantly following up with a blur of mace strokes.

"Stand and fight, bitseach!" shouted Cassán, sparking a round of chants from his followers.

In response, Brianag bared her teeth and attacked. Sweat streamed off Cassán's forehead, stinging his eyes. His muscles burned, his heart pounded, and his lungs cried out for respite. Physical fitness had never been a priority, and that returned to taunt him as he tired rapidly. Lumbering forward in the direction he thought Brianag would be, he felt a sharp pain as

Brianag slammed the iron boss of her shield into the small of his back. The excruciating and paralyzing pain brought Cassán to his knees.

"Yield or I will end you, *brother*," snarled Brianag. The mace poised to crush Cassán's skull drew gasps of "No!" from Brion and Gràinne, although not from the crowds gathered in the courtyard and standing on the ramparts.

"I yield! I yield!" shouted Cassán, much to the disappointment of his supporters, who had hoped for a glorious, if fatal, conclusion.

"Arsehole!" spat Brianag before turning on her heels to return to her ma and da.

Brianag's only warning was the sudden hush of the crowd. She whirled around to watch Cassán snatch, lift, and throw a spear. At the distance between them, a blind man could hardly miss. Brianag twisted and dived to her left while her right hand went to her bròg-éille. She cried out as the edge of the leaf-shaped spearhead raked her shoulder.

On the other side of the arena, Cassán screeched, "Bitseach!" and collapsed to the dirt, gripping his thigh as he tried to staunch the blood flow. A shadow loomed over him as Brianag kicked him onto his back. He felt a wet, muddy boot crushing his throat. "The next time, I'll put the knife in your heart." Brianag spun around. Her intent was to walk away, but she stopped after a few steps. "The Hag's arse!" The crowd became silent as Brianag turned, closed on Cassán, and kicked him in the face.

Brion and Gràinne looked with parental concern and disapproval as Brianag stood before them. "I'm only fourteen. I'm allowed to be irritable when someone tries to spit me on a spear. Is there a druid healer in the fort? I'll need some stitches in my shoulder."

"I'll take you to a healer," said Gòrdan.

A few steps from her parents, Brianag turned. "If that spear had hit my face and scarred me, I would have ended him."

"Go with Brianag, please. I have business to take care of," said Brion to Gràinne.

***

Along with Seonag, Brion marched to where Cassán and his hangers-on congregated. The livid, white scar that carved a gorge through his beard added a terrible aspect to Brion's face and made the group flinch. Cassán winced as his hair was pulled tight and his face brought close to his father's.

"Not only did you try to kill your sister, but before the people, you dishonoured yourself and shamed me."

Brion looked at Seonag. "See to it that my son and his followers are given food for five sunsets and expelled from Dùn Brion. They are banished from the lands of the Na Mèadaidh. If any remain in the fort after three sunsets, execute them."

"Father, no," whined Cassán.

"I have tolerated your behaviour for too long, but no more. I am no longer your father."

* * *

"Do you not think the punishment harsh? Cassán is no warrior and has few skills to serve him outside these walls. Unprotected, many may seek to take advantage of him," said Seonag.

"He tried to kill my daughter—his sister," rasped Brion.

"That was certainly rash. Yet your acceptance and celebration of Brianag likely raised fears of rejection in his mind. That she also ably demonstrated her expertise as a warrior, humiliated Cassán before his friends. Such emotions are hard to control. He is not yet a man." Seonag shook her head. "He also is badly served by his choice of companions."

"I say again: Cassán tried to kill Brianag, and that cannot go unpunished," snapped Brion. "What would you have me do? Strip the flesh off his back in a public flogging?" It was Brion's turn to shake his head. "No. Enmity and a dagger in the back lie at the end of that path. His mother had no qualms about disposing of those who got in her way. This is not the time to discover if Cassán is his mother's son."

"But…" Seonag stopped her words as she saw the look of misery and helplessness in Brion's eyes. The anguish of a father. *Did mine feel the same way when he abandoned me? Does he feel anything now?*

"Cassán will be fine. Once his band have exhausted their food and their bellies shrink and growl with hunger, he will return and ask for forgiveness. This swift kick up the arse will reset his attitude and give us something to build on."

"I pray to the Goddess you're right," said Seonag, yet she had her doubts.

* * *

The curse of the Gaels is a long memory for slights, whether real or imagined. An embittered Gormal Mac Eachdonn sat hunched on his throne. Public humiliation at the hands of Brion, although a score of summers in the past, continued to ravage his body and mind. That he also laid the blame for the execution of his mother, Ceana, at the feet of Conall Mac Gabhann, Brion's brother, by hand-fasting, did not help.

He looked up, hearing a disturbance at the chamber's doors, and watched a young man push past the typical gathering of sycophants, seekers of favours, and those wishing justice. The latter were perpetually disappointed unless they had gold or silver to strengthen their case.

Ten paces before the throne, the envoy dropped to his knee and bowed before Gormal. His face was unfamiliar, but then so were many in this room. A bored Gormal lifted a hand and signalled the messenger to speak. If he did not like the message, the messenger would find his head on a spear and his body in the ditch surrounding the hillfort.

"I bring news of a schism between the rìgh of Dùn Brion and his son. Cassán is cast out and banished from his father's kingdom. He travels with his followers to Dùn Athad, seeking sanctuary… and an ally." The young man bowed and stepped back.

"I thank you for the brevity of your message. Cassán will, of course, be welcome in my home." An expression of grateful relief filled the envoy's mien, for many *rìghrean*—kings—were envious and jealous of other royalty.

Gormal signalled for his shield-man to come closer and whispered in his ear: "Cassán is to be given quarters in Dùn Athad until I decide what to do with him. I have no need of his companions. If they follow a wastrel like Cassán, they're fools. Hire mercenaries to kill those travelling with him. You will then 'rescue' the prince." The shield-man nodded. About to depart, he stopped when Gormal put a hand on his arm. "The messenger is personable and a good ambassador. It's a pity he has to die. Make it quick."

Gormal stood and attempted to straighten up, but many summers of bitterness and little exercise had slouched his shoulders. That caused his spine to curve, leaving a permanent hump on his upper back. He swore yet could not resist smiling. At last, he would soon have a weapon to scourge Brion. With Drostan gone on one of his numerous trips to Gaul, who would stand in his way?

CHAPTER 7

He had named himself the *Seirbhiseach na Fala*—Servant of the Blood. Yet the glory of the title withered when most shortened it to Seirbhiseach— and even that was a mouthful. The High Priest never considered himself in service to anyone, not even to the evil he planned to invoke. Like all zealots, he remained arrogantly confident that he could control that to which he intended to give life. Thus, for a priest, he demonstrated an incredible lack of understanding of malevolence.

Hunched over a wood-and-peat fire, Seirbhiseach warmed chapped, dry hands. His refuge was an inconspicuous wattle-and-daub roundhouse in the settlement of Cùil Daothail. Situated near the north-eastern coastline of Northern Albu, Cùil Daothail was a bustling centre of trade and commerce. The northern clanns considered it neutral territory and protected it because of the wealth it generated.

It was late autumn, and winter winds flowed down the slopes of white-capped mountains. They brought flurries of snow to dance along rutted dirt paths and foretold the freezing cold that would seep deeper into bones and dirt. A scowl twisted Seirbhiseach's thin grey lips. The settlement was less than a sunset's journey from the southern border of the Na Daoine Tùrsach's ancestral lands.

The priest ground his back teeth, although given the diseased and blackened gums in which they were anchored, the act had its perils. In

Seirbhiseach's eyes, the kingdom of the Na Daoine Tùrsach had, like a coveted cornfield, been bartered and divided among the Forest People, the Ravens, and a handful of minor clanns. Worse, his people had disavowed generations of tribal loyalty and willingly embraced their new rulers. Seirbhiseach swore to show them the error of their choice.

Still, the glower on Seirbhiseach's face gradually became a smile of perverse satisfaction when the strains of wailing and crying reached his ears. Mothers mourned their daughters' disappearance and prayed to the Goddess for their return. Fathers threatened revenge and violence. Seirbhiseach huffed. Was the girls' sacrifice not a better way to end the misery of a life that promised drudgery, poverty, and violation? The parents should be thankful their offspring's blood helped nourish a deity who, when risen, would be much more powerful than the Goddess.

Seirbhiseach's eyes lifted as a minion pushed aside the hide covering the entrance. The older priest blinked rapidly at the sudden brightness. He was grateful when the novice priest stepped inside, and gloom secured the chamber.

"Messengers bring news of the arrival of Diadhaidh's granddaughter at Dùn Brion. They also say that she is accompanied by her daughter." The High Priest's eyes glowed violet at the unexpected bonus. One to be queen, one to be sacrificed, and both to be despoiled. The bloodlines would decide each one's fate. Perfect. He looked up as the young man cleared his throat.

"There is more?"

Eager to please, the young priest nodded. "Diadhaidh's granddaughter also travels with a suckling baby." He watched Seirbhiseach's eyes calculate the value of the news. "It is also rumoured that Brion Ó Cathasaigh has exiled his son, Cassán, from Dùn Brion. The prionnsa travels to Dùn Athad to seek sanctuary."

"Praise the Baobhan Sith. Our champion is all-powerful and delivers our enemies into our hands." Again the messenger hesitated. This time Seirbhiseach's response was a curt, "What?"

"There are rumours of bodies drained of blood and chests ripped open in the lower lands of the Ravens."

"Those are our lands stolen by the Ravens," corrected Seirbhiseach. As he waved rough hands over the fire, the High Priest thought for a moment. "I have sanctioned no blood gifts. The mountain loch is a sacred place of sacrifice until our strength builds. However, others may take revenge on enemies by mimicking us. Search them out. I will ensure their death serves a higher cause when we find them." The envoy nodded and, before taking his leave, dropped a few logs onto the firepit. Seirbhiseach nodded his thanks and said, "Go to the crannag. Make sure all is well."

As the door covering flapped back into place, Seirbhiseach scratched his entangled shock of hair. Unwilling to consider that the Baobhan Sith might be acting independently, he shook his head and shouted, "No! I gave life to you. You will serve me." Yet his words sounded hollow. How could he control a being with its rumoured abilities? *It must have a weakness. All creatures, whether men or gods, do.*

✳✳✳

Face flushed with unaccustomed exertion, Cassán bent over, rested hands on his knees, and fought to bring his breathing under control. Blue eyes took in the densely forested and mountainous terrain. He groaned. The landscape between Dùn Brion and Dùn Athad would be similar. Closer to Gormal's stronghold, there would be lochs and marshes to navigate. So far, the weather had been unseasonably temperate and dry, but darkening skies foretold change.

Used to Dùn Brion's comforts and fawning servants and slaves, the trek became a nightmare for Cassán and his companions. Two sunsets into the journey, they had journeyed less than a quarter of the distance. Foolishly squandered, their food supplies were exhausted. Rumbling bellies bore witness that berries and mushrooms were a poor substitute for venison, fresh bread, and hard cheese. Throats that previously guzzled down unlimited quantities of beer and wine resentfully settled for spring water.

Cassán looked at the travellers' faces as they sat around the fire. *Do*

I know any of them? The party of twenty who departed Dùn Brion was already reduced by half its number. There was no profit to be made from a banished prince. Therefore, they struck out north and east, hoping to reach sanctuary and find another fool to leech off. Cassán peered at those remaining. Were they loyal friends, and how would he know? *Seventeen summers, and this is what I have become—an outcast. Brianag is only fourteen and has more sense than me—and a warm cot to lie in.*

Yet Cassán's instinct was to assume the mantle of a victim. *What else do I have?* Over the next few sunsets, his incessant bleating about the unfairness of his plight strained the forbearance of the most tolerant of his followers. Several more drifted away. His band needed a strong leader to guide them. *Did I learn nothing from my father or Gòrdan? Does Brion's blood run through me or not?*

Increasingly marginalised, his authority and value questioned, for the first time in his life, Cassán began to examine his conduct. He looked into his friends' eyes and saw them calculate his diminishing worth. It became obvious that only the expectation of a favourable reception at Dùn Athad persuaded his friends to stand with him.

On the sixth sunset, the group set up camp in the forest east of the Mòine Mhòr. The vast marshlands surrounded Gormal's dùn. In the distance, Cassán spotted the crag and fort silhouetted against the red-orange hue of the setting sun and heaved a sigh of relief. He envisaged sanctuary and a life for which he was better prepared.

That night, thoughts of warm food, cold beer, and a dry cot made the band sleep easier, but not Cassán. Dreams made him toss and turn, yet even in his visions, he remained loath to accept any complicity in his downfall. His father and bitseach of a sister had humiliated him. He deserved sympathy, not rejection and exile.

Yet other uncomfortable thoughts slipped quietly into Cassán's mind and tenaciously dug in. What had he done to command respect? What had he accomplished? Brianag had offered him friendship, but he had spurned that, instead choosing to fight—and be humiliated. *At fourteen summers, she makes a better princess than I am a prince.* On the cusp of dawn, Cassán grudgingly moved closer to what his father had known for a long time: he was a pampered, unpleasant child with no genuine friends.

The band woke to grey skies and clothes stiffened by frost and wet by mizzle. No one among the group knew how to set snares for small animals. Thus, there was no food to break their fast and the dawn was greeted by a round of griping and accusation. The eyes of those nearing the limit of their patience bored into Cassán.

Yet Cassán returned their stares calmly, without acrimony, and stood. "I have come to a decision. I intend to return to Dùn Brion and beg for my father's forgiveness. He is a fair man and will recognise my contrition is genuine. It is your choice whether to follow me or not."

The round of fiery swearing and thrown punches was expected. Cassán had just ended the fools' dreams of comfort and a continued bloodsucking existence.

"*You* might be accepted by Brion. We certainly will not," said the oldest of the group. Yet they had asked for a leader, and Cassán had given them one.

The band had neither posted guards nor prepared even basic perimeter defences. Even in the most peaceful of times, this was stupid and reckless. The roar from the treeline paralysed Cassán's followers rather than sparking them into action. As mercenaries swarmed the camp, several of his followers were still protesting the lack of food when steel permanently opened their mouths. The few who clumsily pulled swords from sheaths were overwhelmed and dispatched without pity.

At the eye of the storm, Cassán spun round and round. He heard the curses of the attackers at the lack of promised plunder. *Who promised such a reward?* He watched as his friends were stripped and mutilated. A few, unlucky to remain alive, were penetrated before their throats were cut. Shouts of "Better than rutting sheep and goats" were accompanied by cruel laughter.

At that moment, Cassán realised how sheltered his life had been in

Dùn Brion. He also questioned the wisdom of Brion's inclination to wrap him in sheep's wool and cosset him from the harshness of everyday life. *Why am I still alive?* No answer came because a blow to the back of his head sent him into blackness.

★★★

Cassán moaned and rubbed the egg-sized lump on the back of his head. As he attempted to stand, a wave of nausea brought him to his knees, making him throw up. He gasped in pain as the stitches from Brianag's knife wound broke and blood seeped from the cut.

Shouts forced him to focus. His first impression was of too many bodies lying motionless on the dirt. Greater clarity and a less blurred vision drew a distinction between his lifeless, naked companions and a larger number of mercenaries. He shook his head, but that only made him puke again.

In the clearing, two men argued. One was tall, burly, and dressed in a warrior's attire. The other was gaunt, sallow-skinned, and wearing well-worn clothing. The latter protested loudly: "We had a deal!"

The other laughed and nodded to several others, who grabbed the miscreant and held him while he was gutted. The slop of entrails made Cassán retch again, which proved painful given his belly was empty. He wiped drool from his chin and, having regained his feet, looked at the chieftain.

"What was the deal?"

The question took the warrior by surprise. He had been told Cassán was a whimpering eejit. Therefore, his instinctive response was a fist to Cassán's chin.

★★★

As dusk fell, Sidheag, for that was the name the Baobhan Sith had chosen, broke through the thin veneer of ice on the surface of the loch's waters. She caused fewer ripples than a fish sipping air. She could have risen at any time of the day or night, but her eyes and skin were sensitive to sunlight.

Thus she felt much more comfortable in the gloom. She also preferred the inhospitable peripheral parts of Northern Albu, where the nights were longer. Naked or clothed, cold had no impact on Sidheag.

Without sufficient nourishment, her body movements were clumsy and uncoordinated. Having hauled herself up and onto the walkway connecting the crannag to the loch's shoreline, she paused to crouch and sniff the air. Thin, greyish-pink lips lifted into a smile, and she advanced towards the building's doorway. Her gait was ungainly, and it seemed as if she walked on the tips of her toes. Sidheag cursed the "gift" of hoofs that set her apart from her sisters.

Three pairs of eyes turned as the wooden door of the crannag creaked open. Their orders were to keep watch on the loch and dissuade intruders. Instead, they chose to stoke the firepit, roast spitted chickens, and guzzle down the ample stock of meadowsweet-flavoured beer. They talked of conquest, plunder, and rape, yet only of the helpless young females kidnapped from neighbouring communities and farms. As priests, they justified their actions as being their right.

They were mentally, spiritually, and physically ugly men with cruel appetites. Few took Seirbhiseach's rambling monologues about raising up a demi-goddess seriously. Still, professing loyalty to Seirbhiseach had given them a path to satisfying their darkest desires. Only a fool would turn from that opportunity.

In the light of the roaring fire and flickering rushlights, they stared at the naked, odd-legged apparition with growing curiosity. Even as their doom walked closer, their thoughts were not of escape but lust at the undressed, gaunt vision before them. Any stirrings of fear in their hearts were overpowered by hardening manhoods and a desire to inflict pain. The laughter that echoed off the crannag's wooden walls chilled them.

"You think that I cannot read your minds. Fools, it does not take the powers of a goddess to discern your thoughts. But enough of this. I am hungry."

✳✳✳

Sitting on the floor, Sidheag groomed herself like a feral cat. As the long, pink tongue cleaned the last traces of blood from her body—the precious liquid should never be wasted—Sidheag smiled. She felt her body become fuller and more curvaceous. Her talons retracted, but her nails remained blood-red in colour, as were her lips. A few more men to feast on, and she would be ready to move *her* plan forward. Content, she purred and curled into a ball on the wooden slats.

∗ ∗ ∗

Before adding the Na Daoine Tùrsach territory, the Ravens' land was mainly inhospitable and mountainous. Hundreds of small farming and fishing settlements dotted the long narrow strip of land that hugged the rugged coastline.

Its people fished in stormy northern seas and frozen lochs no matter the season. Hunters tracked game in the pine forests of the foothills, while those under thirteen summers scavenged for berries, mushrooms, and roots. Twice each year, many would journey to Cùil Daothail to trade furs and the rough, warm, woven fabric made from the fleeces of the hardy sheep that roamed above the forest line.

Since the final battle with the Na Daoine Tùrsach and the division of the clann's domain, the balance of life had changed. The Ravens had annexed land that could be farmed, in which crops could be planted and harvested. Life remained harsh and always would, for the earth resented those who sought to tame and thrive on it. Yet, Blàr's people had widened the narrow chasm between life and death and now enjoyed a small measure of comfort.

The Rìgh of the Ravens looked around him and wondered if that life would change again. Like the other farmsteads he had investigated, the scene did not point to a raid for plunder or slaves. The roundhouses were intact, their thatched roofs unburnt, and nothing had been stolen. Often the embers in the firepits retained life, and the enormous soot-blackened cauldrons still simmered, filling the air with the aroma of soups and stews.

Yet every living being in the small family community—man and beast, wee'uns and the elderly, male and female, about thirty in total—was dead. They lay scattered on the ground, their faces frozen in the horror of their death. All were drained of blood. No doubt they had suffered, and every sign indicated they had been helpless to resist their fate.

Yet there was a difference in their last moments. The females had long thin gashes from ear to ear as if a razor-sharp blade had been drawn across their throats. In contrast, the men and beasts were subjected to un-fettered savagery. Throats were torn out, ribcages cracked open, and hearts removed. Blàr grunted. The only positive he could take away was that the men had not been raped.

Not a religious man, Blàr Mac Artair tugged his thin black braid, fin-gered the blue-black raven feather that hung from it, and looked to the skies for answers. *The Hag, who did this?* And how could a community sim-ply allow themselves to be slaughtered like docile cows? In the pit of his stomach, Blàr feared the answer. As he looked around the farmstead, he growled in frustration. Beyond the carnage, something was wrong.

Blàr looked up as his shield-man approached. "Send out messengers. Raise the army. Gather the smaller communities and farmsteads into the brochs and hillforts." The veteran nodded but did not move away. "Is there something else?" The man nodded and led Blàr across the dirt. Then he pointed. In the mud were a single hoof print and a single paw print. "Shite!" Both men's fears had become real.

"There's one other observation," said the shield-man. He pointed to a young warrior who stood before a group of corpses. His head was bowed and his eyes were red from weeping. "One of his rutting partners, a girl of seventeen summers, lived in the farmstead." The veteran paused. "She is missing, and so is her younger sister."

"The Hag's arse!"

It was as if a blindfold had been removed, and Blàr had an answer that made his belly churn. In each ravaged community, the balance between men and women had bothered him. Now he had an explanation, and it troubled him.

***

Cassán awoke naked in a damp chamber that smelled of piss, shite, and rotting food. That it had a dirt floor and no windows extended the duration and concentration of the stench. Water trickled down walls covered in slime and mould, although if the temperature dropped further, that would cease. The only light came from flickering torches on either side of the door, but they were on the outside.

He rubbed his bruised chin and hoped he could return the greeting one day. *What is the origin of my newfound embrace of courage?* Cassán cursed a growing need to pee. He shrugged, stood in a corner, took his cock in his hand, and sighed in pleasure at the release. Yet, Fate is perverse. In midstream, the cell door groaned and scraped over the dirt floor.

"I see you're settling into your quarters." The mocking tone in Gormal's voice set Cassán's teeth on edge.

Cassán pointed to his lack of clothes and poor accommodation. "There are rules and traditions for the treatment of nobles. Perhaps you have not heard of them. Your hospitality is lacking, Gormal of Dùn Athad."

"You're an outcast. The law does not apply to you. I can do whatever I want to you," said Gormal, twisting the ends of braided whiskers. "Indeed, by banishing you, your father has given me permission." Gormal chuckled at his own jest.

"My father will avenge me."

"I am counting on that. I dislike Brion, but he is an honourable man burdened with a pathetic excuse for a son." Cassán flinched at the insult. "Yet you remain his offspring, and blood is a strong bond." Gormal paused. "I had hoped you would be a useful idiot, but my shield-man tells me you are surprisingly observant. Thus, another approach is required."

Gormal turned to his captain and nodded. Shortly after, men dragged a glowing brazier and a stump of wood into the room. The impact on the chamber's warmth and darkness was remarkable.

"Perhaps I misjudged you."

"I think not," said Gormal. "I require a token to deliver to your father to convince him that you enjoy my hospitality."

"Take my ring. He'll recognise it as one he gave me."

Gormal shook his head. "Unfortunately, a brigand could have stolen it, or you may have traded it for food and lodgings." The smile in Gormal's tone made Cassán uneasy. "I have an alternative and much more entertaining strategy." Two burly guards grabbed Cassán, forcing him to his knees, while another stretched his right arm over the tree stump.

"I had considered a simple finger, but this is more poetic given your father's disability."

Cassán screamed as the blade sliced through flesh and then the bones, gristle, and tendons of his wrist. His vision blurred by pain and tears, Cassán watched his right hand tumble to the floor and felt blood pump steadily from torn arteries. As unconsciousness approached, he shrieked once more as a glowing iron was placed against his stump.

"I would be a poor host if I let you bleed to death." Gormal looked at his shield-man. "Leave the brazier and wood." Then he turned back to Cassán. "See, I'm not totally heartless. You have a seat and will have heat and light for as long as the wood lasts."

As the cell door closed, the pain in Cassán's arm seemed only to increase. Strangely, one thought was uppermost in his head before he collapsed. *I'm left-handed, bastard.*

CHAPTER 8

Generations of Dùn Athad's kings bred the shaggy-haired horses, which were traded across Albu, Ériu, and even Gaul. Indeed, teams of the hardy animals were favoured by Gràinne's chariots. Gormal's messenger sat astride one of these mounts and brought it to a halt a hundred paces beyond Dùn Brion's main entrance. Tied to the animal's girth strap was a rough hessian sack.

Insolence and audacity radiated from the envoy's demeanour as he shouted, "I bring a gift for Brion, Rìgh of Dùn Brion, from Gormal, Rìgh of Dùn Athad." The tone in the man's voice raised the hackles of those standing alert on the walls. Some gripped spears and measured whether a good throw would hit the man. Grabbing the bag's neck, the envoy lifted it up and tossed it towards the gateway. The sack landed with a splash in a pool of muddy water. As the ripples faded, the messenger urged his horse into a fast canter and retreated down the dirt track.

As if holding hot cinders, the gate guard handed the "gift" to Seonag and then dashed to the far side of the courtyard. Stains on the material, the tang of decay, and the slow drip of dark droplets presaged the foulness of the bag's contents. Gripping the sack in her right hand, Seonag took a deep breath, opened its neck, and cried, "No!"

Seonag turned to see Brion, followed by Cearbhall and Gràinne, descend the stone steps from the walkway. Yet she was too late to mask the expression of revulsion and dismay, making the trio stop short. Standing before his garrison's commander, Brion held out his hand. A sense of foreboding thickened the air in Dùn Brion. Reluctant to obey, Seonag set her jaw and shook her head.

"Please, my king. Leave this to me. We can discuss your response later."

"No. Show me." Brion's arm stretched out again. Distressed, Seonag bowed her head.

"I'm sorry."

The howl that followed held accents of guilt, wrath, and promised vengeance. Gràinne placed a hand on Brion's shoulder and felt him flinch.

"I'm so sorry."

Vacant green eyes were Brion's response.

"Take hope. It's a challenge and signals Cassán is alive. Gormal wants to draw you out of Dùn Brion."

Gràinne turned to Cearbhall. "Undoubtedly, the messenger rides hard for Dùn Athad. Take a score of riders and make sure he doesn't make it. Kill any with him but bring the bastard back to us alive."

As Gràinne turned to Brion, she looked around the courtyard and then at Seonag.

"Where's Brianag?"

Shock at the possibility of harm to his daughter snapped Brion out of his immediate distress.

"She's riding with a small group of friends on the Sleagh. It's a favourite place for the young ones who reside in the dùn,'" said Seonag. "They have Gòrdan and a score of warriors with them."

"We should bring them back. I'll take my riders and find them," said Gràinne.

***

He was seventeen summers of age, brash, and full of himself. It was obvious to everyone, including Brianag, that his goal was to add her to his list of conquests. His reputation would soar, and his boasting would climb to new heights if he spread the thighs of Brion's daughter. The young man's only redeeming quality, and perhaps a sign of a future leader, was his prudent choice of close friends. Yet his brazenness blinded him to what everyone else could see: his best friend had captured Brianag's attention.

The gangly young man had a thick mop of copper-red hair and a face full of freckles. Both provided instant recognition. His demeanour was quiet and his eyes watchful. Always at his bolder friend's side, he was the voice of reason until his sword was drawn. Brianag knew, from watching him practise, that his blade arm was strong and the weapon's edge always keen. He had all the qualities of a king's shield-man and battle commander and only lacked experience.

Brianag loved to tease and flirt with him. Her unsubtle suggestions of the activities they could engage in—she was, after all, her ma's daughter—made him blush furiously. Opposites in many ways, laughter brought them together. Hers was unrestrained and rose from her belly to cascade from her lips. His, flowing from his heart, was the deep loch into which her waterfall tumbled.

Gòrdan smiled as he watched the group. All were the sons and daughters of Dùn Brion's nobility. He wondered how they would cope with the adversity life would inevitably bring. *Are they brittle iron or forged steel?* A flicker, a flash of white in the periphery of his vision, made him start. He looked hard to determine the source, but it was gone. Perhaps just a wildflower petal or an early snowflake carried on the Sleagh's breezes.

Yet Gòrdan's gut rarely deceived him, and it churned. "Fasten shields! Unsheathe swords! Protect the girls!" The latter resulted in a growl from Brianag. Yet she smiled when her love became her shield and stood before her.

Fogs and mists suddenly forming on the Sleagh were a common phenomenon. Yet Gòrdan's instincts screamed *Danger!* as a dense cloud formed. It hovered above the ground, and then moved steadily towards the warriors and young people. Iron rims of *sgiathan*—shields—clashed as the shield-wall organised to confront whatever emerged. As the vapour moved nearer, it became less dense.

"Who are *they*?" asked Brianag peering between and over the shoulders of two warriors. At the centre of the mist, ten white shapes shimmered.

"The Goddess preserve us," muttered Gòrdan.

Reports of the Baobhan Sith, carried by traders from Cùil Daothail, had reached the hillfort and been quickly dismissed. Gòrdan feverishly scanned the landscape for an escape route, but his search brought few viable prospects. The plateau was mostly denuded of trees and covered in gorse, heather, and thistles. Brion had destroyed and scattered the walls of Dùn Na Mèadaidh so completely that not even small piles of rubble remained.

Gòrdan's eyes finally fell on a shallow gully to their rear. It was not deep enough to hide in, but if those remaining stood firm, Brianag could use it to ride to safety. He faced Brianag and, in a reassuring but firm voice, said, "You will take your mount and ride for Dùn Brion. You will not look back or hesitate." Gòrdan turned to her companion. "Go with her. You are her shield-man and will die to protect her. Am I understood?" The young man nodded, gripped her arm, and began to drag a furious Brianag to her mount.

Sniggers, insults, hubris, and for many, relief followed the emergence of nine young women from the mist. They were between fifteen and nineteen summers, and none had the physique or carried the weapons of a warrior. What possible threat could they be? Yet the fine hairs on Gòrdan's skin stood as stiff as pine trees. He scowled at his warriors. "Stay alert!"

As she stepped awkwardly from the mist, wearing what looked like a translucent, pearl-white Greek chiton, Sidheag surveyed those before her and laughed. Gòrdan shivered. The laughter held neither the honesty of a child nor the shared secrets of lovers. Instead, this had the bitter taint of malice and promised death.

"The Hag," breathed Gòrdan.

"Neither she nor your Goddess can or will help you," said Sidheag.

The nine females stepped forward at an unspoken signal and raised their arms. Then they opened dark and impossibly large maws containing rows of unnaturally long, thin incisors. From youthful mouths came a sound that was neither musical nor poetic but discordant, chaotic, and lacking any semblance of beauty. Yet, with the strength of iron shackles, it first bound minds and then bodies. For those on the Sleagh, the battle was over before it had begun.

"The females are mine. Kill the men," said Sidheag, "but make them suffer."

Gòrdan's mind screamed as he fought to regain control of his body, but it was as if his feet had taken root in the dirt of the Sleagh. He watched the young girl move deliberately towards him. Barefoot and dressed similarly to Sidheag, she was as beautiful as Gòrdan's daughter, who had just turned sixteen summers.

Her frame was slender but with the promise of future fullness; long golden-red tresses caressed adolescent hips. She had blue eyes. Yet the colour seemed to deepen as she closed the distance between them. When her fingers touched Gòrdan's face, her gaze was black and devoid of humanity. She opened her maw, and he smelled raw bloody flesh.

He felt her teeth caress his throat and could not resist the orgasmic pleasure of her closeness that made his body tremble. When she tore open his throat, Gòrdan's terrible agony began. His eyes and mind remained alert as he watched her maw open to accept his spurting blood. He felt and heard her tongue lap the thick liquid up with a voracious desire. Talons, sharper than the finest of honed blades, flayed delicate strips of skin from his body. He saw her dangle pink slivers from thin, delicate fingers before she placed his flesh into her mouth.

Gòrdan gasped, although the impossibility of that made his mind laugh. She effortlessly ripped open his chest, cracked his ribcage, and plucked out his still-beating heart. His last sight was of her squeezing thick heart blood into her mouth before tossing the organ aside. As the *bean-shìdh* led Gòrdan's spirit away, he glanced back at the massacre. It saddened him that he had no tears to mourn those who had stood and fallen with him.

✳ ✳ ✳

"Surely you did not think you could escape. You are who I came for," hissed Sidheag.

"Run!" shouted Brianag's young protector.

But Brianag was rooted to the spot. Unable to move, she watched her love withdraw his sword and bravely advance on the apparition. She heard Sidheag laugh as if toying with the young man and then screech as the sword slashed. It was followed by a hiss as if a glowing strip of iron had been submerged in water. She could, and should, have frozen his mind and body, but Sidheag's weakness was a dismissive haughtiness for humans.

Helpless to intercede, Brianag observed a pink mist rise as needle teeth tore her love's throat out and long talons sliced through his flesh. Forced to listen to the unearthly guzzling, Brianag watched his eyes die as he was drained of blood. Her ears heard the dull crack of his ribcage broken, and she witnessed his heart removed and swallowed. She would have wept, but her tears were frozen.

Yet of all the horrors Brianag beheld, one vision would always remain. When Sidheag turned to face her, there was no trace of gore on her or her léine. Indeed, the only blemish on Sidheag's body was the thin scar on her left cheek bequeathed by Brianag's protector's blade. And that was scant solace.

"Men are so frail. Like cattle, their only use is as food." Sidheag whispered an incantation, and a mist appeared. "We have much to discuss and should be going."

* * *

Gràinne beat the ground with her fists and wailed as she surveyed the scene. The curling symbols that swathed her body throbbed as if synchronised with her pulse. Animals going to the slaughterhouse met with a better end. Around her, horses snorted nervously and pawed the dirt. Seasoned warriors swore and vowed retribution. Instead of heather and wildflowers, scraps of raw meat and shards of white bone carpeted the ground. Oddly, the air on the Sleagh, for a moment, was still. Perhaps to ensure that none would forget the smell.

The Hag! What nightmare could cause this? Deep within her, an ancient memory stirred, and Gràinne trembled. *Is Brianag among the dead? How would I know?* She howled like a wolf and those who stood with her watched the curling symbols flow like dark rivers. In anguish, Gràinne vowed to the Goddess to drown the highlands in blood. Then she blamed herself. What foolishness or evil had convinced her that coming "home" would be a good idea? Or that Brianag would be safe with her da?

A shout from the riders' ceannairí céad prevented her from descending into blacker thoughts, and she looked in the direction of his arm. A hundred paces from Gràinne, a young woman had appeared out of a mist. A sudden breeze made long hair flare into a yellow-gold corona, framing a face as smooth as porcelain and just as pale. Only her green eyes, blood-red lips and nails added colour to the canvas. Her lithesome body was draped in a long, sleeveless, white léine.

Yet when the girl opened her mouth, the voice was ancient. "I am Sidheag. You are my *'Bhanrìgh Fuil*—my Blood Queen. You are royal and of an untainted bloodline of the Na Daoine Tùrsach. Diadhaidh promised you to me, and hence you are my property. You can freely choose to serve me and be rewarded with great power.

"If not, I will feed on Brianag, and my daughters will slaughter everyone you hold dear. Either way, you *will* serve me. Come to me in your homeland. If she wishes, I may return your daughter to her father."

"Bitseach!"

The laughter in response was chilling in its arrogance. "Come alone or bring your armies. It will make no difference to the outcome, for neither human nor Sidhe can resist or defeat me. The blood of the vanquished will make me stronger."

"Many before you have thought the same. Yet they are no more than dirt, and their corpses feed the maggots," said Gràinne.

"They were pale shadows."

"The fresh scar on your cheek says otherwise." Gràinne's right hand moved slowly to the longsword strapped to her back.

Heat flared in Sidheag's voice. "Come to me, or would you rather I feed my blood to Brianag, and we test whose breast she prefers?"

Gràinne growled like a feral cat and crouched, sweeping the long-sword from its sheath. The pause seemed interminable before Sidheag chuckled. "You are pitiful; you do not have the strength or power to face me and never will. Do what you will to this child. She has served her purpose. Without me, she will not thrive."

* * *

Released and in a daze, the young girl looked around, uncertain and suddenly afraid. Her resurrected thoughts accused her of terrible deeds, and her mouth tasted foul. The léine she wore clung to her body and had few areas not stained with blood. She stretched out her hand. "Please."

Gràinne walked closer, and a look of hope entered the girl's terrified eyes. A few strides more and the longsword's blade arched through the air. Steel flashed red from the setting sun. A blonde head dropped to the dirt as its body fell to the ground.

The violence to one so young drew horrified gasps from the onlookers, some of whom were fathers from Dùn Brion. Gràinne snarled at their disapproval. "What? Which of you would have stepped forward to assume responsibility for her behaviour in the fort? Which of you would have volunteered a bed in your home? Which of you would have let her sleep in the same cot as your daughters?"

Gràinne snorted derisively. "Just as I thought, no one. Now she is the responsibility of the bean-sidhe and the Goddess."

CHAPTER 9

Brion shook his head at the sight before him. A single funeral pyre burned in the centre of Dùn Brion's market square. Mothers, sisters, and lovers wept; fathers and brothers shed a tear and vowed bloody retribution. At Brion's side, Seonag felt the eyes of the bereaved accuse her, but of what? *What could I have done to prevent the slaughter?* Still, she was the garrison commander. Dùn Brion's safety was her responsibility; grief is emotional, not rational. She stood, head held high and straight-backed. Few saw her brush away the tears that escaped her control.

"Thirty men and women butchered, and hardly enough remains for a single bonfire," Brion murmured. No more and nothing more significant was required. Birds and predators had carried off the larger chunks of meat before Dùn Brion's slaves ascended the Sleagh to glean the remaining pitiful scraps of flesh and bone. No one could divine the dead from the missing.

To the side of the courtyard stood a long, wooden bench laden with gore-encrusted weapons, belts, and personal possessions. It awaited kin who had summoned up enough courage to sift through all that was left of their loved ones.

***

In the corner of the yard, sheltered from the mourners, a single man moaned and wept, but only for himself. Two hard-faced guards stood on either side, ignoring his pleas for mercy and water. Gone was the arrogant mien of Gormal's envoy. His band had been overtaken by Cearbhall well before the Mòine Mohr marshlands. Battered senseless by man and beast, they were put down like rabid dogs.

The captured messenger's return to the fort set his foolish conceit in a stark light. Chained to a single pinewood post, his back had been whipped bloody until he embraced unconsciousness. His future was certain—more torture and a slow, agonising death.

On the dirt, at his feet, lay his right hand. It was Brion's savage response to Gormal's "gift." The messenger trembled at the memory of Brion's unforgiving eyes as he ordered guards to stretch out his arm. There was no compassion as the king's sword descended or when the messenger screamed as hot irons sealed his wound. Yet the act imprinted on the man's mind was the deliberation of Brion as he wiped his blade clean.

Gormal's man wondered what tragedy had stayed his painful demise. Yet that would not last. The awful stares of those who passed by foretold a need to inflict pain. Feverishly the man racked his mind for a tidbit of information that would stay his execution.

✳✳✳

Cassán sat astride the bloodstained log and methodically scratched and crushed the growing population of flea bites on his arms and legs. Yet that was not the end of his parasitic invasion. With a sigh of satisfaction, he plucked and squashed another louse from his bush of pubic hair. His victory was fleeting as immediately his scalp started to itch.

The squeal of rusted iron hinges announced the opening of the entrance to his cell. Curious, Cassán looked up. He took pleasure in the grunts and curses of the guards. The wooden door, swollen with dampness, fought their efforts and dug deep ruts in the dirt floor.

A young woman entered the chamber, and Cassán stood slowly and painfully. By her dress, Cassán guessed she was one of Dùn Athad's serving wenches or slaves. *Is there a difference?* He watched her look around, screw up her nose at the stench, and squint her eyes to pierce the gloom.

With a sigh of exasperation, she shouted, "How the Hag am I to obey the king's orders if I can't see more than an arm's length in front of me? Fetch torches." A heated discussion between the guards ended with a curse and stools dragged across the hallway's stone floor. A short time later, two entered and placed rushlights in several sconces. As they exited, they glared at the girl and promised retribution.

The young woman watched Cassán glance at the open cell door and shook her head. "I would not advise what you're thinking. You're in no state to get past me, let alone the two brawny guards outside this door or the two more at the hallway's end."

"My father would tell you that bravery is not in my character."

She paused to consider her words. "Those closest to us are often mistaken, and with the Goddess's help, every man or woman can change. However, there is also reality. This room lies in the bowels of Dùn Athad. There are no exterior walls and no connecting doorways. The only way out of here is by Gormal's orders—or if you're dead."

"That's cheery. What other words of wisdom do you bring me?"

"Just this. A pleasant manner will achieve more than sarcasm; feeling sorry for yourself will lead to poor decisions." The words were harsh, yet Cassán knew they were true.

"I apologise." Cassán lifted his arm. "Yet perhaps you will allow me a little self-pity. I've had none from my visitors so far." Cassán looked down. "And until now, the darkness has covered my nakedness and embarrassment."

A tear began its journey down the girl's cheek but was quickly flicked away. In the flickering torchlight, Cassán missed the act. She shrugged slender shoulders, moved closer, and pointed to the stump. "Please sit. Gormal has commanded me to care for your wound. He does not wish you to die from infection since, for the moment, you're a valuable asset." She gave a smile, which Cassán thought made her face look beautiful, even with the smudges of dirt.

Cassán put her at about seventeen summers. Whether wench or slave, life would not be easy for one of her age in any noble's dùn. A closer look at the girl's léine showed accumulated stains, both front and back, and in places that pointed to abuse. Cassán's cheeks reddened at how he knew of such things, and his ears burned as he recalled the protests and tears of similar girls in Dùn Brion. He, and his friends, had a lot to answer for, but only he was alive to remedy the wrongdoing. His sigh was long and full of contrition.

"Deep thoughts?"

"Only regrets."

"It's not your fault that you're in these circumstances."

"Sadly, it is."

He watched as she took a pace back, walked around, and inspected him. He felt like a slave on the auction block. Anger and embarrassment reddened his cheeks, but he bit back a retort. *Progress?*

She unwound the rags covering the stump of his arm, and he inhaled sharply as the rough material pulled dead flesh from the still-raw wound. "Sorry," she muttered, yet continued regardless. The salve she spread over the injury cooled the sundered flesh. Cassán wondered how much of the burning sensation was in his head. The balm also held a sting. Cassán chuckled, recalling an old druid telling him that medications were useless if they did not taste awful or cause pain.

"Your face looks better when you smile." She stood up with a soft groan as she finished. Cassán noticed the dirt on her knees.

"I'm sorry. I should have let you sit."

She shook her head and smiled. In the flickering rushlights, he imagined her eyes were green and that the flames picked out deeper red highlights in the long braids. "It is easier for me to kneel while attending to the wound." The young woman then pointed to the weeping, ragged knife wound. "Do you make a habit of gathering scars?"

Cassán shook his head at another memory of his stupidity. "It was my younger sister—half-sister—who did this."

"We have something in common. My sister's an evil bidse, too."

Another shake of Cassán's head. "No, she had every right. I'm not a good person."

"We'll see."

He observed her clean his thigh wound and close it with new stitches. Surprisingly, it did not hurt, which made the girl's brow furrow. *Why?* Silence descended on the cell but broke when his nurse said, "Gormal has ordered me to tend to you when I finish my other duties. It may not be every sunset. The next time I'll bring salve made from plants for the flea bites."

She paused as if choosing her words carefully and shrugged. *There's no sense in me coddling him.* "Next time, I'll bring a fine, bone comb that I use for lice." She felt Cassán's embarrassment. "I might have to scrape the hair from your head if it's heavily infested, but better that than disease." Cassán squirmed as she made a point of looking at his cock and balls. "There, too."

Then she smiled and said, "Shite! I almost forgot these." She rummaged under her léine and produced two apples. She laughed. "I have big tits but not that big." She glanced around as if checking they were not watched. "I expect the food you get is little more than the slop they feed the swine. I work mostly in the dùn's kitchens and will try to bring small morsels of something better."

"Thank you. If you're to be my healer, I should know your name."

"It's Eimhir. I should go now. My advice is don't antagonise your captors. Get strong and never give up hope." With that, Eimhir turned and exited the chamber.

She had walked only a few paces when Cassán heard a slap and Eimhir cry out. The sound of a table scraping across the stone floor followed. Harsh, lewd voices deliberately loud enough for Cassán to hear rasped, "It's time for our payment."

Grunts of brutal rutting and gasps of orgasmic release were interspersed with unheeded pleas for pity. Cassán imagined the sound of Eimhir's tears falling on the wooden bench and the stains they left.

Realising that her face was not smudged with dirt but bruised by fists shamed him. Head hung down, Cassán wept for those who had suffered because of him.

Still, when Cassán looked up, shame had turned to fury, and his eyes were steel-blue with promised revenge. His retribution list was quickly growing beyond his ability to fulfil the oath. He needed help. *I need my da.* The realisation was sobering.

***

Brion, Seonag, Cearbhall, and Gràinne looked at the two guards who lay in the frost-sprinkled mud. Daggers sprouted from their throats and chests. "She's good," said Gràinne. Seonag nodded in agreement.

"She?" queried Brion.

"Who but a woman, and likely an attractive one, could get close enough to kill two guards and do this?" All looked on the slumped corpse of Gormal's messenger, still hanging on the chains that bound him to the post. Gràinne pointed to where the man's cock should have been.

"The bitseach enjoys her work," Gràinne paused, smiled grimly, and pointed. "She used a sharp blade to cut his cock and balls off. Shock and blood loss would have silenced him. Thus, stuffing them in his mouth was a warning to others. A deep, long slash across the belly, and a shorter one upwards, let his guts escape. Finally, she cut across his throat, slowly." Gràinne indicated the throat tear. "She also switched blades. The jagged lines of the cut mean that she used a dull knife. A mean lady.

"She's almost as good as Iasg," muttered Gràinne, drawing a quizzical look from Brion.

"You may not remember Iasg. She's the hand-fast partner of the most accomplished assassin in Gaul and is also exceptionally skilled in that pro-fession." Brion looked at Gràinne, trying to understand how this was rel-evant to the bodies lying before them. "She's the partner of your brother, Beacán."

Genuine shock fell on Brion's face. How could the quiet, introverted brother he knew be a famed assassin?

"For what it's worth, he and Iasg are incredibly happy and have a lovely family. Neither is particularly delighted at their profession, but very few would challenge the claim that they are the best at their trade. Indeed, I wish they were here now and not in Ériu with your nieces."

Gràinne paused to chide Brion. "There are such things as fast ships and horses. The journey between the coastal settlements of Southern Albu, Aremorio, and Gaul is well-known and well-travelled by tin and other merchants." Gràinne sighed. "You've been alone in Dùn Brion for too long. Few here are close friends and none, save Cassán, are family. When this is over, you should consider whether being the rí of Dùn Brion is worth being estranged from those who love you."

Brion looked to Seonag. "Do we have anyone in Dùn Athad?" It ended Gràinne's uncomfortable digression, and she smiled.

Seonag shook her head. "We have tried, but Gormal and his garrison commander are not stupid. The ones I sent lie in the stronghold's dungeons or the ditches as food for the wolves."

"It seems Gormal's spies are more competent than ours," said Brion, ignoring Seonag's flushed cheeks. "Are there more of Gormal's people in Dùn Brion?"

"We always knew the probability of spies or traitors taking Gormal's gold." Seonag dipped her head. "Yes, and there's likely more than one." The heat in Seonag's face rose. *Have I done anything right in his eyes?*

"Yes, but I doubt you anticipated an assassin and a very skilled one. Double the guards. Triple them on those whom you consider targets. Revisit the list of who may be spies. Talk to our informants among the citizens and slaves. Find the bitseach and any others who support her. She may be the leader, but I doubt she acts alone." Brion tugged on his beard. "Then we can decide how to use her."

"I want her dead and her body in pieces—small pieces," said Seonag.

The wrath in Seonag's words and demeanour elicited a nod of agreement from Gràinne and a curious look on Brion's face. "Patience. I, too, want her dead. Yet she may be of more use to us alive. Until then, we find her, watch her, and feed her useless information."

Seonag nodded stiffly, made an excuse, and walked away.

***

"My priority is Brianag," said Gràinne quietly but menacingly. "I will have vengeance on the bitseach who took my daughter. No one will stop me, and patience is not one of my virtues."

"She is *my* daughter, too," retorted Brion, but Gràinne had already walked away.

In her chamber, Gràinne slumped in a chair that was as utilitarian as the dùn. Yet the comfort she needed could not be found in a seat. Fingers twisted in anguish as she repeated the events of the Sleagh over and over in her head. Could she have done anything to prevent Brianag's abduction? *Yes!* Her mind shrieked accusingly. *You should never have come home. What did you expect? The nightmares were a warning, and you ignored them.*

Head in her hands, tears cascaded down her cheeks to splash on the stone floor. After a while, Gràinne looked up, but her red-rimmed eyes saw beyond the room's beams. "Please, Ma. I need you."

***

In the fort's stables, Ealasaid wrapped the long, fur-lined cloak closer around her. The building provided shelter from the wind and icy rain that had begun to fall. Still, the early morning air held the chill of a harsh winter, and she was grateful for the warmth trapped within the garment. That it also hid her bloodstained léine and triubhas was a bonus.

Since before dawn, Ealasaid had held her position, out of sight of the trio inspecting the slain guards and messenger. She needed to understand their reaction, as it would help determine her next moves. A long finger scratched her arched nose, shedding tiny flakes of dried blood. The messenger was of no consequence. He was one of her useful eejits in Gormal's employ. Serendipity selected him to deliver Cassán's hand and sealed his fate. His death was inevitable to sever any links to her.

Yet the group was altogether too calm. Where was the anger, the shouted commands, the calls for vengeance? At one point, when the Na Daoine Tùrsach bidse turned, the assassin felt her stare and almost fled. That, however, would have been a mistake, and she was much too accomplished to make such a fundamental error.

Instincts inherited from her late father and king of Na Mèadaidh, Finnean Mac Sèitheach, scratched at her mind and raised the fine hairs on her neck and arms. Ealasaid's heartbeat was steady, and she had no fear as she watched and planned her next move. *That is my throne that you sit on, Brion, and I will bring you to your knees.* There would definitely be a reaction to her murders. The residents of the fort would demand it. But what form would it take? Coldly she considered her small team. *Who will make a suitable sacrifice?*

Ealasaid gave a long sigh. If she stayed much longer, her fat-arsed hand-fast partner would be screaming to be fed and pampered. When this mission was over, he would die—slowly. As for her twin daughters, she might allow them to live a few more years. Yet they had almost cost Ealasaid her perfectly apportioned figure. Surely, she deserved some recompense for the pain of the births and the hard work she had put into regaining her curvaceous shape.

✳✳✳

As the sun set in the western sky, two women, both strong, fierce warriors, stood on the stone ramparts—each solitary and deep in the turmoil of their minds. A lone raven called from the forest, startling them from their thoughts. They were not alone. Gràinne smiled. She liked Seonag and recognised another who suffered even in the depths of her troubles. She walked to where Seonag stood.

"None of this is your fault. Yet you are the garrison commander, and enemies will use this to assign blame and make you the path to achieving their ambitions." Gràinne gripped Seonag's shoulders and held her gaze. "Those you have previously thought loyal may not support you as they once did. You try to hide your feelings for Brion, but I see the disappointment in your eyes and demeanour." Gràinne inhaled. "I also see how Brion looks at you, but he is a rí, and recent events colour his perception."

Seonag shivered as a night breeze swept across the wall.

"Your fate is in *your* hands. Few would blame you for leaving Dùn Brion. The ríthe and warlords of Southern Albu and Gaul are always eager to recruit experienced warriors. If you choose this path, I will provide a pair of swift horses." Gràinne paused. "Or you can stand and fight for what you want and value… and love. In that case, I hope you have the strength to endure."

"People say you're the future bhanrigh of Dùn Brion," said Seonag. The bitterness in her voice saddened Gràinne.

"It is never wise to take heed of gossip. More often than not, it is proven wrong." Seonag's misery pained Gràinne, and she wanted to hug the warrior. Instead, she turned and strode away.

"I will fight," mouthed Seonag into the wind, inhaling deeply to settle the turmoil within herself.

CHAPTER 10

To Brion, the weather conspired with the Goddess to underscore the gravity of the occasion. Late autumnal, purple-grey skies laden with snow and sleet glowered. Thunder rumbled in the distance, and lightning flashed randomly. All were portentous elements.

The gathering of the rìghrean and bhanrìgh—few would dispute Gràinne's right to the title—was born of necessity, and they assembled in Dùn Brion's Great Hall. The host, due to the stronghold's central location, was Brion. However, assuming his usual roles as pragmatist and conciliator was impossible.

Unsurprisingly, Brion was agitated due to the kidnapping of his son and daughter. Deserved or not, a burden of guilt sat on his shoulders. *Why did I not consider Cassán's fate when I made him an outcast? Could I have done more to protect Brianag?* Blàr and Drostan looked at Gràinne warily. Lost in thoughts of Brianag, she ignored them. Seonag glared at Drostan, but the others were too preoccupied to notice.

★★★

"My brother, Brandubh, and sister, Mòrag. How are they? Well, I hope." It had been a score of summers since the royal family of the Ravens had gathered at their father's funeral pyre. The laudable effort by Blàr to drag some sense of common ground into the conversation foundered when Gràinne's eyes misted. Blàr knew the answer would not be to his liking.

"Brandubh, Rí of Clann Ui Flaithimh and the Ravens, died a hero in battle. His last moments were in his sister's arms." Tears rolled down Gràinne's cheek, splashing the oak table before her. "I was privileged to fight at his side."

Blàr's fingers combed shoulder-length ginger hair and stroked the single raven feather hanging from a thin, black braid. Never a demonstrative man, Blàr's lips moved as he silently whispered a prayer to the Goddess. "My sister?"

Gràinne heaved a sigh of relief, and her eyes brightened. "Your sister lives. She is a great warrior and an even greater mother." Blàr's brown eyes widened at the thought of the wayward sister he knew being an exemplary mother. "Mòrag is the hand-fast partner of Torcán Ó Dubhghaill, and they both reign happily as rí and rígan in southern Gaul." At that, Blàr and Brion exhaled sharply. A more tempestuous partnership they could not envisage. "Torcán is devoted to Mòrag, and she to him."

Drostan looked to Blàr, who nodded and answered the unspoken question. "By the laws of the Ravens' succession, Mòrag ranks higher than me and is the rightful bhanrigh, should she choose to return." Blàr smiled at the question he knew was in the minds of those present. "I will not stand in her way. I was never meant to be rìgh, and it is a position I would gladly pass on."

"I very much doubt Mòrag will return," said Gràinne. "She has her own kingdom with Torcán. Sorry." With a sad smile and a sigh, Gràinne continued. "Too many brothers and sisters rely on distant memories, forgoing embraces and kisses. When we get past our present tribulations, Mòrag would be overjoyed to see you. I doubt you're as poor a sailor as me."

Blàr smiled. "Thanks. Your rebuke is well-founded and accepted."

Gràinne bit her lip and looked at Drostan. She had departed Gaul before Conall's battle with Rome, and some premonition held her back from asking the question on her lips. Still, Drostan had a discerning eye for people's behaviour and motivations. He saw Gràinne's discomfort, and it was not difficult to recognize what she needed to ask. As for Gràinne, Drostan's expression and the look in his eye gave her an answer she did not wish to hear.

"Your father, Fearghal, died at the Battle of Alia. By all accounts, he killed more than any other that day." Drostan pulled on an earlobe thickened by many fights and paused as if pondering a mystery. "Yet his body and longsword were never found. His daughter, Neamhain, mysteriously disappeared on the same day, as did the Sidhe, Mongfhionn." Drostan grunted. "But then that is typical of her entrances and exits."

Gràinne sobbed at her loss, yet she had a knowing smile when she lifted her head. "Believe what you will. They live in my heart and in a realm I may visit."

* * *

Inevitably, the mood of the meeting descended into acrimony and accusation. The hands of the kings' and queen's shield-men hovered over pommels smoothed by use as they moved to protect the ones they had sworn to defend with their lives. At Brion's side, Seonag scowled a warning at Drostan.

"Stand down," growled Drostan to his shield-man. The signal, followed by the nodded heads of Blàr, Brion, and Gràinne, saw the guardians appear to relax. Yet their eyes told a contrasting story as they measured potential allies and enemies.

"Why are you here and at this specific time?" Drostan barked at Gràinne. Before she could answer, he looked at Brion and rumbled, "As for you, you've known of Brianag for a long time. If you wanted to meet your daughter, Pytheas would have arranged ships to bring *you* to *her.*" Drostan's single, intense amber eye stared at Gràinne, and he returned to his original question. "Again, what are your intentions?" Drostan's usually blunt demeanour now had the sharp edge of challenge.

"I did not know of the trouble between Brion and Cassán," said Gràinne.

"A druid's answer!" said Drostan. "You knew of the rising of the blood priests of the Na Daoine Tùrsach."

"Only in dreams and visions. They may have been long-buried memories needing resolution." Gràinne lips pursed, not believing her own words.

"You journeyed based on night frights and a desire to bring Brianag to Brion." Drostan shook his head. "I don't believe you. Something else plays here."

Gràinne frowned at Brion and snapped at Drostan, "I thought Brianag would be safe with her father in a stronghold surrounded and protected by the armies of the vaunted Forest People. Obviously, I was mistaken."

Brion and Drostan started at her words, Brion with guilt at not protecting Brianag, Drostan at the insult Gràinne had delivered. Yet Blàr was not concerned with the ill-tempered duel. His eyes were drawn to the flowing sigils on Gràinne's face, her eyes, which had darkened, and her white-knuckled grip on the table.

He tapped the table with his dagger's pommel, commanding Brion and Drostan's attention. "I think we should remember that we are kings and queen and calm the Hag down," Blàr spoke softly but with authority and inclined his head in Gràinne's direction.

"Shite!" breathed Brion and Drostan. "What is she?"

***

Drostan looked at Blàr and said, "Bring us up to date on events in the north-east."

"A cycle of the moon past, nine girls, all around fifteen summers old, were taken from the villages and farms near Cùil Daothail. They have not been seen since." Blàr continued, "Yet this is not the full story. Over many moon cycles, scores of young females have disappeared, likely to feed the priests' bloodlust and other depravities. Rumours abound of the rebirth of the Baobhan Sith. Fools, power-seekers, and the dissolute flock to her banners."

Drostan slumped in his chair. "I had hoped such times were in our past." Straightening up, Drostan looked pointedly at Gràinne. "You are the only pureblood of Diadhaidh's lineage. Yet, Brianag and her sister may suit the High Priest's lust for power. And the younger ones would be more mal-leable." Exasperated, Drostan shook his head. "What madness drew you here to put your daughter and the people of this land in peril?" Gràinne and Brion exchanged the briefest of glances.

"What have you not told us?" Drostan asked.

"The Baobhan Sith's name is Sidheag, and she has taken Brianag," said Gràinne.

"The Hag's bony arse! This is worse and moving faster than I thought," said Blàr as he listened to Brion's and Gràinne's tale of Brianag's abduction. He looked at Drostan, who shook his head as if not wanting to believe his ears. "This time, we may be unable to stop the bidse." Blàr addressed Gràinne. "At least your grandmother, Diadhaidh, was human. The Baobhan Sith has bided her time well, moves freely across the land, and has gathered her daughters—her Brood."

"I will not allow any harm to come to *my* daughter," growled Gràinne.

"In the past, the Na Daoine Tùrsach followed the priests like lambs to the slaughter and committed unspeakable atrocities. What makes you think it will be different this time?" asked Drostan.

"Because they never had me as their queen," retorted Gràinne.

"They also never had a fully risen Baobhan Sith," snarled Drostan. "Some say she is more powerful than the Aes Sidhe from whom many sus-pect she came."

"No! That cannot be," said a white-faced Gràinne.

"My daughter was not the only one snatched from us." The quietness of Brion's words cut through the ascending crescendo of accusation and riposte.

"He is his mother's son and a wastrel. He has always been such. The Goddess has done you a service. Accept it and focus on the real problem," growled Drostan.

The ominous silence that followed Drostan's judgment was broken by the scrape of Brion's throne over cold, grey stones as he stood. "If you want a war with Dùn Brion and the Na Mèadaidh, you're going in the right direction. He is my blood. No matter his faults, he did nothing to deserve the pit of vipers he has fallen into or his treatment. The boy is no more than a fidchell piece in a game between Gormal, me—and *you.*"

Another chair grated on the flooring as Gràinne stood and walked to stand by Brion. "I stand with Brion."

Alongside Gràinne, Seonag and Cearbhall nodded. "So do we."

"Enough of this nonsense," said Blàr, staring at Drostan. "Who among *your* sons and daughters are innocent lambs or paragons of virtue? Would you let any of them languish in Gormal's dungeon or Sidheag's crannag? I don't think so." Seonag's eyes widened at the mention of Drostan's daughters. She quickly regained her composure, yet Gràinne did not miss the glances shared between her and Drostan. *What is going on here?*

Drostan's eye gleamed, making its green flecks more prominent. The long scar on his face, a gift from a bear, twisted as he smiled. "Well, that's settled that matter. We're united—both children or none. Now, what is the plan? Winter is almost upon us."

The crackle of logs in the chamber's firepits and the sweet aroma of burning peat helped soothe the tempers of those in the room.

"As Drostan has stated, Samhain is a quarter cycle of the moon away. The passes to the highlands are already almost impassable, and heavier snowfalls are on the way," said Blàr. He shrugged. "Indeed, I will find it challenging to return to Cùil Daothail. Yet, the Ravens are in great danger should the blood priests of the Na Daoine Tùrsach prevail." Looking at Gràinne, he said, "I'm sorry, but barring a miracle, I think getting to your daughter before Imbolg will be impossible."

"Then I will ask the Goddess for a miracle," said Gràinne.

"Blàr, you should plan on holding Cùil Daothail until Imbolg. I suggest you travel to the settlement at first light and prepare for a siege. Sadly, Cùil Daothail is the main food source for the bidse and her followers—human or not."

Drostan looked around the table. "Does anyone know if the bidse has any weaknesses?"

"The 'Bhanrìgh Fuil is her weakness," said Gràinne, although she wondered where the thought had come from. In her head, Gràinne heard the cackling voice of one who was neither Diadhaidh nor Sidheag. *I'm going mad.*

"Then we're in deep shite!" retorted Drostan. "For who knows what side that creature, if she exists, is on?"

"She exists," said Gràinne softly.

***

"Now to our other problem: Cassán. At least this resolution is in man's realm and will be settled by swords." Drostan looked at Brion. "You and I should have dealt with Gormal long before this, which is on us. I will add five thousand to Dùn Brion's army. How many can you levy?"

Brion looked at Seonag. "Definitely two thousand, maybe three. Given enough time, that could grow to five thousand with warriors from the outer settlements," said Seonag.

"Time is not on our side," responded Gràinne. "Would a score of my riders help to spread the word?" At an enthusiastic nod from Seonag, Gràinne turned to Cearbhall. "Coordinate with Seonag. You'll need guides from the fort. Hopefully, they'll be good riders, too."

"We still have a major obstacle to overcome," said Drostan. "The Mòine Mohr. Gormal's dùn is surrounded by boglands, and few know the paths across it. And if we successfully traverse the marshes, we still have the bluffs that Dùn Athad sits on and the hillfort's walls to climb. That bastard can sit inside Dùn Athad and laugh at us." Drostan snorted. "Besides, who fights in winter?"

"When will the bogs freeze over?" Everyone looked up at Gràinne's question. Brion looked at Drostan, who shrugged.

"A cycle of the moon after Samhain, the bogs will be solid enough to walk on. How does that help with besieging the dùn?" said Brion.

"We don't have to besiege Dùn Athad. We just have to make them think that's our plan." Gràinne turned to Brion. "How much do you know of your sister Mórrígan's reputation?" Brion's eyes widened as Gràinne explained how his sibling had earned the title of An Fiagaí Dorcha—The

Dark Huntress.

"I doubt I can reach the terror Mórrígan inspired, but I can make life in the settlements that look to Gormal for protection a living nightmare. With the outcry from his subjects, he'll find it hard to remain within the walls of Dùn Athad."

"Does the bastard care for his people?" asked Brion.

"This does not solve the issue of Cassán. At the first sign of a siege or mass attack, Gormal will kill the boy… and painfully at that." Drostan's apparent new-born concern for his son brought an ironic smile to Brion's face and an expression of helplessness.

Brion looked at Gràinne. "Like you, I need a miracle from the Goddess."

***

As the gathering paused to relieve bladders and allow the servants to re-fresh the food and drink, Drostan took Gràinne aside. Gruffly he said, "I'm no go-between. However, I have a message from your Thracian prince." Gràinne's eyes widened. "Amodocus has agreed with Pytheas for him and his men to travel to Northern Albu. He likely set sail shortly after me."

Gràinne smiled. "That's the first good news I've received since leaving Massalia."

***

The group had barely resumed their seats when the Great Hall's heavy oak doors crashed open, flung aside like driftwood. Only the shadows cast by the flickering torches on either side of the door indicated that anyone was there. With one long stride, a tall, grey-cloaked figure stepped inside.

Swords whispered as they were drawn from wool-lined scabbards. Drostan grasped the axe that always lay within reach and balanced it in his hands. Warriors who previously stood along the hall's heavy tapestry and banner-covered walls formed a shield-wall and moved to intercept the intruder.

"Do you think these could stop me?"

The mocking voice held a tone of undisguised authority, which, on this occasion, appeared to be tempered with humour. With a flick of a slender wrist, the hood was flung backwards. A mass of blonde, almost white, tresses with thistle-pink highlights was released.

"Ma!"

It was debatable which event astounded those who gathered the most: the dramatic entrance of the Sidhe, Mongfhionn, or the way Gràinne tossed her chair aside and ran to the door. The strong embrace captured Gràinne's relief at Mongfhionn's presence. It also made the recipient expel a sharp "Ooof!" and smile broadly, a rare phenomenon.

"You have many questions, Daughter, but first, we have serious things to discuss. Introduce me to those with whom I may not be familiar."

A beaming Gràinne walked before Mongfhionn to the high table and announced, "I present the Lady Mongfhionn of the Aes Sidhe." Ripples of delight were tempered with hints of consternation among those seated and standing. After a short pause, Gràinne added, "And my mother—by adoption."

"Cease all talk of adoption, child," gently chastised the Sidhe. "You are as much a daughter to me as Neamhain."

Brion rose from his throne and bowed. "Welcome to Dùn Brion. I was much younger when we last met, my Lady. Although my memory might deceive me, you do not appear to have aged a single sunset." Brion sighed. "However, I suspect your presence points to us being in even deeper trouble than we know."

Mongfhionn dipped her head. "Thanks for your compliment and welcome. Sadly the answer to your supposition is yes, you are."

Beside Brion, Drostan said, "Bloody Aes Sidhe. A bigger group of interfering women it'd be hard to find."

"I cannot give you back the eye you lost, Drostan, but I *can* take the light from the one that remains." The tone of the Sidhe's voice was chilling, and Drostan's amber eye glittered in anger.

CHAPTER 11

Cassán shivered uncontrollably in a cell where the water leaching into the walls had already frozen. Yet his eyes brightened as the dungeon's door opened, and Eimhir stepped in. That she was accompanied by a chorus of shouted promises of brutal rutting after her visit made Cassán wince.

Head held high, Eimhir approached Cassán but stopped short as she saw his trembling. Her first thoughts were that he had developed a fever from an infection. Yet she also observed that he was not sweating. A hand on his forehead and a glance at the chamber's ice-covered walls, and she had her answer.

"I want heat brought in here immediately, or I will go to Gormal, and you can explain why his prisoner froze to death," she shouted.

More curses and threats followed as an iron brazier was carried into the chamber, filled with wood, and set alight. Standing her ground, Eimhir said, "This fire will be kept going day and night. Or, as the Hag is my witness, I'll see Gormal knows how you brought an important prisoner to the gates of Mag Mell."

"You risk too much by caring for me," said Cassán. "I do not wish you to visit again." His voice told Eimhir how much sorrow his words brought, and she smiled. Cassán's behaviour, certainly in her presence, was at odds with the common gossip she continued to hear about the prionnsa. Eimhir shrugged. Rumours are rarely a reliable source of information.

Seeing her shoulders lift, Cassán assumed Eimhir had agreed to his proposal. Unsuccessfully, he tried to disguise his sadness. A hand on his head, the gentle ruffling of his hair, and a smile on her lips told Cassán he had misjudged his healer.

"Ewww!" exclaimed Eimhir, quickly withdrawing her hand and squishing several lice between her fingertips. "Sorry, but I have no choice." A quick hitching of her léine revealed a pale thigh to which a blade was strapped. As she withdrew the knife, it gleamed in the torch and firelight. Cassán flinched… and then looked perturbed.

"How did you conceal that?"

Eimhir smiled at Cassán's disquiet. "Men rarely see anything but my big arse when they mount me." With a twist of her lips, she said, "For them, I'm a treat. They're more used to rutting sheep and goats."

A boyish grin spread across Cassán's face. "It's not that big."

"And how would you know that?"

"Informed observation." Cassán attempted to divert the conversation from its natural conclusion. "I don't want you to suffer humiliation and hurt on my part. Please make this your last visit."

Touched by Cassán's concern, Eimhir stretched out her hand to touch his head but recoiled at the thought of the livestock in his hair. "Look, in my station, being used by men and some women is part of life. Many are destroyed by this, while others are strengthened.

"Yes, there is no doubt that your guards will lift my léine and rut me when I leave, but my *maighdeanas* was taken when I was little more than a child. A bath in cold spring water will cleanse me. If something else is needed, there are those nearby with knowledge of herbs and plants.

"Consider also that your jailors have a harsh life and look forward to their use of me. They have no desire to see my visits cease and that allows me more freedom. Keep it from your mind, for I need you strong in body and spirit."

Cassán looked at Eimhir oddly, and she wondered what was going through his mind. Finally, he said, "From your speech and manner, I know you're not low-born. How did you become a servant in Gormal's dùn?"

Eimhir's face took on a furious look, making Cassán wonder if he should have kept his mouth shut. "My bidse sister betrayed me. She was never one to tolerate a rival, although I could never fathom why she perceived me as one. When I was fifteen summers, I joined a group of mercenaries." Eimhir smiled. "I'm very good with blades." Cassán gulped as she held up the dagger.

"My band were paid to defend a settlement that was being persecuted by Gormal's thugs. We were travelling to take up positions when we were ambushed. Only a few of us survived. Gormal took great delight in telling me who sold us out. It transpired that my sister was one of his spies." Eimhir lifted her hands. "And here I am."

"I'm sorry."

"It's in the past, and I don't like to think about it." Eimhir inhaled and exhaled slowly. Then she raised the blade and smirked. "If that was an attempt at putting off the inevitable, it didn't work." Cassán groaned.

The knife's edge was honed sharp and cut through Cassán's red locks quickly as he perched on the log. The smell of brimstone made his nose crinkle as Eimhir tossed his tresses onto the brazier. "We'll burn the bastards." Cassán wondered if it was just the lice to which she referred. "This may hurt." The warning came as the blade scraped his skull to remove the last vestiges of hair. Cassán flinched several times as he felt the dagger nick his skin. Each time Eimhir said, "Sorry," but she never stopped.

At last, Eimhir said, "Finished!" She rolled her neck, cracked finger joints, and stretched cramped muscles.

"That wasn't too bad," said Cassán.

Eimhir smiled. "I'm only done with your head." She looked pointedly downwards.

"No!"

Cassán watched with a terrible fascination as Eimhir's blade deftly denuded his manhood and balls of hair untrimmed since puberty. Many thoughts tumbled into his newly shaven head, not the least that it would be unwise to move to relieve the cramp slowly spreading across his arse. Yet her touch on his cock and the caress of his balls overrode all but one, which became obvious.

"*That* is not making my task easier."

"Sorry," murmured Cassán, feeling his face flush.

"Be a shame to waste it, though. Consider this a reward for good behaviour," whispered Eimhir before her mouth opened and her head dipped.

***

It was dark when Brianag awoke on a cot of rushes, straw, and meadow-sweet. Yet that meant little in the highlands, for it could be morning or night. She shivered and exhaled, watching her breath float like a tiny cloud before her. She pulled the heavy wolf fur closer, grateful for its warmth.

The royal crannag was surrounded on all sides by mountains. It sat far from the loch's shore, connected by a wooden walkway. As such, the structure was exposed to freezing winds, rain, and heavy snowfalls. Winter drew near. Perhaps it was already here. Soon the lake would freeze, and the weather would worsen. Brianag thought about her home in Southern Gaul, and a tear rolled down a cheek flushed pink from the cold.

She looked around and shuddered again at the sight of her companions. Dressed only in long white *léinte*, the nine "daughters" of Sidheag stood in a circle around her but distant, with their backs to the crannag's curved wall. On seeing that Brianag was awake, the females glided closer.

Were they curious? Did they have any human emotions, or were they empty vessels filled with Sidheag's venom and hate? And why just nine? More to the point, could they be killed? Their silence and vacant eyes made the hairs on Brianag's arm stiffen. Even with the warmth of the pelt, Brianag continued to shiver, and her teeth chattered. How long had passed since her abduction? Where were her ma and da? Many questions filled her head, but Brianag had no answers and scowled in frustration.

"The cold will get worse… much worse. As you see, it does not affect my daughters or me." Brianag started at the voice. "I can make the cold go away. You will feel neither cold nor heat with just a few drops of my blood. Consider it a gift, a kindness. There would be no terms attached."

Brianag snorted her disbelief. "*Póg mo thoin*—Kiss my arse! Bitseach."

"When your fingers, toes, and nose are white and feel like wax, and their tips turn black from frostbite; when the choice is which limb to sever or death, you will change your mind." Sidheag chortled. "Never let pride cloud your judgment. None of us is totally without redemption."

"Bitseach!"

Sidheag glanced at her daughters. Silently they moved to the door and exited. "We will talk later, but I have work to do." An elegant hand swept in a semicircle. "You are free to explore. You can try to escape, but that will be in vain. Even now, the passes are almost blocked by snow. And I will always know where you are."

CHAPTER 12

"Gràinne's and my children are missing…" began Brion.

"Brianag is *my* granddaughter," snapped Mongfhionn, her milk-pale cheeks flushed red. It was an ominous start to the conversation.

"My apologies," said Brion. "May I continue?" He took the brusque dip of the Sidhe's head as consent.

"My son, Cassán, is captured by Gormal and his hand delivered as proof. I expect he languishes in one of Dùn Athad's dungeons and will be used as leverage against me in the near future.

"However, that is a human tragedy, which will likely be resolved by bribery or men and women in battle." Brion reached for a jug of spring water, poured a measure into a small bowl, and sipped. This was not a time for wine and beer.

"Brianag's kidnappers, all female and apparently little more than children, killed veteran warriors without mercy and left little more than scraps of meat." Brion acknowledged Blàr, who sat across from him. "According to Blàr, the priests of the Na Daoine Tùrsach are abroad. Many girls and young women are missing and likely have been sacrificed.

"Rumours of the Baobhan Sith, a name previously used to frighten children into obedience, infest the highlands." Brion looked to Gràinne. "According to Gràinne, our foe is called Sidheag." Brion held the Sidhe's eyes without flinching, and for that, she smiled.

"Who or what are we dealing with, my Lady?"

For a moment, Mongfhionn hesitated. It was uncharacteristic and did not bode well. Feeling more comfortable on her feet, the Sidhe stood and began a slow walk, back and forth, along the length of the long table. To Brion, it appeared that she was marshalling her thoughts. *But for what, and why?*

"The Baobhan Sith, or Sidheag as you know her…" The words hung in the air before descending like a deluge of freezing water on those present. "…is my sister."

"I warned you. Bloody interfering—and dangerous—*bidsean.*"

"And I warned you, Drostan Ruadh. You live and rule by the consent of the Aes Sidhe, but others would gladly take your place. One of them, and you know who *she* is, may well serve the Forest People better." Mongfhionn's eyes glittered like polished obsidian as she glared at Drostan. "Debate is one of man's strengths. Arrogance and ignorance are not." While Drostan fumed, the rest chose to examine their fingernails or push morsels of food around clay plates.

"By sister, obviously I mean one of the Aes Sidhe. Sidheag was the first of us created, but she was flawed. The imperfection in her design was the need for blood to sustain her physical form. That soon became a thirst Sidheag could not control and now has no desire to limit. She will lose her powers if she stops feeding on flesh and blood and that Sidheag will never countenance."

"Could this get worse?" muttered Brion.

"It could and likely will, Brion Ó Cathasaigh. Sidheag became enamoured with some of the darker elements that inhabit the deep places of all creatures, whether man, god, or demi-god. Humans name this 'evil.' It twisted Sidheag's mind and made her the horror she is now." Mongfhionn's pink tongue flickered over full, red lips, moistening them. She looked at a chalice of water but shook her head.

"The rest of the Aes Sidhe, apart from a few of Sidheag's acolytes…"

"Shite! There's more of them!" This time it was Blàr who interrupted.

Mongfhionn shook her head.

"Not anymore. Sidheag could not tolerate rivals and so she destroyed the others. However, she does need a channel to be fully formed and powerful. The Priest Queens of the Na Daoine Tùrsach provided that." The Sidhe peered thoughtfully at Gràinne. "Sidheag needs A 'Bhanrìgh Fuil, conceived by untainted parents. That may be our only advantage." Gràinne looked uneasy.

"Sidheag amassed a terrifying amount of dark power and sustained it by blood. She became too much for the Aes Sidhe to control." Mongfhionn's long sigh presaged her next words. "We asked the Goddess for help. For the Aes Sidhe, that was a bitter pill to swallow, and, of course, the Goddess had her terms."

"Can we bring the history lesson to a close? Can *you* kill the bidse?" asked Drostan, having recovered some composure.

"No." The answer was not what those gathered expected or wanted to hear. "A Sidhe cannot kill another sister." Mongfhionn ground her teeth. "Hence why we were forced to ask the Goddess to intervene."

"The Hag's hairy arse!" Drostan's sentiment was shared by those around the table.

"The Goddess banished Sidheag to the depths of the Otherworld and eternal isolation. Being fickle, she also added what she considered a whimsical touch. Personally, I think the Goddess knew the Otherworld could not hold Sidheag forever. Hence, she marked Sidheag by transforming her feet into deer hoofs. Sidheag has a unique walk and is even more bitter because of it."

"We found hoof and wolf prints at some of the murders," said Blàr.

"I'm not surprised. Being a Sidhe, Sidheag can transform into an animal or bird. Most of us use that gift sparingly, but Sidheag always had a fondness for her wolf form." Mongfhionn finally took a sip of water. "Her pack always numbers nine, symbolising perfect power among the Celts and Gaels. All are female and inherit many of her abilities. Yet they are husks, expendable, and will die if Sidheag ceases to exist."

The Sidhe looked around the men seated. Her smile was unnerving and mocking. "To Sidheag, a man's only use is as food. She can and does rut with men but thank the Goddess, can never bear their children. Who knows what monsters they would be? Whether she enjoys the act, no one has lived to tell." The Sidhe paused and looked at Blàr and Drostan.

"Sidheag is ambitious and driven by revenge. I believe her immediate goal is to reign over Northern Albu. However, that will not constrain her desires or insatiable blood lust. Once secured, she will inevitably cast her eyes on the rest of Albu.

"The immediate threat is to Cùil Daothail. Sidheag cannot be allowed to secure that settlement and with it unfettered access to the lowlands." The Sidhe shook her head and looked at Blàr. "I may be able to throw some obstacles in Sidheag's path and provide tactical advice. However, you will have to hold the settlement until Imbolg—and maybe longer. Until a more permanent solution can be found. Your task will not be easy."

Turning to Drostan, Mongfhionn said, "The warriors you planned to give Brion against Gormal must, instead, be sent to reinforce Blàr at Cùil Daothail." Brion gasped at the implication, but the Sidhe shrugged. "As you said, yours is a human problem. Sidheag is not and must take priority. I'm sorry."

"What about A 'Bhanrìgh Fuil?" asked Blàr.

It was the question Mongfhionn had dreaded. She looked at Gràinne with a mother's concern. "I have things I need to discuss with my daughter. We should take a break."

✳✳✳

Later, the meeting of Northern Albu's royalty reconvened, and the Sidhe addressed them. "After her grandmother, Diadhaidh's death, Gràinne became the only surviving royal. She is the rightful Bhanrìgh of the Na Daoine Tùrsach." Mongfhionn looked at Gràinne. "She is not A 'Bhanrìgh Fuil—the Blood Queen—*yet*."

"More riddles," growled Drostan. "Tell us something we can use to defeat the bidse." The Sidhe's eyes narrowed, and she glared at Drostan.

Brion and Blàr sighed, frustrated at Drostan's animosity to Mongfhionn. Brion sensed that Mongfhionn's patience was a dry well.

"You are not helping," said Brion to Drostan. "Let the Sidhe speak."

"I agree," added Blàr. "The Lady knows more about unnatural things than we can ever hope to glean. We need her information… *and support.*" Taken aback at his allies' criticism, Drostan's jaw set in silent defiance.

"Thank you. Socially, physically, and by lineage, Gràinne fulfils the criteria for a Blood Queen. She is a pureblood, untainted by other tribes. Blood Queens had to be conceived by a Na Daoine Tùrsach mother who was a virgin until a hand-fast partnership was arranged. Gràinne was conceived by Diadhaidh's daughter and her partner, Caol. Her lineage can be traced back to the original A 'Bhanrìgh Fuil.

"However, Diadhaidh perceived her daughter as a future rival. She was sacrificed to quicken Sidheag's return and to eliminate the threat to her throne. There is no other candidate for the Blood Queen and, due to Gràinne's lifestyle and choice of rutting partners, there will be no more."

Gràinne squirmed in embarrassment and hissed, "Ma!"

"Gràinne is Sidheag's final and only chance for sustained and unlimited power." Hard eyes looked at Gràinne and calculated her value. "She is also our only chance of defeating the abomination."

Gathering her thoughts, or more precisely determining what should be revealed and what should remain unsaid, Mongfhionn paced the stone floor. "In their early days, the Na Daoine Tùrsach were a minor tribe of priest-kings and queens, firmly matriarchal, cannibalistic, and perpetually under attack. To survive and flourish, they needed a powerful ally." The Sidhe smiled. "The original Blood Queen was brutal but cunning and never trusted Sidheag. She knew that, like a wild beast, the apparition needed to be controlled. Thus she proposed an arrangement.

"Sidheag agreed to protect the Na Daoine Tùrsach. In return, the queen gave Sidheag form through blood sacrifices. During negotiations, the queen sacrificed enough blood to make Sidheag visible but insufficient to give her physical form. If Sidheag wanted form, which was her deepest desire, then there were 'terms.' She could never kill a current or future Blood Queen, and the singing of the Tuireadh would bind her. Sidheag, desperate for form, agreed. Yet the Blood Queen knew that Sidheag would escape the terms and conditions if she could.

"Subverting the agreement became Sidheag's focus. The major weakness of humans is their short life. Sidheag had no such restriction and could concentrate on the 'long game.' Thus, over generations, Sidheag gave the Blood Queens what they desired—wealth, health, and victory over enemies.

"With each generation, the fear increased that Sidheag would withdraw her munificence. The Blood Queens became weak-minded, conceding to her suggestions, and the cult of priests became loyal to Sidheag. Thus, she had effectively reversed the original arrangement." Mongfhionn lifted a cup from the table and sipped the cool water.

"Problem solved," said Drostan. "We set a trap for Sidheag, Gràinne sings the Tuireadh to bind her, and we remove the bidse's head with an iron blade."

"A simple solution put forward by a simple man," retorted Mongfhionn.

"Not helpful," muttered Brion as Drostan bristled at the insult.

"Were you not listening when I said Gràinne is not A 'Bhanrìgh Fuil yet?" said the Sidhe.

"How does she become A 'Bhanrìgh Fuil?" asked Brion.

Mongfhionn's answer was a shrug of her shoulders. She looked at Gràinne with a mother's concern. "Only Gràinne knows that. You have had more visions recently, haven't you?" Gràinne nodded. "And have, I suspect, been visited by the first Blood Queen. Listen to her, but be wary. Do not trust her."

"Shite! I've so many people in my head. Perhaps I'm doomed to madness," said Gràinne.

"So basically, we hold Sidheag at bay until Gràinne becomes the Blood Queen, whenever that is. Not exactly a great plan," remarked Brion.

***

As the meeting broke up, Drostan drew Blàr aside. "This cannot be allowed to happen again. When Sidheag is vanquished, the Blood Queen's line must end."

"I hope you're not suggesting what I think you are," retorted Blàr. "Did you not listen to Mongfhionn? Gràinne is the last of the Blood Queens. There can be no more."

"I do not trust any of the Aes Sidhe, and Mongfhionn is at the apex of their hierarchy. They have always had a self-centred agenda. How can we know the Sidhe speaks truthfully?" said Drostan. "Gràinne cannot be allowed to survive this war."

"I will not have the blood of an innocent on my hands or conscience."

"The blood of innocents has already been spilt to feed the Baobhan Sith."

"That is on Sidheag's hands, not Gràinne's," said Blàr. "Think on this, Drostan. How will you prevail against the Sidhe's wrath if you murder her daughter?" In answer, Drostan turned and stomped out of the room.

***

A cloaked figure stepped from the shadows, startling Drostan as he paused outside the door to his quarters. The expressionless face of Mongfhionn and the gleam in her obsidian eyes sent a shiver along his spine. His hand went to his belt loop, and he cursed. His axe lay on the table in the Great Hall.

"You plot against my daughter, and yet expect no retribution. You may have deserted your daughter, but I have no intention of abandoning mine. I am disappointed, Drostan, for I did not think you so foolish or short-sighted." Mongfhionn's hands reached out to touch Drostan's face. "I warned you I could take the light from your remaining eye."

"No!" gasped Drostan, realising he could no longer see the torches in the hallway. He was alone… and blind.

CHAPTER 13

394 B.C.—Winter—Samhain

The philosophy that no one is irredeemable met its foil in Ealasaid Nic Finnean. Madness could not be attributed to her, for her thoughts and actions were as clear as mountain spring water and sharp as the blades she wielded. Still, if Ealasaid had qualities to be admired, they were her patience and single-minded determination to achieve the goal she set for herself.

Her driving desire was simple: to wrest the throne of the Na Mèadaidh from Brion and return it to the true ruler of the Na Mèadaidh—herself. If Ealasaid could visit pain and death on those who had deprived her of her birthright, it was no more than justice and deserved retribution. Her activities, no matter how minor, were never unplanned or lacked purpose. Like her father and former Rìgh of the Na Mèadaidh, Finnean Mac Sèitheach, she was a twisted, cunning, and cold-blooded killer.

Ealasaid tolerated winter only because of a hedonistic love for the warmth and the feel of the thick wolf fur draped over her shoulders. It was dusk as she traversed Dùn Brion's yard on her way to the stables. With agility and deliberation, she skirted the growing number of ice patches and ridges of frozen mud. A turned or broken ankle was not on her agenda. Ealasaid smiled at all she passed and smugly congratulated herself.

The reason for Ealasaid's conceit, if she needed one, had little to do with the season. She had the perfect disguise. Over five summers ago, when she was seventeen, her appearance in Dùn Brion had caused little comment or gossip. Undoubtedly a beautiful and striking woman, Ealasaid bathed in others' admiration and was taken seriously by no one. "Nice tits and arse but as dense as Dùn Brion's stone walls" was the common perception.

Ealasaid saw no reason to persuade them otherwise. Her choice of partner, a low-born man who would not be recognised even in a small crowd, surprised and disappointed her many suitors. That said, the hand-fasting contract never put any constraints on her need to satisfy her baser cravings. Thus she took multiple transient rutting mates.

Following the murder of Gormal's envoy and his guards, Ealasaid had kept a low profile. Dùn Brion's guards and patrols had been tripled, and every nerve in her body screamed *Danger!* Dwellings inside and outside the fort were continually searched. Residents, primarily females, were taken for further scrutiny.

Gossip from the garrison confirmed that Brion and Seonag were looking for a female killer. *How do they know? Is it a ruse to draw me out?* The slow, steady arrival of warriors from the Na Mèadaidh's outlying settlements troubled Ealasaid as Brion assembled his army. The numbers assigned to track down the assassin and her team increased the threat of discovery.

The dùn celebrated the festival of Samhain. Boars turned slowly on iron spits; hundreds of amphorae of wine and casks of beer were cracked open. Ealasaid's pert nose wrinkled at the smell of woodsmoke, fat, and roasted flesh. The sounds of joyful celebration grated on her ears. Still, the feasting provided a distraction and welcome respite from Brion and Seonag's investigations.

A sacrificial goat had been selected, and she drew him into the stable's shadows. The young man—more a boy—nodded furiously, eager to please one he obviously desired. He took the blade proffered for "his safety" and, about to move away, stopped when a hand was placed on his forearm. Her smile enthralled him, and he watched her fur and then her léine fall to the straw.

His hands appreciated the swell of her ample breasts and the soft curve of her belly. One hand slid downwards to comb her lush bush, and soon his fingers opened her and plunged into her wetness. She felt his manhood harden and rub against her lower abdomen. He seized her firm, round arse cheeks and, lifting her up, slammed her against one of the stable's rough wooden uprights.

She smirked at what her hand-fast partner would think of the inevitable scratches on her back and the tale they told. She would taunt him with the marks and ask him to remove the unavoidable wooden splinters. She would laugh at his protests, knowing he feared losing access to her body. *Coward. Weakling. I'd think more of him if he beat me bloody.*

The strength of the young man's grip surprised Ealasaid, and she gasped involuntarily when he lowered her onto his manhood. Danger and imminent death had always heightened Ealasaid's sensitivity and increased the flow of lubrication. She moaned as he impaled her. His curses and cries as her nails dug into and raked his back raised her desire.

There was no foreplay, no finesse, just increasingly faster and deeper thrusts. The sustained vigour of his youth drove her to a climax. Yet there was no sentiment, no meeting of hearts. Thus, Ealasaid was glad when he grunted and emptied his seed into her with one final thrust. She had other things to do, other priorities.

She watched him walk from the stable. His back seemed straighter, and his step had a swagger, for he had a tale to brag about. In his memory, Ealasaid lay on the straw and listened to the stabled horses nicker as she played with her swollen labia. After bringing herself to an explosive climax, she stood and slipped on her garments. She thought it a waste that she had not rutted the boy before this evening and a pity that his end would be excruciating.

Ealasaid consoled herself that her subsequent actions would give the boy a fighting chance. Blade in hand, she moved through the joyous Samhain crowds. In her wake, she heard the cries of anguish and felt her hands wet. Time to return home and ensure her children were settled for the night… and get a bath. Young men were not known for their prudent choice of rutting partners, and she did not want to catch anything.

✳ ✳ ✳

Seonag and Brion stood alone on the ramparts in the moonlight. Senses were heightened by the smoky scents of bonfires combined with feasting and rutting. The time and location, supported by the sounds of celebration and frivolity, were perfect for romance. Yet since the kidnappings, tension and dishonesty about their desires had formed a deep chasm between them.

Over the past five summers, and since Seonag's promotion to shield-woman and then commander, fort gossip pointed to and even favoured, a more personal relationship between king and protector. Neither did anything to dissuade the rumours. The unspoken assumption had been that its release would be in one of their cots.

That it still remained unsaid was the problem. Few questioned their courage in battle, yet Brion and Seonag were cowards regarding love. Furthermore, since the abductions of Brianag and Cassán, an edge of distrust had slipped through a door that should have been firmly closed long ago. They were ships docked alongside the same jetty, but the currents threatened to take the vessels in different directions.

On this night, their friction broke, but not with honesty and declarations of love. From Dùn Brion's courtyard, a crescendo of discordant noises joined the revelries—those of terror and panic. Joy and laughter were replaced by screams and tears. "The bidse is clever," snarled Seonag. Brion nodded, exhaled a weary sigh, and shouted to the guard towers and those waiting below.

"Watch all who leave by the gates. Whoever it is, I want them alive and standing before me in the morning."

The two turned to descend the steps to the yard, and two pairs of eyes met in the moonlight. Yet the spark between them had no tinder to ignite a fire.

"After you, my rìgh."

Brion dipped his head and placed a booted foot on the first step. "Shite!" he muttered, not referring to the disruption of the Samhain celebrations.

Unseen by Brion, a solitary tear rolled down Seonag's cheek.

***

It was barely past sunrise when a shout of, "Sound the alarm! Warriors to the ramparts!" came from the southern gateway's guard towers. Across the dùn, men and woman hurriedly donned armour, grabbed sgiathan and weapons, and climbed rough, stone steps to their posts. Along the battlements, braziers were lit. Great cauldrons, filled with hot cinders, oil, and water, simmered and smoked.

"What next?" muttered Seonag. The fort was still anxious about the Samhain deaths, and the perpetrator remained at large. Alongside her, Cearbhall gripped the stone wall and watched.

The source of the alarm was a large band of riders who had crossed the Abhainn Dubh river to the east and were proceeding at a slow canter in Dùn Brion's direction. Yet the mounted warriors' demeanour lacked any sense of urgency. Soon they approached the long, winding dirt track that ended at the hillfort's gates.

The group's horse tack and fittings glittered in the morning's weak, wintry sunlight. The leader, obviously a tall, well-built man, wore a domed helmet with a high and forward-inclined apex and protective cheek and nose pieces. A thick crest of bronze feathers embellished the helmet from the tip to its chainmail neck ribbon. The rest of the horsemen wore similar, if less extravagant, head coverings.

Each rider carried a round wooden shield on his back. They wore breastplates, armbands, and greaves. Most of these were leather, and a few were bronze and highly polished. Even the horses had patches of chainmail to protect their more vulnerable parts. Like many of the age, they wore their wealth: thick gold torcs, and bands and bracelets of copper, gold, and silver.

"The Hag's scrawny arse!" Seonag prowled up and down the stone walkway like a large lince. She looked at Gràinne, who had just appeared on the walkway, and muttered, "I thought your riders were well-armed."

The half-smile, half-smirk from Gràinne and Cearbhall's hand over his mouth caused Seonag's eyebrow to arch. Still, Seonag's observation was correct. The horsemen carried a virtual armoury on their mounts and the spare horses each warrior led. Heavy iron darts, skull-crushing maces, vicious long and short curved swords, spears, bows, and full quivers of arrows were the visible part of their weaponry.

Before long, Brion joined the trio. "Rut the Hag! I never expected Gormal to attack this soon... or at all. Is it foolishness or clever strategy? Where did he get the horses? Shite! They must be mercenaries. The bastard!"

The flamboyantly attired leader walked his horse to within fifty paces of Dùn Brion's gates, removed his helmet, and scratched a head of damp, thick, black locks. Finally, he flicked a covering of powdered snow from his shoulders and, in a deep booming voice, called out, "I am Amodocus, Prince of Thracia. Is this the fort of Brion Ó Cathasaigh, King of the Na Mèadaidh, and brother of Mórrígan, Queen of Clann Ui Flaithimh?"

"He seems to know a lot about you," said Seonag. Perplexed, Brion just grunted. The Thracian's next words deepened the mystery.

"I am looking for Gràinne Ni Fearghal, Queen of the Na Daoine Tùrsach," shouted Amodocus. Then with a broad smile of white teeth against dark skin, he added, "I know of your laws of hospitality. We have journeyed a long way, and my warriors would appreciate food, drink, and a warm cot."

Brion turned to Gràinne; she and Cearbhall were moments too late to disguise the broad grins on their faces. "I take it that you know something about this?"

In answer, Gràinne ran to the guard tower on the right side of the front gate and peered over its lip. Turning to Brion, she smiled and, with a touch of smugness, said, "It appears my heavy cavalry has arrived."

"Let them in," commanded Brion. To Seonag and Cearbhall, he said,

"The prince will be quartered in the Great Hall. See that his men and horses are placed with Gràinne's people. I suspect that they are well-acquainted with her warriors."

* * *

The skies were filled with blue-grey clouds, threatening an imminent snowfall. Sunset and darkness were not far off, but it was already night for all intents and purposes. Arms crossed, Seirbhiseach listened to the novice priest's tale of the strange events that had taken place at the crannag. The High Priest scowled, wondering if he had given too much responsibility to the young man.

According to the acolyte's account, the three who had been left to guard the building were missing. In the torchlight, he pointed to splashes of dark stains on the floor. A recently slept-in cot also suggested another warm body had visited the structure. Unwilling to accept the obvious, Seirbhiseach searched for an explanation that did not conclude that he had lost control.

The splash in the water drew a sharp contrast against the silence of the loch and its environs, drawing Seirbhiseach's attention. He exited the crannag and stepped onto the wooden bridge. The apparition rising from the water seemed to hang in the air before stepping onto the walkway.

As it walked towards him, the gait appeared odd, but in the gloom, he could not comprehend why. The perfectly apportioned body held a pale blue tone in the half-light. Hair, blacker than night, hung in long tresses touching the creature's arse and hips. Thin, magenta lips curled in a cruel, mocking smile as it spoke.

"My name is Sidheag. I am your goddess. You will obey me fully and without question." The words startled the priest. It had never crossed his mind that the nightmare could have a name, personality, or sex. The Baobhan Sith had not fully arisen in generations, and descriptions of her physical appearance were more fanciful than factual. In his mind, Seirbhiseach had envisaged a spirit subservient to him. For the first time, he began to question this assumption.

"Firstly, there will be no more sacrifices of girls or females of any age—unless I personally carry out the pleasure."

Seirbhiseach observed that talons had taken the place of Sidheag's fingernails; he heard an ominous clicking as she stretched long, artistic fingers. A shuffling noise behind Sidheag made the priest squint his eyes. He watched nine females appear on the jetty. Where had they come from? Why had he not seen them before? And who was the limp body they carried between them?

The High Priest opened his mouth to demand that the apparition obey him. He had brought her to life, and she owed him obeisance. Seirbhiseach also was unhappy with her curtailing his abuse of the young girls. That was one of the deep pleasures he enjoyed. It was his right.

"A *servant* has no rights unless I give them."

Sidheag's voice was not loud. Likely it was not even spoken. Yet Seirbhiseach felt its lash more painfully than a knotted whip. For the first time, fear and seeds of doubt sprouted in the priest's mind. He considered that nourishing the apparition might not have been his wisest decision. The priest trembled at the reality of controlling her. How would he subjugate her to his will? The cackling laugh confirmed that his thoughts were open to her.

"You were never in control, but you may be useful to me. Remove all ideas of conquest or confinement from your thoughts, or I will feast on your emaciated body… now."

Bathed in the silver rays of the recently risen moon, Sidheag stepped towards the group of priests who accompanied Seirbhiseach. Her footsteps sounded as if a pony pranced along the wooden boards. "At least you brought me a gift," she murmured. The priests stood frozen as Sidheag's finger traced and savoured the strong, if increasingly rapid, pulses in their necks.

A protest formed in Seirbhiseach's mind but failed to connect to his mouth. Unable to move, he watched razor-sharp talons slice effortlessly through flesh and arteries and a cavernous maw open to drink. Yet none protested, and soon all lay lifeless and drained of blood. Sated, Sidheag licked her lips and chin with a long, fleshy tongue and sighed.

"Next time, bring more. My daughters also need feeding." "Follow," said Sidheag, and he did. "We need to discuss my strategy to subdue this land."

Seirbhiseach nodded, for he had no speech on entering the crannag. He watched as Sidheag's daughters laid Brianag on the cot. The girl's skin looked pale and had the sheen and colour of wax. Her body shivered, and her teeth chattered uncontrollably. She appeared drowsy, fading in and out of consciousness, and slurred any attempt at speech. *What has happened to her?*

"I warned her about trying to escape, but the stupid child still tried. She is fortunate we found her; even then, she was almost dead from the cold." Sidheag stared at Seirbhiseach. "You will be responsible for her well-being when I am not here. If she dies, so do you."

As Sidheag and her Brood left the crannag, Seirbhiseach wondered how many thousands would be sent to recover Brianag. Panic rose in the priest's gullet and climbed higher when he heard Sidheag's mocking cackle.

✳✳✳

"I have travelled from the Great Sea to meet my rival and settle this contest, once and for all. Do we fight or just get drunk?" Amodocus' voice boomed across the chamber as he strode down the middle aisle of the Great Hall. On reaching the table, he grasped Brion's arm as if they were long-lost brothers.

The angry looks that ricocheted from Seonag to Brion to Gràinne prompted Amodocus to flash a broad smile. Against his dark-olive skin, his teeth looked starkly white. Arms spread wide as if in apology, he grinned mischievously. "Or maybe I am mistaken, and there is no contest."

The tall, strapping Thracian looked at Gràinne and politely asked, "Where is my daughter, Heilasa? Where is Brianag?"

A cry from an infant wrenched from the nipple she suckled on answered his first question. The second brought anxious looks, prompting him to ask, "What is wrong?" Amodocus listened with incredulity and fury to a recounting of the kidnapping of Brianag and Cassán. He pointed to Brion and asked, "Why are you not storming the fort of this Gormal?"

Brion stood mutely, angry and embarrassed at a stranger pointing out his apparent procrastination. Seonag stepped forward, hand on the hilt of her sword, but Amodocus held her stare and shook his head. "Don't. I would not like to see such beautiful tresses covered in blood or your head severed from your neck." A hand on Seonag's arm and a shake of Brion's head forestalled bloodshed but did little to reduce Amodocus' ire, which he turned on Gràinne.

"This man's son means little to me, although his lack of action does not fit with what you told me about him. However, *your* dithering on a rescue for Brianag is of more concern." Amodocus turned around and called out to his shield-man, who leaned against a wooden upright ten paces away. "Get my men mounted and armed. We ride at first light." The Thracian's brown eyes once more held Gràinne's stare. "You can ride with me… or not."

"No!"

The appearance of Mongfhionn should not have surprised anyone. All knew she had a knack for sudden entrances. Yet all jumped at the sound of her voice.

"My Lady." Amodocus bowed as Mongfhionn's long stride placed her swiftly at the long table. "I last saw you at the Battle of Alia and recall your extraordinary departure." Amodocus' jaw set, and he held the Sidhe's eyes without flinching—a remarkable feat by anyone's reckoning. "I hold you in great affection and respect, but do not stand between my family and me. Upon that way lies death for one of us, and I do not fear that end." Amodocus tugged his short, curled beard. "Yet I suspect I have not been told the full story if you are here."

Mongfhionn smiled and inclined her head. It was not often anyone confronted her, and she found Amodocus' attitude honest and refreshing, if imprudent. "Listen, Thracian, and then make up your mind. I will not stand in your way."

✳✳✳

The silence of Drostan's chamber was broken by the rustle of Mongfhionn's cloak. Drostan slouched in an oversized carved chair, morose and in a huff. Studiously, he avoided enquiring about her presence and reached out to grab the jug of water from the side table. His aim was poor, and the vessel fell to the floor, shattering into a hundred pieces. He cursed in frustration.

Irritated, the Sidhe spoke first. "Your friends have implored me to be merciful. That is not my nature, and you threatened my family."

"Bidse!"

"Is their faith in you is misplaced, and an old hound can neither learn new ways nor take sound counsel? In that case, I will leave you to your rage and self-pity." Drostan heard the cloak swirl as Mongfhionn turned. "And to your *permanent* blindness."

"Stop!"

"I do not take orders, at least from humans. Temper your tone."

"Please. Stop. What is it you want from me?"

"Ah, that's better. Now we can have a conversation. Let's begin by discussing Seonag."

CHAPTER 14

Ealasaid's hand-fast partner served as the garrison's quartermaster, a key position in any armed force. Yet he constantly bemoaned his low-born status. Nobility was not his birthright, and thus far, his tenure in Brion's army could only be described as unexceptional. No longer, if he ever were, a warrior, he could not increase his wealth by heroic acts or battlefield plunder. Therefore, he amassed riches by having his thumb in every crooked pie.

Indeed, his only notable accomplishment proved to be the capture of Ealasaid. Still, if he had considered that with his head and not his manhood, he would have asked, "Why?" However, that was a question to which he feared the answer. He sensed she despised him, and their children, but chose to ignore the murderous darkness in her eyes. With every fibre of his body and spirit, he desired Ealasaid, yet he feared her more.

In truth, Ealasaid tolerated her mate because he had peripheral access to those who sat at the high table. Hence, the couple received invites to the social gatherings of the high and mighty. Yet more than that, he had an immense network throughout the army. Most in that chain had unsavoury reputations and an eye for profitable, and sometimes violent, mischief, which suited Ealasaid perfectly.

Ealasaid knew she needed to deflect attention from herself and her activities. Thus, she propagated a campaign of rumours that Seonag had lost the confidence of Brion. The strategy, sustained by more frequent access for her partner to the bounty between her thighs, proved successful. Fibrous roots sprouted and spread quickly in her partner's feeble mind. In turn, he spread Ealasaid's claims among his networks. Since it was hard to miss the recent tension between Brion and Seonag, the gossip had a kernel of truth and thus was all the more plausible.

∗∗∗

Ten warriors, eight men and two females, blocked Seonag's path. She recognised most of them. All wore the look of experience and carried scars from many campaigns. The hard-bodied fighters also had a history of poor judgment and insubordination. Therefore, they had no chance of advancement under Seonag's command.

The group's leader, Sionn, persuaded by Ealasaid's gossip and access to her *pit*, had convinced himself that he had an opportunity for rapid advancement and enrichment. It was not difficult to recruit others who were like-minded. On a damp, chilly morning, Sionn stepped forward and pronounced, "You have lost the confidence of Brion, Rìgh of Dùn Brion. Resign your post as Commander of Na Mèadaidh's army. Let someone more worthy assume the position."

Still, Seonag's belly laughter surprised Sionn and insulted his self-esteem. "Let me guess, one of you brave warriors thinks they can take my place. How will that work when you're dead?" Seonag's lips curled into a disquieting sneer. "Fools! Has your leader explained that if I don't kill you, Brion certainly will? Kings need trusted servants, not traitors."

A rumble of disgruntlement filtered through the group. Sionn had assured them that being outnumbered ten to one would cause Seonag to yield. However, they had not counted on Seonag's mounting frustration with Brion. Seonag was in the mood for a fight, if only as a distraction from her relationship with Brion. Hence, she ignored negotiation or submission and said, "I'm going to kill you."

Troubled looks settled on the faces of Sionn's supporters. Belatedly, they wondered at the wisdom of publicly confronting Seonag. Still, Sionn calculated that the sacrifice of his comrades to give him victory was a good trade. He would inevitably find his chance to strike and deliver a mortal wound in the melee. His hand grasped the hilt of his sword and drew the weapon a hand's length from the scabbard. "No more words."

The response was unexpected. Seonag looked up at the winter-grey sky and then at her clothing. The arrogance in her demeanour riled Sionn. "I am unarmed." She pointed to the ramparts, where the confrontation had caught the curiosity of those with nothing better to do. "None in Dùn Brion will support your rebellion if you murder me. I will get properly attired. Meet me at the centre of the courtyard at meadhan-latha." Seonag smiled again. "That should give you enough time to make arrangements— for your funeral pyres."

Seonag's boots crunched over the frost-hardened ground as, head down and muttering a string of oaths and curses, she strode back to her quarters. *I should have taken Gràinne's offer.* When she reached the steps of the building, a man stepped in front of her. Startled, Seonag's hand went to her knife.

"That won't be necessary," said Cearbhall. "Plainly, the numbers are against you. Since Gòrdan is no longer with us, perhaps you would allow me to assist. I can provide counsel if you do not permit me to fight along-side you."

Seonag smiled and dipped her head.

"In that case, may I suggest a few changes to your armour?"

✳✳✳

Called to the ramparts by Gràinne, Brion stared aghast at the unfolding scenario. Instinctively he called the watch commander to his side, but a hand touched his arm before he could issue orders. Gràinne shook her head. "Your equivocation and inability to declare your feelings for Seonag has prompted this."

Gràinne looked into Brion's eyes. "I cannot understand your hesitancy. It is not in your nature; therefore, I can only suspect other things are at play." Pity filled Gràinne's face, and she said, "Seonag has no choice other than to face the challenge. Better she dies while standing her ground than forever looking over her shoulders."

"Brianag and Cassán were taken under her watch. Have you forgotten?"

Anger flared in Gràinne's eyes. "How can any blame be assigned to Seonag? What could she have done to counter Sidheag? How can she be held accountable for Cassán? It was *you* who banished him against *her* counsel." Gràinne looked into Brion's eyes. "If she survives this trial, beg her forgiveness, or set her free. That is the least she deserves."

Standing a few paces from the duo, Amodocus grunted. The sound provoked raised eyebrows. "I hadn't realised that you were such a philosopher and observer of men and women. You should reflect on how your counsel might be applied to us."

Gràinne's cheeks flushed. Disregarding the awkward moment, Amodocus smiled and pointed to the courtyard.

"If anyone is taking wagers, my gold is on the lady. Look how she walks."

✳✳✳

Cearbhall stood at the weapons table and helped Seonag strap an oblong sgiath to her left arm. The shield also had a metal hand grip, but Seonag instead grasped the thick oak shaft of a battle *sleagh*—spear. She breathed deeply, inhaling, and exhaling several times. The act steadied her nerves, although its real purpose was to get her comfortable with her new armour. She balanced a javelin in her right arm and nodded to Cearbhall. Firm, steady hands settled a plain battle helmet of bronze and iron over Seonag's blonde braids.

"Keep moving. Show no mercy. Remove the main threats first. The Goddess go with you."

Seonag crouched and turned slowly. In turn, she held each of her opponents' eyes and examined the expressions on their faces. After completing her first cycle, she knew she had to kill or cripple six. Experience told her the others would break and run.

Hypnotically smooth in motion, Seonag rose from the crouch and hurled the javelin. A warrior staggered backwards. His throat, ruined by the weapon, gushed hot blood over his nearest companions. They swore at him and pushed him aside.

Settle down, Seonag chastised herself, for she had aimed at the warrior's chest. Then she quickly switched the spear held in her left hand to the now empty hand.

With a feral snarl, Seonag gripped the sleagh near its butt end, and swung the weapon in a wide arc parallel to the dirt. At thigh height, her goal was to make her attackers jump back, giving her more space to manoeuvre. The strategy worked, but one opponent was too slow. She felt the leaf-shaped spearhead carve through flesh and the scrape of its tip on bone. A cry of pain rang out.

In an instant, Seonag was in her adversary's face, a growling nightmare. Her grip slid up the smooth shaft, and she thrust upwards. The spearhead pierced the soft flesh under the warrior's chin and kept on its path, bursting through the top of the man's head. Seonag roared, although not in victory but in frustration.

The spear's tang, captured by the man's skull, refused to be pulled free quickly. She grimaced as several heavy blows landed on her back, and her ears rang from strikes on her helmet. Releasing the spear, she rolled free and deftly caught the axe thrown by Cearbhall. Once again, Seonag swung around to face her opponents.

Assuming she would retreat, the group closed in. Instead, Seonag charged forward, slamming the iron boss of her sgiath into one of the females. She heard her opponent's shield crack. *Poor quality will always let you down.* The warrior's hesitation was fleeting and costly. Axe in hand, Seonag punched the fighter on the nose and heard the crunch of broken bones.

Tears blinded the woman, and the sudden gush of blood and snot made her choke and spit. Seonag screamed as she raked her enemy's face from eye to chin with her chainmail glove. *Thanks, Cearbhall.* The young woman screeched at losing her beauty and vision and crawled away from the fight.

An axe bit into Seonag's shoulder with enough force to buckle her knees, and another hooked over her sgiath to wrench it from her. With her arm temporarily dead, Seonag's axe slipped from her grasp. Only the leather loop on the weapon's shaft kept it within her reach. Seonag gritted her teeth and clung to the shield.

She rolled to the side but could not avoid more axe and sword slashes. Seonag felt her leather cuirass loosen and knew its protection was almost gone. Her arm tingled painfully as feeling rushed back into the limb. Yet grasping the axe still remained beyond her.

Instead, slithering on the frost-covered dirt like a demented viper, Seonag lashed out with her feet and oblong sgiath. She smiled grimly at the yelp as its iron rim smashed a knee. *Another one removed from the fight.* Yet the axes and swords kept striking as she tried to roll away and rise to a crouch. She felt her arms and legs wet and prayed to the Goddess that it was sweat, not blood.

A hand stretched out, and Seonag tugged a dagger from her boots. She stabbed upwards, although more in desperation than strategy. A deluge of blood soaked her hand, and she heard the wailing for a ruined manhood. The pounding on her shield continued, but finally, she staggered to a crouch. Seonag felt her leather armour loosen. Even the iron scales between the layers of boiled leather could not maintain the cuirass's integrity.

Blade slashes ripped her triubhas and the flesh beneath, and Seonag screamed more in anger than pain. She cursed Brion, and on the ramparts, the king flinched. More blows to her back threatened to bring Seonag to her knees, but she gritted her teeth and set her jaw. She could not let that happen, for there was only death down that path. And so, breathing harshly, she stumbled to her feet, lashing out with the sgiath, and finally gripping her axe. Around Seonag, the crowd of onlookers was hushed. *Do I really look that bad?*

"Yield! You cannot fight on. Your armour lies in tatters, and blood flows from many cuts," said Sionn.

"Fool!" yelled Seonag and flung her axe towards her opponents. It was not a throwing axe, so its tumbling flight was erratic. Still, the weapon buried itself in an assailant's boot. Smeared with blood and gore, Seonag's appearance was terrible, and her smile nightmarish. "Six of your band are dead or crippled. Look at the rest. At least two have lost their taste for the fight and will run at the first chance."

Seonag grinned through a mask of dried blood and watched Sionn glance around. Fear had slipped into his eyes. "Your error was allowing me to rise and rest, even for a short time. Kill without mercy or die." While talking, Seonag edged back to the weapons table. She tossed her broken sgiath aside and, with it, the remains of her leather armour.

Sionn smirked until Seonag ripped her tunic off and turned, gripping a longsword in two bloody hands. However, it was not the weapon that made Sionn start. Rather, it was the silver-grey sheen of the half-sleeve chainmail covering Seonag's torso down to her hips.

"*Bidse!*"

"*A ghlaoic*—fool! I am your death."

In the hope of escaping judgment and certain death, the remaining assailants scattered into the crowd. Thus, only Seonag and Sionn stood in the fighting circle. Sionn settled his sgiath on his arm, balanced his sword, and walked towards Seonag. His demeanour spoke of arrogance and hubris as he watched Seonag drag her sword behind her and limp towards him.

"I didn't think it would be this easy," he taunted.

"*Tha thu a' bruidhinn tro d'asal*—you talk through your arse!" spat Seonag.

She examined every movement of her opponent and every detail of his weapon and armour. Briefly, she looked up and caught Gràinne's eyes and shuddered. They were black. A quick dip of the head communicated Seonag's thanks. The sword she wielded belonged to Gràinne and was a hand longer than Sionn's. Seonag prayed to the Goddess that it was strong from hilt to tip. She only had one chance.

Longsword lifted high, and with a fearsome battle cry, Seonag charged.

Taken aback, Sionn responded by stopping, bringing his shield across his chest, and bracing himself. His eyes widened as he watched Seonag abruptly stop beyond his sword length and saw the steel blade descend. Sionn was a tall, muscular warrior, and Seonag knew his shoulders were too broad to be fully protected by his shield.

With a scream and the last of her strength, Seonag brought the end of the blade down on Sionn's right shoulder. Leather split, flesh and muscle gave way, and bone shattered. Sionn tried to get his sword into play, but his arm hung loose, attached by strings of muscle and tendons. He swung his sgiath at Seonag, but blood spurted from the sundered arm and his strength faded.

Dropping the longsword, Seonag unsheathed a knife and circled behind Sionn. He screamed, "Bidse!" as he felt the razor-sharp blade slice across the back of his thighs and fell to his knees.

"Yield, bastard!" Having recovered the longsword, Seonag laid its tip against the disabled man's throat. She felt the blade tremble with the blood pulsing in Sionn's artery.

"I yield," said Sionn through gritted teeth.

"The Hag, but I don't believe you," said Seonag. Sionn's eyes opened wide. "Once a traitor, always a traitor."

"No!"

With the last of her strength, Seonag drove the longsword into Sionn's throat, to its hilt. Sionn's body seemed uncertain as to what was expected of it. Eventually, the weapon's weight tipped the balance, and the corpse tumbled to the side. Shortly after, Seonag collapsed to the ground. On the ramparts, she heard a howl of "No!"

Before blackness took her, Seonag whispered, "Too late, my king."

✳✳✳

Brion's voice boomed from the parapet, "Find those who started the scurrilous rumours about the loyalty of my garrison commander. They will suffer a much worse fate than these conspirators." Turning to the watch commander, and in a voice clear to all, Brion said, "Find those who attacked Seonag and still live. Hang the schemers on the walls. When they are dead, throw their bodies onto the rocks below."

Ealasaid stood at her hand-fast partner's side among those who had crowded the gallery to get a better view of the fight. After Brion's words, she glanced at her mate. He trembled; sweat flowed from his brow and down his chubby face. *Perhaps now would be a suitable time to relieve me of this arsehole.*

Instinctively, Ealasaid scanned the battlements, but she felt her eyes drawn to a grey-cloaked figure who stood a head taller than most. Shivers ran up and down Ealasaid's spine as glittering black eyes held her gaze and full red lips formed a terrible smile.

"No!" she gasped and fled the ramparts. *When did a Sidhe arrive?*

✳✳✳

Confined to the dùn's healing rooms by the druids, Seonag had a constant stream of visitors, with one exception—Brion. Truthfully, it was not that Brion did not care but that he was at a loss as to what to say. Seonag sighed. *He could stand silent by my cot, and I would be happy.*

Seonag smiled as Gràinne strode into the chamber. After a few moments of conversation, Seonag took Gràinne's hand. "I'll take those horses now."

"Are you sure?"

Seonag nodded. "What is there here for me? Just memories of what might have been." The glum look on Seonag's face made Gràinne's eyes mist over.

"When you're well enough to ride, come see me."

In the shadows outside the room, Brion clenched his fist in frustration and anger—at himself.

CHAPTER 15

Unusually subdued, Drostan slumped in the large, carved chair. His calloused palms polished the seat's wooden arms, and his demeanour spoke of defeat and resignation. The fire, often mirrored by his shock of red hair, slumbered, or perhaps had gone cold. His flesh appeared ill-fitting for his frame, and his hair had lost its vibrancy. Yes, the Sidhe had returned sight to his one eye, but now Seonag was on his mind.

Brion looked around the room as if expecting to see the bean-sidhe assigned to guide Drostan beyond the veil. "You need to do something about this," he hissed at Mongfhionn. "A defeated Drostan, at best, is no use to our campaign and, at worst, could doom us."

"He is his own man and the author of his misfortune. His father, Failbhe, was no friend of the Aes Sidhe, yet he respected our role and led the Forest People wisely. None can constantly disparage the Aes Sidhe and hope to be ignored." Mongfhionn paused to consider her words. "My sisters have less patience than I do. If I had not argued many times on his behalf, the maggots would have feasted on Drostan long ago." Brion lifted his hands in frustration.

"If Drostan wishes to constantly grasp thistles and wallow in self-pity, I will find a new rìgh for the Forest People. He has sons, daughters, and more than a few bastards that would gladly sit on his throne. Some might even be good, or better, rulers."

"I'm sure you can, but by the time that is settled, Northern Albu will be under the heel of Sidheag. There will be no Forest People, no Ravens, and no throne to fill. Or have you forgotten about your *sister?*" retorted Brion. Mongfhionn's eyes flared at Brion's verbal slap.

"I know of one who could take the throne of the Forest People on the next sunset—and so do you," snapped the Sidhe. "And she would be much more amenable."

The crash of a heavy axe head on the oak table startled everyone except Mongfhionn. "I can hear you, bidse," growled Drostan. "Iron can cleave that head from your shoulders. You are not immune to death, Sidhe."

"But you will be in the feasting rooms of Mag Mell long before that sharp edge kisses my skin, and a bhanrigh will sit on the throne of the Forest People," countered Mongfhionn. "Choose your destiny, Drostan. Do you want to die a martyr to self-pity, erased from the lore of your people, or the rí who fought Sidheag?"

"Bidse!" snarled Drostan, gripping his axe shaft firmly in his massive hands.

"A man of few words and seemingly fewer actions."

"You are wrong. A king who kills a Sidhe will never be forgotten."

"Try it," said Mongfhionn. Yet there was a glimmer of a smile on her ruby lips, and tongues of fire danced in her dark eyes as she stood, oak staff in hand, ready to fight.

A heavy slap to Drostan's back drew a loud "Ooof!" from him, and a great belly laugh from Amodocus. It also made all around the table jump. That someone of the muscular frame of Amodocus, and the only one in the room who towered over Drostan, could move so quickly and silently brought gasps of surprise.

"This is the best entertainment I have witnessed since I departed Thracia over a score of summers ago." Amodocus pulled on his beard, and humour fled his expression. "Still, it also brings back memories of the squabbling that led to my tribe's downfall. I pray to Artemis and Ares that those around this table fight as well as they argue."

"For pity's sake, is life with the Aes Sidhe so intolerable that you need to come here and pick a fight—at this time?" asked Brion, glaring at Mongfhionn. He turned to Drostan. "As for you, apologise to Mongfhionn. You went too far, and you know it." Brion stared at Mongfhionn. "And you accept it." Both adversaries growled.

"I'll take that as your agreement. Now can we get back to settling on a strategy?"

***

Eimhir entered Cassán's cell to hear loud grunts and heavy breathing. Momentarily, she wondered if one of the dùn's *strìopachan* had slipped into the chamber. To her surprise, the thought did not please her. However, she quickly cast that aside when Cassán rose from the dirt and walked towards her. He was smiling and covered in a sheen of sweat.

"It confounds me that I remember the lessons Gòrdan valiantly and persistently tried to drum into my head. He contended that every man would eventually find himself imprisoned but that, even in small spaces, a man can and should keep himself fit." Cassán's eyes took on a distant look as if wishing things were different. "I owe him much more than an apology when we next meet." He saw sadness in Eimhir's eyes. "What?"

"Gòrdan is dead."

"No," whispered Cassán and slumped onto his log.

"It is rumoured around Dùn Athad that he and his men were slaughtered protecting Brianag."

"My sister?"

"She was taken. The armies of the Na Mèadaidh, Forest People, and Ravens are gathering. A great battle at Cùil Daothail is expected."

"The Hag's arse! And I'm stuck here. Why didn't you tell me of this sooner?" Anger flushed Cassán's cheeks. "So, I am left to languish in Gormal's dungeons." It would have been difficult not to miss the bitterness in Cassán's voice. He shrugged in resignation. "I'm a wastrel. Brianag is worthy of rescue."

The angry and disappointed response from Eimhir startled Cassán. "You are Brion's son and his blood. Of course, he will attempt to rescue you, and many will die—possibly even your father. Gormal knows this. What else did you expect?"

Cassán propped his head with his hand, and his face was filled with regret when he looked up at Eimhir. "It's all my fault. Better Gormal had sent back my head."

One more time, Eimhir inspected Cassán. The young man had changed markedly from the fat arsehole of his reputation. A diet of dungeon slop and the small amounts of more nutritious food she had smuggled in had dramatically decreased his weight. But for the first time, she observed that the exercise regime he had taken up had transformed a gaunt body to one having a sinewy strength.

"This is no time for self-pity or noble thoughts of martyrdom. It is not your fault. It is Gormal's," said Eimhir. Her mien was stern when she knelt before Cassán and took his hand. "Yet it is time we discussed your escape from Dùn Athad. Imprisoned, you are a problem for your father and restrict his options." She smiled. "While not in perfect condition or health, you look in good enough physical condition to survive my plan."

Cassán looked at Eimhir warily. "Survive your plan? That sounds ominous. Can we not just kill the guards and make a run for it?"

Eimhir chuckled and shook her head. "It would be impossible to overcome the guards. Recent events have made Gormal more cautious. He has increased the number of your guards to four outside the cell. The same number secures the door at the top of the steps, which leads into the dùn. One unfortunate blade strike, and we would be undone.

"Besides that, we would have no time to hide the bodies. The alarm would sound, and we would be trapped inside Dùn Athad." Eimhir smiled at Cassán's crestfallen expression and caressed his shaven head. "No, we will need to be more creative.

"Do you trust me?"

The guarded mien returned to Cassán's face. His eyes narrowed as he observed Eimhir. "Do I have a choice?"

"Not really."

✷✷✷

Ealasaid scowled, which made her face appear quite unattractive. Then she glowered upon realising that this did not fit the façade she had carefully developed. The source of her annoyance was hearing the cries of her dupe as he was dragged across Dùn Brion's entrance.

The young man had lasted a pitifully short time after sunrise before Brion's warriors captured him. Would he break under torture? Of course, he would. Everyone did. The question was, how long would he hold out and therefore, how long did she have to kill him or escape?

Killing Gormal's messenger, tied up and left in the open with only two guards, had not been much of a challenge. This time, however, she suspected that any prisoners would be taken to the deeper dungeon cells, which would present a much greater test.

It was meadhan-latha when another commotion in the yard caught Ealasaid's attention, and she had her answer. Two squads of warriors entered the garrison's quarters. Soon, two people—a man and a girl—were hauled from the building. "The Hag!" swore Ealasaid, for she knew both.

The young woman screeched her innocence as she was dragged over frost-hardened dirt towards the dungeons. The man's demeanour, however, spoke of an acceptance of his fate. Yet Ealasaid watched as his gaze scoured the yard for options, and she smiled. She had trained him well. "Be patient. An opportunity will always present itself," she muttered, willing him to accept her guidance.

The dungeon's entrance was reached by stone steps under the Great Hall. As the man came closer, his head swivelled, and his eyes filled with fear. "No. Remain calm and in control," Ealasaid hissed. She sighed in disappointment when her accomplice broke free of his guards and ran towards the gateway. What plan did the fool have? A scream rent the air, and the man stumbled. Face down on the yard's thin sprinkling of snow, a red stain blossomed from slashes to the back of his thighs. The guard's blades had slashed almost to the bone. A kick to his head sent Ealasaid's assistant into the blackness.

"Arsehole!" snapped Ealasaid. She needed time to think. All was not lost. One of Ealasaid's charitable duties ensured that prisoners were cared for while awaiting judgment. Thus, access to the cells would not be an issue, for she was well-known. Additionally, those on guard duty are chosen for brawn, not brains. Presented with her undoubted allure and a body designed to satisfy the basest of their desires, most men's minds focused on the opportunity to rut her.

Whether there were two or three guards, it did not matter. She could handle more than one man. Indeed, she had done so before—and enjoyed the experience. Ealasaid smiled. What man expects a blade in his eardrum or his throat cut when about to climax? It would get bloody, but someone else's gore had never bothered her.

Still, she would have to move quickly. At best, her fellow conspirators might last until the next sunrise, but could she take that risk? Ealasaid stopped at the stables before going home. She had arrangements to make and decisions to take.

✶✶✶

Several sunset or more, Brianag could not tell, had passed since her failed attempt to escape. During that time, she had passed in and out of consciousness. Her memory had worrying gaps, and she found it challenging to forge a path through the fog of confusion that had occupied her mind.

Why do I not feel hungry? Who fed me? Brianag looked under the heavy wolf hide and felt heat rise in her cheeks. *Who undressed me?* A strong smell of stale sweat assaulted her nostrils. She sniffed her armpits and snorted. *They could have bathed me.* Her nose, having awakened, now crinkled as another scent made its presence known… piss and shite. The flush in Brianag's cheeks deepened from embarrassment and the realisation that she lay in her body fluids and waste. *The Hag if I'm going to ask the bastards for new straw.*

An itch on her arm briefly distracted Brianag before she returned to her situation and surveyed her companions in the crannag. Sat by an open fire pit, the priest, Seirbhiseach, rocked back and forward and mumbled incomprehensibly. Meanwhile, Sidheag's daughters stood ten paces away in a circle around Brianag. Brianag shivered, but not due to the cold. Her lips pursed. *Why do I not feel the cold?* No answer came, for Brianag had slipped back into unconsciousness.

✳✳✳

"Get out of her head, bidse. Unlike you, she is not a weakling and, with my help, will not be easily manipulated by the Baobhan Sith. Go and do not return." Diadhaidh looked at her ancient ancestor and, momentarily, considered standing her ground. One defiant look into the soulless, red eyes and at teeth and nails stained with blood, and she fled. The Ancient One spat in disgust. "You were never a Blood Queen."

It seemed to Gràinne that she had watched a duel, albeit a one-sided one. She should have been relieved. Her dreams were not as crowded, if only because the Ancient One had banished Diadhaidh. Now her visions were of two ghastly apparitions—Sidheag and the crone who claimed to be the first Blood Queen. *She must be who she says she is, for why would anyone wish to be so ugly in character and form?*

"Can I defeat Sidheag?"

"Alone, no."

"With the Sidhe?"

The Ancient One cackled. "No."

Gràinne bristled at the mocking tone of her ancestor. She thought of Brianag, her shoulders slumped, and her fingers wrestled with each other. "How can I defeat the bitseach?"

"Become the Blood Queen."

"I am the Blood Queen."

"No, you're the Bhanrìgh of the Na Daoine Tùrsach, and that is not enough."

"Then what?" Despair and helplessness seeped into Gràinne's voice.

"Learn the Tuireadh."

"I know the Death Chant," snapped Gràinne.

"No! You do not. You know only what Sidheag allowed—a child's version with no power."

"That's it? I learn an ancient form of the Tuireadh, and then I can defeat Sidheag?"

"No, but it's a step forward."

"Then what?"

"Use your brain, child." Impatience made the Ancient One's face grow fiercer. "Think of our tribe's earliest beginnings and the name you wish to claim."

A vision suddenly appeared in Gràinne's head.

"No!" she shrieked. Lathered in sweat and breathing heavily, Gràinne woke and sat up in her cot.

"More nightmares?" queried Amodocus, but Gràinne was speechless.

CHAPTER 16

"Are you sure about this?" Gràinne looked genuinely concerned. "With Amodocus' hundred added to mine, I can give you ten or twenty riders to accompany you. It's too dangerous to travel alone."

"Thanks, but no. I know the landscape; besides, I'd be terrible company," said Seonag. She looked at Amodocus and smiled. "Amodocus has provided me with strong horses and enough weapons for an army." Seonag then turned to face a miserable Cearbhall, but he had few words for his feelings and simply embraced the warrior.

"Take care, my lady. I hope you find what you're looking for and that we meet again."

"Where will you travel? South to the great hillforts? Across the seas to Aremorio and Gaul? The Great Sea?" asked Gràinne. Seonag pursed her lips as if not wishing to divulge her thoughts. Her hand was grasped and a brooch pressed into it. "Should you journey to Gaul and Conall's kingdom, present this to Mórrígan. You'll find a warm welcome."

Tears blurred Seonag's vision as she muttered, "Thanks," before mounting her red chestnut horse. Taking up the reins, she walked the beast and its companion towards the gateway and exited Dùn Brion.

✱✱✱

On Dùn Brion's ramparts, a lonely and wretched figure watched Seonag ride away. At the sound of footsteps, he turned to see an irate Gràinne hurtling towards him. The slap rocked Brion, forcing him to fall on his arse on the icy walkway.

"You bastard! She only wanted you to ask her to stay. Was that too much to expect? The Hag! Did I ever really know you? Do you have a heart?" Gràinne turned about and was only a few paces away when a voice full of anguish stopped her.

"She turned east after leaving the fort. She turned east, Gràinne."

"The Hag, no! She's going to join Blàr to defend Cùil Daothail."

* * *

On Dùn Brion's ramparts, guards and the curious watched Gràinne's and Amodocus' chariots and riders assemble outside the stronghold's gateway. Snow drifted in the soft breeze and swirled around horses' hoofs, prompting a game of "stamp the snowflake," which increased the chiming and jangling of reins and tack. It was just after dawn and the rising sun added to the pageantry, bathing anything metallic in warm reds and oranges.

Only the grim appearances of riders and leaders suggested the activity was not a celebration. These were the faces of men and women riding to war and knowing they might not survive. Sat astride their great horses, swathed in wolf and bear hides, they looked like giants, and many were. In battle, the warmth of their furs would be sacrificed for the freedom of movement. The heat of the fight would keep them warm.

Alongside the great fighting horses were strings of smaller, shaggy-haired ponies. All carried essential supplies, and all snorted with disdain at the prancing of their bigger brothers. They knew there would be no campaign in the snow-covered landscape without them.

One angry man stood with his arms spread wide, furiously remonstrating with Gràinne. Face flushed by cold winds and fury, Cearbhall once more pleaded not to be left behind. Gràinne had given him his orders the last sunset. The decision, born of pragmatism, did not include him and his men taking part in the raid. Gràinne judged it impossible for foot warriors to move and strike fast over vast areas covered in snow.

"There will be other battles, Cearbhall. Likely too many," said Gràinne.

Cearbhall shook his head and bitterly countered, "You have made me break my oath to your father. That, I cannot forgive." Cearbhall's final, blunt words echoed in Gràinne's ears before he turned and strode back through the dùn's gates.

"He is loyal. When he ponders your decision, he will get over his anger." Amodocus' arm across her shoulders comforted Gràinne, but only for a moment. She shook her head.

"He made my da an oath never to leave my side and, if needed, to die for me." Tears filled Gràinne's eyes. "I made him break that promise. Even if he absolves me, how will I forgive myself?"

With unfortunate timing, a crunching footfall made Gràinne and Amodocus turn to face the gateway. They watched as Brion and a guard of ten strode towards them. "I have a request." Gràinne, still angry at Seonag's treatment, scowled. "With your permission, I would like to appoint Cearbhall as the acting garrison commander in Seonag's absence. He is the most qualified in the fort."

"No!" exploded Gràinne. "You drive Seonag away, and now you seek my senior ceannairí céad as her replacement. You go too far, Brion, and ask too much."

"It makes sense," asserted Amodocus, not flinching at Gràinne's hard stare. "He's a veteran warrior with no command. Do you want him and his men to go to Cùil Daothail like Seonag?" Brion and Gràinne flinched at the reminder of Seonag's destination.

"Agreed," said Gràinne reluctantly.

∗∗∗

Ealasaid straddled her partner and slowly removed her léine. In the torchlight, she was pleased as her hand-fast partner's manhood hardened at the sight of her body. Radiating a musky fragrance, she slowly lowered herself onto his cock. Still, the drool trickling from one corner of his mouth countered any pleasure, eliciting only disgust.

He moaned loudly as she rode him, and so did she. The immediacy of a bloody and violent death had increased the wetness between her legs. She rode him harder and harder until her orgasm overwhelmed her, and she felt him explode inside her.

As he lay panting in a sheen of perspiration, she lifted herself off him and took his cock in her hand. He moaned with anticipated pleasure. Instead, Ealasaid grasped the blade beside the cot and, in a smooth stroke, castrated him. His screams were cut short by the rag she stuffed into his mouth.

Blood soaked through the straw and furs of the cot and spread across the grey stone floor. The volume was unsurprising. Ealasaid dismembered her hand-fast partner and while he remained sentient. The extreme nature of his death would serve as a warning to any who would betray or pursue her. However, more than that, Ealasaid felt he owed her the pleasure of a prolonged and bloody death.

As Ealasaid washed the blood from her body, she shivered at the water's coldness but welcomed the sharpness it brought to her mind. In the next room, her twin daughters, who were ten summers old, lay sleeping. That they were a lover's and not her hand-fast partner's offspring brought a smile to blood-red lips. *Fool!*

But what to do with them?

* * *

Ealasaid's urgent need to escape Dùn Brion was hastened, although not due to the dismembering of her partner. An innate sense of survival rang alarm bells in her head. Brion had changed the dungeon guards to Gràinne's veterans under Cearbhall's command. Their numbers and experience tipped the balance, and Ealasaid knew that the fort had become too dangerous for her.

Thus, on the cusp of sunrise, three gathered at a small gateway in Dùn Brion's northern wall. Every stronghold has a minor exit, an escape door, used when events take a drastic turn for the worse. This one opened onto a narrow track carved into the crag, barely wide enough for a single horse.

A small, obese man with a pockmarked face exited the small guard post and nodded to Ealasaid. A heavy pouch of gold changed hands.

"Horses wait outside the gate, and others have been arranged between here and your destination." The man weighed the pouch in one hand. His grin was cruel and toothless. "Our original arrangement was for one horse and one person." He nodded to the girls and leered. "They'll cost more. Or you can leave them with me to use or sell."

Ealasaid growled but knew protest would be useless. Another pouch exchanged hands, and the quartet entered the narrow tunnel to the gate. She watched the locking bar slide from its rebate and smiled as the doorway opened. "Girls, you go first. Tread carefully and keep tight to the rock." Ealasaid watched her daughters exit and turn to their right. She turned to the ugly man.

"I don't like people who change deals. However, more than that, I don't like fat arseholes with big mouths."

Having judged a thrust to the man's ample belly would risk not being fatal, Ealasaid's dagger punched through the man's throat. Apart from the gurgling noises as he drowned in his own blood, his demise was quiet. A final slash across his neck ensured he had no chance of survival. The murder was efficient and swift, allowing Ealasaid to step back before the red torrent splashed her travelling clothes. As he died, she reclaimed her bags of gold.

CHAPTER 17

Blustery winds and heavy snowfalls swept over Cùil Daothail as Blàr, and his warriors arrived. The King of the Ravens swore, yet not at the weather or the snow already mid-calf deep. That was normal for the season. As if seeing the settlement for the first time, Blàr realised that Cùil Daothail sprawled over a massive, level site. Of more concern, it appeared to be indefensible.

"The Hag's tits! Show me something positive," he bellowed into the wind.

The settlement, a half-day's walk from the bay and coast to its north, was surrounded by dense pine forests. Yet its expanding population necessitated clearing large tracts of land close to the community's core. Cùil Daothail had begun as the centre of ironworking in north-eastern Albu. From there, it expanded into the production of tools, weapons, and crafts, quickly establishing itself as a prosperous and growing trade hub.

Considered neutral territory by the tribes of Northern Albu, Cùil Daothail served one purpose for its ruling council and citizens: creating wealth. Rarely did they think of defences or the possibility of being attacked. Blàr surveyed the settlement and pointed out the only bright light to his shield-man: the community's ancient centre.

Square and measuring three hundred paces along each side, a single stockade protected it, but no guard towers or ditches. Northerly winds whistled through the many gaps where timber pilings had been repurposed or burned as fuel. "It's a start," grumbled Niall, Blàr's shield-man and second-in-command.

He pointed to the forest. "There's no shortage of wood. We can use the timber already cut down from the land clearing, and we have over two thousand warriors as labour. More when the rest of our army drifts in, and Drostan's contingent arrives." He tapped the ground with a staff. "And the dirt is not fully frozen. Digging will be hard but not impossible."

Blàr smiled at his commander's optimism and said, "It's time to inform Cùil Daothail's council that their lives are about to change—forever."

* * *

In the wee hours of the morning, Brianag tossed and turned in her cot and kicked the wolf furs to the floor. Brianag favoured her ma's bedtime attire—nothing. Yet, although naked, she did not feel the cold, and that caused her to frown. The loch had already frozen over, and knee-deep snow covered the ground. Harsh northern winds rolled down the mountain slopes to lash the crannag. The dwelling swayed and creaked but refused to bow to the elements.

Cut logs and bricks of peat burned in the crannag's central firepit. Still, the creepy *tuili*, Seirbhiseach, a heavy fur draped over his shoulders, sat huddled over it, hogging its warmth. The dark stains on the wooden floor made Brianag shiver—although not with cold. Why did she not feel the chill?

An itch on her arm distracted Brianag from contemplating her companions. Absentmindedly she scratched it and puzzled at the minor cuts, some new and some healed. Curiosity caused her to look downwards. Besides the redness she had rubbed, Brianag saw several cuts, each less than a fingernail's length, on other parts of her body. Some had already healed. *What is going on?* Then it dawned on Brianag. "The bitseach!" she yelled.

The outburst startled Seirbhiseach but had no effect on Sidheag's nine daughters, who stood motionless and silent. "Did you really expect me to let you stubbornly freeze to death?" This time the voice of Sidheag startled Brianag, but only because she sensed that the Baobhan Sith was far away. Yet the words she had heard were clear and in her head.

"You lied!" shouted Brianag.

"A mother always has to do what's best for her offspring. Did you wish to freeze to death following your escapade? By all accounts, it is not a pleasant way to cross the veil."

"You are not my mother and never will be, bitseach."

"That is yet to be decided. One day you will beg for my embrace."

Brianag sensed irritation in Sidheag's tone and chuckled at her victory.

"Don't fight me, Brianag, or I will take what I need. However, in this case, I had no need to go against your wishes." This time, it was Sidheag's turn to laugh. "*You* gave me permission, albeit your mind was somewhat confused due to you having almost frozen to death."

"Liar!"

"Think what you will, Brianag. The truth is you only live because of me."

Brianag felt a painful shriek in her mind, making her head throb painfully. *Great, now I have two voices in my head.* Still, she recognised the new voice and smiled through gritted teeth.

"You!" snarled Sidheag.

"Did you think the Aes Sidhe would stand aside and permit your evil to grow unchecked?" asked Mongfhionn. "Go back to the depths or be destroyed, *sister.*"

"Not another family fight," groaned Brianag.

"I will have Brianag, and I will have Gràinne. A Blood Queen is owed to me."

"A blood oath promised by a queen addicted to power is a foundation built on quicksand. Release the child. She is not A 'Bhanrìgh Fuil, and you know it." Brianag bridled at being called a child but wisely decided that this was not the time to assert her maturity. "Retreat, and I will permit you to live."

Mongfhionn's face transformed to that of the Hag, and the foulness of the Otherworld flowed with her words. Brianag gasped, realising for the first time that she could see the face of the Hag. It was a sight she could have lived without. Furthermore, she fought hard to keep control of her stomach as it churned at the stench flowing from the Hag's maw.

"Harm one hair on my daughter's or granddaughter's head, and you will suffer oblivion. But before that, you will experience unimaginable pain. That is my promise, Sidheag."

"You do not frighten me, old woman. I am much stronger than I was and am certainly too powerful for you. Gràinne is my property, and, in the end, Brianag will choose me."

"You are more foolish than you once were, Sidheag. Madness has infected you and will be your downfall. *I* will come for Brianag, and you will stand aside."

A high-pitched scream, immediately taken up by the nine daughters, rent the air before Sidheag and her Brood fled the crannag.

***

Seirbhiseach rocked back and forth on his stool, repeatedly muttering, "What have I done?" In his head, the Sidhe had allowed him to glimpse the Hag and hear her terrible voice.

"I will take care of you later, priest, and I promise it will not be pleasant. For now, you might have some use. Watch over the child. Whatever harm comes to her, I will visit on you a thousand times."

"Do you have to keep calling me child?" This time, Brianag could not resist the rejoinder.

Mongfhionn chuckled but breathed easier at the fight in Brianag's tone. "Forgive me. When you're as ancient as I am, everyone is a child." In her mind, Brianag felt the Sidhe struggle for her next words. "You will be rescued." Brianag's trusting smile broke Mongfhionn's heart. "*But* you will have to endure for a season. Battles must be fought, and many will die for you and your ma."

Devastated, tears rolled down Brianag's cheeks. Yet she did not cry for herself. She thought of the young man and others who had already died and would die for her. "Perhaps it would be better if I had passed beyond the veil," she whispered, her voice tiny and trembling.

"Your concern for others is laudable. However, it is an option I will never entertain for you—or your ma." In Brianag's mind, Mongfhionn drew herself up. She looked like a giant raven with a blonde crest. "Sidheag, as you have already guessed, has fed you her blood and taken some from you. That is why you can feel and hear her. It also makes it easier for me to talk to you.

"Unfortunately, what you know, she also knows. Thus, I cannot give you more details. Suffice it to say, you will be freed. Do not let go of that promise no matter how dark things appear."

To Brianag, the Sidhe seemed reluctant to go. "I understand, Grandma. Do what you need, and the Goddess go with you."

"This I can do for you." With a wave of Mongfhionn's hand, Brianag fell into a deep sleep and dreamed of her ma and better days.

* * *

Blàr had demanded that Cùil Daothail's council should convene. As sunset loomed, twenty surly members stood before him. In their expressions, he saw antipathy, anger, and frustration at the disruption of their business. Perceiving little to be gained from being pleasant or watering down the bitter wine he would force them to drink, Blàr shouted over the din of their conversations. "The Baobhan Sith has risen!"

The statement drew chuckles of incredulity and whispers of "Old women's tales."

Blàr snapped back, "Are you blind to the murder and blood-drinking of young girls? In Cùil Daothail, I hear the wailing of mothers. Are your ears filled only with gold?" Silence fell on the chamber, apart from a few who continued to mutter, and Blàr noted who they were.

"Open your eyes to things other than profit. The Baobhan Sith and her followers intend to attack and overwhelm Cùil Daothail. This is the gateway to the lowlands and beyond. Alone, you cannot hope to defend yourselves. The apparition, also known as Sidheag, has no mercy and will not negotiate. She will slaughter males of any age, consume their flesh, and drink their blood. As for your daughters, death will be a mercy should she add them to her Brood."

Knowing his next words would be like a spark to tinder, Blàr said, "From this moment, Cùil Daothail is under *my* command. I have two thousand and five hundred warriors with me. Five thousand more from the Forest People are expected. Cùil Daothail is where we will make our stand.

"The walls of the ancient core of Cùil Daothail will be strengthened. Only those trades needed for war will be permitted to remain within the stockade. All others should leave." Blàr paused before adding. "Every building outside the stockade will be burned and razed."

To no one's surprise, the Council Chamber erupted in anger. Blàr was not unsympathetic. For many, he had announced the death of businesses built over generations. "What do you expect us to do?" asked Cùil Daothail's Council Leader, his tone as bitter as *caisearbhan*.

"I would like workers to help strengthen Cùil Daothail's fortifications and for those men and women capable of fighting to stand with us." Blàr glared at the council members, and many shrunk from his gaze. "However, I expect you will take what wealth you can carry and flee to save your own skins." Only the blind and deaf could not see and hear the disgust in Blàr's expression and voice.

✳✳✳

Gormal continued to refuse Cassán garments. Thus, he remained as naked as the day he was birthed. The official explanation that Gormal did not want Cassán to use the material to hang himself, while plausible, ignored that Gormal's nature tended to pettiness.

Still, in normal times, nakedness was not a significant issue for the Gaels. When Eimhir visited, having no clothes did not bother Cassán, unless his guards had neglected to refill his brazier. On this day, Cassán would have liked to clothe himself, if only to appear less of a bumbling eejit.

"You want me to do what?"

Eimhir sighed. To her, the plan seemed rational. "There are two ways out of here. One is that we fight our way out. That has a high probability of death—for both of us. The other path is if you are already dead—or appear to be.

"Once your corpse is found, Gormal will rant about it until he grows weary. Likely, the guards will be executed. But being of no further use, he'll have you thrown into the ditch that surrounds Dùn Athad. I will find and revive you, and we will escape to safety."

"This potion made from crushed plants you wish me to take. Have you used or seen it applied before?" The look on Eimhir's face gave Cassán his answer. "Shite! You haven't. Why should I trust you?" The hurt in Eimhir's emerald eyes stopped Cassán from digging a deeper hole for himself.

Exasperated and in a voice that held an unusually harsh edge, Eimhir snapped, "You trusted me with your balls!" Then in a softer tone, she said, "Rumours are spreading throughout Dùn Athad that Gormal already grows tired of you. Furthermore, there are reports that a force has departed Dùn Brion and is travelling in this direction.

"Gormal no longer needs you to draw your father out of Dùn Athad," said Eimhir. "It is also likely that the thought of sending Brion your dismembered corpse teases his vengeful mind." Eimhir's jaw set. "Choose now. A chance of escape or a certain and painful demise." Eimhir had grown fond of Cassán; hence, it deeply wounded her to be cruel, but what choice did she have?

To ameliorate the tense atmosphere, Eimhir added, "I am assured that the mix of plants and herbs will work. One potion to make you sleep deeply and appear dead, the other to revive you. It is simple." *If it works and I can find you in the ditch.*

Cassán shrugged in resignation. "When?"

✦✦✦

A quarter cycle of the moon following the meeting of Cùil Daothail's council, Blàr and Niall stood on the settlement's stockade. They watched long lines of Cùil Daothail's people trudge north and east to the coast or south and west to the lowlands. "How many stayed?" asked Blàr.

"More than I expected and less than needed. Maybe five hundred men and women," replied Niall. He shook his head in disbelief. "They would rather perish in the snows than fight for their homes."

"Let the army drink, eat, and rut tonight. It will be their last celebration for a long time, and for many, it may be their last."

CHAPTER 18

Brion sat across the table from Cearbhall. From their demeanours, both men had other things on their minds. "I need a garrison commander. You, and your hundred, require a purpose. I spoke with Gràinne before she departed, and she will agree to any agreement we reach." Brion saw no sense in conversational frills, so his tone was abrupt.

The look in Cearbhall's dark-brown eyes and an almost imperceptible shake of the burly warrior's head told Brion his run of disappointments had not ended. "Thank you for the offer, but I must decline. My warriors and I leave for Cùil Daothail in three sunsets. The settlement needs us more." Cearbhall stamped a booted foot on the stone floor.

"Dùn Brion stands on solid rock and is built of the same, and the garrison's warriors are strong. We both know that Gormal cannot prevail if he foolishly attacks this stronghold. Appoint from within the army's ranks. It would be a better plan. I can point you to several who will make excellent choices if you wish." A disappointed and resigned Brion inclined his head.

Both men were relieved the awkward conversation had passed without acrimony and any tension had dissipated. Cearbhall grinned and said, "I have a gift from Gràinne. In her haste to ride, she omitted to hand it over." A surprised Brion watched Cearbhall stand and walk to the door. He returned with an obviously heavy sack and, with a grunt, dropped it onto the table. Gripping the bottom of the bag, Cearbhall emptied its contents onto the table.

"She gifted me pieces of iron?"

Cearbhall laughed. "Not just any parts. These are special. They are the fittings for the bolt throwers placed on the ramparts of all Conall's hill-forts." Cearbhall paused, and a look of sadness fell on his face. "However, once used, they will change the shape of war in Northern Albu—forever."

The moment of reflection lasted only a few moments before Cearbhall chuckled. "They will, however, put the fear of the Hag up Gormal's arse. My men and I will show you what is needed and train your warriors to use the machines. Your blacksmiths should have no problem reproducing similar parts."

***

Gràinne's and Amodocus' mounts pawed at the soft snow. The horses nickered happily as yellowed teeth ripped and chewed the clumps of grass uncovered. From a low rise, the couple surveyed the farmstead. There was nothing unique about it. A large roundhouse with a steeply sloping thatched roof dominated the large enclosure. Probably it housed several generations of family and a few animals.

Two smaller buildings, one on either side of the main dwelling, were used for storage, tools, and any slaves they owned. Off to one side stood a large wooden barn, which, from the noises, housed the farmer's livestock and a couple of horses.

It was just after dawn and still gloomy. Snowflakes drifted in the light breeze, and the air was sharp and clear. The noise of a family breaking their fast echoed in Gràinne's ears. Mothers, fathers, brothers and sisters, babies, and those whose life hung on by the grace of the Goddess shared the day's first meal. All were unaware of the watchers.

"No unnecessary deaths, and leave any girl of Brianag's age or young-er alone. I'll cut the balls of any man who disobeys me." Amodocus rolled his eyes. In Gaul, Mórrígan had given him similar instructions, and his re-ply to Gràinne mirrored the counsel he gave to Mórrígan.

"How do you expect us to successfully terrorise Gormal's subjects without rape and enslavement?" Amodocus manoeuvred his horse alongside Gràinne's chariot, avoiding the long curved blades. He patted and stroked the mount's black velvet shoulders as he leaned over. "As for not killing them all, better they die quickly by our blades than a lingering death in the snow and ice as they try to reach Dùn Athad."

"Their lives will be in the hands of the Goddess, not mine."

"You cannot wash their blood from your hands that easily," replied Amodocus.

Gràinne deftly side-stepped the debate. "We cannot take prisoners or slaves because we have no place to keep them, and they will slow us down. Kill any who resist. Burn the buildings to the ground and slaughter the livestock." Gràinne thought for a moment. "However, if there are healthy horses, secure them and load them with fresh meat and corn."

Unblinking, Gràinne held Amodocus' dark stare. "Our warriors may rut the older girls, mothers, grandmothers, and even the men if they wish. *But* leave the babies and children, boys and girls, untouched. Am I clear?" The Thracian shrugged and placed a horn to his lips. Moments later, two hundred horses crashed through the farmstead's perimeter fence. Shortly after, the screaming started.

* * *

Ealasaid snapped at her daughters, making them cower against the wall of the small roundhouse. It was not for any particular transgression. They were children who were cold and hungry. Constantly, they asked why they had been dragged from their warm home and forced to travel in winter. Reasonable questions unless you were their ma. That they also continually asked about their da and when he would join them infuriated Ealasaid.

"Get dressed. Eat your oatmeal and berries, and drink your milk. Be ready to leave by the time I get back with the horses, or I will leave you here, and you can fend for yourselves." Tears and sullen looks were the girls' responses.

The roundhouse was the second overnight shelter. Ealasaid had arranged for three such places of respite, food, and fresh mounts between

133

Dùn Brion and her destination. Two small *bàtaichean*—boats—were also secured to cross the narrow *caolas*—straits—and loch waters.

She gave herself a pat on the back for her planning, which was well-deserved. Even with winter snowfalls, Ealasaid had reduced the journey to five sunsets. Walking, the trek would have taken at least a quarter cycle of the moon, and, in this season, they likely would have perished. With age her daughters would appreciate the care she had taken to make the journey more pleasant. Instead, they continued to complain, and she threatened harsher punishments.

Later, the trio walked a short distance from the small cove where the *bàta*—boat—had dropped them. Ealasaid turned to her daughters, smiled, and pointed to a copse of oaks. "Shelter there. I must pay the *fear-bàta*—boatman—for his services." As she approached the man, she heard him sing a love song. His voice was deep and rich. She recognised the ballad and smiled. It reminded her of a time when she had had few cares, many suitors, and a father.

The fear-bàta bent over to tidy his fishing lines. Even in winter, he hoped to catch a few fish for his partner's and children's evening meals. The fresh snow dampened Ealasaid's footfall, and she was at the man's back before he heard a soft crunch and began to turn.

The blade's tip and edges were honed sharp and punched through the nape of his neck, exiting his throat. A vicious twist and slash almost severed his head. As his blood splashed the snow, Ealasaid, always a practical woman, nimbly stepped around him, reached into his garments, and reclaimed the gold she had paid him.

Using water from his skin, Ealasaid washed the man's blood from her hands and smiled. The owners of the roundhouses where they sojourned had suffered the same fate. "No loose ends and gold saved," she muttered as she trudged up the slope to the thicket of trees and her daughters. So far, it had been a successful escape.

⁂

His face puce with rage, Gormal stomped, ungainly, to and fro along the ramparts of Dùn Athad. He railed at his shield-man and garrison commander, called Madadh, and pointed to the throng of refugees at the gates. All demanded entry to his fort. Then he looked to the north and east. Spittle sprayed from dry, cold-cracked lips as he watched black curls of smoke ascend to smudge the winter skies.

It had started seven sunsets ago with a single black trail, but each day brought sightings of more burnings. Worse, the farmsteads and small settlements were not all in the same location. Had Brion attacked? Gormal shook his head. *Who fights in winter? Yet how much danger am I in?* By now, the Mòine Mohr marshes were frozen, so he had lost the protection of its deep peaty waters. Gormal again swung around to face Madadh and pointed to the growing swell of those displaced from their homes.

"Refuse these vagrants entrance to my home. Turn them back. Kill as many as you need." Gormal saw reluctance on Madadh's face. "Do you refuse my orders?"

"Your instructions are understandable my king, if born out of anger rather than careful thought." Madadh, a few summers older than Gormal, had been at his rìgh's side for twenty summers. Thus, he knew Gormal's moods and the risk of opposing his commands. Still, he dipped his head and said, "However, it may not be a prudent decision… at this time."

Before Gormal exploded, Madadh pointed to the crowds and continued: "The warriors who make up the garrison that protects you, and Dùn Athad, have family members in that crowd. They will be outraged if you refuse entry to their mothers, fathers, sisters, brothers, and lovers." Madadh's arm swept in a half-circle. "Whoever attacks us deliberately strikes at the farms and communities nearest Dùn Athad, where most of your army has kin. In their place, I would do exactly the same."

"What do you advise?"

"Throw open the gates of Dùn Athad and let all enter. I will have a score of my men inspect them. Those who can't prove kinship with the army will be asked to leave."

"Asked?"

Madadh smirked. "Perhaps 'encouraged' would be a better word."

"How do you intend to resolve our main problem?"

"Rumours and reports from those chased from their homes point to a well-armoured warband of horsemen and chariots. Some report many dark-skinned warriors, but that could just be fertile imaginations. That they are mobile explains the wide range within which they strike. They burn buildings, rape the females, slaughter livestock, and kill anyone who defies them. They don't take slaves—yet I suspect only because of the burden of guarding them."

Madadh paused. "It is clear that they intend to terrorise your people, which is why you must keep the army firmly on your side." The garrison commander tugged at his bushy red beard and whiskers. "Let me take five hundred out to meet and destroy them. I'll choose those who have lost homes and family members. They will be highly motivated and we'll depart at sunrise."

Gormal shook his head. "No. You will remain at my side in Dùn Athad. We don't know who, in the chaos, has slipped into our midst. Choose a suitable chieftain to lead the five hundred and offer whatever reward is needed to sustain his enthusiasm." Madadh dipped his head. "Resolve this quickly. Dùn Athad's grain and meat resources are finite. With this population to feed, we'll need to ration food in a quarter cycle of the moon and will starve by Imbolg."

✳✳✳

"It has to be now," said Eimhir. "The fort is in an uproar because someone is burning and pillaging the nearby settlements and farmholdings. Throngs of people demand entry to Dùn Athad. This will provide cover for our deception."

"Surely, in the confusion, we can just slip past a few guards and escape the fort?" Cassán still did not fully support Eimhir's plan and grasped at any straw.

"These troubles will make Gormal shift priorities. He may decide your usefulness is over."

"Do you know who's attacking?"

"It is rumoured that it is a mounted warband from Dùn Brion."

"Mounted? Are there chariots spoken of, too?" Eimhir nodded, but what she perceived as Cassán's procrastination made her noticeably anxious. "It must be Gràinne, my half-sister Brianag's mother. At Dùn Brion, only she leads a band of riders and chariots. But why isn't she chasing after Brianag's captors?"

Cassán held out his hand. "Give me the first potion. I must be gone from this place—one way or the other."

✶✶✶

Their eyes met as Eimhir pushed through the crowds awaiting entry to Dùn Athad. Eimhir's were the deepest green; of the other set, one eye was blue and the other hazel with flecks of amber. It was a unique and unmistakable mix.

"*You!*" snarled Eimhir, and her hand went to the sheath on her thigh.

The reaction from Ealasaid was instantaneous and remarkably similar, with one exception: she growled, "*Sister!*"

A surge of the crowd towards the gateway forced the sisters apart. Both cursed and sheathed their blades. In their final shared look, each swore death to the other. The daughters of Finnean Mac Sèitheach had never been loving siblings. Ealasaid grasped her daughters' shoulders, making them cry out at the vice-like grip as they were propelled through Dùn Athad's entranceway. Eimhir returned to her mission: to locate the body of Cassán before he froze to death.

✶✶✶

The only movements Cassán could make were involuntary tremblings as the cold invaded his exposed flesh. Shortly after he began to regain consciousness and the ability to think. At that point, Cassán came to a sobering conclusion: "The deceiving bitseach." Yet a smile had forced his frozen lips apart.

A steady, if light, snowfall wrapped him in a thin, white shroud. Still, the large snowflake that settled annoyingly on his nose promised much more and heavier snow. Cassán wanted to sneeze or blow the flake from his nose, but that was beyond his capabilities. *Shite! I'm going to freeze to death.*

Eimhir fast approached panic as she tramped along the outer edges of Dùn Athad's ditches. The skies were a dark grey and purple, promising much more snow. Sunset loomed but she carried no torches—a flaw in her planning. The light from the numerous braziers on the ramparts provided little help. Eimhir thought she had walked at least two-thirds of the trench's perimeter. That gave her hope, and she prayed to the Goddess it would not be long before she found Cassán. Yet she was also afraid. What if she had missed him?

Scuffling sounds nearby made Cassán twist his head. That he could do so surprised him. Perhaps the potion's effects wore off at a quicker pace. Growling sounds made him look in their direction. A young wolf held a head in its jaws and worried it. Cassán recognised the slowly disintegrating face of one of his guards.

Ten paces away, an older she-wolf barked, and the younger one dropped its plaything and padded to where she stood. *Maybe she found the guard's body.* Cassán would have panicked, but the cold had numbed his body and mind into accepting his fate as a meal for wolves.

The she-wolf's call startled Eimhir. "The Hag's bony arse!" she swore, and her heart pounded furiously. *Another flaw in my plan. What was I thinking?* Packs of wolves always made their way to Dùn Athad's ditches during winter. It was a good food source, especially if the season was harsh. However, at the beginning of the wintertime, the animals could afford to be more selective of their food and targeted fresher meat first.

"Shite!"

Eimhir calmed her breathing, waited for the next wolf call, and prayed to the Goddess she was not too late. When a howl broke the silence, she dashed towards the sound. She also prayed again that it was the right wolves. In the dimming light, Eimhir saw a large animal paw and sniff at a white shape, and she screamed. Armed with only a short blade, it was doubtful she could fight off a ravenous wolf, yet Eimhir kept going forward and yelling.

A pair of amber eyes watched Eimhir, and a low growl escaped the beast's mouth. Then from about twenty paces away, a wolf barked and was followed by another. "The Hag! How can I fight more than one with only a dagger?" Still, the other wolves sounded younger; the she-wolf growled once more at Eimhir before disappearing into the gloom.

"You took your time," said Cassán and then, with what he hoped was a straight face, added, "When do I take the antidote?"

"Pòg mo thòin!" Eimhir's reply was short, rude, and infused with heartfelt relief.

"If only I could." Cassán hoped his face formed a grin, although it looked more like a painful grimace.

"Can you move anything apart from your head?" Cassán glanced downwards with a smirk. "Or that?" Eimhir looked around to make sure they had not been discovered. "I've stored supplies at a nearby farmer's hut. We should be able to get to it shortly after sunset." She sighed. "But I can't carry or drag you by myself, although I *will* try."

"So much for the perfect plan." Cassán chuckled at Eimhir's discomfort. "Sorry, I couldn't resist that. Help me sit up and let me lean on you. I think my muscles are more frozen than suffering from the potion's effects. If you can help me start moving, I can keep going." Cassán paused and looked at his naked body. "I hope you have some warm clothes in the hut. I don't want to lose any more body parts."

✳✳✳

A fire crackled in the firepit, radiating fragrances of woodsmoke and peat. Cassán inhaled deeply, hardly believing he had finally escaped from Gormal and the awful stench of the dungeon. He shifted under the heavy furs to get comfortable. Yet he felt warm and safe, and most of the feeling in his body had returned. Occasionally, his skin felt as if stabbed by a thousand tiny pins. Feeling his eyelids heavy, he knew sleep was not far off. Yet one thing bothered Cassán—how could he thank Eimhir? With that thought,

Cassán drifted into a peaceful slumber.

In the wee hours of the morning, Cassán woke to the sound of wood being added to the fire and instantly felt guilty. Why had he not thought of it? Was he still a self-centred arsehole? He listened to the soft padding of feet on the dirt floor and froze as the hides that covered him lifted and the air rushed in. Then he felt a warm, naked body cuddle next to him and his heart thudded in his chest.

"Face it. The 'new' you was never going to make the first move," whispered a husky voice that sounded nothing like the Eimhir he knew. "But surely you're not going to make me do all the work?"

When Cassán rolled on top of her, Eimhir had her answer. The rutting and riding were indelicate and frantic. Still, the climaxes were a welcome release of pent-up emotions from their recent trials. For the rest of the night, Cassán promised to acquaint himself with every piece of Eimhir's body and how she liked to be pleased.

"You know, for someone with only one hand, you're a pretty good lover," Eimhir purred.

"Bitseach!"

***

The door to Brion's chamber slammed open, and an angry Drostan filled the doorway. "Where's Seonag? Where's my daughter?" roared the king of the Forest People.

Brion was at first taken aback and then embarrassed at the omission of Drostan from those who were informed of Seonag's departure. *Shite!* "She left after her recent challenge and rides for Cùil Daothail."

"No!" Drostan glared at Brion. "Why did you not stop her or forbid her to go?"

"That's a father's job, but he has been missing in her life for some time."

"I left Seonag in your care for her safety. I love her and trust you."

"I love her, too, and I think she loves me." The simple statement startled Drostan. "My oath to you prevented me from telling her. If I had told her, she would not be travelling to Cùil Daothail," said Brion. The bitterness in his voice was unmistakable. Drostan slumped in a nearby chair.

"What can we do?" asked Drostan.

"It's too late to do anything. We failed her."

CHAPTER 19

Muzzles wet with blood and strings of flesh hanging from red-stained incisors, Sidheag's pack trotted away from another small settlement and another slaughter. As with the others, she left one traumatised survivor alive to spread the tale of the Baobhan Sith's bloodlust and revenge.

In the days following each massacre, priests visited neighbouring communities to deliver a message. Join the Baobhan Sith's horde—it could hardly be called an army due to its lack of organisation or discipline. The alternative was an unpleasant death. To no one's surprise, the recruiting strategy proved highly successful.

In the crannag, Brianag tossed and turned in her cot. Each sunset, Sidheag fed her more blood, resulting in the growth of her unnatural connection with the Baobhan Sith. The cost was Brianag's weakened link with Mongfhionn. Thus, the adolescent felt more alone and abandoned with each feeding. Furthermore, Brianag's desire to resist diminished, which she found depressing.

Sidheag no longer needed to feed blood to Brianag while she slept. In daylight, razor-sharp talons opened Sidheag's veins, painlessly. Brianag soon ceased to fight against the dark blood that dripped slowly from Sidheag's wrist and past her waiting lips. Any resistance was pointless, so why bother?

It pleased Brianag when Sidheag visited the crannag because it gave her respite from her nightmares. When the apparition hunted with her Brood, Brianag experienced every talon slash, tear, and bite of human flesh. Every breath she took stank from raw and decaying human meat. The gouts of blood that painted Sidheag's body felt hot on Brianag's skin. Disturbingly, the gore no longer made her stomach churn.

In the beginning, Sidheag's bloodlust made Brianag feel unclean. Now her skin flushed pink, and her breathing became shallow and rapid. The sensations rippling through her body reminded Brianag of the release she obtained when her fingers rubbed and played with her pit. Brianag screamed *No!* in her mind at finding pleasure in Sidheag's abominations. Yet it was becoming harder to cry out or even to want to shout.

The Siren voice of Sidheag urged Brianag to surrender. To renounce those who once loved but had now abandoned her. To accept her fate. Yet what was that? What was she becoming—another abomination? Sidheag promised peace of a kind. Welcoming the inevitable became almost impossible for Brianag to withstand. In desperation, Brianag called out two words, "Grandma! Ma!" and collapsed.

***

Brianag's call pierced Mongfhionn like a dagger to the heart and increased her sense of helplessness. A powerful, if not the strongest, Sidhe, she had never had to fight a battle where she felt so outmatched and outmanoeuvred. Sidheag continually set barriers to her entering Brianag's mind, and when Mongfhionn broke one, another took its place. "The bitseach is playing with me!" she shouted and continued to pace the stone floor of her chamber.

Much against her better judgment, she had asked her "sisters" of the Aes Sidhe for additional support—another Sidhe, perhaps. They had dithered and procrastinated. Excuses as transparent as the lightest of linens were put forward. "Bloody politics!" Mongfhionn bellowed. Her fellow demi-goddesses had long lost sight of their purpose, and Sidheag's rebirth had thrown them into disarray.

Petty jealousies made many yearn to see Mongfhionn brought to her knees. Some even thought that Sidheag, rather than evil, was simply misunderstood and could be reformed. Mongfhionn gritted her teeth. She would not beg. Yet her shoulders sagged, for she knew if it meant saving Gràinne or Brianag, she would prostrate herself and accept any terms.

That said, whether demi-goddess or human, all knew and feared Mongfhionn's retribution. Vengeance on those who refused to support her was inevitable, terrible, and not bound by time—for that was her nature. The Sidhe gripped her oak staff, drawing from its ancient strength. Yet without the powers of the Blood Queen, Mongfhionn knew any battle with Sidheag would inevitably fail. *Will I have to choose between Gràinne and Brianag?*

"Call on me, and I will come, Mother."

The small voice startled the Sidhe, and her heartbeat raced. She knew each tiny nuance of the words spoken and smiled. It belonged to a young and precocious talent destined to reign over the Aes Sidhe. As yet, because of her age, she was unfettered by the rules of the Aes Sidhe. Mongfhionn shook her head.

"I will not risk the loss of another daughter, Neamhain."

"You can call on me, and I will come, Mother. Or you can be stubborn and try to protect me. Either way, I *will* come. Brianag is *my* blood, too." Mongfhionn smiled at the grit in Neamhain's voice and imagined a delicate jaw firmly set.

"Please, give me more time," pleaded Mongfhionn. She felt Neamhain's resignation and acceptance… and disappointment.

⋆⋆⋆

"Enough! I will prevail over the bitseach." Mongfhionn stormed from her room and strode down the hallway to Brion's quarters. The heavy oak door almost came off its hinges as she threw it open.

"The Hag, Mongfhionn! Are we under attack?" asked a sleep-befuddled Brion.

"Brianag is in terrible danger. I am going to Cùil Daothail at sunrise." Mongfhionn's face took on a look of vulnerability, which made Brion anxious. "Humans think I am all-powerful. I am not. Even with my powers, I, alone, cannot defeat Sidheag. Yet I cannot sit on my arse in Dùn Brion."

"Gràinne?"

"She will soon know of Brianag's distress. Brianag's mind and body are undergoing changes, the end of which no one, not even Sidheag, can predict. That bitseach plays with fire."

"That's not what I meant, and you know it," said Brion.

The Sidhe's shoulders slumped fleetingly. "To defeat Sidheag, we will need a fully developed A 'Bhanrìgh Fuil."

"What does that mean?" rasped Brion with increasing impatience. "Speak plainly."

"The original Blood Queen made a bargain with Sidheag to balance their powers so that neither dominated. Gràinne has to accept that agreement." Brion shook his head, frustrated at Mongfhionn's unwillingness to reach the point. Exasperated, the Sidhe said, "The early Na Daoine Tùrsach were cannibals. Draw your own conclusions."

"No!"

Mongfhionn held Brion's eyes in a stern gaze and said, "*You* are on your own. The fate of Dùn Brion is in human hands… *yours*." The Sidhe swirled around and paused. "Where does Drostan sleep?"

As the chamber's door slammed shut, Brion sat up. Sleep had fled, and he had much to consider. He prayed to the Goddess that Cearbhall would change his mind. A door slamming in a far hallway made him chuckle.

"I pity Drostan."

★★★

"*Brianag!*" Gràinne tumbled from the chariot's open cret but fortunately landed in a drift of soft snow. When Amodocus reached her, a face frozen in terror looked into his eyes.

"I'm losing her," stammered Gràinne, tears streaming down her cheeks. Even Amodocus' embrace could not console her. "I should have gone after Brianag and not listened to my ma."

Amodocus watched, deeply troubled, as the colour of Gràinne's eyes turned as amber as an eagle's and then opaque until obsidian. Sitting upright, she appeared to stare at a distant place. In her head, Gràinne saw the Sidhe and heard her voice.

"I was wrong, daughter. I am going to Cùil Daothail immediately. Follow me as soon as you can. Together, we will find Brianag and end the abomination."

Gràinne blinked slowly and looked at Amodocus as if trying to assemble her thoughts. To the Thracian, her eyes now held tongues of fire and the sigils on her face and arms flowed like deep, dark-blue rivers. He watched her lips open, and from deep within Gràinne came a long undulating howl. It was immediately taken up by packs of wolves in the forests surrounding Dùn Athad, sending shivers up and down Amodocus' spine.

"We finish this mission today. No mercy. We kill every living being that crosses our path." Gràinne looked into Amodocus' eyes. "Then we ride for Dùn Brion and thence to Cùil Daothail. Brianag is in grave peril." The Thracian's face set into a grim mask as he turned to face the riders.

***

In the crannag by the frozen loch, a sleeping Brianag smiled, and a watching Sidheag mouthed, "No."

***

Gràinne watched and relished the third small settlement burn to the ground. Thick black smoke curled upwards, and the stench of charred flesh clogged the nostrils of Gràinne's riders. In the small square, the snow was stained red from the scattered bodies. From children to the elderly, no one had been spared. No living creature survived—neither man nor animal.

Whispered news of Brianag's peril had trickled through the riders. All were veterans skilled in war, yet as they gathered to ride from the community, they looked at each other. Each was fiercely loyal to Gràinne and Amodocus, but they were neither outlaws nor mercenaries. Bloodlust resided in Gràinne's eyes and the day's wanton slaughter stuck in their throats. All feared the Goddess's retribution for their crimes.

Amodocus recognised the signs and took Gràinne aside. "The slaughter and need to inflict pain are understandable, but how do they help Brianag?" The Thracian gripped Gràinne's shoulders, forcing her to look into his eyes. "Ask our warriors to slaughter another farmstead, and they will refuse. They still have honour and will not become like those they fight against."

"You?"

"I will always stay at your side."

Gràinne grasped Amodocus' arm. About to grudgingly accede to his advice, a flicker of movement across the Mòine Mohr caught her attention. Gràinne turned to face her riders and pointed to the line of warriors steadily tramping over the frozen bog. "Will you fight for me one more time?" Gràinne's mien was grim but resolved. "When we return to Dùn Brion, I promise you can freely choose to ride with me to Cùil Daothail and our likely deaths or not."

In her mind, Gràinne heard the hissing voice of the Ancient One: "They are not who you need to please. There is only one path to harness the powers of the Blood Queen. Without my help, you will never see Brianag again. The Sidhe cannot stop Sidheag."

***

Ealasaid was furious and had been in that state since she had crossed Dùn Athad's gateway. Her repeated assertions that she was a spy in Gormal's employ had been derided and then summarily dismissed; likewise, her request for an audience with the king. Furthermore, she faced being thrown out of the hillfort because she had no kin in Gormal's army.

Thus, Ealasaid resorted to an old tactic, lifted her léine, and exposed her arse. The invitation to the young chieftain who commanded the inspection squad accepted, Ealasaid forestalled her imminent expulsion from Dùn Athad. It was a pragmatic decision and, for Ealasaid, an easy one.

The young warrior was hardly going to refuse the gift of her body since she was of infinitely better quality and more experienced than his regular rutting partners. That said, Ealasaid enjoyed the hard-bodied warrior's manhood thrusting into her with unrestricted brutality. Hence, his name sat further down the list of those she would kill later.

Added to his physical attraction, it transpired that nepotism—he was kin to Gormal's shield-man, Madadh—gave the young man his current position. Therefore, between rutting sessions, she whispered in his ear about her desire for him—and a meeting with Madadh. Ealasaid saw that as a stepping stone to what she wanted: an audience with Gormal. The gullible chieftain proved no match for Ealasaid's wiles and powers of seduction.

More rutting, this time with Madadh, bore fruit and Ealasaid finally secured her audience with Gormal. Had Madadh known more about the viper he had let gain access to his king; he would have strangled her. However, being a practical woman, had Ealasaid sensed trouble, she would have slit Madadh's throat and sought another means of entry.

Now, head held regally high and body sheathed in a shimmering white chiton, Ealasaid strode along the middle aisle towards Gormal. She smiled, accepting the gasps of desire and admiration, for the delicate garment hid little of her considerable assets. Coming to a halt ten paces from the king, Ealasaid smiled as she awaited the signal from Gormal to speak.

"I am Ealasaid Nic Finnean, daughter of Finnean Mac Sèitheach and the rightful queen of Na Mèadaidh." Some gasped in horror, others in admiration at the announcement.

"I have come from Dùn Brion and have news of Brion's strengths and weaknesses. I think we should discuss our mutual hatred of Brion and how we can reclaim the throne of Na Mèadaidh for its rightful queen—me." With a bow, Ealasaid ended her introduction.

"Why was I not informed of the lady's status?"

The sharp tone in Gormal's voice did not bode well for Madadh, and the commander glared at Ealasaid. While she returned his stare with a gracious smile, her eyes promised death should he oppose her.

"Dismiss the congregation. The lady and I will continue our discussions in private."

***

With less than a sunset, before he intended to depart for Cùil Daothail, Brion's request for an urgent meeting surprised Cearbhall. Hence, he entered the room with a look of curiosity—more so when he found that the only other person in the chamber was the Sidhe. She paced the room in a state of agitation as if wanting to be elsewhere.

Brion opened his mouth to speak, but Mongfhionn cut him off and pointed a long finger at Cearbhall. In a characteristically blunt and definitive tone, she said, "*You* will stay and help Brion defend this stronghold. That is the end of this discussion."

Having declared her demands, Mongfhionn forced a benign smile onto her lips. In a less authoritative tone, she added, "Your desire to go to Cùil Daothail is admirable and courageous." Cearbhall dipped his head in modest affirmation. His eyes widened when the Sidhe continued, "Yet, there, you will make no difference, and the most likely outcome will be the deaths of you and your warriors—for no gain."

Mongfhionn looked at a discomfited and irritated Brion. "Make your arrangements with Cearbhall." Then she turned to face Cearbhall. "My daughter's and granddaughter's lives are at stake. Do *not* oppose me on this."

"Do I have a choice?" grumbled Cearbhall.

"Of course you do. Humans always have a choice." Mongfhionn's smile was almost a pleasant sight. "You can become Brion's battle commander or die… *now*. Ask Drostan if you doubt my powers." A sense of relief appeared to settle on the Sidhe, and she walked away from the table. As she reached the door, her head turned, but, this time, the Hag peered from under Mongfhionn's hood.

"Mongfhionn's weakness is that she has mercy within her heart. I do not, and they are my kin also."

"Some things never change. She always makes great entrances and exits," said a rueful Brion. "Now, let's talk strategies. The Sidhe has insisted on your remaining, which means the battle will not pass us."

CHAPTER 20

"Tactics?" queried Gràinne. "They look about five hundred strong."

Amodocus smiled, relieved that a measure of sanity had returned to Gràinne. "They have chosen the battlefield poorly. In any other season, the advantage of the marshland would be a challenge for our riders. Now the land and bog are frozen hard, and the landscape is level. We should test their shield-wall's strength and willingness to stand."

"We should kill everyone and send a parting message to Gormal."

Gràinne's matter-of-fact tenor elicited a raised eyebrow from Amodocus. Had he been too hurried in his earlier assessment? As if sensing his reticence, Gràinne snorted. In a voice loud enough for all to hear, she said, "They are warriors, not farmers or tradesmen, and like us, are paid to fight and, if needed, to die. Surely that causes us no problems." The roar and slap of swords on shields gave her their answer.

***

Dùghlas, the chieftain who led the five hundred, clapped cold hands together and wished for a stool near a roaring brazier and a bowl of steaming hot beef stew. A veteran of many skirmishes yet few significant battles, he knew the drills and commands and understood the heat and frenzy of a fight.

Thus, Dùghlas looked with concern at his enemy compared to the mix of warriors under his command. Could his five scarred *ceannard-ceud*—leaders of one hundred—keep the young hotheads under control and the shield-wall solid?

The tribal elders told stories of the deep, bone-numbing freezes that had begun many generations past and still continued. The Mòine Mohr marshes had always frozen, but not to the extent that horses and chariots could traverse them safely. Dùghlas knew the battlefield was neither his choice nor ideal, given that they faced mounted warriors.

On either side of Dùghlas stood a young man and woman. He constantly found himself snapping at the young man to stay in line. "An eager arsehole," grunted the veteran. Looking for glory and plunder, he had all the marks of one whose actions got others killed. The girl was about the same age, no more than a score of summers. Yet her stance was that of an experienced warrior, and her leather armour, sgiath, and weapons were well maintained. He heard her stamp her feet and smiled. Then he bellowed.

"Stamp your feet, move your arms! Stretch your limbs. I don't care if your cocks or tits freeze and fall off, but I want you able to fight."

He expected the enemy to dismount before the attack. It was the traditional approach of the Gaels. Yet, usually, only leaders rode into battle, but in this warband, all were mounted. Dùghlas' gut told him that his optimism was unfounded. Still, he smiled when the riders closed to five hundred paces and dismounted. His warriors well outnumbered their adversaries.

∗∗∗

"I propose an alliance between our kingdoms…" began Ealasaid.

"You have no kingdom," retorted Gormal.

Ealasaid reddened and ground her teeth at the insult. It was the first time she had met Gormal. She studied him intensely and was unhappy with her impression: a malformed and slack-jawed rìgh whose brutality disguised his lack of substance. By reputation, his father, Eachdonn Breac, had been much more formidable. Sadly, his weakness was being an honourable man.

Her expression became one of amusement as she wondered if Gormal knew his father had been betrayed by his hand-fast partner, Ceana.

She was Finnean's sister and Ealasaid's aunt. A smile ghosted on Ealasaid's lips. *So much for principles.* The Sèitheach women had a natural talent for deception and death. She wondered momentarily about her sister. *Is Eimhir a killer like me?*

"I am informed you are a passable spy, if focused on your personal quarrel with Brion, rather than my kingdom." Gormal smiled unpleasantly. "You may visit with the one who recruited you following this meeting. The wolves will not have devoured all of him." The king stretched his head forward like a *clamhan*—buzzard. "You have little to bargain with except your body. I can find many strìopachan with similar assets, but who will cost me much less than you."

"Brion is Rìgh of the Na Mèadaidh only by the dictate and army of Drostan. He is unloved, and many will desert him once it is known that I, the true bhanrigh, have returned."

"I hear only the fantasies of a spy and assassin with royal ambitions. Had I known of your lineage, I would have had you killed."

Ealasaid dipped her head and watched Gormal's fingers absent-mindedly stroke lank, auburn tresses. His hair was threaded with blond—a gift from his mother. Then she looked into and seized his green eyes with her unique look. Gormal tried to avert his gaze, but Ealasaid refused to surrender.

"Drostan will shortly lead his warriors into battle at Cùil Daothail, leaving Dùn Brion unprotected. Proclaim my right to the Na Mèadaidh's throne, and Brion's army will splinter. If we're fortunate, he'll face an insurrection. At the least, he'll be left with a weakened force." Ealasaid smiled. "Now, do we have an alliance?"

***

"Slings!" roared Amodocus.

"Rut the Hag," cursed Dùghlas and shouted, "Back three rows raise shields! Keep the wall tight." His hoped-for traditional fight evaporated as his enemy unwound slings from around their waists and loaded them from the pouches slung on their belts. The whirring of long cords of braided wool against the muffled sounds of boots on snow seemed extraordinarily loud. The crash and clatter of thousands of missiles—a mix of stones and iron bullets—resounded across the Mòine Mohr.

"Hold your position!" bellowed Dùghlas at the rising number of yelps as stones found flesh. "The sgiathan will protect you, and our enemy can only carry a small number of stones." The veteran heaved a sigh of relief when the bombardment stopped. He looked around his four lines of warriors and shouted, "Ceannard-ceud move the wounded to the rear rank."

"Mount up!" boomed Amodocus. "Walk to two hundred paces."

Dùghlas' hopes were raised and dashed as he watched the warband mount and dismount. The enemy was near enough for him to discern their faces and weapons. He shuddered, for, like many, he had dismissed the rumours of dark-skinned warriors. Yet here they were. That said, their colouring bothered Dùghlas less than the weapons they carried or that the horses they rode were huge and protected by chainmail.

"Quiet!" he shouted to quell the increasing rumbles of anxiety within his ranks. His unease rose as he watched the riders unsheathe bow staffs, string the weapons, and take long black arrows from the quivers tied to their mounts. *Shite!* "Brace for missiles. Keep the wall tight. No gaps!" Dùghlas' respect for his enemy grew with each tactic. "They are well-led," he muttered.

The distance was beyond that of a killing shot. Hence, the clouds of arrows arched high in the air before descending on Dùghlas' contingent. Warriors cursed as thousands of barbs punched through wooden sgiathan to tear and scratch exposed skin. This time the shrieking told of real pain, of shafts finding and penetrating targets. Against shields, stones were an inconvenience to be suffered. Arrows brought death and injury.

Once more, Dùghlas shouted, "Hold the formation. Keep the shield-wall strong. Injured to the rear. Bring the dead to the front. They can be used as a barrier. Our time to fight will come." The last declaration was sent with a prayer to the Goddess that it was true. A cheer from the front row caused Dùghlas to shake his head.

After exhausting their supply of arrows, the riders remounted and cantered back to where three chariots waited. Dùghlas' band's glee was short-lived as a horn resounded, the enemy turned, and the horses charged. "The bastards just wanted enough space to reach a gallop," spat Dùghlas and then shouted, "Lower spears! Stand firm!" His warriors heaved a confident sigh of conviction and shouted battle cries. Dùghlas knew it was little more than fantasy to believe that horses would not charge a line of spears—but it did help morale.

★

A second sunset passed when Cassán and Eimhir stumbled across the snow-covered body of the fear-bàta murdered by Ealasaid. Crimson snow marked the man's final resting place. Fortunately for the duo, his small boat, held by the ice that had formed around it, had remained in place. "I suspect this is my sister's work," spat Eimhir. "It's where I would have had a bàta land."

"She does appear to treat people as disposable," said Cassán. "Although we should thank her for the boat. It will shorten the length of our journey." The angry stare from Eimhir stopped him from saying more. "Or perhaps not." Cassán pondered for a moment before asking, "Would she have hired a fear-bàta to cross the next loch in our path?"

Eimhir nodded. "Yes, and I can guess where she might have crossed that stretch of water." Eimhir grimaced as if suddenly having a sour taste in her mouth. "We're probably going to find a murdered boatman there, too." The young woman twisted strands of her rose-gold hair. "I'm not sure I should accompany you to Dùn Brion."

"What? Why not?"

"I am Finnean Mac Sèitheach's daughter and Ealasaid's sister. Those are not great references. We should be realistic."

"The Hag with realism! I'll be with you." The look on Eimhir's face was unconvincing. "Oh, I see. I'm the spoilt wastrel who has been banished and is under sentence of death." Cassán took Eimhir's hands and worried about how cold they felt. "We will enter Dùn Brion and face my father together. Agreed?"

Eimhir dipped her head and said, "We've a short time of daylight left and should take advantage of the calmer weather before resting for the night."

* * *

"Stand, you fool!" snarled Dùghlas.

As he watched the riders close on the shield-wall, the order was barked at the young man to his right. A patch of yellow snow showed he had lost control of his bladder. Still, in battle, that was not uncommon. Why on earth did the ceannard-ceud put him in the front row? If gold had bought his place, Dùghlas would see both men punished—if they survived.

Shouts in a language they did not understand reached the shield-wall. Still, it was not difficult to imagine their meaning. It was the same for all battles—taunts, curses, appeals to gods, threats of castration and rape were common to all warriors. At least on horses, they were spared the flaunting of arses and cocks—although not breasts.

Dùghlas' nerves jangled, and his heart pounded at the unearthly ululations of the apparition who stood unclothed on the leading chariot. *Naked, in this weather.* Dùghlas shook his head in disbelief. Twenty paces from the shield-wall, the riders divided and charged, right and left, along the outer perimeter of the formation.

For a brief moment, Dùghlas thought his spears had caused the riders to change tactics. The javelin that suddenly sprouted from the young man's chest proved that wrong. Why had the eejit lowered his sgiath? Each rider carried six javelins and six heavy darts, which they hurled with practised ease at Dùghlas' ranks. It was the moment that the real screaming began.

"Rear rank turnaround, lower spears, and face the bastards!" Dùghlas's command was sensible but too late. Unprotected by shields, the rear and right sides of any formation are the most vulnerable. Javelins and darts bit savagely, and the shape became increasingly ragged until it broke into clumps of fighters. It was then that the chariots' spinning scythes took their toll. When the riders and chariots had exhausted their missiles, a hunting horn sounded, and they withdrew.

"They've been reduced to about three hundred warriors in a loose formation. Their leader has held them together surprisingly well. Many would have turned and run by now," said Amodocus.

Gràinne nodded and then looked upwards. The light was fading fast. "End it the way we discussed," she said in a voice cold as ice.

Astride his black horse, Amodocus held a mace in his right hand and a curved rhomphaia in the left. Directing his mount with short phrases and nudges of his knees, he rode at a fast canter at the point of a battering ram of Thracians. Behind them galloped Gràinne's riders and, off to the side, her three chariots.

Dùghlas had not considered that each horse weighed over seven times their riders' weight. Hence, they were as much a threat, if not more so, than those who rode them. The Thracian ram hit Dùghlas' depleted ranks, scattering the foot warriors like chaff in the wind. Following in their hoof-steps, Gràinne's riders divided into two and fell upon their hapless adversaries with slashing swords and long-handled axes.

Meanwhile, the chariots ploughed a bloody path along the right flank and wheeled around to do the same for the rear row. Body parts flew and were scattered over the ground. In the bloody melee, white snow became a crimson slush of gore and mud as riders slashed with blades and bashed with flanged maces. Still more of Dùghlas' command was injured by the lashing hoofs of the horses.

The shrieking and cries of his command resounded in Dùghlas' ears and would remain with him for the rest of his life. Back to back, Dùghlas and the young woman, who had stood courageously at his side, slashed upwards at blades that swung at them from a great height. Even riders dislodged from their mounts were found to have much superior armour to his own.

Soon the screams of agony became hoarse shouts and whimpers for mercy. Dùghlas and the girl stood defiant at the centre of a small circle of warriors. Yet soon, it was just the two of them. *How could five hundred warriors die or be severely injured so quickly?*

"I am sorry," said Dùghlas to the girl. She looked at him without understanding as he gripped her shoulder and thrust a dagger into her chest. "Better to die by my hand than to be raped by these bastards." As her eyes dimmed and her last breath fled from her body, Dùghlas gently lowered her to the ground.

With a grunt from sore muscles and exhaustion, he stood up straight and looked into the face of Amodocus. The mace crushed Dùghlas' skull, but given Amodocus' strength, his death was swift, if brutal. Beyond the veil, he met the young woman, and they entered Mag Mell's feasting halls together.

"Kill the injured and behead them. The last thing we need is vengeful spirits." Gràinne paused for a moment before adding, "Leave their leader. He is mine." She ignored Amodocus' questioning look and said, "Our warriors can keep any spoils they may find. But tell them to be quick. I want away from here very soon."

✶✶✶

The gloom of dusk provided Gràinne cover as she sought out the leader of Gormal's contingent. Beside him lay the young female warrior. The wound that had ended her life was obvious, as was the evidence that she had not wielded the blade that sent her to Mag Mell. "An honourable man indeed," she muttered. "I wish I had known you."

Gràinne exhaled a long, mournful sigh. "Forgive me, Goddess." The dagger's blade glinted red in the sunset. Fortunately, its edge was keen and easily cut through flesh and muscle. She felt the knife scrape the sternum and saw the white bone. Gràinne glanced around. She did not have an axe to break the bone quickly. Therefore she grimaced and reached into the corpse's bloody chest, cracked the ribs protecting the heart, and ripped the organ from the cavity.

On her knees and gagging with disgust, Gràinne lifted up the vessel and opened her mouth. Thick heart blood flowed between her open lips. Barely keeping her belly from puking, she gritted her teeth at what she must do. *I must finish it for Brianag.* Sharp incisors bit into the muscle and tore a chunk loose. Tears streamed down Gràinne's face as she swallowed the morsel of flesh.

Movement at the edge of her vision startled Gràinne. She grabbed her sword, rising from her knees. The revulsion in Amodocus' eyes wounded Gràinne deeply. "I will do anything to save Brianag. *Anything.* Stand with me or leave now."

Amodocus moved towards Gràinne. That he still held a mace in his right hand made Gràinne grip her sword tightly. He smiled sadly, dropped the weapon, and embraced his distraught lover. It seemed an age until the convulsions that wracked Gràinne's body subsided.

Hands on her shoulders, Amodocus gazed into Gràinne's eyes and could not stop a shudder. In the past, he had seen her eyes black, which was a terrible vision. Yet now her gaze was blood-red, and was a truly horrific sight. Gràinne looked at Amodocus curiously, but he smiled and shrugged. "You should rest. We ride for Dùn Brion at first light."

⁎⁎⁎

On her way to Cùil Daothail, Mongfhionn cantered to a halt. "Oh, Gràinne, my daughter, what have you done?" Eyes that rarely cried misted over. Yet the Sidhe also knew that now there was a chance to stop Sidheag.

In the crannag on the frozen loch, Sidheag screeched, "The bidse!" and cursed the Ancient One.

CHAPTER 21

In the high, snow-capped mountains and valleys of north-eastern Albu, Sidheag's campaign of terror and death, together with the missionary zeal of Seirbhiseach's coterie of priests, created a storm wave of support. Miscreants, bandits, and mercenaries grasped the opportunity for nefarious activities and plunder.

The inclination of ordinary citizens was one of resignation. Who could stop the Baobhan Sith, her Brood, or her growing army? Better to be on the side of Sidheag than horribly mutilated and used as food. Parents with daughters reasoned that, by supporting Sidheag, they could prevent their offspring from becoming one of the nine. That was wishful thinking, for Sidheag would dispose of and take whomever she wanted.

In the crannag, caught between threats from Mongfhionn and Sidheag, Seirbhiseach rocked back and forward on the stool beside the fire-pit. Clumps of white hair torn out by the roots littered the floor. Realising that he was a minor and very disposable, piece on the fidchell board grated on the High Priest and kept him in a state of permanent fear.

His command of his priests, who had grown in number to over one thousand zealots, was tenuous. Constantly, he tried to uncover any weakness of Sidheag. His reward was her mocking laugh before his body convulsed in pain. He had no secrets from her.

A moan drew Seirbhiseach's attention to the cot and the tormented sleep of Brianag. The Sidhe had commanded him to protect her, but how? The vivacity and defiance in Brianag's formerly bright, emerald-green eyes had been extinguished. She lay naked in the cot. The heavy furs and coverings, used when she first arrived, lay scattered on the floor, tossed aside as useless.

Each day, Sidheag dripped blood into Brianag's open mouth and forced the High Priest to watch. Given his nature, it was a cruel punishment. On occasion, Sidheag would feed on Brianag's blood. Yet it surprised Seirbhiseach that the apparition restrained herself to a few drops each time. *Why so little? What need had Sidheag of Brianag's lifeblood?* His hopes rose.

This morning, Seirbhiseach watched Brianag roll onto her back, and his innate lasciviousness surfaced. He leered at her young body, and drool dribbled from one side of his mouth. In the brief time she had been at the crannag, Brianag's adolescent body had developed into one shapelier and more softly contoured. She radiated a sensual aura at odds with a girl of barely fifteen summers. Was this another "gift" from Sidheag? Seirbhiseach snarled. *Her young body should be mine to use.*

However, Sidheag and Mongfhionn had threatened terrible retribution if Seirbhiseach so much as breathed on Brianag. Frustrated, he stroked his manhood and stared a while longer. With a sigh, his desires were temporarily satisfied, and he turned back to the firepit. He fought to focus his remaining mental abilities on the only thing Sidheag had left him: a desire for revenge that burned hotter than the fire before him.

✳✳✳

Brianag was lost. She barely knew who she was or what she did during the days and long nights. A shiver trickled along her spine, not from the cold but at the increasingly vivid and nightmarish visions that haunted her sleep. *Are they all in my mind?* It was a question to which she had no answer or at least none she wanted to acknowledge.

She looked down at her body and did not recognise it. She saw the curvaceous shape of a well-nourished, older girl. In the beginning, she had infuriated Sidheag by refusing to eat, and, in her mind, she still felt committed to her protest. Yet she craved raw, bloody meat. Brianag had never enjoyed overcooked food. Now, unless blood dripped from the carved slice, she felt unsatisfied. Cutting meat she also saw as a waste of time. She wanted to rip the warm flesh from the sacrifice while it still lived.

In a rare moment of lucidity, she glanced at her hands and gasped, "No! Please, no." Her fingernails were stained red and tiny slivers of meat clung accusingly between flesh and nail. Desperately, she tried to remember, but that was like moving through honey. Only her dreams gave her any clarity, but those images horrified her. Surely, it was not her killing and feasting on warm flesh and blood.

"No!" she cried out again. Brianag feared the truth. Yet she also felt guilty about how enjoyable her new appetites and shape felt.

* * *

"It is so dark in here," said Neamhain. Two small feet padded along the twisting hidden paths in Brianag's mind, seeking a sanctuary, a place of light in the darkness that shrouded her sister's thoughts. Neamhain sobbed at Brianag's suffering and her constant, unrelenting torment. The young girl inhaled deeply and bit her lip, knowing her mother would be furious. Still, how could she leave Brianag to fight by herself? Neamhain knew Brianag would fight for her.

Eventually, Neamhain found a refuge, a den where evil had not extinguished the light and sat down. "I can work with this." Her attention concentrated on Brianag, and she whispered softly, "I am here, Brianag. I will never leave you alone, but you cannot give in. You have to fight with me."

In her sleep, Brianag smiled and murmured, "Thanks, Sister."

* * *

"Take us to Seonag. She knows who I am," said Cassán. He hoped his voice sounded calm and reasonable. However, he had become more anxious the closer he and Eimhir got to Dùn Brion. The two tall, beefy gate guards looked Cassán up and down and then repeated the process for

Eimhir.

"Seonag is no longer the king's commander and has left Dùn Brion."

As the pair stood at the gateway, a group of curious guards approached the gates. "Must be a quiet day for us to get so much attention," muttered Cassán, unable to keep his irritation to himself. The guards bristled, and hard stares replaced curiosity.

"Are you trying to get us thrown into the dungeons?" hissed Eimhir.

"Sorry." Cassán smiled and looked at the taller of the guards. Then with a graciousness he did not feel, said, "I am Cassán Mac Brion, son of Brion, Rìgh of Dùn Brion, and the Na Mèadaidh. Please take me to my father."

Once more, the guard inspected Cassán as if he were a prize horse. He shook his head. "You're never that fat, spoilt bastard. Anyway, Cassán is banished from Dùn Brion. If you are who you claim, then you're an outcast, and I could kill you without consequence."

The sentinel nodded to his comrades. "Take this pair to the dungeons." Then he looked at Cassán. "Just be thankful we're having a 'quiet day,' and I don't want to clean your blood from my sword."

"Did you have to mention dungeons?" asked Cassán as the pair were dragged across the yard to the cells. Eimhir's glare stopped further stupidity. As the duo crossed the courtyard, one of the gate guards turned to his comrade.

"Didn't Cassán have his hand cut off by Gormal?"

The sentinel nodded and shrugged. "So what?"

His friend pointed to the receding back of Cassán. "He is missing a right hand."

✴✴✴

Sunrise came and went, and meadhan-latha neared. Cassán, narrowly avoiding a wooden splinter from the rough wooden bench, turned to Eimhir. "At least they let us share the cell, and it seems a bit more pleasant, and the food is better than at Dùn Athad." He shivered. "Although a brazier would be welcome before we freeze," he shouted. Cassán put his arm around Eimhir and pulled her closer for warmth.

"Better accommodation or not, prisoners rot in dungeon cells until they die or are taken from them to be tortured and executed."

"My da would not do that to us. He's a fair and honourable man, which, regrettably, I found out rather late." Another reassuring squeeze and Cassán added, "You'll see. We'll be fine." Thankfully, Eimhir did not see the glance upwards or hear his silent plea to the Goddess.

✳✳✳

Outside the cell door, two men listened and watched through a small grille. "I find it hard to believe that is my son, either by temperament or appearance. What happened to his hair?" Brion turned to Cearbhall and, in a low tone, said, "Have them brought to the small reception room."

Then Brion smirked. "But don't make it seem it's for a happy reconciliation. I'm sure the Goddess won't begrudge me a few more moments of retribution for the grief he's caused me." Cearbhall smiled and dipped his head.

✳✳✳

Cearbhall could barely control his grin as a protesting Cassán, and his companion were dragged across a yard of slush, ice, and mud. Yet the new garrison commander was impressed by the restraint shown by Cassán. By reputation, the "old" Cassán would be screaming and threatening dire consequences for his treatment.

The guard, one of those who had first greeted Cassán, had been both chastised and well-briefed on his role. Hence, as he stopped at the door to Brion's chamber, he turned and said gruffly, "These are days of turmoil, and the rìgh's temper is changeable. Your arrival, if you are who you claim, may have exacerbated it. Good luck."

"It is what it is," said Cassán as the guard led Eimhir and him into the small reception room.

A small rectangular table sat in the middle of the room. In a smaller version of his throne, Brion sat straight-backed. To his left stood

Cearbhall, whom Cassán knew to be one of Gràinne's ceannairí céad. A frown creased Cassán's brow. He had only been gone three or four cycles of the moon, yet he sensed significant changes in Dùn Brion. He bowed deeply, as did Eimhir, and said, "It is good to see you again… Father." The grunted response gave Cassán little comfort.

"You, I *may* know, but who is this?" barked Brion, peering at Eimhir. In truth, Brion was shocked at the change in Cassán and hardly recognised the gaunt, shaven-headed young man who stood before him. Additionally, Cassán's body language suggested a depth to his son that had been former-ly absent. *Wishful thinking.* To give himself time to think, Brion focused on Eimhir.

"Well?"

It was the moment Eimhir had dreaded, and a truthful answer might see her lose her head. She straightened her shoulders, held her head high, and spoke. "I am called Eimhir. The Goddess brought Cassán and me to-gether during his sojourn in Gormal's dungeons."

"That is all well and good, and I'm sure more details will be fleshed out later, but your reticence to tell me your full name is disturbing."

Eimhir inhaled deeply and exhaled. "I am Eimhir Nic Finnean, daughter of Finnean Mac Sèitheach, whom I believe your sister, Mórrígan, killed."

"The Hag!" exclaimed Brion and Cearbhall. The rìgh stared at Cassán. "*You* saw fit to bring the daughter of Finnean into my stronghold? The stay in Gormal's dungeons improved your physique, but did it addle your mind?"

Cassán's face flushed an angry red, and he stepped forward to defend Eimhir. The action did not go unseen by Brion, as did Eimhir's hand on Cassán, which halted his intent.

"I should also say that my elder sister is Ealasaid Nic Finnean. She is one of Gormal's spies," said Eimhir. "I suspect you may know of her, but you may not know that she is in Dùn Athad. I saw her briefly when we were escaping. She likely seeks an alliance with Gormal. My sister's heart burns with the fires of vengeance and thwarted ambitions to be pro-claimed queen of the Na Mèadaidh."

Eimhir frowned. "I have never sought, or will ever seek, to be Bhanrìgh of the Na Mèadaidh. Believe me, or not, my father's death was more than justified, and my sister's will be, too." Then she smiled and stepped forward to stand at Cassán's side.

"The Hag's arse, Cearbhall. Will our litany of ill omens never stop?"

"If we are not welcome, Father, I would ask for better clothing, two horses, and food for five sunsets." Cassán held his father's gaze without flinching.

"Don't be an eejit, boy. Your arrival is the best news I, and this fort, have had in a long time." Cassán's and Eimhir's jaws dropped as Brion and Cearbhall broke into broad smiles.

"This was all a test," said Cassán. His voice held a hint of annoyance.

"Of course it was. Did you expect to walk through the gates of Dùn Brion as if you had never left? How could I know what creature resided in a body I hardly recognise? Or whether you had taken Gormal's gold?" Brion dipped his head towards Eimhir. "And given her lineage, she may have been another assassin."

Brion looked at Cassán's right arm, and his expression became one of pain and sadness. "Does it hurt?"

"Occasionally. Often, I think, probably like you, that I still have my hand." Cassán looked at Eimhir. "Without Eimhir's care, I would have lost the arm through disease and, with it, my life. She suffered great humil-iation and abuse in attending to me. Her escape plan…" The edges of Cassán's lips lifted. "…was somewhat unconventional but, as you can see, successful."

Brion smirked. "Who was responsible for the lack of hair?"

"It was keep the lice or lose the hair." Cassán chuckled and scratched the short red stubble. "I'm actually quite used to the shortness and may keep it. No maintenance and no trouble in battle." The last words raised the eyebrows of both king and his commander.

"But what are we to do with *you*?" Brion once more held Eimhir's gaze while simultaneously silencing Cassán with a raised hand and a shake of his head. "In my judgment, Eimhir is more than capable of speaking for herself."

Eimhir bowed and took a step closer to the table. The sudden flash of white flesh and the blue-grey glint of steel drawn from the sheath strapped to her inner thigh drew sharp gasps from all in the room. Cearbhall swept his sword from its scabbard. The sound of Eimhir's blade piercing the oak tabletop and the reverberations along its length as the weapon quivered to a standstill prompted exclamations of relief and a few curses.

"For a start, your guards should search prisoners more diligently. I suggest you appoint me as your shadow, for this should never have happened—even in a private audience, no matter who the guest is. You are a king. Assassins, like my sister, will be paid substantial amounts of gold to murder you."

Roars of laughter and relief echoed off the room's stone walls. Brion pointed to a table laden with food and drink. "We shall celebrate my son's return and discuss new beginnings."

* * *

As they left the room, Cassán tapped Cearbhall's arm and took him to the side. "I was dismayed to hear of Gòrdan's death. I had hoped to redeem myself and earn his respect by being a better student for him. Perhaps you would train me. I fear war will soon be upon us."

Cearbhall smiled and nodded. "It would be my pleasure, my prionnsa."

CHAPTER 22

393 B.C.—Winter

"I will not ask why you are here, but I am delighted to see you," said Blàr.

Calf-deep snow carpeted the double stockade. It was early morning, and Blàr turned to watch Seonag crunch her way through the crust of ice. Like two ice-breathing dragons, Blàr's and Seonag's breath shimmered white and sparkled in the dawn sun before dissipating. Seonag smiled at Blàr's justified pride in what his men had achieved. Under challenging conditions, they rebuilt, extended, and added a second row of stakes to Cùil Daothail's fence and dug a deep trench along its perimeter.

That said, Blàr's eyes held a deep sadness as he pointed out the charred skeletons of Cùil Daothail's former residents. The lives of those who had resided and conducted their business outside the community's stockade had changed irreparably. Still, they were not the only ones to suffer. Inside Cùil Daothail's strengthened walls, homes and workshops had been repurposed for war.

"You had no choice," said Seonag.

"True, but it still angers me. I doubt Cùil Daothail will ever recover."

Seonag dipped her head. Then, on some unknown impulse, maybe to feel part of the fort and its garrison, she tapped the blade of her sword on the tip of a fire-hardened stake. It echoed as metal on metal. Puzzled, she rapped the weapon against several others. All produced the same metallic sound.

"I was not aware of your talent for alchemy."

Blàr chuckled and shook his head. "The history and wealth of Cùil Daothail are built on the production and working of iron. In fact, the settlement sits on ancient iron deposits." Seonag's face told that she had no idea where Blàr was going, and he laughed loudly. It was a good laugh from deep within, yet it also sounded as if he had little to be happy about recently.

"Among the many rumours, it is said that Sidheag and her Brood are susceptible to iron. That would not be unbelievable, for the Aes Sidhe are well-known to be wary of iron. When she was last in Albu, Gràinne killed the abomination known as Kartimandu with an iron-tipped spear. Thus, based on the principle that it can do no harm, every pole has iron nails and spikes hammered into them. That includes the stakes in the ditches surrounding Cùil Daothail."

"What size is our garrison?"

"The fort is square, with each side five hundred paces in length. Currently, I have four thousand men and women, which should give us a double shield-wall along the battlements. I expect another thousand to drift in over the next moon cycle. The five hundred Cùil Daothail residents who remained will form our reserve. My guess is that Sidheag's army will attack from the north. Hence, you and I will take charge of the northern defences."

Seonag nodded. "Drostan?"

"The last messenger from Drostan reported that he and an army of five thousand are moving through the forests towards us."

"Thank the Goddess, it's winter. With so many warriors, this fort would soon stink in any other season. Do you think we'll need them?" asked Seonag.

"Sidheag and her Brood cut through and slaughtered Gòrdan and his men like a sharp knife through *gruth*. I've heard that Gòrdan's warriors didn't unsheathe their weapons. That is worrisome. The bidse continues to butcher communities across north-eastern Albu who won't bend the knee and join her."

Blàr paused and said, "We often argue about Drostan's pragmatism and ruthlessness. Yet without the armies of the Forest People, how will we stop Sidheag?" With a sigh, he added, "Let's hope whoever succeeds Drostan wields the power of the Forest People wisely."

Seonag blushed and sought to change the direction of the conversation, which was getting too close to home. Blàr put her flushed face down to the cold breeze scouring the ramparts. "How many can Sidheag put in the field?"

"Current estimates, which change each sunset, are between ten and twenty thousand." Blàr sighed. "Perhaps your decision to come to Cùil Daothail was not the most prudent."

"One piece of land is as good as another to die on," replied Seonag.

* * *

The blare of horns announced Gràinne and her warband's arrival at Dùn Brion. It was quickly followed by bellows from the guard towers and the groans of heavy gates that begrudgingly consented to open. The gaily coloured chariots, a stark contrast against the grey stone fort, entered first, followed by the riders.

"See that the horses are fed, watered, and brushed. When that's done, you can feed, drink, and rut until you can't walk, but in two sunrises, I ride for Cùil Daothail—with or without you," shouted Gràinne. With a nod to Amodocus, the pair strode towards the broch. Waiting on the uppermost step into the building were Brion, Cassán, Cearbhall, and Eimhir.

Gràinne recognised Cassán, but only because of his missing hand. "I'm glad *your* son has returned." There was no mistaking the bitter tone of Gràinne's voice. "He looks as if he has undergone a remarkable physical change. Let's hope it reflects an attitude that does not fade with adversity."

Eimhir bridled at the slight and growled like a mother lince protecting her kits. Cassán's hand on her shoulder reduced Eimhir's anger and drew Gràinne's attention, prompting a reluctant smile. "*You* bear a semblance to a murderous bitseach I came across recently."

"I am Eimhir Nic Finnean, and the bidse is my sister, Ealasaid."

Eimhir's lips curled into a smile at the surprise in Gràinne's mien. However, both women brought their demeanours under control quickly. The irritated look Gràinne shot Brion elicited only a shrug. As she stepped forward to climb the short series of steps, Gràinne found Eimhir blocking her path.

"Please, leave your weapons at the door. One of *my* guards will see that they are well looked after. They will be returned to you when you leave…" Eimhir smiled and added, "…with keener edges."

"Who do you think you are, bitseach?" Gràinne's face coloured like a slapped arse.

With a smile as sweet as honey, Eimhir replied, "I am the head of Rìgh Brion's personal security. *No one* comes into his chambers armed." Eimhir looked Gràinne up and down. "And I mean *all* your weapons, even those hidden underneath your léine and triubhas."

Another quick inspection and Eimhir added, "That also includes the jewelled daggers disguised as pins in your thick tresses. I can lend you a thong for your hair. You may, of course, retain a dagger for food—as long as it's shown openly."

"I think good wishes rather than confrontation may have achieved a better result," whispered Amodocus in Gràinne's ear. He bowed to Eimhir and began to unbuckle his weapons' belts.

"I will deal with you later," hissed Gràinne.

Gràinne's eyes drew a disconcerted look from Brion. The usual golden-amber colour had a red tone as did her sigils. He looked at Amodocus, who mouthed "Later" and shrugged. Gràinne glared at Eimhir, only to find her gaze countered by emerald gems. With a snarl of resignation, Gràinne began to disarm. Once finished, she put a foot on the second step but faced Eimhir's raised palm.

"If, like me, you carry a small blade sheathed in the cleft between your arse cheeks, then please remove it. Searching you would be embarrassing for all but the men."

"If we don't kill each other, our destiny may be to become friends," said Gràinne, climbing the steps.

"I would prefer the latter," responded Eimhir, "but will not shrink from the former." She reached out a hand. "Truce?"

To everyone's relief, Gràinne smirked, grasped Eimhir's forearm, and nodded. "Agreed. Now, where's the food? I'm starving."

As they mounted the last step before entering the brock, Gràinne turned around and smiled at Cearbhall. There was a strain of regret in her voice when she spoke. "I see you've made good use of the iron fittings I left."

He dipped his head and indicated the tall ballistae mounted on Dùn Brion's ramparts. "We are ready for Gormal."

"Do you have the second sack?" Cearbhall nodded. "Good, I'll take it with me to Cùil Daothail."

* * *

"I should accompany Gràinne to Cùil Daothail."

The room narrowly avoided descending into an uproar at Cassán's words. Eimhir's hand went to her mouth to prevent a scream of denial. Brion was much less restrained.

"That is out of the question," he barked. "Your place is here—at my side."

"She is your daughter and my sister. One of us should be in Cùil Daothail." Setting aside emotions, it was hard to argue against Cassán's logic. Thus, a change of tack was needed. Cearbhall pushed his chair back, placed calloused and scarred hands on the table, and looked into Cassán's eyes.

"No one here questions your wishes or your bravery. "However, consider that you have just returned from a long stay in Gormal's dungeons. There you suffered the loss of your hand and, apart from what Eimhir smuggled in, consumed a meagre diet. Even the escape likely still takes a toll on your body." Cearbhall looked at Cassán and said gently but frankly, "You are not ready for battle."

171

Cearbhall watched Cassán's jaw set and knew the young man's pride edged him closer to ignoring all counsel. "You asked me recently to train you in weapons and battle tactics. That I will do, but it will take time. Here is my proposition. I will train you, and when *I* decide you're good enough, I will give you my blessing and one hundred warriors. At that time, you may travel to Cùil Daothail."

Cassán looked suspiciously at Cearbhall. The veteran growled, "I will not allow any man or woman to doubt my honour or honesty. Agree with me or challenge me."

"I do not like this, but it is a fair exchange. Accept it," said Brion.

Cassán looked at Cearbhall and bowed. "I meant no slight. I apologise and accept."

Seated at the long table, a chieftain whispered in his neighbour's ear: "Are we sure that person is really Cassán?"

Later, Gràinne crossed the chamber to stand before Cassán. "When I meet with Brianag, I will tell her of your brave offer, and, as I do, she will agree that she has a brother of whom she can be proud."

＊＊＊

Drostan Ruadh revelled in the smell of the pines but cursed when he inhaled deeply and felt the hairs of his nostrils freeze. The trees in the depths of the ancient forest were giants, and survival meant they were widely spaced. Above, the evergreen canopy of pine and oak provided an almost impenetrable barrier against the elements. Thus, only a light sprinkling of snow lay on the thick carpet of decaying debris or gathered in small drifts against boles and moss-covered rocks. Most of the woods' residents slept, so the air was eerily quiet.

Five thousand warriors, armed with clubs, spears, and axes, moved quickly and silently through the forest. All had furs or *bratan* draped over bare shoulders and torsos. The coverings were for sleeping and for when the campfires slumbered. They were suffered as an inconvenience and would be cast aside during battle.

The winter had been long, and the fighters' faces and bodies were milk-pale, apart from the swirling tribal and family designs painted in shades of blue and white. All wore brightly coloured *triubhas* held up by cords of braided wool. It was their retort to the season's gloom.

"It's a lot of warriors," muttered Drostan. Yet measured by the forest's magnificence, their numbers were pitiful and easily lost in its immensity. Bare feet—the Forest People held the use of *brògan* in disdain—measured each step. On this day, the forest's nervous tremors were felt by the warriors and communicated to the army's communal consciousness. The ageless woods were anxious, as was Drostan. The Forest People had never known or sensed the woods to be as worried in his and his father's lifetimes. It was as if the forest feared for its continued existence.

As dusk fell, messengers were sent to the five cohorts, each comprising one thousand men. The divisions walked in a loose chevron formation with Drostan's group at its point. Scouts from each band ranged far ahead to alert the army to potential troubles. The force was about four sunsets from the crossing at the Abhainn Nis river. From there, a morning's jog would see them at the gates of Cùil Daothail.

As the camps were set up, a tall, gangly warrior approached Drostan and whispered in his left ear. "What? Speak up!" grunted Drostan. The man smiled and spoke into Drostan's right ear. The rìgh of the Forest People's hearing was not as sharp as it used to be. Indeed, since his youthful fight with a bear had left him blind in his left eye, Drostan was also practically deaf in his left ear. Most times, the loss only caused him mild irritation, for he had become an astute reader of men's faces—and their lips.

"None of our scouts have returned—from any cohort. We should prepare for trouble."

Drostan nodded. "You know my orders."

✳✳✳

Brion watched Gràinne depart Dùn Brion with mixed feelings and high misgivings. After his talk with Amodocus, he wondered if the vivacious and irresponsible girl he once knew had been devoured by a darker creature—A 'Bhanrìgh Fuil. What did it mean, and where would it lead? *Will*

173

I be forced to meet her in battle one day? He prayed to the Goddess for insight.

The only bright light appeared to be Amodocus. Larger than life, only the Thracian seemed able and strong enough to ground Gràinne. Brion again prayed to the Goddess that this would continue. The thought of an unfettered, blood-seeking Gràinne made him shiver. But then, in a similar vein, so did his sister, Mórrígan, and she had conquered her darker self.

At least she will have the Sidhe at her side. Yet the more Brion thought about that pairing, the more unhappy he became. Unrestrained, Mongfhionn would create and wade through lakes of blood to avenge her loved ones. She had done it before in retribution for her sisters' deaths. Brion sighed. At one time, he had dreamed of an idyllic life with Cassán's mother. That had ended in disaster; perhaps, inevitably, so would his reign as Rìgh of the Na Mèadaidh. *Do I care?*

"Watch the yard. That might put you in a better frame of mind."

Brion smiled at Eimhir's astuteness and turned to observe Cearbhall and Cassán. Then he chuckled. "All is not lost. I have found a son and, perhaps, a daughter." Eimhir blushed at Brion's observation but offered no protest.

＊＊＊

The blood-curdling howl froze the men around Drostan—literally. Soon the refrain was taken up by the voices of nine others. He swirled around and saw statues, not warriors. *Shite! Is this what happened to Gòrdan? And why am I unaffected?* True, he heard a Hag-awful buzzing in his ears, and his movement was a little sluggish, but he could still move. Grunting with the effort, Drostan pulled his axe from the leather loops on his back. *It must be the bidsean's wailing.*

Drostan watched as nine young females emerged from the forest depths and arrayed themselves in a semicircle. Cavernous maws opened, but was that in his mind? They began to chant, though they used no words. The tone and language raised the fine hairs on his neck, and Drostan felt the sound ripple through his warriors.

The realisation hit Drostan like a club. Only a tiny number, apparently as deaf as he, resisted the song of Sidheag's Brood. He roared to those in the rear where the unearthly chant had not touched: "Cover and plug your ears. Send messengers to the other bands."

Then Drostan turned around and shouted, "Those who can still move, stand with me." Drostan felt the bean-shìdh beside him and growled, "Not today, bidse." He watched Sidheag's Brood move closer and heard the sighs of his men as more were enthralled. Surrounding him, a hundred grim-faced warriors prayed to the Goddess and gripped weapons.

One of the young women screamed, but her voice held notes of pain this time. Drostan's face creased in a smile of grim satisfaction. She had trod on one of the many three-pronged, iron thistles sown in a circle around the camp. Drostan took ten long paces forward and looked into the innocent face of a girl who could have been his youngest daughter.

He roared, "I am not deceived, bidse!" and swung his battle-axe. A head crowned with long, red hair flew high into the air and fell at the feet of her sisters. For a moment, her sisters looked at each other as if unsure what to do. Drostan turned and bellowed one word: "Iron!"

From the deep forest came a long ululating scream of anger that caused blood to seep from ruptured eardrums. But was that a bad thing? The Brood stood straight and opened their mouths to magnify Sidheag's rage. Another, this time a beautiful, young redhead, took a step forward into the field sown with iron. Once again, Drostan's axe swung. No blood flowed, and no cry of pain resounded as Drostan's double-headed weapon split her skull and gouged a path between her breasts.

"Do not cross the field of iron," bawled Drostan. "Let them come to you. Show no mercy. They are not who they once were." Grim-faced warriors steeled themselves to face an enemy who could have been their daughters. Compelled by Sidheag, the Brood moved forward, but their howling turned to shrieks as iron thistles pierced bare feet.

Alongside Drostan, warriors tossed clubs aside and swung axes or lunged with spears. Three more of Sidheag's daughters fell. Startled, those remaining looked blankly at each other as if not understanding or knowing what to do. "You should have taught them how to think, bidse!"

Drostan's taunt was instantly followed by Sidheag's screech of wrath. This time the Brood did not step forward but took several paces backwards. In the place of their song came the shouts and war cries of Sidheag's human army as they surged forward. "Retreat!" roared Drostan as he ran through rows of men and women slowly recovering from the thrall of Sidheag's daughters.

⁕⁕⁕

At sunrise, Drostan's remaining divisions broke their fast in silence. In the gloom of dawn, Drostan and one hundred warriors returned to the original campsite of his warband. Many tossed their morning meal onto the forest floor. The smell and sight of the slaughter made the stomachs of veteran warriors heave. While the carnage was terrible, it was made worse by the bite marks on the bodies and the signs of flesh torn from corpses while they were still warm.

"Four young women, even with Sidheag's power, did not do this," spat Drostan.

Cannibalism among the Celts, although frowned on and rare, was not unknown. The savagery Drostan saw was on a scale never witnessed in the lore of the Forest People. As he inspected the butchery, hoping to find some source of hope, Drostan came across the husks of Sidheag's five daughters. They were already decayed beyond recognition.

"*Strìopach!*"

Unsurprisingly, the meeting of Drostan and his chieftains was sombre. They had lost eight hundred comrades, and few had lifted a weapon to defend themselves. "At this rate, if we make it to Cùil Daothail, we'll be lucky to have two hundred warriors," stated one noble. It was not a comforting sign, given that the man's disposition usually tended to be overly optimistic.

"We have no choice. If we retreat, we'll suffer as many deaths and lead Sidheag's pack into our homes. For our children's sake, we must forge ahead." Drostan paused and scratched his head. "But we need better tactics. I'm open to any suggestions.

176

"We know the brood doesn't like iron and prefers to attack after sunset. Also, the priests and followers are human and can be killed like any other. How do we separate them from Sidheag and her pack?"

A female chieftain shook her head and said, "They all must die. Sidheag, her Brood, her priests…" She paused. "…and their human followers. This time, the taint of blood worship cannot be allowed any mercy. From the youngest baby to the eldest, the Na Daoine Tùrsach must be exterminated." None protested.

It was meadhan-latha when once again, Drostan's army set off in the direction of Cùil Daothail. As usual, Drostan strode ahead of his warriors. Not long after they set out, one of his closest advisors caught up with him. "You should send messengers back to our home settlement. The *Comhairle-Chatha*—the High Council—should know who your successor will be… just in case."

Drostan nodded and smiled grimly as he recalled his last conversation with Mongfhionn. "They already know Seonag is my heir."

***

As Sidheag and her remaining daughters walked among the army encamped at the edge of the pine forest, she was uncharacteristically agitated. The Baobhan Sith was furious that those she considered cattle dared to challenge her. In the camp, many looked at bloody hands and picked shreds of human flesh from rotting teeth. What madness had taken hold of them? Yet others relished what they had done and wanted more.

In fear of her inevitable wrath, men and women dropped to their knees, studiously avoiding her eyes. Mothers and fathers kept their daughters well out of sight, for all knew Sidheag would soon wish to make her Brood whole again. Theirs was a vain hope. They had made a bargain with evil, and their sacrifices and prayers to the Goddess were spurned. What did they expect—forgiveness, absolution?

Yet the initial attack had been successful. Drostan had lost one-fifth of his warriors in a single skirmish, although at the cost of five of Sidheag's daughters. Sidheag snarled. Drostan had proved unusually imaginative or inspired in his choice of iron as a defence. As for his poor hearing, she cursed Serendipity's mischievousness.

The young priest had ambitions to supplant Seirbhiseach in Sidheag's favours. Thus, he enthusiastically embraced and copied the carnivorous appetites of Sidheag's Brood. After initially vomiting several times, he began to appreciate the taste of human blood and flesh. As Sidheag stood before him—and, since he was barely average height, towered over him—he smiled.

He felt long talons caress his chin and then tilt his face. Sidheag examined his bloodstained teeth and the splashes of gore on his face and cloak. The priest gulped at the disapproval on her face. "You are my priest. You represent me to the people. Clean yourself up, or I will feed on you." The man nodded and felt droplets of cold sweat trickle down his spine.

"Tomorrow, *you* will lead the attacks on Drostan and will not cease until his army is destroyed. Fail, and I will eat your flesh and drink your blood."

CHAPTER 23

Drostan stared at the flames and imagined Sidheag screeching and burning in excruciating pain. With him around the campfire were his chieftains. Of the original ten, only four remained. All bore fresh scars and tired eyes. Due to the incessant howling of Sidheag's pack, few had slept since the first attack. In wolf form, the four remaining daughters continually circled the perimeter of Drostan's much-reduced force. Still, the Brood stayed beyond the reach of the circle of iron spikes sown around the encampment.

The gnarly king shook his head. He had lost almost three thousand men and women. "Ideas? I'm open to suggestions," said Drostan.

"We have no defence against the Brood and its mistress. The song makes statues of our warriors and leaves them helpless meat. Iron kills them, but once we cross the iron perimeter, all of us…" The chieftain smiled at Drostan. "…except the few that are mostly deaf, are at the mercy of the bidsean."

"So we just lie down and die?" asked another chieftain, whose pock-marked face and fresh cuts were luridly highlighted by the flames.

"No. We attack," said the female warrior.

Drostan looked at the speaker and smiled, yet there was regret in his eye. Teàrlag was the only female chieftain of the Forest People. She had fought, and still fought, many battles to secure that honour. Drostan wished he had more of her ilk, yet his biggest regret was not spending more time with her. At least they had one shared memory, their daughter.

Drostan's eye held Teàrlag's steel-blue gaze and his eyebrow lifted. "If we stay here, we will die," Teàrlag spoke bluntly. "If we wait on Sidheag's next attacks, we will die, which would be a tragic waste of brave warriors. Better to die fighting than be a meal for the strìopach and her bidsean."

Teàrlag rubbed her chin, leaving it smudged with blood, dirt, and ash. "They always attack at night or in the gloom. There must be a reason for that. I say we wait until meadhan-latha and run for the forest line. Once beyond the trees, the light will be brighter, even in winter. Then we fight until we reach the gates of Cùil Daothail—or die."

"Seems sensible," said the pockmarked chieftain, dipping his head. "It will be an honour to fight alongside you."

"Is it not an honour to fight alongside me?" Drostan's eye glittered in the firelight.

The warrior laughed. "Of course, it is, my king. But if I'm honest, she's a better fighter than you, so I'll be safer in her company." Drostan dipped his head and chuckled. A cough halted the brief merriment, and all looked at Teàrlag.

"There is one more thing we could do. If we cannot hear, Sidheag cannot enthral us." Eyes widened around the fire, for none knew if Teàrlag was serious, but the glint in her eye was ominous.

✶✶✶

Seonag and Blàr stared into the gloom of a new dawn and in the face of northerly winds that peeled the skin from raw faces. Along the ramparts of Cùil Daothail, battle horns reverberated. Hundreds of braziers were hauled into place and set alight. Warriors dashed to their assigned positions, stamping snowdrifts into packed ice, and slamming spears against sgiathan. The thick furs draping their shoulders would be cast aside when battle commenced.

To Blàr's surprise, the direction of the attack came from the west and the dense forests over which Drostan ruled. Expecting an assault from the north, he had positioned his forces accordingly. A mouthful of curses and snapped orders to his chieftains, and the imbalance was addressed.

Yet what concerned Seonag were the numbers of the enemy. She scowled and said, "This force is too small to trouble our warriors or the stockade. Why?" In response, Blàr grunted. "Not an early morning person, are you?" queried Seonag. A ripple of laughter spread along the ramparts. Blàr grunted again, but the dimples in his cheeks had deepened.

Still, Seonag's observation rang true, and that worried Blàr. He estimated that being generous, the attackers numbered about one thousand. As they charged across ground cleared of trees, many looked as if they had come straight from tending fields of crops. A good percentage carried pitchforks instead of spears; few held shields or wore any armour.

"They can't be serious," he muttered.

"Where's Drostan?" Seonag asked the question in both of their minds.

"He's likely coming behind them. That would be a good trap." Seonag nodded, although not very convincingly. The king of the Forest People was two sunsets overdue.

"Thanks." Seonag smiled at her assigned shield-woman. The warrior's face seemed carved from pink granite, and she was as tall as Seonag, although more heavily muscled. The warrior tightened and balanced Seonag's armour and shield with brusque efficiency. Then she inspected Seonag's weapons belt before handing her a blackthorn-shafted spear. Seonag smiled at her curt grunt of approval and knew her protector would never be more than a few paces away.

Blàr looked down into the yard and shouted, "Reinforce the gates. None of the bastards gets inside." The sound of heavy timbers slamming against the entranceway drew a smile. Then he called out, "Save your spears. Let the ditches do their work."

✳✳✳

To keep her daughter from being chosen for Sidheag's Brood, the girl's mother had cropped her long blonde hair and tightly bound her blossoming breasts. Taken into the forests, she was forced to scream and shout until hoarse. Barely sixteen summers old, she looked and sounded like an adolescent boy. As a disguise, it proved successful. Perhaps too successful.

On this morning, as the sun painted the winter sky with vibrant reds and oranges, the girl and a thousand others ran across the field towards Cùil Daothail. She had often stayed in the settlement with her family, especially during the feasts of Bealtaine and Lugnasad. The young girl smiled at many happy memories and then frowned at one.

On one visit, a handsome young man, ten summers older than she, had seduced her with stories of his undying love. The wine he coaxed her to drink was heady. With only feeble resistance, her léine was lifted, and she was penetrated. It was another first, although not for him. He conquered and moved on. Occasionally, she wondered whether they would ever meet again. She felt the spear in her hand and ground her teeth. *It would not work out well for him.*

The girl's thoughts splintered as she heard the roar of the horde. *Is that my voice shouting battle cries?* The young woman looked up and saw the walls of Cùil Daothail and the helmets and spears of many warriors. Suddenly she was frightened. This was not the friendly trading centre she knew. Her nostrils filled with the smell of burning and ashes. Where were the homes and places of business? Where was the scent of food roasting or stews simmering in the enormous black cauldrons? Where were the laughter and sounds of music and singing?

As Cùil Daothail's stockade loomed large in her vision, she panicked and tried to stop and turn around. Her efforts were futile. Wild-eyed men and women, with mouths spewing hate and spitting drool, surrounded her. Fear gripped her, and she lashed out with her spear. A man bellowed as the *ceann-sleagha*—spearhead— tracked down his cheek. A fist swung and caught the girl on her cheek. She staggered a few paces before being lifted by the crowd and propelled forward.

The young girl floated like a feather and her nightmare was over. She looked without understanding or recognition at a girl's broken, bloody body hung up on a sharpened stake. Beside her, the bean-shìdh smiled and said, "Come." Her long blonde hair restored; the pretty girl took her guide's hand.

***

Few attackers reached Cùil Daothail's stockade, and even fewer managed to climb it. The stronghold's ditches quickly filled with hundreds of the dying. Then came the cries of those begging for mercy. It reached a crescendo and then fell as the *mnathan-shìdh* began to reap the harvest until only the whimpering of those pleading for release remained.

Hundreds of braziers provided warmth and light on the walkway. Snow and ice melted in circular patches around the fires. Inspecting the shield-wall, Seonag stamped through a slurry of blood and snow. The defenders of any stronghold, whether built of stone or wood, always have the advantage. Only vastly superior numbers, or an enemy from within, will tip the balance in favour of the attacker. On this occasion, Sidheag's force had neither, and that bothered Seonag. Several of Sidheag's "warriors" lay dead at her feet, stabbed by her spear. Many more had been bundled over the fence and finished off by the ditch's stakes.

"They didn't even have scaling ladders or hooks," growled Seonag, her mouth sour from the butchery. "Why? They didn't even match us for numbers."

The answer came in a long wail from the forest. Yet it was not a cry of defeat and soon became an abhorrent, cackling laugh. "I will choose the time of your death, and it is not today." Sidheag's voice was as clear as the water from a mountain spring and sent shivers throughout Cùil Daothail's garrison.

"The bidse is playing with us like a wolf with a mountain hare," said Blàr.

"Often, the wolf is disappointed," replied Seonag.

***

It was not a happy relationship and, would end in death. Whose had yet to be decided. Gormal did not trust Ealasaid, considering her a potential threat. For her part, Ealasaid regarded everyone as a threat. She briefly considered rutting Gormal as a political strategy but thought his body and mind too repulsive—even for her.

Thus she focused on business with Gormal while encouraging Madadh's support by providing full access to her body. That proved to be of a pleasurable if limited duration. It transpired that Madadh's hand-fast partner was Gormal's sister. The lady cowed Madadh with threats of demotion or an extended stay in the dungeons. Ealasaid admired the lady's strength and satisfied her carnal needs with the young chieftain she had met earlier.

"We need to foment rebellion among the Na Mèadaidh," stated Ealasaid.

"It's winter. Anyone with common sense wants to stay close to a roaring fire, eat, and rut. Imbolg and spring are only a few cycles of the moon away. We will wait until the snows recede."

"Without Drostan, Brion is weak *now*. He won't be in the spring when the campaign in Cùil Daothail is over. Without an insurrection to weaken its garrison, Dùn Brion will be challenging to overcome. Like Dùn Athad, the stone fortress could hold out for an unlimited time." Ealasaid glared at Gormal. "Brion and his bidse have shamed you and slaughtered your warriors and people. Do you want revenge or not?"

"You go too far," snapped Gormal, but he halted his guards' approach. After a moment's consideration, he smiled and asked, "What do you need?

"Twenty riders and forty of your hardiest horses. They will visit the settlements along the Sleagh and announce my arrival and claim to the throne of the Na Mèadaidh. Those communities were always loyal to my father and likely still are. I can raise an army of two or three thousand from them." Ealasaid paused as she tried to slow down her racing thoughts. "They also have full access to Dùn Brion and can carry my message into the heart of Brion's stronghold."

Gormal grunted. He had no confidence in Ealasaid's claim that the Na Mèadaidh remained loyal to the memory of Finnean and would rise up. *A dead king is simply that—a dead king. Still, she might be a useful distraction.*

Furthermore, giving her horses and men was a small price if it would re-move her irritating presence. He dipped his head to Madadh. "See that the lady has what she needs." Then Gormal held Ealasaid's stare.

"Do not bother me again until the feast of Imbolg."

* * *

The terrifying and plaintive cries, the constant retching and vomiting on the crannag's wooden floor, proved impossible for Seirbhiseach to ignore. The pungent, sour smell of puke stained the air. A half-eaten carcass lay alongside a growing pool of vomit, spotted with lumps of raw flesh.

Sidheag had taken Brianag from the crannag that evening and returned at sunrise, lying her senseless on the cot. With a smile of satisfaction, and before departing the crannag, Sidheag threw the bloody remains down to be within Brianag's reach. Was it left as a snack—or a reminder?

Seirbhiseach scratched his newly shaven head. During his recent tor-ment, he had pulled out so much of his white thatch that it looked silly. Hence, he had taken a sharp blade to what remained. It was a disconcert-ing change, which had the bonus of startling the echelon of priests below him. They stared at his gaunt face and red-rimmed eyes, and in their gaze, Seirbhiseach saw something long past—fear of him.

Another moan and another splash of vomit brought Seirbhiseach's attention back to Brianag. After leering at her young body, he refocused his senses on their predicaments. Her face was covered in slowly drying gore, and her teeth were bloodstained. The High Priest observed strings of raw meat lodged between her incisors and stuck to bloody fingernails. Worryingly, the latter had an increasing resemblance to Sidheag's talons. Brianag's blood-painted torso bore streaks of red from her breasts to her thighs.

Sidheag's High Priest felt something long-buried swell up from within. Was it compassion? Perhaps. *She is a brave child. Much more courageous than me, for she still fights while I do nothing. I'm disgusting.* His thoughts frightened Seirbhiseach, and he wondered where they had come from. *What if my redemption is bound to hers?*

Seirbhiseach's lips curled in distaste at what he was about to do, and he muttered, "Needs must." He threw the carcass into a snowdrift, then cleaned up the puke- and gore-covered floor. Lifting the unconscious Brianag in his arms, Seirbhiseach laid her on an old hide. Removing her gore-soaked bedding, the priest replaced it with clean straw and dried meadowsweet.

The next phase drew from a strength Seirbhiseach did not think he possessed. He carefully and thoroughly cleaned the blood evidence from every part of Brianag's body with warm water and damp cloths. He washed and combed her hair and cleaned her teeth. When he had finished, he stood and admired his work before lifting and settling her back into the cot. The bloodstained pelt and towels he tossed into another snowdrift.

"She will think the memories of hunting and killing are no more than another of Sidheag's nightmares." Yet Seirbhiseach's hopeful words were more of a prayer.

✳✳✳

Before they emerged from the forest, Drostan glanced at Teàrlag. Their faces held expressions of deep love and profound regret. Both mouthed words that only they could understand. Drostan's face broke into a grin and a bushy, red eyebrow raised. Teàrlag shrugged her shoulders. It was a logical stratagem if brutally delivered.

With a bellow of defiance, the warriors of the Forest People, long adept at fighting under the dense, green canopy of the woodlands, broke through the wildwood and entered an alien landscape of calf-deep snow, gorse, and heather. On their heels, Sidheag's horde shrieked. The response was understandable.

Drostan's force had broken into four divisions and scattered. It was the only change Drostan had made to Teàrlag's plan. His warriors were divided into groups led by Drostan, Teàrlag, and the other two remaining chieftains. Never one to shrink from battle, Drostan commanded the rearguard. The tactic was sensible, although, for those who took the tail position, survival was in the hands of the Goddess. But then, was that not always the case?

Cùil Daothail and safety of a kind was less than a half-day's fast march, but that seemed a long way. Sidheag's horde swarmed from the treeline, outnumbering Drostan by at least ten to one. Infuriated by Drostan's tactical change, Sidheag and her pack howled like wolves but remained in the gloom of the canopy.

Warriors stopped mid-step as the Siren song invaded their minds. Drostan swore at the Goddess, the Aes Sidhe, the Hag, and the spirits of the forest as fighters surrendered without raising a weapon. He roared at his men to keep going.

Yet from the woods came another screech of wrath as Sidheag realised how few a number the newly enthralled represented—barely enough to feed herself and her Brood. Fuming, she ordered her daughters into the field. They needed to be closer.

✳✳✳

The black horse appeared from nowhere, rising up before Sidheag's Brood. It sported a blaze of white on its forehead shaped like a fork of lightning. The horse did not whinny, snort, or squeal but, like its ride, seemed to growl when it opened its mouth. Hoofs, as strong as iron, stamped the ground. The cloaked apparition sat astride the blood-red dillat appeared to have no face or one so dark as to be invisible.

As the hood was flung back, white hair that touched bony arse cheeks flared out. Those watching saw it was not the creature's face that was black but its foul maw. Sidheag's remaining daughters opened their mouths to confront the Hag, but long, skeletal fingers pointed at them and roared, "Enough!"

Cut from the source of their power, the daughters of Sidheag looked from one to the other. A scream from the forest gloom could not restore the broken link. "Go to the unseen depths of the Otherworld where you belong, bitseacha. Today only humans will fight," said the Hag.

From the forest's depths emanated a shrill voice. "A minor victory. I have Brianag, and you cannot be the Hag for long before she overwhelms you, and you cease to exist. In the end, I shall prevail."

"Maybe. But not today, bitseach." The Hag swept the oak staff over the four who stood motionless. "Enjoy your demise," cackled the Hag. "I will."

Horrified miens spread over the usually expressionless faces of Sidheag's Brood. Rooted to the ground, they felt and watched ice slowly cover their toes and spread upwards. Larynxes were crushed as ice strangled Sidheag's daughters before encasing their heads.

The Hag admired her crystalline sculptures and snapped her bony fingers. In an instant, tiny icicles invaded and burst every cell until all that remained were blood-red statues—and they would soon melt, even in a winter's sun. Only the apparition heard their final sobs.

***

Light-headed, Mongfhionn shuddered and fell from the horse onto a snowbank. Sidheag was right. She could only transform into the Hag for short periods. In her state of semi-consciousness, deep in Mongfhionn's being, she heard not the awful cackling of the Hag but a voice of seductive power and reason.

"You cannot defeat Sidheag, and even with A 'Bhanrìgh Fuil, there is no guarantee of victory," said the Hag. "Yet you know that is within my powers. I can make you ruler of the Aes Sidhe and of men, Mongfhionn. I can safeguard Brianag, Gràinne, and Neamhain forever. Think of all the good you could do if you kneeled to me."

"Shite! Two bitseacha!" said Mongfhionn and drifted into the black.

***

Drostan saw the face of the young woman for a mere moment. It was not the plainest he had ever seen but was made uglier by the hatred that poisoned her eyes. It was an unblemished face until he swung the battle-axe and carved a deep, diagonal trench from temple to chin. Death startled her, but she looked hopefully at the bean-shìdh who appeared before her. Then she screamed in terror as she was dragged to the gates of the Otherworld.

Sidheag's corruption had put the girl far beyond any hope of redemption.

Yelling and screeching, Sidheag's horde streamed from the forest, but they were momentarily confused by Drostan's tactics. Then they made a fateful and surprisingly shared decision. Like a flock of birds, they swirled as if catching a warm updraft and then, as one, swooped on the rearmost contingent of Drostan's army.

"Turn and face the bastards!" roared Drostan. It was a sensible command. Why show the enemy your back when you can die facing them? "Shields!" he shouted, and the clang of wood and iron rims sounded. One hundred warriors wide and five deep, Drostan's division slowly and steadily retreated in the direction of Cùil Daothail.

Drostan's warriors were, without question, the better fighters, a fact many of Sidheag's army discovered when their flesh was sundered by axe and spear or crushed by clubs. Quality and bravery make for epic tales recounted by *seanchaidhean* over campfires, yet count for little when vastly outnumbered. Surrounded, Drostan's five hundred formed a double circle and began to build a berm of corpses.

Like many born into poverty and disadvantage, the twins—brother and sister—had joined Drostan's army when they were fourteen summers. Now twenty summers old, they were considered veterans because they had survived. Warriors rarely celebrated attaining thirty summers. If they did, it was attributed to cunning or having the Goddess's favour rather than swordsmanship.

As a wintry sun rose high in the sky, the siblings stood on either side of Drostan and vowed to protect the king at all costs. The circle of blood-soaked warriors had shrunk. Over half had joined the protective berm of bodies that reached the waists of attacker and defender. The brave who died taunted the enemy's dead and watched as their spirits were dragged weeping into the Otherworld by the mnathan-shìdh. It was a victory of sorts.

The young man grunted as a spear sundered his upper arm's gold and silver bands and tore his flesh. His sister glanced at him, but he smiled and brought his club down on his assailant's skull. It was not the first cut he had taken—most of his exposed flesh, like his sister's, was slick with gore.

Her weapon of choice was a sleagh, and few in the army could rival her skill. She stabbed, slashed, and bashed—the butt end of the spear had been personalised with an iron cap and several iron rings. The young woman quickly lost count of the number her spearhead sent beyond the veil.

Chillingly, she grinned through a mask of blood. Thus, the slavering priest who brandished an axe and stood before her was momentarily startled by her frightening expression. "Bidse!" he screamed, and her gorge rose at the foul stench of his breath. It was an opportunity, and she drove the leaf-shaped ceann-sleagha into his mouth.

The priest's eyes widened at the impossibility of the woman's act. He was one of Sidheag's chosen, born to rule at her side. The warrior twisted her spear viciously and pulled it free, along with his jaw. Before the bean-shìdh yanked him to the Otherworld, his last memories were of the terrible pain and the young woman's grinning face. He would never see her face again, and his eternity of agony had hardly begun.

Once more, the circle shrank. Fifty warriors remained, although a good proportion were injured or exhausted. Muscles cried out for rest and relief. A sword or axe, even a club, is not a light weight to wield in a lengthy battle and certainly not constantly. Any leather armour—and few of the Forest People wore this, favouring the protection of the curling symbols painted on their flesh—lay in pieces.

Brother and sister glanced at each other and smiled. Each knew the other's thoughts and that the bean-shìdh would soon call their names. The young man prayed to the Goddess that his sister would live, and the lass did the same for him. A gasp and a curse ripped them from their petitions.

In horror, they watched Drostan slump to his knees and then, with a roar, rise; the axe arched, and his opponent's head flew from his shoulders. Blood gushed from the headless corpse before it fell to the side. Yet the red torrent made little difference to the siblings' or Drostan's appearance. Gore seeped and flowed from myriad cuts. The one-eyed rìgh breathed harshly and fought to speak. "It has been my honour to fight by your side." Once said, Drostan slumped to his knees in the crimson slush.

"Grab the king!" shouted the girl. Her brother put Drostan's arm over his shoulders and started to drag the rìgh to the centre of the circle. In the distance, they heard the sound of a horn but shook their heads. *Too many strikes to the head.*

✳✳✳

A backwards glance and the realisation that Drostan's end drew near prompted Teàrlag to howl and call for the battle horns to sound. The three remaining divisions could have continued their path and reached Cùil Daothail. Yet it was not the Forest People's way to desert their king. And so, they turned and attacked against impossible odds.

Undoubtedly an act of valour and sacrifice, it would have been a senseless throwing away of lives had not the sound of blaring horns cut through the air. As Teàrlag's warriors battered and slaughtered their way to Drostan, Gràinne's and Amodocus' riders and chariots carved a bloody furrow from the west. Alarm rippled through Sidheag's army, and as one, they turned and fled back into the forests. Still, shock rather than force of arms and numbers defeated them.

"The Hag!" said Gràinne as she kicked and threw corpses aside to reach the centre of the battle. A young man and woman lay across Drostan with hands clasped as if to protect the king and cross the veil together. Alongside the trio knelt Teàrlag. She tore at blonde hair matted with blood and cursed the Goddess and the Aes Sidhe. Teàrlag had found Drostan, but she kissed and hugged a dead lover and sobbed for missed chances.

"I think we're missing something," said Gràinne to Amodocus.

The tall Thracian removed his helmet and dipped his head. "If only we had arrived sooner."

"We'd be dead, too."

"But it would have been a glorious end."

"Dead is dead, and we have daughters." Gràinne paused to think. "We should send a rider back to Dùn Brion. Brion must be informed. Perhaps he knows who will reign in Drostan's place."

191

CHAPTER 24

The warriors on Cùil Daothail's ramparts murmured as the line of blood-splattered Forest People trudged across the entranceway and into the stronghold. Haunted looks, uncountable scars, and blood-encrusted ears marked the fighters' bearing. The latter caused a ripple of consternation along the fort's walkway. For the first time, the garrison saw the enormity of the task set before them.

"Take these men and women to shelter. They are brave beyond what you can imagine. Get them a hot meal, beer, and a cot to rest on. They will also need new clothes, weapons, and armour." Sat astride her tall mare, Mongfhionn's voice boomed out, echoing off the dùn's walls. "Pray, when the time comes, you are as courageous."

"Not exactly a rousing call to battle," muttered Blàr.

Blàr and Seonag watched the Sidhe walk her black horse at the van's rear. Alongside Mongfhionn limped a tall woman. Her blonde hair, still in battle plaits, was matted with blood. Yet even from a distance, all could see her eyes were raw from crying. With one hand, she grasped a staff for support; with the other, she gripped the hand of the one carried on a litter by four tall warriors. In the rearguard, Gràinne's chariots and riders followed.

The king of the Ravens shook his head. Solemn was an inadequate word to describe the procession. As the litter crossed the gateway and entered Cùil Daothail's yard, Teàrlag glanced up. Two pairs of matching blue eyes met. Moments later, a scream rent the air. Seonag, followed by her shield-woman, sprinted along the walkway, and scrambled down wooden steps to the gateway.

Totally confused, Blàr looked to Niall, who shrugged his shoulders. By the time both men had reached the end of the walkway and were about to descend the steps, the litter came into view, carrying a red-haired man. "The Hag, no!" breathed Blàr, recognising the gore-covered features of Drostan Ruadh.

Yet it was Seonag's heart-breaking cry of "Da!" as she threw herself across Drostan's body that sent shockwaves around Cùil Daothail.

***

That evening, the immense funeral pyre of Drostan Ruadh, Rìgh of the Aos na Coille, the Forest People, burned brightly and fiercely as befitted the man's life. Around the fire, leaders and chieftains of the clanns represented bowed their heads. At their centre, two women held each other and wept while another watched.

As morning broke, the purple-grey dawn sky looked more menacing than usual. The faces and thoughts of those gathered in the roundhouse mirrored the threatening skies. Out of respect for Drostan, no one wanted to break the silence. Yet a descent into despair would serve no purpose and would cede the highlands to Sidheag.

Mongfhionn pushed her seat aside and stood. "We mourn and miss Drostan." Eyebrows were raised at the irony. "Drostan and I had our differences, but even I can appreciate the bloom of a thistle and its prickles. He was a great king but a better man. He loved his people, and they loved him."

Blàr thought he caught a look of regret in the Sidhe's eyes before she quickly resumed her porcelain mien. The Sidhe straightened her back and spoke sternly: "The time for remembrances and celebrations of Drostan's life must wait. We have a war to win, and that will not be easy."

Looking up from his contemplations, Blàr said, "Perhaps we should start with introductions." He looked at Seonag. "I'm not sure I know who you are. Did Brion?" There was no anger in Blàr's voice, yet Seonag sensed the recent revelation vexed him. She placed her hands on the table, but a hand on her shoulder halted her from rising.

"I present Seonag Nic Drostan, daughter of Drostan Ruadh."

"Well, that's a revelation, although not an unpleasant one. And that is rare in these times," responded Gràinne before asking, "Did Brion know?"

"Yes."

Blàr's eyes widened, and his face flushed angrily. "The Hag! Was I the only one who didn't know?" He did not get an answer as Mongfhionn forged ahead.

"Drostan and Seonag's mother thought to keep Seonag from the politics of the Forest People's High Council—and her brothers. Hence, they sent her to the best stronghold in Northern Albu—Dùn Brion." The Sidhe looked at Seonag and raised an eyebrow. "Neither considered what other complications might arise or that Brion would steadfastly keep his oath." Seonag's cheeks flushed, and she glared at Mongfhionn.

The Sidhe ignored Seonag and made another announcement. "By the consent of the Forest People's High Council and with a little nudging by the Aes Sidhe, Seonag will succeed her father. When our current troubles are quelled, she will be officially elevated as Bhanrìgh of the Aos na Coille." Mongfhionn's obsidian eyes glittered at the shocked looks around the table.

"If anyone here challenges this, speak with me privately, and I will hear your arguments." The Sidhe's full lips thinned into a dark smile. "If you are dissatisfied, I assume you know the consequences."

"Today is full of surprises on many levels, but surely few will disavow Drostan's wishes," said Blàr, and then he looked at Seonag. He smiled, stood, and bowed. "May I be the first to congratulate you, Seonag, Bhanrìgh of the Aos na Coille? Long may you reign over the Forest People."

Seonag smiled and then shot a hard look at Mongfhionn. Her words proved difficult to speak as she simultaneously ground her teeth. "I wish someone had informed *me* of my 'elevation'."

"No matter, it is done. You are more than capable of the job, but only time will convince you of this." The Sidhe turned to Teàrlag. "I mourn your loss, but your daughter needs your support."

"Daughter!" gasped Blàr. "Are there any more revelations?"

Mongfhionn laughed and inclined her head to the warrior. "I present Teàrlag Nic an t-Sionnaich, hand-fast partner of Drostan. Some of you will know her brother, Carmag, who was Drostan's battle commander and also had oversight for Cùil Daothail."

"Shite!"

"Why, Ma? Why was I kept in the dark?" Seonag's emotions spun between anger, sorrow, and tears for missed chances.

"Drostan and I loved each other deeply, but two fires cannot occupy the same space for long before one overwhelms the other or they destroy each other. Rightly or wrongly, a decision was made." Teàrlag gulped to tamp down her roiling emotions.

"With you as Bhanrìgh, Drostan and I hoped to spend our later years together." Tears filled Teàrlag's eyes, but she fought them back. "At least I was with your father at the end, and we will meet again in Mag Mell." Teàrlag breathed deeply before adding, "However, if we don't find a way to defeat Sidheag, that might be much sooner than I anticipated."

Teàrlag looked at Seonag's brawny shield-woman and smiled. "If you permit, I will be my daughter's shield." The warrior, plainly disappointed, bowed. "Yet, a bhanrìgh has many enemies. You would honour us by standing at her left side." The beaming smile gave Teàrlag her answer.

"How many did you lose?" asked Blàr. He did not wish to bring the meeting back to a gloomy discussion and did not want to hear the answer.

"Four thousand warriors. All brave men and women. Many were slaughtered like cattle. Against humans, we can prevail, but we had pitiful defences against the bidse's and her Brood's song." Teàrlag scratched at a patch of dried blood on her earlobe and smiled soberly. "I'm not sure causing temporary deafness is a viable battle strategy."

"Rut the Hag!"

"Food and refreshments will arrive shortly," said Blàr, hoping to ease the meeting's atmosphere. "We have a long day of discussion and planning ahead." He looked at Gràinne and Amodocus. "My apologies for not greeting you sooner. Needless to say, I'm pleased to see you. Mounted warriors and chariots could be a critical advantage—even in the snows."

Blàr tugged at his single raven feather. "However, I have no room in Cùil Daothail for the four hundred or more horses accompanying you." Silence briefly descended until Amodocus stood.

"Horses are hardy animals and, if housed in a basic shelter, will tolerate the cold. Tomorrow, if you give me some men who know the area, I'll scout the forest south of Cùil Daothail for a suitable clearing. Can I assume that, besides our warriors, you will provide the labour needed to make our mounts comfortable?"

Blàr smiled. "Of course."

"Before we eat, I have a gift for you and a task for your blacksmiths." Gràinne dipped her head, and a warrior walked forward and laid a sack on the table. "Let me explain about ballistae."

✳✳✳

In the crannag, Brianag's nightmares continued to infect her sleep. *Are they visions or memories?* Her stomach cramped, her jaw ached, and her chest felt bruised from endless retching. As she looked around the cavernous room, she saw no evidence of vomiting and heaved a sigh of relief. Additionally, her bed of straw and meadowsweet, although slightly damp from sweat, was otherwise perfect. Perhaps it was just a bad dream, yet the images seemed vivid. Her stomach churned at the possibility it might be real.

Something wedged between her back teeth annoyed her, and she tried to pry it loose with her fingers and tongue. Finally, she extracted the offending item and looked at it. Held between her fingertips was a short piece of wood fibre. Had someone cleaned her teeth? Who?

There was only Seirbhiseach in the crannag with her, and he had never shown her any kindness. That one end of the sliver was tinted red concerned her. Brianag prayed to the Goddess that it was her blood.

"Where are you, Ma? Where are you, Grandma? Why have you not come for me? Have I been abandoned?" Brianag's questions and her plea to the Goddess made Seirbhiseach look up. Brianag's heartfelt sense of being deserted brought a tear to his eye, although he quickly wiped it away.

Suddenly Brianag screamed. It was as if someone had driven a spike into her head. She felt blood stream from her nose and splash her breasts. Seirbhiseach rose from his stool, uncertain what to do, but a power forced him to the floor. Brianag called out for Gràinne and Mongfhionn, but only Sidheag answered. Like a viper, a mocking voice, bereft of pity or mercy, slithered into her mind.

"You are alone, and you are mine. They will not come for you because they have other priorities." Sidheag cackled. "Drostan is dead by *my* hand. When my daughters are replenished, Cùil Daothail will fall, and I will have your mother."

"Replenished? Why would they need renewing?" A spark of defiance rose in Brianag's heart. "Who killed the bitseacha?" In spite, Sidheag stabbed cruel talons into Brianag's head. The young woman collapsed to the floor, screaming in pain, and felt her body wracked with uncontrollable spasms and tremors.

"Think well of the freedom *I* have given you, child. For I can take it away and make you one of my nine. You forget that it is your mother I need. Your only use is to force her to kneel to me."

Brianag knew Sidheag was not in the crannag, yet she felt the dark eyes of the apparition on her. "You have no colour, daughter. I will take you hunting with me this night. Some warm meat ripped from the bone and a long drink of blood will set you right."

Brianag trembled at the mocking laugh and gasped, "No, please, no." Why wasn't her ma or grandma here to help her? Was Sidheag right? Had they deserted her? *The bitseacha.* The thought entered her head before she could stop it. *No, they love me. Yet why have they not come for me?* Brianag sobbed, and her cot became wet. *I'm not strong enough to resist Sidheag. Should I yield? Who would blame me?*

✳✳✳

In a tiny room in Brianag's mind, veiled to Sidheag's corruption, Neamhain sat and sobbed at her sister's suffering. She worried that she might be too late to help her. "I'm sorry, Mother," she whispered. Then the Song of Neamhain began, and the room seemed brighter.

Brianag smiled and whispered, "Thank you, sister."

In the distance, Sidheag screeched.

✳✳✳

In Cùil Daothail, Mongfhionn sat upright in her cot. "No, Neamhain. Please, no." Then the Sidhe cursed her sisters of the Aes Sidhe for their equivocations and politics and, true to form, swore retribution. Fortunately, Mongfhionn bit her tongue before also damning the Goddess to the Otherworld. That would have been a terrible mistake.

Like a bear, Amodocus' muscled arms held Gràinne and fought against her thrashing and screaming. The Ancient One's gift allowed her to see into Brianag's mind. Thus, she experienced her daughter's torment and waning faith for the first time. Blood-red eyes stared into Amodocus' as Gràinne said, "I swear, I will bring rivers of blood to this land if Brianag is harmed." He held her tightly until she sobbed herself to sleep.

✳✳✳

Eimhir drew Cassán to the side. These days it was hard to pry him away from Cearbhall and his training. Yet during the nights, she appreciated his hard body and the additional weight that better food had given him. Still, with all the exercise, Cassán's build remained lean and sinewy, and his stamina had improved. Eimhir blushed at the last thought. Glancing around to ensure they were not being observed, Eimhir whispered, "We need a meeting with your father—Cearbhall, too."

Cassán looked curiously at Eimhir. He knew something had been bothering her for several sunsets, and he prayed it had nothing to do with him. She had taken to her new role like a fish to water, but like the pink-fleshed *bradáin,* she was stubborn and had no fear of swimming against the river flow.

Was having second thoughts? That worried Cassán because he could not imagine being without her. He nodded and looked to the sky. "It's almost meadhan-latha. I'll grab Cearbhall and meet you in my da's chamber. While we eat, you can explain what is worrying you."

✶✶✶

"My informants tell me that riders are visiting all the settlements and farmsteads along the northern and southern sides of the Sleagh. Their message is that the rightful ruler of the Na Mèadaidh, Ealasaid Nic Finnean, has returned to claim her throne."

"Well, that's spoilt lunch," muttered Cearbhall.

Eimhir smiled. "From what I gather, the envoys have had a mixed reception."

"Why would any side with Ealasaid? Since Finnean's death, the Na Mèadaidh have had a much better life under my rule. Why throw that away? It doesn't make any sense," said Brion.

"The communities along the Sleagh were always favoured by Finnean's benevolence. Some miss the wealth and positions of power and influence. Some nobles are related to Finnean and therefore have a blood allegiance." Eimhir held Brion's eyes. "When our troubles have passed, it would be political to reconsider the reallocation of key roles."

Brion smiled and nodded. "Keep my enemies close."

Eimhir shook her head. "I was thinking more of reconciliation and washing away old grievances." Brion frowned at being scolded.

"How many can they raise against us?" asked Cassán, if only to redirect the discussion.

Eimhir pursed her lips. "Two, maybe three thousand at the most. My information is that the lands north and south distant from the slopes of

199

the Sleagh remain loyal—mostly."

"Mostly?" Brion's eyes met Eimhir's. She sighed.

"It is likely that some settlements along the Sleagh will remain steadfast. And it is equally probable that a few of those to the north and south will be swayed by opportunities for plunder and to settle old scores."

"Dùn Brion will stand with the king, and no besieger can breach its walls. We can outlast any rebellion, large or small."

Eimhir shook her head at Cearbhall's optimism. "Certainly, a good proportion of the garrison comes from loyal families. But all the Na Mèadaidh have unfettered access to Dùn Brion." Eimhir thought for a moment. "And there will always be troublemakers looking for an advantage. Look at how quickly they ganged up on Seonag." Eimhir saw Brion's face flush and muttered, "Sorry." Brion tugged at the ends of his auburn braids.

"So what's our strategy? Do we have to wait until Gormal attacks to find out who stands with us?"

"No," said Eimhir. "My band will watch for signs and try to identify the potential leaders of an insurgency. Only those known to be loyal will be assigned key duties, like guarding the gates or the ballistae. We will identify, isolate, and marginalise our enemies. Those we are certain are against us, we will execute. There can be no quarter given to traitors."

"But how do you know those in your band are as loyal as you are?"

Eimhir shrugged at Brion's question. "In life, nothing is certain or as it seems. I will watch for small signs."

The discussion was nearing a close when a great commotion outside the room ended with a booming voice declaring, "I must see Brion, Rìgh of Dùn Brion." Eimhir's hand went to the blade strapped to her thigh. She relaxed as the messenger, clearly one of Amodocus' Thracian riders, entered the small chamber. His size immediately made the room look smaller. Bowing to Brion, the warrior laid a ring on the table. Brion recognised it as Gràinne's and knew she rarely took it off.

Alarmed, Brion asked, "Is Gràinne hurt? Surely, she's not dead?"

The envoy shook his head, although when he recalled Gràinne's eyes, he shuddered. "No, my leader is in good health. She and Amodocus arrived safely in Cùil Daothail." Then he straightened his back, removed his helmet, and bowed again. "With regret, I must report that Drostan Ruadh, Rìgh of the Aos na Coille, is dead. He, and four thousand warriors, were killed in a battle with Sidheag's army before reaching the settlement."

Eimhir reacted first. "Does anyone else know of this?" The messenger shook his head. Eimhir looked at Brion and Cassán. "Given our conversation, this needs to be kept within the walls of this room. We likely have at the most, a cycle of the moon to prepare for an attack by Gormal. Sidheag may already have sent messengers to him."

The ambassador coughed, and four faces looked up. "I have one more report. Hopefully, you will find it to be better news. Seonag Nic Drostan is the new Bhanrìgh of the Forest People."

"The Hag! Seonag is Drostan's daughter and now bhanrigh," exclaimed Cearbhall and then looked at Brion. "Did you know of this?"

"I knew she was Drostan's daughter but was sworn to secrecy."

Cearbhall slapped his forehead. "The Hag's arse! Seonag didn't exactly leave Dùn Brion on good terms. Perhaps we have more problems than just Gormal and Sidheag."

CHAPTER 25

Mongfhionn gripped Gràinne's arm with such ferocity that she yelped and grumbled that she would have bruises later. Still, the combination of fear, helplessness, and promised retribution in the Sidhe's eyes frightened Gràinne.

"What is it, Ma? I've never seen you like this."

The Sidhe epitomised awful power and promised blood vengeance to all who defied or harmed those under her protection. Plucking up the courage, in a small voice, Gràinne asked, "Is it Brianag? Has something terrible happened?"

The Sidhe, having regained a semblance of composure, shook her head, and drew Gràinne into her arms. The rarity of Mongfhionn's emotional response drove Gràinne's anxiety level higher. While her ma did not lack compassion, rarely were her emotions open to public scrutiny.

"It is…" The words seemed to catch in the Sidhe's throat. "… Neamhain." Gràinne's eyes widened as her mind churned with many possibilities, most of which were unpleasant. "While we planned strategies, Neamhain took action. She has gone to help her sister."

"The Hag! No," gasped Gràinne. Then she frowned and asked, "How could Neamhain find Brianag, but we couldn't?"

Mongfhionn smiled and shook her head. Gràinne was simultaneously relieved and disappointed at the gesture. "You should know Neamhain and me better, my daughter. We are Aes Sidhe and not bound by the usual laws of nature." That Neamhain was considered a Sidhe surprised Gràinne, for she was the daughter of Mongfhionn and the very human Fearghal.

The Sidhe inhaled deeply as if marshalling her thoughts. "Neamhain has hidden in Brianag's mind. She seeks to comfort and protect her sister from Sidheag's influence and seduction."

"Shite!"

The Sidhe nodded. "Exactly. Neamhain is only eleven summers. She has considerable talents, but she cannot comprehend Sidheag's powers. If the bitseach uncovers Neamhain's sanctuary, she can destroy her in this world and that of the Aes Sidhe." Mongfhionn shuddered and wrung her hands. This time it was Gràinne who opened her arms to give comfort, and to Gràinne's surprise, the Sidhe put up no resistance.

"We need to find Sidheag's hiding place, destroy it and the bitseach, and rescue our daughters," said Gràinne.

Mongfhionn nodded. "We should consult with Blàr and his chieftains. Perhaps there is a pattern to the disappeared girls and slaughters of farmsteads and settlements." The Sidhe bit her lip. "The winter is not truly my domain, but I should be able to help with the weather."

Gràinne dipped her head and gave her ma a squeeze. "Perhaps Sidheag still uses the same loch as in Diadhaidh's time?"

The Sidhe shook her head. "I think that would be extremely foolish of the abomination." Mongfhionn's brow furrowed, and then she hissed like a viper. "Yet, until she obtained her physical form, Sidheag would have had to live in the waters of her birth—or those connected to them."

Expressions of determination and hope settled on the Sidhe's face. "We need to talk to Blàr. His people will know which rivers flow into and out of Diadhaidh's loch. And which waters are fed by them."

Both women breathed easier. They had a plan.

At that moment, Cùil Daothail's war horns sounded.

★★★

Winds had scoured Cùil Daothail for five sunsets, carrying blue-grey clouds heavy with snow. Clothed in heavy furs, the lives of those who stood sentinel on the ramparts were cold and uncomfortable. However, during snowstorms, an assault on the walls was unlikely.

On this day, the garrison awoke to a new dawn of silence, pale blue skies, and a weak sun. The storm had passed, but there were no celebrations. Blàr looked out from a guard post on the northern wall and saw a landscape whose whiteness hurt his eyes. On the western stockade, Seonag stood in awkward silence with Teàrlag. Her mother was the first to speak.

"We do not have the luxury of time to discuss recent events…" Teàrlag pursed her lips. "…or our relationship. Both can wait until the Goddess decides if we live or die in Cùil Daothail. Yet you are now the Bhanrìgh of the Forest People. As with Drostan, that comes with authority and heavy leadership responsibilities."

Seonag's blue eyes widened. "You're not suggesting that *I* take command of Cùil Daothail?" Her jaw set. "That would be very unfair to Blàr."

Teàrlag smiled and shook her head. "Quite the opposite. My counsel would be to fully support Blàr as commander. He is a brave man with a good head for battle tactics. By all accounts, he has shouldered the duties of the Ravens' throne, a position that I hear was thrust upon him, much better than anyone expected. Listen to him, but remember you are the bhanrigh, and your opinion must be considered. Only accept if you are confident in Blàr's tactics." Seonag nodded and heaved a sigh of relief.

"Now, tell me about Brion."

It was the moment Seonag realised her mother had returned. Thankfully, the *barrr ewww* of a war horn allowed her to evade answering. The source of the alarm was the appearance of Blàr's farthest-ranging scouts. While the pair looked exhausted, their mounts had given all. Sadly, their reward would be a sharp blade and being added to the fort's food stores. Around the table, the leaders of Cùil Daothail's defenders and several shield-men and women awaited the envoys' report.

"How many do we face?" asked Blàr.

"The number is difficult to gauge." One messenger looked at his comrade, who dipped his head in agreement. "Not less than twenty thousand, we think."

"The Hag's tits!" exclaimed Cearbhall and then muttered, "Sorry." He was not, of course.

"We estimate that about half of the army are farmers and tradespeople. Most are unhappy with Sidheag's rule but are terrified of what she will do to them and their families if they don't follow her." The scout paused before adding, "We reckon about five thousand are fanatics, including several thousand priests. The rest are mercenaries, outcasts, and thieves looking to pillage, rape, and take slaves."

"When will they arrive?"

"Further north, the storms are fiercer, and the snows deeper. Many passes are blocked, and communities are still digging paths out of the drifts. I estimate we have a half-cycle of the moon before they reach Cùil Daothail's stockade." The relief around the table at some good news was palpable until the scout added, "However, those who attacked Drostan in the forest are still close by and number at least five thousand."

Blàr called Niall to his side.

"Stand the full garrison down but double the guards and patrols."

＊＊＊

The slatted wooden floor was awash with blood and vomit. Seirbhiseach shook his head and grimaced at the stench that permeated the crannag. Once again, he settled his stomach for the task ahead and gathered strips of cloth and pails of water before crossing the room to stand by Brianag's cot.

As usual, Brianag tossed and turned in the bed as she fought the demons that infested her mind. Although her body no longer reflected her age, the priest considered Brianag an infant helpless to resist Sidheag's games. *How much longer can she fight?* He had no answers to help her or himself.

Seirbhiseach recoiled as his toe touched the pool of blood that seeped

205

from the half-eaten corpse. In and of itself, the sight was a troubling development. Previously the remains left for Brianag, after a night's hunting, had been animals of increasing size. Not so on this day. The corpse was a boy, only a few summers younger than Brianag.

Why? Had Sidheag felt the need to blood Brianag with humans? Yet, perhaps it was a deception to cause Brianag more turmoil. A look at the cadaver and Seirbhiseach had his answer. The teeth marks piercing the young boy's skin and the bite-size on the gnawed bones were those of an adolescent. By Seirbhiseach's reckoning, it matched Brianag's bite. He searched for an alternate rationale and posited that one of Sidheag's daughters had killed the boy and left the body in the crannag. Yet the priest could not convince himself.

Seirbhiseach bent over to grab the corpse and instantly was thrown onto his back and straddled by a furious Brianag. Blood-infused drool flowed from her mouth, splashing his face. Red-stained teeth, which appeared longer and more pointed than usual, caressed his throat. His Adam's apple bobbled up and down as his fear rose.

"Mine," hissed Brianag. "Touch it, and I will rip your throat out and feed on you."

With a strength born of panic, Seirbhiseach grabbed Brianag's arms and forced her off his chest. Rolling her over, he sat astride her belly. *Thank the Goddess, she doesn't have Sidheag's or her Brood's physical power—yet.* "Fight this bidse! Or else you are lost forever," said the priest while keeping a firm grip on Brianag's arms. "Fight!"

The beautiful song that echoed around the crannag was clear and soothing but impossible. There was no one else present. Was it in his head? How? Brianag's eyes slowly lost their deep, almost black, colour, returning to their natural green. Yet the orbs were dull and lacked vitality, sharply contrasting with how she had first entered the crannag. With a sigh, Brianag passed out.

"Thank you," whispered the priest as he laid Brianag on a fur and then braced himself to clean up the mess.

Neamhain wept, but kept on singing.

* * *

Eimhir smiled as she lifted a clay bowl to her mouth and sipped the cool spring water with relish. Increased trading with ships from Gaul and the Great Sea had changed the people's expectations, hopefully for good. She turned to Cassán and caught his eyes before standing to address Brion.

"I have no good news. Dùn Brion is already awash with gossip of a challenge for the throne of the Na Mèadaidh. There are allegations that you are a usurper set on the throne by Drostan. Rumours of rebellion flourish like seeds in good soil. It is the same in the communities across your domain. The people are divided."

"The situation, while not unexpected, has developed faster than I anticipated," said Brion. He glanced at Cearbhall, who nodded in agreement. Then Brion smiled at Eimhir. "I appreciate your respect, but you do not have to stand when among friends. Leave that to occasions that require ceremony." Eimhir beamed and took her seat.

"I think the time for subtlety and consideration of others' perspectives is over," said Brion. "I'm open to ideas on how we deal with an insurrection if it transpires. I'm still hopeful that, like a breeze, it will pass. Yet how do we know who is on our side?"

"Invite Ealasaid and Gormal to visit for negotiations. When they are within range, end them with bolts from the ballistae," said Cassán.

Cearbhall groaned. As they broke their fast earlier, he informed Cassán that, even though he judged him ready, his plan to travel to Cùil Daothail would have to wait. Needless to say, Cassán was unhappy, although this time, he understood and kept his anger and disappointment under control.

"That would be one option," responded Brion diplomatically, "and has its merits. I will bear it in mind, especially if war is officially declared. However, at this time, it would make the bitseach a martyr." He looked around the table. "Any other suggestions?"

Cearbhall looked at Eimhir, and she nodded. "Eimhir and I have spoken on this. She is confident as to who stands with us. This needs to be

207

brought into the open, even if it divides us further. Your leaders and their people must make a choice." Cearbhall paused to sip from his cup. "Call a meeting of the chieftains of the Na Mèadaidh. Make each one swear an oath of loyalty before the others. Those who will not make the vow or do not attend can be assumed to be on Ealasaid's side."

"Will the rebel nobles not just lie?" asked Cassán.

Brion shook his head. "An oath witnessed by the druids is a serious commitment before the Goddess. Few will risk a trip to the Otherworld rather than Mag Mell." Brion rubbed his chin. "We will make it clear that any who do not wish to pledge loyalty may leave Dùn Brion unharmed."

Eimhir opened her mouth to speak, but a raised palm from Brion halted the action. "Correct me if I'm wrong, but I think you were about to say that you have a list of those who certainly will not support me. Correct?" Eimhir dipped her head. Brion looked at Cearbhall. "Have you chosen Cassán's *chomhairle?*"

"There are a hundred, plus a well-seasoned ceannairí céad, that I would recommend." Cassán bore a disquieted mien during a conversation, seemingly about him but about which he remained in the dark. His chair scraped the floor as he poised to protest. The same palm that greeted Eimhir stayed Cassán's retort. Brion's eyes turned to Eimhir again.

"As far as possible, continue to collect information." To Cearbhall, he said, "Send messengers to all the communities of the Na Mèadaidh announcing that in half a cycle of the moon, there is to be a meeting of chieftains and nobles. They should say it is to discuss a potential war with Gormal, although most will see through the subterfuge."

Brion paused, set his jaw, and held Eimhir's gaze. "After that meeting, you will inform Cassán who needs to die and where they may be found." Eimhir nodded and looked at a surprised Cassán.

"I guess it's official who's the boss." His broad grin assured everyone in the room that Cassán had no issues with his orders or commander.

As the meeting broke up, but before she exited the room, Brion placed a hand on Eimhir's forearm. "I have put a terrible burden on you. You will never have full information and will make wrong choices. Innocent men and women will be killed. However, no blame will be placed at your feet. That is a rìgh's responsibility."

As Eimhir walked down the hallway, she reflected on Brion's words and muttered, "True, but it will be me who looks on the faces of the dead in my nightmares." She sighed. *How did I end up as the conscience of the Sèitheachs? I doubt Ealasaid has such thoughts or visions.*

⁎ ⁎ ⁎

The first sign of the impending attack was the howling of Sidheag and her pack as they reconnoitred the outskirts of Cùil Daothail in wolf form. Yet they kept to the gloom of dawn and dusk and the night's blackness. Mongfhionn thought that was understandable. The days had been frigid but unseasonably sunny.

Mongfhionn smiled. Others of the Aes Sidhe were much more adept than she at moulding the winter season to their wishes. Her domain was the lightning, the storm, and the wind. Still, she was not inexperienced. She chuckled at the weapon she had kept in her quiver. The crunch of steps in the snow made her turn. Red lips opened to reveal perfectly white teeth.

Gràinne rolled her eyes and thought it unfair that the two people she loved, Amodocus and Mongfhionn, had teeth that could be seen in the dark. That said, the Sidhe was much more circumspect about showing them off. "You hear the wolves?"

The Sidhe dipped her head. "She is being much more cautious than her nature normally allows. Drostan must have hurt her ambitions more than she anticipated. I suspect his use of iron and Teàrlag's practical brutality surprised her." The Sidhe swept her hand over the fort. "I'm impressed by Blàr's novel use of iron in constructing Cùil Daothail's stockade and ditches. That the settlement is built on ancient iron deposits may yet be an advantage, too."

"Do you recall using painted designs to prevent Kartimandu from enthralling our army in the Battle of Mai Dún?" asked Gràinne. "I think it was either your or Mórrígan's idea." Mongfhionn nodded. "Can you devise something similar for here? We can't just make everyone deaf by punching their ears."

The Sidhe paced back and forward along the walkway before returning to stand before Gràinne. "I believe I can create such a design." Gràinne heaved a sigh of relief until Mongfhionn dampened her enthusiasm. "Kartimandu was only a *fuath*, although a rare evolution of that species. Sidheag has her beginnings as a powerful sister of the Aes Sidhe.

"The symbol might work on her Brood, but she is much stronger than they." At Gràinne's downcast look, Mongfhionn smiled and cupped her chin with a delicate hand. "It is, however, an excellent idea, and I should have thought of it. But we will need more than one arrow in our quiver.

"What is your knowledge of the Tuireadh?"

The question rocked Gràinne on her heels, for the Ancient One had asked her the same question. She hated the Death Song of the Na Daoine Tùrsach. It brought unpleasant memories, and she seemed to be another person on the rare occasions when she sang it. "Why do you ask, Mother?" Gràinne's eyes were full of suspicion and trepidation.

"Like you, everyone assumes the Tuireadh is an incantation that brings death and disaster or celebrates blood lust. That is because your grandmother, Diadhaidh, and her blood priests chose to interpret the chant in that manner because it suited them."

Gràinne scratched her scalp and grimaced at the flakes of dead skin that floated downwards. She wondered where the Sidhe's thoughts were going.

"Also, most only sing the first half of the Tuireadh."

"But how does this help us to fight Sidheag?"

"There is an ancient tale among the Greeks of a *seanchaí* named Orpheus whose song was so beautiful that it countered the song of the Sirens who sought to destroy his friends." Mongfhionn smiled at Gràinne's puzzlement. "What if you and I can use the Tuireadh to challenge Sidheag's song?"

"But I don't know the words," said Gràinne.

"The Ancient One does."

✳ ✳ ✳

"We must attack now. My spies inform me that at least half of the Na Mèadaidh support my claim to the throne. Brion is weakened by Drostan's death, and his allies, including the Sidhe, Mongfhionn, are under siege in Cùil Daothail. The snows are packed hard and ideal for warriors and horses to travel over." Ealasaid could not hide her frustration at Gormal's reluctance to act decisively and his constant procrastination.

"And *my* spies tell me that *your* sister sits beside Brion and ruts his one-handed son. And that she provides Brion with counsel regarding who he can trust. By reputation, her network appears as good as, if not better than, yours. Whether she is also an accomplished assassin has yet to be demonstrated—or perhaps none of her targets is alive to tell tales."

Ealasaid's cheeks flushed red in anger, although more about the mention of her bidse of a sister. She opened her mouth to speak but was stopped by Gormal's raised hand. "*My* informants report that Brion has called a meeting of the chieftains before the feast of Imbolg. I dislike Brion intensely, but if you think he is stupid, you gravely underestimate the man. Like his sister, Mórrígan, he has a ruthless streak." Gormal's shoulders hunched, and his long neck bent to peer like a great clamhan at Ealasaid.

"If your envoys are as foolish and loose-tongued as I am led to believe, Brion already has a good idea of who will desert him. We will wait until after the feast of Imbolg to decide when to attack." As Ealasaid opened her mouth, Gormal snapped, "You are dismissed."

Furious, Ealasaid stormed from the chamber. Hearing Gormal's laughter ringing in her ears, she promised to end his life as soon as she sat on the throne of the Na Mèadaidh.

211

CHAPTER 26

In the distance, thousands of flickering torches traced the bank of the Abhainn Nis. The vista was breathtaking, bathed in silver-blue moonlight and framed by a clear night sky and pristine blanket of snow.

"Why does evil have to be so beautiful?"

Blàr puffed out a cloud of tiny ice crystals and sighed at Seonag's observation. "They're not all evil. Many are afraid; others are weak-willed and easy prey for malevolent leaders."

"Tell that to those who died alongside Drostan," snapped Seonag. "There will be a reckoning, and blood will flow. That is my promise."

Blàr dipped his head and said nothing. Platitudes, even those well-meant, would only insult Seonag's grief. He considered putting an arm around her shoulders. Yet, he discounted it as sending the wrong signals or being open to interpretation. But would it? *What happened between Brion and Seonag?* He sighed, breathing more ice particles into the air. They sparkled in the moonlight before disappearing—just like his courage.

"Deep thoughts?" asked Seonag. The heat had gone from her voice.

"More a reflection on missed opportunities and lost nerve," he chuckled. Seonag caught the sadness in Blàr's voice and wondered what he alluded to.

"Do you think the bidse will attack tonight?"

"Normally, I'd say no. Only thieves and assassins fight in the darkness, but Sidheag is neither normal nor human. From talking to Teàrlag, she may be sensitive to sunlight." Blàr gripped the wooden stockade, and Seonag watched him look to the west. "Like me, you can hear the wolves' howling. She is assessing our strengths and weaknesses. According to Mongfhionn, that is unusual for Sidheag, so perhaps we should take it as a compliment."

Blàr stopped and thought for a moment. "To answer your question, yes, I think they will attack in the deep darkness, between *meadhan-oidhche*—midnight—and sunrise."

"From which direction?"

Blàr scratched his whiskers and tugged a narrow earlobe flushed red from the cold. "There are only two possibilities. The Abhainn Nis is about two hundred paces wide, but the water currents are slow and gentle. However, the river is too wide to swim and too deep to walk across. They'll have to use the old bridges.

"One pair is downstream, directly north of us, where there is an island. The other is upstream, to our west, and uses a large sandbank to span the river. I think they'll cross upstream and attack from the west." Blàr snorted. "We'll soon know. They'll have to move shortly or lose the chance to attack tonight."

"Our defences?"

"It's too late to add more physical fortifications, but I think we've done well. As to bodies, with your warriors, the garrison stands at over five thousand, and most are veterans."

Seonag winced at Blàr's reference to her fighters. Had Drostan been forgotten so quickly? She shook her head. *Don't be a stupid bidse.* A conversation to Seonag's right drew her gaze to where two were deep in conversation. "What do you think Gràinne and Mongfhionn are cooking up?"

Blàr shrugged his shoulders. "Who knows? The Sidhe has never been a great communicator, more a brutal one. Gràinne has changed, but I can't put my finger on its manifestation. Amodocus is unusually tight-lipped when the subject is broached, which is ominous." Blàr paused. "Gràinne is obsessed with getting the job done in Cùil Daothail so she can go after

Brianag. I hope Brianag is found unharmed, for I shudder to think what will happen if she is not."

The Raven's king paused and said, "Like you, they have promised and undoubtedly will exact a terrible retribution. I doubt either will care who from." Blàr paused and held Seonag's gaze. "What about you?" Angry and embarrassed, Seonag's face flushed at Blàr's candour. In answer, she walked away.

***

Gràinne looked at Mongfhionn before turning to face Amodocus. "Mongfhionn has a new strategy to execute and has prevailed on me to stay in Cùil Daothail. That puts you in charge of the riders and chariots." Amodocus dipped his head.

"My suggestion is that you wait in the forest. You'll hear the signal and know when you're needed. After that, your task is simple—kill anyone outside Cùil Daothail who gets in your way." Gràinne's instructions were met with a rib-crushing embrace and a flash of teeth before Amodocus turned and strode away.

On the walkway, Blàr, Seonag, Teàrlag, and their protectors bellowed out commands. In the half-light of dusk, hundreds of braziers were set alight. Soot-blackened cauldrons filled with water, oil, pitch, and embers bubbled and smoked on the fires. Men and women tugged protective coverings stiff from frost from the ballistae, tightened the skeins, and stacked bolts against the stockade. There were originally ten on each wall, but Blàr, wagering on an attack from the west, had repositioned ten from the other ramparts to the western stockade.

Along the fence, two ranks of warriors, men and women, smirked at each other. The strange white sigils the Sidhe had demanded they paint on their faces clashed with the usual arrays of tribal paint. Facing west, Gràinne and Mongfhionn stood and waited.

"I'm going to freeze my arse off," complained Gràinne. She referred to the nakedness of both women since both had dropped their cloaks to the snow. In her head, the Ancient One cackled.

"Nonsense, child. There was frost on the ground when you fought naked against the Gaiscedach on the walls of Lugudunon. Have faith in your true armour." The Sidhe smirked. "Besides, many of these men and women will die. Let them journey to Mag Mell with a smile and fond memories of our arses and breasts." Mongfhionn inspected Gràinne more intensely, making the young woman blush.

"You need to put weight on. I can see your ribs."

"Ma!" Around the pair, men and women chuckled.

* * *

The man was twenty summers old and wore a farmer's sculpted body. From sunrise to sunset, hard labour in harsh conditions had turned weak flesh to muscle on his bones. His hands were large and ingrained with honest dirt. Hazel eyes, flecked with green, pointed to intelligence at odds with his lifestyle. Frustration resided in his eyes. He wanted to find his way in the southern lands but had buried ambition under duty to his family.

His eyes also held worry and fear. He glanced at his sister, who was three summers younger and shuddered. He remembered the sobbing of his mother and the impotent curses and threats of his father, grandfather, and brothers when Sidheag chose his sibling as her daughter. The young man spat. Chosen? What choice did she or any of the family have?

Now, dressed in a flimsy white léine that flapped around bare feet, she walked with her eight "sisters" at the head of Sidheag's army. He spat again, drawing curious looks from those around him. They shuffled to distance themselves from him. Sidheag did not tolerate rebellion, and none wished to become the abomination's, or her Brood's, next meal.

Still, the young man was past caring and bellowed his sister's name: "Malmhìn!" *Yet is she my sister anymore?* What lived behind deep blue eyes that now seemed blacker than night? His hopes soared as he watched her hesitate, turn, and glide towards him. Fearlessly he advanced to meet her. Around him, the horde parted and drew away from the young man.

"Return to us, Malmhìn. Return to those who love you." The young woman looked curiously at him, perhaps puzzling over a deeply buried memory. She moved closer until he could feel her putrid breath caress his face. His stomach churned, but he quelled the urge to vomit.

He whispered, "Sister," and embraced her. She felt warm and uncomfortably sensuous as she pressed hard against his body. He felt every soft curve as she moulded herself to him. Her soft moans were filled with seduction. "No, Malmhìn, this cannot be between us," he whispered. The young man tried to push her away, but her embrace had the strength of iron chains and would not release him.

In the distance, he heard Sidheag cackle, and he shivered. Malmhìn looked into his eyes, and the young man realised this was not the sister he loved. He sent prayers of intercession and forgiveness on her behalf to the Goddess.

Pain cut his supplications short as razor-sharp talons sliced across his belly and upwards. He heard his guts slop onto the snow and felt blood pump from a torn artery as she bit his neck. The final torment before the bean-shìdh took him was to hear the abomination lap up his blood and feast on his warm flesh.

Sidheag shrieked. The Brood turned and fell on those who had stood close to the young man. Not even the slightest taint of defiance would be tolerated.

∗∗∗

Blàr turned to Niall as war horns reverberated along Cùil Daothail's ramparts. The stocky veteran perceived his role as the king's protector and had reluctantly agreed to take charge of the ballista teams. His hesitancy and angst were perfectly understandable. Still, under Gràinne's and Amodocus' counselling, Niall had drilled the bolt-thrower units until they could load and fire accurately—even in the dark.

On the parapet, Mongfhionn turned to Gràinne and whispered, "Not your time yet." The Sidhe lifted her arms and called out her supplication to the Goddess. As the melodic incantation rose and fell, the banners and flags along the stockade fluttered. By the time she reached the climax of her song, the easterly wind had whipped her long hair into a corona around her head, and the emblems cracked like whips.

"Kill the bidsean," growled Blàr to Niall as they watched the line of torches move closer to Cùil Daothail's walls. As the enemy passed a line of tall standing stones, recently pounded into the earth, Niall shouted, *"Pitch!"*

Along the western rampart, bolts, with strips of cloth wrapped below the iron heads, were dipped into pales of pitch, and set alight. The slap of missiles rang out sharply as they were placed in ballista grooves. "Fire!" bellowed Niall, and twenty fiery bolts launched into the night. As the missiles left the machines, Niall's teams were already repeating the process.

Sidheag's army had little warning and less understanding of the weapon. Only a faint whoosh of displaced air heralded their arrival. Cùil Daothail's closeness to the fragrant pine forests masked the sweet smell of resin—hence the attackers' shock when the volley slammed into stacks of wood already soaked in pitch. All exploded in a blaze of fire, raining burning brands down on those closest. The snow melted and steamed under the intense heat, and Sidheag's horde fragmented, swerving to avoid being scorched.

"Now we can see the bastards, not just their torches," grunted Blàr as he turned to Seonag and Teàrlag. Seonag looked at her mother's grim face and wondered if that was any advantage. On the stockade, Niall roared until his voice became hoarse and then continued to bellow an unintelligible stream of sounds. Still, the ballista teams knew what was asked of them and answered with salvos of bolts.

Arrayed before the army, Sidheag's Brood opened their maws and wailed. Sidheag had dismissed Teàrlag's use of temporary deafness as freakish and unsustainable. Thus, they were assured, if indeed they could feel emotion, that their voices would enthral Cùil Daothail's defenders. The tactic had never failed.

This time, Mongfhionn's blustery, easterly wind plucked the voices from the nine, dissipating their song until it was a mere whisper. From her vantage point, Sidheag raged and ordered her Brood and army forward. Then she watched in surprise and perhaps a frisson of fear, as a volley of flaming bolts shattered her newly reformed Brood.

Was it hubris or error that made the Baobhan Sith position her daughters ahead of the horde? Dressed in white and lit up by enormous bonfires and moonlight, they were a distinctive target and well within the range of the ballistae.

The bolts had two types of iron heads: leaf-shaped to slash and shear and spike-shaped to penetrate. Niall's second and third barrages sheared limbs and decapitated heads from the Brood. Five bloodless husks fell to the snow. Of the four still standing, half had shrapnel burns. Again they raised their hands and screamed into the night, and again the wind silenced them.

At another time, the fiery bolts might have appeared festive. To Sidheag's horde, it seemed as if the horrors of the Otherworld had been unleashed. Aided by Mongfhionn's winds, hundreds of flaming missiles slammed into their ranks. Burning pitch clung to clothes and flesh, turning many into human torches. The pungent smell of brimstone rose as long tresses of hair blazed.

Bolts impaled and sliced through unarmoured flesh, cleaving heads from shoulders and limbs from torsos. In the silver moonlight, pristine snow became a slush of black gore as arm's-length iron spikes locked groups of two or three together in a macabre dance. At least they had companions as the mnathan-shìdh hauled them away to an eternity of torment.

Stunned, Sidheag's army milled around in the bloody slush. In a panic, they turned around as if to flee but were halted by fanatical priests. A shriek from Sidheag gripped their minds and pointed them again at Cùil Daothail.

Blàr beamed at Seonag, who looked shocked at the ferocious power of the ballistae. Yet both knew that the death toll was negligible compared to the size of Sidheag's army. In normal circumstances, a human horde would have turned and fled, but this was hardly a typical battle.

As the swarm flowed across the snow towards Cùil Daothail's walls, the war machines continued to hurl bolts into their midst, ploughing deep, bloody furrows in a field of flesh. Sidheag's remaining daughters walked forward but were now protected by human shields.

"They're almost at the next defences," said Blàr. For a moment, he regretted that Gràinne had sent Amodocus from the fort. The riders were experienced archers and could have kept selecting targets when the ballistae, unable to depress further, fell silent. After a moment of reflection, he shook his head. No. They would be much more valuable on their horses.

Shrieks of pain rent the air as hundreds tumbled into deep ditches and were impaled. Two lines of trenches, placed at one and two hundred paces from Cùil Daothail's walls, had been excavated, populated with fire-hardened stakes, and camouflaged. Many of those to fall were Sidheag's torchbearers. As they died, the lights guiding the horde were snuffed out.

Yet that was not the end of the suffering as volleys of flaming bolts descended on the farther ditches. Pitch-soaked straw covered the bottom of the trenches and burst into flames, creating scars of fire in the snow. "The most effective traps are the simplest," muttered Blàr.

"She has no pity and no mercy. Thousands of dead are nothing to her. Like cattle, she will drive them to our walls."

Blàr barely restrained himself from jumping at Mongfhionn's voice. There had been no sound of feet on snow and ice. "When they reach the berms of earth on the far sides of the ditches, Gràinne and I will attack." Blàr dipped his head, but the Sidhe placed a hand on his arm. "At that time, I will have to let the wind go, and Cùil Daothail will be at its most vulnerable."

✳✳✳

Imbolg was seven sunsets away and the proposed meeting of the Na Mèadaidh chieftains sooner. Thus, the quartet of Brion, Cassán, Cearbhall, and Eimhir met daily to review Eimhir's reports. Brion looked to Eimhir. At first, she made to stand, but remembering Brion's words, she smiled, and kept her seat. Eimhir's manner was business-like, and her report was concise.

"I am reasonably sure who you can count on and who will not support you. Those in the "don't know" category represent about one-quarter of the nobles, which is not good.

"Many tread a diplomatic path, waiting to see which way the wind blows before planting their spear in the dirt. A substantial group have long-standing claims or disputes that have not been settled. Thus, they are un-enthused, although not antagonistic." Brion grunted at Eimhir's less-than-subtle rebuke.

"I have taken the liberty of inviting that group to Dùn Brion and promised them a hearing before the main meeting." Eimhir heaved a sigh of relief as Brion nodded and smiled. Kings often had prickly tempera-ments. "One way or another, we'll soon know who is on your side."

"How does it look from your perspective?" asked Brion, turning to Cearbhall.

"I've refreshed Dùn Brion's garrison and used it to filter out malcon-tents. Those clearly loyal have also been allowed time to visit their families. Morale is high." Cearbhall smiled at Eimhir. "Based on Eimhir's intelli-gence, most of those currently within our walls are deemed loyal."

After a pause to take a few gulps of beer, Cearbhall continued: "Cassán and I have overseen increased weapons and tactics training, and he has taken command of the ballistae. We have assigned specific posi-tions and command areas based on Eimhir's information. The need and placement of temporary accommodation for the warriors accompanying each chieftain have been managed." Cearbhall inclined his head in Cassán's direction.

"My *caomhnóirí* will act as the stronghold's security force. We will re-strict all chieftains' and noble's retinues to ten warriors plus a reasonable number of slaves, servants, and partners. Those who protest too much, if not already on Eimhir's enemies list, will join that group." Cassán's face took on a troubled and distasteful look.

"After the meeting and guided by Eimhir, my warriors will become assassins."

CHAPTER 27

Twenty steps from Mongfhionn, oblivious to the cold, Gràinne paced back and forward, twisting her fingers endlessly. *I cannot let myself be controlled by another entity.* Gràinne knew Mongfhionn continuously battled the Hag, and she feared what Brianag, with Neamhain's help, fought against. *Where will it end if I give in to A 'Bhanrìgh Fuil?* The cackling laugh of the Ancient One did little to improve to reduce her turmoil. *Get out of my head, bitseach!*

"You don't understand," whispered the Ancient One. Gràinne sensed a disappointed shake of her head. "And you have little time to gain wisdom." It seemed as if a less menacing demeanour settled on the Ancient One. "You *are* A 'Bhanrìgh Fuil. It's not about giving in. Until now, your life has been a lie, a deception of your own making."

The Ancient One chuckled. "As for me dominating you, please tell me how. Unlike Mongfhionn or Sidheag, I am a spirit... an old memory. I have no power save my knowledge, which you can accept or ignore." Gràinne imagined her ancestor braiding long grey hair as she sought to marshal her thoughts. "I should have ended Sidheag, not negotiated with the bidse. Generations of the Na Daoine Tùrsach have been cursed by my stupidity and lust for power.

"You have the chance to remedy my crime." The Ancient One chortled. "Although I don't think it will be enough to release me from the Otherworld. The Goddess is a vindictive, unforgiving bidse. You would do well to remember that."

A movement to her left made Gràinne turn, and she faced Mongfhionn. Disquiet flickered in the Sidhe's eyes before she regained total control. In the moonlight, her daughter's eyes looked black as night, as did the curling sigils that swathed her body. Yet Mongfhionn knew that was a trick of the light. Gràinne's eyes and designs were blood-red.

"Shall we begin, daughter?" Gràinne nodded and lifted her arms.

✳✳✳

Clear and full of power, the songs of Gràinne and Mongfhionn ascended to the night sky, and so did the fury and howling of Sidheag. Their enthrallment weakened, Sidheag's army stumbled and staggered in confusion. The remaining Brood members, their voices nullified by the Death Chant of the Na Daoine Tùrsach, appeared unsure how to respond.

Whether to keep a grip on power or accrue personal wealth, the zealots and the pragmatically invested in Sidheag's force grasped the danger. Thus they resorted to more traditional ways to sustain the momentum of the attack. Like sheep and goat drovers, they shoved, kicked, and killed as they herded the flock towards the chest-high berm edging the final ditch.

On Cùil Daothail's walls, Niall's bolt throwers fell silent. Their teams grabbed shields, spears, and blades and stepped into the shield-wall. Beyond the stockade, the agonising cries of hundreds assaulted the ears of the defenders. Pushed by the horde's momentum, they tumbled onto the ditch's forest of stakes. Sidheag filled the trenches with their bodies as if they were no more than dirt.

The more experienced among the besiegers bellowed orders and called for trees to bridge the trench and ladders to scale the fence. As the stockade trembled under the assault, volleys of javelins and darts were thrown in a seemingly never-ending hail of missiles. Terrified men and women screamed. Yet Cùil Daothail's stocks were not infinite. First, the barrage slowed, and then it ceased.

Prayers of thanks to the Goddess were released by the besiegers, but she had no interest in their entreaties. Willingly or not, they had chosen their side. Forever stained with darkness and corruption, they had to be cleansed from her domain.

A torrent of boiling water, pitch, and oil cascaded over the stockade, escalating the attackers' screams to a terrifying level. Many on the walls stuffed wool in their ears to dampen the cries. Yet, it proved impossible to remove the pitiful shrieking from their minds once heard. The sounds would haunt their dreams for many summers.

The maimed suffered doubly. Unlike a sword slash or club bash, the torrent of horror left bodies mutilated, burned, and scarred. Cruelly, the cascade left many victims alive and those around them, even friends, embarrassed to look upon their hideous forms. The Goddess gave them a foretaste of how they would suffer in the Otherworld.

✴✴✴

In the forest, Sidheag fought to control and direct her anger. Some long-buried instinct made her lift up her arms to the night sky. She snarled. Who in the heavens would favour her petitions? Sidheag's four daughters stood between the melange of priests, veterans, farmers, and artisans. Mirroring their mistress, they lifted up their hands.

The songs of Sidheag and the Brood ascended to do battle with the Sidhe and A 'Bhanrìgh Fuil. While the chants nullified each other, Mongfhionn knew the tactics were an imperfect solution. Inevitably, cracks appeared, and through these, the Siren songs of Sidheag and her Brood slipped through. Along the walkways, the foolish who had scorned Mongfhionn's design froze, enthralled by Sidheag and her daughters.

At a long wail from Sidheag, the remaining Brood members glided forward with unnatural speed and purpose above the slush of battle gore and snow. They screeched as wood, spiked with iron, burned their feet and hands. But Sidheag's mind compelled them forward.

Those defenders, paralysed by Sidheag's song, could do nothing. Their minds screamed *Danger!* as the Brood's faces appeared above the stockade and their feet on the walkway. The swiftness of their talons, slashing and ripping the enthralled defenders' flesh, ended their suffering. Others, stunned into hesitation, died as the four swept along the parapet, slaughtering scores with contemptuous ease. However, the besieged were fortunate. Their deaths were swift, for the abominations were driven to kill, not to feed.

"Get those bidsean off the wall!" roared Seonag.

Along with Blàr, Teàrlag, and their brawny protectors, Seonag dashed to the small group whose cavernous maws were filled with needle-like teeth and the promise of death. The foul stench from their mouths caused the band to pause to quell roiling stomachs. Then with spears extended and expressions set in grim determination, they advanced on the four. On the other side of Sidheag's daughters, another group of defenders moved to cut off the abominations' retreat.

Mongfhionn looked at Gràinne and, for the briefest moment, stopped her anthem. "Join your friends. I will try to keep Sidheag occupied." Gràinne dipped her head and gathered up her weapons. The Sidhe whispered, "Force the bitseacha into the square." Mongfhionn smiled at Gràinne's raised eyebrow. "Trust me."

Gràinne cast a backwards glance at the Sidhe as she ran to join her friends and instantly offered a prayer for strength to the Goddess. What she observed was worrisome. On the Sidhe's face were the marks of two battles: the strain of her duel with Sidheag and lightning-fast flashes of the Hag attempting to break through.

"Drive the bitseacha into the courtyard," bellowed Gràinne.

She was surprised that the others obeyed without question. Yet in the darkness and flickering torches, Gràinne could not see the fear of A 'Bhanrìgh Fuil in their eyes. Prodded by the tips of iron spearheads, the Brood snapped and snarled. The reaction from Sidheag's previously emotionless executioners surprised their tormentors.

An ancient memory called to Gràinne, and she stepped forward. "Cease! I am A 'Bhanrìgh Fuil. You will obey me."

Whether Gràinne's declaration stunned the Brood or her companions more was open to discussion. Blàr's expression promised they would speak later. Yet the four daughters hesitated, and that was long enough for Blàr and Seonag to close on them. Teeth bared and snarling like wolves, three were forced closer to and over the edge of the walkway.

Sensing the fate of her daughters, Sidheag's ululations railed against the Sidhe, battering her like a shield. Yet even the Baobhan Sith's powers were not unlimited. She could not fully control her army and daughters and fight Mongfhionn. Frustrated, Sidheag made her choice, shrieked, and her army renewed its assault on Cùil Daothail's walls.

✳✳✳

All but one of Sidheag's daughters fell from the parapet, landing with uncanny skill on the snow-covered dirt. However, one chose defiance and shrieked at an advancing Blàr. With a snarl, he thrust forward with his spear, impaling the monster. Yet, skewered on Blàr's spear, she raged and spat at him while pulling and dragging herself along the wooden shaft.

An arm's length from Blàr, long talons lashed out, tearing flesh from his face. The claws on her other hand found soft belly flesh. Blàr grunted and stumbled to his knees. With his last strength, he grabbed a sword and slashed at the apparition. Blàr's blade was swung in desperation but guided by the Goddess. Half of the young woman's head and part of her shoulder were cleaved and her body collapsed to the parapet.

"No!" yelled Seonag and ran to Blàr.

The Ravens' king clutched his belly in a vain attempt to prevent his guts from escaping. A torn, bloody face smiled at Seonag, and he shook his head. Pointing to the square, he said, "You have command. Kill the bidsean. Hold the walls." As a tearful Seonag turned away, Blàr looked up and smiled at the bean-shìdh who stood before him. She reached out a hand to grasp his.

"Blàr Mac Artair, your brother and father await you in Mag Mell."

✳✳✳

The small group dashed down the steps to the yard, stopping abruptly at the remnant of Sidheag's Brood. Oddly, Sidheag's daughters had barely moved from where they had landed. Furthermore, any effort to reposition seemed laboured, and their faces twisted as if in great pain.

"It's the iron," said Gràinne. "Old Cùil Daothail was built on ancient iron deposits." She nodded to her companions and then spoke to the three females. "You are helpless, and Sidheag cannot help you." Sweeping her longsword from the sheath on her back, Gràinne faced the young women. "I am A 'Bhanrìgh Fuil, and you should have heeded *my* words."

The sword glinted in the moonlight as Gràinne cleaved the first of the daughters' heads. Seonag and Teàrlag followed her example, and soon three heads lay in the snow. Yet there was no time for celebration as a great uproar rose from the walls.

"Back to the parapets! The bidsean achieved their goal. We are breached," shouted Niall.

⁎

Hesitation in battle kills. The shield-walls around the four sides of Cùil Daothail's battlements wavered, although their indecision was understandable. Warriors expect to fight warriors, even if a large part may be no more than adolescents with weapons. Those on the stronghold's ramparts faced farmers and farmers' wives and children.

Worse, many opposed people they knew, were friends with, or whose daughters they rutted. Others faced kin. And so, many delayed their blades only to be impaled on pitchforks, slashed by hoes, and bludgeoned by hammers. Hundreds died before Cùil Daothail's defenders realised these were not the people they knew or had grown up with.

Seonag, Gràinne, Niall, and Teàrlag strode along the blood-soaked walkway, stabbing, slashing, and bellowing, "Fight or be killed!" Yet perhaps the sight of their comrades lying dead on the parapet proved the most effective incentive. Jaws set and teeth ground, the edges of sgiathan clashed as the garrison's shield-wall pulled together. Most had retained a javelin or spear and stabbed over, between, and through the waisted, oblong shields.

The flow over the stockade seemed never-ending. Scores of Sidheag's army were speared and thrown back over the wall and into the ditches. Yet hundreds took their place.

"This cannot go on. We've already lost a third of the garrison, either dead or severely injured. Many are exhausted. Sidheag has not sent her best warriors in, and that is worrisome. I'm open to suggestions," gasped Seonag as she plunged her spear into another farmer's throat.

"Do you trust me?" asked Gràinne.

Seonag inspected Gràinne, and her eyebrow arched. Of all those on the ramparts, Gràinne appeared to be the only one gaining in strength and not covered in blood. "What do you suggest?"

***

The first faint hint of dawn breaking the blackness of night was a thin line of purple-grey on the horizon. Mongfhionn felt the imminence of sunrise and heaved a sigh of relief. It was doubtful whether she could keep her chanting going for much longer and restrain the Hag, let alone Sidheag.

In the forest, Amodocus smiled broadly when Cùil Daothail's war horn's deep *barr-ewww* reverberated across the battlefield. His riders, restless at not joining the battle, checked weapons and walked their heavily armoured mounts to the edge of the tree line.

***

"Open the gates!" bellowed Gràinne.

Then she turned to a blood-splattered Niall. "Have the ballistae ready. I trust you'll know the right moment." Gràinne smiled. "Choose badly, and you'll face a very angry Amodocus."

It took only a few blinks before Sidheag's forward army realised that the great western gates of Cùil Daothail had swung open. Expecting a trap or diversion, the attack stalled for a brief period. Then, mindless and screaming, they flowed across the dirt bridge and rushed the dùn's entranceway. Like a dam breaking, they poured in, and spread out.

At the far end of the yard, two rows of shields—one thousand warriors—led by Teàrlag stood resolute. They were the bait and proved an irresistible target. The horde charged towards them. Yet as they closed on the shield-wall, the unswerving unity that drove them on appeared to falter, as if they were caught in two minds.

"It's the iron," said Gràinne to Seonag. Then, raising her longsword, she roared, "Spears! No mercy! Slaughter the bastards!"

Two thousand missiles, launched from the ramparts, fell like winter hail on Sidheag's army, turning the dirt into blood-red slush. The screaming started. When the barrage halted, Teàrlag's shield-wall, like a giant meat grinder, marched forward, battering, hacking, and slashing anything that moved. Their spears thrown, half of those on the walkways joined Teàrlag in the brawl. The remainder held their position to repel any more besiegers.

The earth trembled along Cùil Daothail's ditch as eight hundred hoofs pounded the snow into hard-packed ice. The unfortunate still on the berm were brushed aside onto the stakes below. Bellows and battle cries filled the air as Amodocus' riders threw heavy darts and javelins into the vanguard of Sidheag's remaining army.

Cries of battle joy rose to meet shrieks of agony when the riders wheeled around and galloped along the forward flank of Sidheag's depleted horde. Maces bashed skulls, and long rhomphaiae slashed flesh to the bone as Amodocus led his warriors to attack the fraying frontline. Amodocus had cleaved the attackers from those in the dùn.

Towards the rear of Sidheag's rattled army, a lone voice rose up and shouted, "Retreat!" The refrain was quickly taken by the horde, and they turned about.

Amodocus turned on his horse, looked at the western wall, and roared, "Now!"

Instantly, twenty ballistae cracked and clattered as a volley of bolts was flung at Sidheag's retreating force. It was followed by the slap of another score of missiles placed into the firing grooves. Ten rounds were shot at Sidheag's army before it was out of range, and Niall bellowed, "Stop!"

From the forest, Sidheag screeched in fury as her army fled the battlefield and the sun rose above the horizon. On the walls of Cùil Daothail,

Mongfhionn ceased her song and grasped the stockade for strength before collapsing to her knees. She muttered a gruff "Thanks" to the warrior, who retrieved her cloak and laid it on her shoulders.

***

Dawn broke over Cùil Daothail. In the forest, Sidheag took stock of her army. Over ten thousand fighters were dead or severely injured and unable to fight. Under her instructions, the latter group had already been corralled into pens and designated as food. The lucky ones, at least in this life, were those who had friends with a sharp blade. Since none would ever pass through the gates of Mag Mell, their relief was temporary, and their sojourn in the Otherworld eternal.

All knew that Sidheag's immediate priority was replenishing her Brood with fresh stock. They also knew the futility, and potential consequences, of trying to hide or disguise any potential candidates. Sidheag's senses were designed to identify the flesh of young females. Therefore, all waited in sullen resignation.

***

In Cùil Daothail, Seonag could taste the funereal atmosphere as she gazed around the stronghold. The garrison had suffered badly and lost at least a third of its warriors. More would die from disease and infection. "The Hag's arse," she spat. "Drostan and over four thousand dead in the first battle and now over two thousand dead in Cùil Daothail." She shook her head and muttered, "Another attack and we're done for."

"She won't attack—at least not here." Seonag started at Mongfhionn's voice.

"Why can't you have a footfall like a normal person?" snapped Seonag.

"I am not 'normal'," said the Sidhe. She looked around as they were joined on the parapet by Amodocus, Gràinne, Niall, and Teàrlag. "Good. Now that we're all here, we must agree on a future strategy. We have some, but not much, time. Sidheag needs to gather a new Brood, feed them and herself, and re-evaluate her strategy. Both sides have suffered grievous losses, and the victor is undecided.

"At first light, Amodocus, Gràinne, and I will ride for the mountains and Sidheag's crannag. Blàr gave us a good indication of where the loch might be." The mention of Blàr was met by a round of curses and vows of retribution. In Seonag's case, tears ran down battle-smudged cheeks.

"There's a practical matter to be decided." This time it was Teàrlag who spoke. Her expression held the sadness of one who had recently lost a hand-fast partner and a friend. "Who will lead the Ravens?"

"It has to be Niall. He was Blàr's shield-man and knows the warriors better than us," said Seonag.

Niall lifted his hands up in protest. "I am low-born and no rìgh."

"We're not looking for a rìgh—yet." Mongfhionn's tone was sharp, having been diverted from what she considered more urgent matters. "The Ravens need a battle commander, and you're it. Live with it. A rìgh can be decided on later."

Teàrlag pointed to the yard, which was carpeted with thousands of bodies, and then swept an arm over the landscape. "What do we do about the dead? I suppose we could leave them for the wolves and ravens."

"Our fallen should be burned on funeral pyres outside Cùil Daothail," said Seonag. Then pointing to Sidheag's dead, she snarled, "They don't deserve respect. Pile the bodies in the square. Soak them in pitch and oil, those in the ditches, too, and burn them to ash." Pausing to calm her bitter inner turmoil, Seonag looked at Niall and added, "Burn Cùil Daothail to the ground and scatter its ashes. The site is an abomination."

Teàrlag placed a hand on Seonag's forearm and squeezed it gently. "Well said, daughter." Then she turned to Mongfhionn. "Where will the bidse attack next?"

"There's only one other stronghold in Northern Albu of strategic importance," answered Mongfhionn.

"Shite!"

CHAPTER 28

393 B.C—Spring

Brion chuckled, causing the eyebrows of those present to arch. Yet his perspective was not focused on the parade of petitioners looking to resolve long-time disputes or receive what they considered deserved recognition and reward. It was the obvious uneasiness of Eimhir. Looking like she had a burr on her arse, she constantly changed position. Yet Brion knew it was not due to physical discomfort.

In the highly organised society of the Gaels, everyone knew their place. At heart, Eimhir was a young woman with strong opinions and un-challenged bravery. She also was very traditional. Brion caught her gaze and held it. "I recall informing you that, in private, you had no need to stand in my presence and could dispense with the use of my titles and un-warranted fawning. Yet my intent was to make you more comfortable, not less. Have I failed?"

Eimhir's eyes widened in shock and embarrassment, and her cheeks flushed at Brion's perceptiveness. The boyish chortling of Cassán and Cearbhall only deepened her colour. She opened her mouth to protest but was halted by a raised palm. "I need you to give me sound counsel. If you wish to stand or walk around the chamber, dip your head to me, or call me whatever honorific you are happy with, please do. I need your mind and talents focused on our many problems, not etiquette."

With a smile and a modest bow, Eimhir pushed her chair back and stood. "Thank you, my king. I think better on my feet."

The atmosphere in the small chamber eased, and Brion said, "Well, the meetings went better than I'd hoped for." He smiled and looked around the room, expecting agreement. Yet the demeanours of Cassán, Cearbhall, and Eimhir did not appear to reflect his optimism. Disgruntled, he shook his head. "What am I so obviously missing?"

Cassán scratched the stubble on a recently scraped head and tugged at the winter growth on his chin. He was not convinced that a beard suited him, but Eimhir liked it, and that was good enough. Additionally, it meant not having to shave until Bealtaine. "I agree that the negotiations went well, Father..."

"But?"

"We have the problem of how to deal with the three who remain unsatisfied." Cassán inhaled deeply, and it was apparent his next words would be distasteful. "Do we dispose of them before or after the main meeting? We have from this sunset until meadhan-latha before the full gathering of the chieftains."

"Can we keep the news of their demise from those attending?"

Eimhir shook her head. "That's unlikely. Cassán's warriors could kill the three and their entourages. However, the likelihood of several escaping our net is high. I recommend we wait until after the gathering. One or two may change their minds."

"I thought I was the optimist."

✳✳✳

The only one of her kind, Sidheag was lonely, but did she understand that emotion? Undoubtedly, the responsibility for her lack of companionship could be laid at her feet. She had killed all who bore any semblance to her or coveted her powers. Her sisters of the Aes Sidhe, the jealous bidsean, had cast her out, leaving Sidheag without friends and at the Goddess's mercy.

Indeed, the blame for her bloodlust should be laid on the shoulders of the Aes Sidhe. They chose to exile rather than understand her. She could have made them more powerful. Perhaps even stronger than the Goddess. Why could they not see her qualities? *How can I be evil if I am just following my nature? And it is not as if the Aes Sidhe or the Goddess are innocents.* Sidheag huffed. *They have bathed in more blood than I could ever hope to achieve. It is so unfair.* Sidheag barely refrained from stamping a cloven foot.

"Why did you, my closest friend, abandon me? I needed you, but you chose to side with my enemies." It was the closest to genuine emotion that Sidheag had ever acknowledged. Yet there was little hint of remorse in her words. Mongfhionn had chosen wrongly and needed to be punished, along with any she held dear. Sidheag looked at Brianag and relished her victory. She had a weapon to use against A 'Bhanrìgh Fuil and Mongfhionn.

To Sidheag, the difference between her and Mongfhionn had become stark. Undoubtedly Sidheag was the more powerful entity, but the humans gladly fought alongside the Sidhe. Sidheag could call on no such loyalty. For the Baobhan Sith, it was about control, slavery, and, of course, food. The humans feared both demi-goddesses, but they would fight and die for the Sidhe.

Sidheag paced the forest clearing, although that did not fully describe the half-prance, half-walk of someone with hoofs, not feet. Agitated at not winning the Battle of Cùil Daothail, she took consolation in the thousands of dead. Her enemy had been significantly weakened, if not vanquished.

However, of more immediate concern was Gràinne's unwelcome ascension to the throne of A 'Bhanrìgh Fuil. To their dismay, the famed demi-gods and goddesses of the Tuatha Dé Danann had found the key to their existence ultimately lay in human hands. Defeated in battle by the ancestors of men, they were exiled to the mounds and underground halls. They took a new name—the Aes Sidhe, to cover their shame.

So it was for Sidheag. Her relationship with the matriarchal society of the Na Daoine Tùrsach had been born out of necessity. Undoubtedly a powerful demi-goddess, circumstance and survival had forced Sidheag to come to an accommodation with a minor tribe with an affinity for blood sacrifice and cannibalism.

Sidheag ground her teeth as she recalled the first Blood Queen. Sidheag had given her visions, which promised power and protection of the Na Daoine Tùrsach and victory over their enemies. Yet the Ancient One was a cunning, shrewd, and brutal woman who had bound Sidheag to uncomfortable conditions.

By Gràinne's grandmother's time, to all intents and purposes, Sidheag had neatly circumvented the roles and terms previously agreed. None challenged her because she permitted them to indulge their worst lusts and desires. *Humans are selfish, have no spine, and are constrained by their short lives and passions.*

In Gràinne, a new, stronger A 'Bhanrìgh Fuil had arisen in the mould of the Ancient One. The Tuireadh had already been turned against Sidheag and threatened her existence. Sidheag's ominous laugh stiffened the fine hairs on the napes of those around her. *Humans are notoriously sentimental about family, and I have Brianag.*

✳✳✳

"Are you sure about this?" asked Eimhir.

Brion dipped his head, although the action had an air of disappointment and resignation. That was understandable. He had reigned over the Na Mèadaidh for over fifteen years. Even Brion's harshest critics acknowledged that the tribe had prospered. His rule was fair and within the law; what more could be expected of him? Yet now, Brion faced the likelihood of a insurrection because of Ealasaid. Eimhir ground her teeth and cursed her bloodline.

Dùn Brion's Great Hall was packed with nobles and chieftains. Many were friendly or open to persuasion or bribery, but a sizeable number were enemies. Also, any conversation was complicated by history. The Gaels rarely forgot or forgave longstanding feuds, and the desire for revenge always bubbled below the surface. Silence fell as Brion's throne scraped the stone platform.

Arms outstretched, Brion inhaled deeply, and his voice boomed out. The lower walls of the chamber, concealed by tapestries and drapes, dampened echoes. Yet the sound rose above that mark and carried whispers, which floated above those gathered. "Welcome to Dùn Brion. I find it sad that these gatherings are only called in times of turmoil… or impending war." Unease rippled through the congregation. "Yet in two sunsets, I am confident we will celebrate Imbolg with steadfast hearts."

Turning to each of those seated alongside him, Brion adopted a business-like tone. "Over the autumn and winter, many things have changed at Dùn Brion. Hence, introductions are in order. Firstly, I introduce my new garrison and battle commander, Cearbhall Ó Domhnaill. He has been seconded to us from Gràinne Ni Fearghal, Bhanrìgh of the Na Daoine Tùrsach's army." At Cearbhall's raised eyebrow, Brion shrugged.

"Where is Seonag? Why is she not your battle commander?" The shout was mischievous and amplified by many others.

"Seonag Nic Drostan…" Brion paused to let the name sink in before continuing, "…the daughter of Drostan Ruadh has assumed the throne of the Forest People. Her father, and four thousand warriors, died in a battle with the army of the Baobhan Sith in the forests to the west of Cùil Daothail." The shock of Brion's statement stunned the nobles into silence. Most had dismissed reports of the Baobhan Sith's return as rumour and wild speculation.

Savouring the impact of his declaration, Brion smiled at Cassán, who stood. "On a more pleasant topic, this is my son, Cassán Mac Brion." A current of astonishment accompanied by gasps of disbelief circulated the room. Most had known Cassán as an obese wastrel who had been cast out by his father.

Brion chuckled. "Those who knew him will see that he has changed considerably." Then the king's demeanour changed dramatically. "He was captured and held in Gormal Mac Eachdonn's dungeons. The same bastard who also cut off his hand." Visceral shouts of "No!" and calls for revenge rose from the floor. At Brion's raised hand, the audience fell silent. "My son and I will have our retribution… soon."

A quick nod in Eimhir's direction made her stop wringing her hands, but it came too late to prevent her from biting her lip. Cassán's hand on her shoulder steadied her, and she stood. "This is Eimhir, who rescued Cassán from Gormal's cells. I have appointed her as commander of my personal security." Relieved at some good news, a great cheer rose, and goblets were banged on wooden tables.

The respite was brief when Brion added, "Her full name is Eimhir Nic Finnean. Some of you may know the family name." Eimhir ignored the gasps of suspicion and fear and concentrated on those who tried to shield their true feelings. In this, she was aided by an army of serving wenches who chose that moment to descend on the tables, ostensibly to refill beer jugs. Each had been briefed to listen carefully and note each table's conversations.

The rolling announcements had served their purpose, creating an air of unease among the assembly. Eimhir stood as the babble subsided. "As our rìgh has said, I am Eimhir Nic Finnean, daughter of Finnean Mac Sèitheach, formerly king of the Na Mèadaidh. He was, as you will recall, an insane, murderous bastard, executed by Mórrígan, rígan of Clann Ui Flaithimh and also known as An Fiagaí Dorcha." Eimhir smiled as many recollected both the king and his executioner.

"Many of you have been visited by envoys from my sister, Ealasaid. She aligns herself with Gormal against Dùn Brion and seeks to claim the throne of the Na Mèadaidh. Ealasaid is not to be trusted. She is a murderous, duplicitous bidse. We will not allow her ambitions to succeed. Ealasaid and Gormal will be confronted, defeated, and sent to the Otherworld."

Eimhir looked to Brion, who stood and said, "Northern Albu is in great turmoil. Many lives have already been sacrificed. Sadly, much more blood will be spilt. To survive, the Na Mèadaidh must be united under one banner and one rìgh." Brion stared at his nobility. "Today, you have a choice to make. Kneel and swear fealty to me as your rightful rìgh or leave Dùn Brion as my enemy. There is no other choice."

* * *

"You have to go, sister."

In the small sanctuary of her mind, Brianag looked at Neamhain and wept. Neamhain set her jaw and shook her head. "I will not desert you, and you cannot force me to. Neither can Sidheag."

"I cannot bear you to see my fall. My path is a dark and foul journey to a place from which I may never return. We both know that I cannot resist Sidheag forever, but I may be able to make her fear me." Brianag put her arms around Neamhain and held her tightly. "Remember me as I was, sister. Please, go now. I hope you will be waiting for me should I return."

In the crannag, Brianag wailed inconsolably as darkness overcame her sanctuary, and nothing good remained. Then her jaw set, and she padded across the room to Seirbhiseach. Violet-red eyes looked into ones as black as night, and he flinched. "We should talk, priest."

Seirbhiseach nodded but wondered curiously at the clicking noise. He gulped as he watched crimson talons grow from Brianag's fingers. Yet when she smiled, that was much worse. Brianag's adolescent teeth had been overthrown by rows of long, needle-pointed incisors.

Far away, and each in her cot, the Sidhe and Gràinne sat bolt upright and cried out, "We're coming!"

"Too late," came the reply. A tear rolled down Brianag's cheek, and then she locked them out of her mind.

✷✷✷

In his heart, Seirbhiseach knew there would be no redemption. He had been a willing fool in the resurrection of the Baobhan Sith. The blood she continued to spill stained his hands. Added to this, the threat from the Sidhe hung around his neck like a kern stone. Yet as she commanded, he had protected Brianag. For that, the priest hoped Mongfhionn might speak to the Goddess on his behalf. Perhaps the Goddess might find a place of lesser torment for him in the Otherworld.

As he observed Brianag's manner, the priest became more terrified of her than of the Sidhe or Sidheag. His mouth trembled as he recalled their recent talk—the black eyes that held him and refused to release him, her deep red lips, and the needle-like teeth.

Seirbhiseach's heart pounded in his chest, and he could barely control his breathing at the sound of her talons clicking. His stomach roiled at the stench of decaying flesh when she came close enough to breathe on him. More than this, the cold, pitiless manner in which she spoke would have blanched his hair, had any remained—and if it were not already white.

Comfortable in her nakedness, Brianag stood before him, radiating a primaeval sensuality. Her body was many summers older than when she first arrived at the crannag. Yet Seirbhiseach's manhood remained un-moved, and drool did not dribble down his chin. Fear had replaced lust. Once more, he prayed to the Goddess, and again, he expected no answer.

＊

As she entered the crannag, Sidheag glanced to where Brianag lay and pursed her lips. *What a pity she's not a pure blood.* This night, before fleeing the loch, she would take Brianag hunting, and the young girl would cross a final threshold, from whence there was no return.

She observed the miserable priest, moaning and rocking as he warmed his bones at the firepit. His usefulness had ended. Sidheag hissed in dis-appointment because his body had hardly any blood or meat. He would provide only fleeting nourishment for her. *I will give him to my new daughters to practice feeding.*

Her attention was momentarily diverted by rumblings of discontent from outside the crannag. Five hundred priests cursed the cold. Hoping to forestall frostbite, they clapped hands and stamped feet on the wooden jetty. Sidheag smiled. They were the dregs of her priesthood but would serve her purpose.

At Sidheag's clip-clopping steps on the wooden floor, Brianag smiled and rose from her cot. It was a twisted, uneven smile as her jaw had not fully adjusted to her new teeth. She walked, with a sensual sway of her hips, to where Seirbhiseach sat. The High Priest ignored her until she hissed, "Stand, priest, and face your Mistress." Seirbhiseach rose slowly, and Sidheag growled. Seirbhiseach turned to face Brianag, not her.

"We have a traitor in our midst, Mother." Brianag smiled at Sidheag, and the apparition started, for behind Brianag's full red lips were rows of needle-like teeth. "He thought to use me as a weapon against you. A silly idea, of course, although he did divert your attention from my training. Yet as you can see, that proved to be quite ineffective." Brianag's long talons clicked before she caressed Seirbhiseach's throat.

Sidheag dipped her head, yet within her obsidian eyes were glimmers of suspicion, wariness, and a hint of fear. Brianag's professed loyalty had been expected and inevitable, but the timing was Brianag's, not hers. The fine hairs on the Baobhan Sith's nape stiffened. *Why can I not see into her mind?*

"He is yours to deal with, *daughter*."

"Find peace, priest," whispered Brianag in Seirbhiseach's ear. "For what it is worth, I thank you."

The priest smiled at Brianag's deception. The girl had changed. Whether for the better, only the Goddess knew. He felt his head tilted, and needle-sharp teeth seized his flesh. His throat was gone in seconds and his belly opened by razor-edged fingernails. Blood streamed over Brianag's breasts and down her belly. She turned to Sidheag with strings of meat trailing from her teeth.

"Not much meat on him, but his blood does feel pleasantly warm on my skin."

Brianag turned to face the always-present Brood. "You may have the remains." Sidheag's eyes narrowed. A growl rose from her belly and escaped through tightly pursed lips. Her new daughters obeyed Brianag without hesitation. In her impatience, had she given Brianag too much of her blood?

Sidheag's eyes widened with sudden realisation. Until Brianag, she had never fed her blood to any other. Certainly, not one whose veins had the blood of A 'Bhanrìgh Fuil and an impure human. "No!" she gasped. *What have I created?* Sidheag shook her head. She would deal with the adolescent later and destroy her if needed. At this time, she urgently needed a real army and commanders experienced in war. Her undisciplined horde required structure, and she knew where to find it.

"More training would be a waste of time, Brianag. We leave for the west immediately. We will feed on the way."

✶✶✶

It was meadhan-oidhche, and several braziers burned brightly in the small chamber. The ebb and flow of light from the mix of oak and pine, the warmth, and the pleasant pine scent imbued the room with an atmosphere perfect for a romantic evening. That was dispelled when Brion ordered servants to place rushlights in the iron sconces nailed to each wall. Those present needed illumination, not subtle lighting.

"What is your report?" Eimhir had dreaded the question. She stood, placed her palms on the oak wood table, and looked each man in the eye.

"The good news is that over three-fourths of the nobles swore fealty to the king, which is better than I expected. The bad news is in two parts. Firstly, from my sources, I believe three spoke falsely when making their oath. Secondly, including this group, the disloyal number a dozen chieftains. Most are minor, but a few have substantial armies. I reckon they can field upwards of two thousand men."

"That means we have over three thousand warriors to defend Dùn Brion, which is a reasonably good outcome," said Cearbhall. "Plus, we have the bolt throwers."

"Can we reduce our enemy's numbers?" asked Cassán, looking at Eimhir. Her brow puckered, for she knew what he was asking.

"Most of those who refused to swear loyalty to the rìgh departed Dùn Brion hastily after the ceremony. Apart from those whose homes, farmsteads, and villages are at the most westerly end of the Sleagh, the rest are too distant to strike." Eimhir bit her lip, tasting salt and iron. "The three who spoke falsely are camped beyond the dùn—with their families and guards."

She looked at Cassán. "I will go with you and direct your men."

Cassán shook his head and said, "You have done enough. Stay here and rest."

Eimhir's jaw set. "If I am to cause their death, the least I can do is to be there when they are executed."

As Cassán opened the door to follow Eimhir from the room, Brion quickly crossed the chamber to stand at his side. "They all must die—young and old, male and female. Others who have given their oath falsely must fear retribution." Brion inhaled deeply and softly said, "Perhaps Cearbhall and I should lead the men."

Cassán gave a wan smile in the flickering rushlight and shook his head. "A son must learn how to be a king."

✷✷✷

The scattered corpses were an ugly blemish on the pristine snow surrounding the crannag. Yet, they did not bleed long before they froze. It was spring, but that would not be felt for several cycles of the moon in the highlands of north-eastern Albu. The skirmish—it hardly deserved to be called a battle— did not last long. Five hundred ill-equipped priests proved no match for the Sidhe or Gràinne and her riders.

Mongfhionn and Gràinne strode along the long bridge to Sidheag's crannag while Amodocus supervised the disposal of the priests. That said, this amounted to little more than rolling or tossing the bodies onto the still-frozen loch. Come the thaws of spring, the remains of the cadavers not devoured by wolves would sink below the cold, deep waters.

Neither woman expected to find Brianag or Sidheag. Brianag's last bitter cry still rang in their ears. Yet could they ignore the faint flame that flickered in their hearts? With a deep breath, they entered the crannag and confirmed their fears. The only occupant of the residence was the frozen, emaciated body of Seirbhiseach. The cause of his death was evident, but not who had disembowelled him and torn out his throat. Still, as Mongfhionn inspected the body, she had her suspicions.

"We will make the bitseach pay in ways she can never comprehend," snarled the Sidhe.

"And just how will that help Brianag, Mother?"

The bitterness in Gràinne's voice pierced the Sidhe's heart. No response from her would give Gràinne comfort. "We know where Sidheag is going. You and Amodocus should ride for Dùn Brion. I will go to Cùil Daothail and inform Seonag and Teàrlag that they should march west to the stronghold."

"Inform?" Gràinne's lips curled.

"No matter the words. They must go to Dùn Brion, or we will lose everything."

"I already have lost everything."

A furious Mongfhionn grabbed Gràinne by the shoulder and shook her like a sack of grain. "No, you have not," hissed the Sidhe. "Until I see her corpse, I will not give up on Brianag. You also have Heilasa and Amodocus." Gràinne flinched at Mongfhionn's ferocious mien.

"I have no time for whining self-pity. We made decisions. They could have been better, but we will live with them, learn from them, and make better ones in the future. At worst, we will dispense retribution."

"Bitseach!"

"Yes, I am and always will be. But who would A 'Bhanrìgh Fuil rather have at her side when going to war?"

✳✳✳

"We lost a chieftain," said Eimhir.

"A friend of the three?"

Eimhir shook her head. "No, I had counted him as loyal to us. I spoke with him this morning. He informed me that he had no issues executing the three traitors whose heads are spiked on the walls." Eimhir paused, looked at Brion, and continued, "However, he said the slaughter of their families brought dishonour on the Na Mèadaidh… and you. He has withdrawn his support and, with it, five hundred warriors."

"When his lands and property are seized or burning under Gormal or Ealasaid's rule, it will be too late for honour," retorted Brion.

CHAPTER 29

Ealasaid surveyed the gathering army and then turned to face Gormal and Madadh. Her sardonic expression needed no words, but she could not resist commenting. "This is all you can muster. I make it no more than five thousand warriors—and that's being generous. How many are veterans and not children ripped from their mothers' tits?"

Gormal's demeanour grew darker than the early spring storm clouds, although, in Northern Albu, the season was little different from winter. "I will not leave Dùn Athad defenceless."

Ealasaid's lips curled upwards. In the pre-storm light, both men thought her quite unattractive. Still, Ealasaid's mood mirrored the thunder and lightning rolling down the high mountains.

"The campaign has yet to start, and you're already preparing for defeat." Ealasaid straightened her shoulders, pulled herself up, and glared at Gormal. That she towered over Gormal made him uncomfortable, and he pulled his fur closer to disguise the reaction. As for Madadh, Ealasaid sneered at him, contemptuous of a man who let himself be cowed by his hand-fast partner. *How did I arrive at a place where I needed these weaklings?*

"I do not see the army of the Na Mèadaidh," countered Gormal. "Where are your vaunted thousands loyal to the memory of your beloved father? How is the rebellion going? Is Dùn Brion in turmoil?" Gormal paused and hissed through the gaps in his crooked teeth, "I think not."

"They will meet us on the plain north of Dùn Brion," snapped Ealasaid, diverting attention from her growing nervousness. Her informants had fled Dùn Brion after Imbolg, and their final messages were not comforting. Sympathetic nobles and their families had been slaughtered, and chieftains were forced to swear allegiance. The rumours of a warband led by her sister and Cassán burning farms and settlements loyal to her father raised her apprehension. Yet, Ealasaid's lips thinned in a grim smile. The terror created by Eimhir was precisely the strategy she would have executed.

"Know this, bidse, I know what has taken place in Dùn Brion and among the Na Mèadaidh. Far from being weakened, Brion has consolidated his power and is well-positioned to withstand a siege. In our favour, however, Northern Albu is in turmoil, and no help is coming to his rescue. Now is the only opportunity to dethrone that bastard, but many will die before his surrender or death." Ealasaid opened her lips to speak, but Gormal's raised hand stopped her.

"You have undoubted talents as an assassin and a whore," said Gormal. He smirked as Ealasaid's cheeks blushed at the insult. "But know this: my chieftains and commanders have orders to make you die very painfully, should anything happen to me. Even should the fault not lie at your feet." Gormal's smile was cruel and smug when he added, "You live only because I live."

✳✳✳

As the pyre for Blàr flared against a night sky devoid of moon or starlight, a sombre trio stood, heads bowed. Each was an island surrounded by stormy seas of conflicting responsibilities and thoughts. At their backs, the charred ruins of Cùil Daothail smouldered. Dark smoke curled upwards, unseen but felt by the scents of smoke and charred flesh.

The group mourned the thousands who had died—fathers, mothers, sons and daughters, lovers, and youth. Many wondered whether the battle had been a futile attempt to hold back the inevitable. The sound of barking diverted their attention beyond the slowly disappearing walls of Cùil

Daothail. Packs of scavengers foolishly fought over carcasses preserved by the freezing weather. There were many more bodies to devour than their bellies could hold.

"Snap out of it!" Mongfhionn's interruption startled the group. Her callousness brought angry flushes to smoke- and blood-smudged cheeks. "Now is not the time for grieving. If you want to join Blàr, stab yourself and fall onto his pyre. There is a battle to be fought and won."

"It's after sunset. We can't travel in the darkness," retorted Teàrlag to a chorus of agreement.

"Yes, you can. Do you think Sidheag's army waits for the dawn? No. They are already several sunsets ahead of you." Mongfhionn gripped Seonag and Teàrlag's eyes—an impossible feat, given the darkness. Yet, both women felt unable to break the Sidhe's spell. "Choose which of you will journey to the Forest People and who will march to Dùn Brion. The Forest People need to be alerted, an army raised to defend Dùn Brion, and the rest escorted to the high forests."

"We've already lost five thousand warriors and a king. Is that not enough?" snapped Teàrlag.

"If Sidheag is not stopped, you will lose ten thousand more—and the strongest clann in Northern Albu will be no more. Who do you wish to sit on the Forest People's throne—Seonag or Sidheag? Choose whether to be food or warriors. There are no other options."

"I will take what remains of the Ravens' and Forest People's armies in Cùil Daothail and march for Dùn Brion," said Seonag.

"Is that wise?" asked Teàrlag.

Seonag shook her head. "No, but it's sensible. The Forest People's Council will be persuaded better by you than by one they haven't seen in many summers." Seonag looked at Niall. "How many wagons do we have?"

"Only ten have full teams of oxen."

"Dismantle twenty ballistae and load the parts onto the wagons. Burn the rest." Niall dipped his head.

"What of Gràinne and Brianag?" asked Seonag.

"Gràinne and Amodocus ride for Dùn Brion. I have a pair of horses for Teàrlag to speed her travels." Mongfhionn turned abruptly and swung up onto her black mare. She faced the group with a face flitting horrifyingly between the Sidhe and the Hag. "Do not disappoint us." The chill in her voice froze everyone's blood.

"What troubles me is that she never spoke of Brianag," said Seonag, putting the others' thoughts into words.

✳✳✳

Standing on Dùn Brion's ramparts, Brion looked north, screwed up his eyes, and scowled. A hard day's walk in the distance, the densely forested mountains of the Forest People rose up. On this sunrise, they were shrouded by gently undulating ribbons of low-lying mist. To the south-west were similar but closer hills. None scraped the skies like the great peaks of the far north, but few could climb them without being out of breath.

To the north-west was the start of the vast plain between the highlands and the lowlands. The land remained carpeted in slowly receding snow and lakes of slush. "That's my problem," he muttered. Predominantly flat and thickly forested with alder, oak, and pine trees, the long plain formed the only viable access to Dùn Brion. Gormal's army could approach the fort unseen by staying in the trees.

Brion turned at the heavy footfall of Cearbhall and smiled. The burly warrior could never be accused of being dainty or light-footed. As if guessing Brion's thoughts, Cearbhall gave a great belly laugh. Then, reading Brion's expression, he said astutely, "There's no sense worrying about where they might be. We'll see them when they reach the meadowlands."

The rìgh nodded. The pastureland to the immediate north of Dùn Brion was immense. A man at a leisurely pace would take from dawn to meadhan-latha to traverse the strip of land. Dùn Brion's garrison would know the scale of the challenge when Gormal's army broke from the forest cover.

Horn blasts and shouts at the southern gate prompted the two men to run to the wall.

"Open the bloody gates, or I'll tear them down!" The voice was clear and commanding. Brion rolled his eyes. Only one person would announce themselves in that manner.

***

"Summon the chieftains and nobles to the Great Hall. I wish to look them in the eye." Mongfhionn brushed past Brion and Cearbhall as if they were little more than tall grass bending to a stiff wind. As if recalling something, she turned and barked another order. "Send a messenger to Cassán and Eimhir. Order them to return to the fort along with their chomhairle."

Brion bristled at the presumption and disrespect. The Sidhe had no patience for fools. However, this time her manner seemed to go beyond that and into the realm of distrust and suspicion. *What happened in Cùil Daothail?*

"Your choice is simple, Brion, Rìgh of Na Mèadaidh, and the same one I gave Drostan. Obey me, or I will remove you." An imperious yet oddly fragile-looking hand stopped whatever words Brion formed from leaving his lips. "Gràinne and Amodocus will arrive in three sunsets. Seonag should arrive with the remnant of Cùil Daothail's defenders in seven sunsets. Either of those would make a suitable replacement for you. Perhaps even Cassán."

"You cannot impose your will on a free people," exploded Brion.

"I can, I will, and I have," spat Mongfhionn. "Choose who you would rather serve—the Baobhan Sith or me. There is no other choice. Believe me, I am the lesser of two evils."

"What of my daughter? What of Brianag?"

"She marches with Sidheag. Willingly, I suspect," snarled Mongfhionn. "First, we will deal with Sidheag. Then *I* will decide what is to be done about Brianag."

Brion's anger flared. "She is Gràinne's and my responsibility, not yours, my Lady."

"That was when she was human. Whether she still is, remains to be

247

tested." A brief mask of despair covered Mongfhionn's face as she beheld Brion's stricken mien. "I am sorry."

As the door closed, Brion slumped in his seat. To Cearbhall, the king looked suddenly frail and older. Brion looked up at Cearbhall. "What sort of father am I? I failed my son, but the Goddess gave me a second chance. Now, I have failed my daughter. Mongfhionn says she has become a monster." His head in his hands, a flood of tears splashed the oak table. Yet when he looked up, Brion's demeanour was one of grim resolution. "I refuse to give up on Brianag. No matter what she may have become, she is my daughter."

✳✳✳

"What is your plan, *Mother*?" asked Brianag.

That she had a daughter who spoke to her unsettled Sidheag's usual disposition. Furthermore, the taint of disrespect in Brianag's voice was undisguised. It jangled what substituted for Sidheag's nerves. Had she been as impertinent to Gràinne? Were all human adolescents ill-tempered and argumentative? Sidheag looked to her Brood, who gnawed contentedly on the bones of a dozen malcontents. *These are malleable, obedient, and expendable.*

The Baobhan Sith growled. Observing her daughters drew another comparison with Brianag. Her skin had lost the golden glow of a life in the lands of the Great Sea and now shone pale as goat's milk. Yet she did not look sickly. The evidence was a body resembling Sidheag's curvaceousness more than an awkward girl of fifteen summers.

Brianag's long, thick tresses of auburn hair proved the perfect foil to her pallor. Her cheeks were a pleasing shade of pink, set off by piercing, deep emerald eyes that became almost black when she hunted. "Hunted," hissed Sidheag. Yes, Brianag hunted, and yet that made Sidheag uneasy. Brianag tended to be a solitary predator, but sometimes the Brood followed her—without Sidheag's permission.

However, Brianag's pick of human prey, most of whom were healthy leaders, disturbed Sidheag. The fact that she made a choice at all irritated the Baobhan Sith. The Brood ate whomever and whatever Sidheag commanded. Brianag appeared to eat with a purpose. *What is her plan? Does the bidse think she can take my place?*

"Mother, you didn't answer me. What is your plan?" The mocking formality of Brianag's use of "Mother" caused a rumble of irritation that began in Sidheag's stomach and progressed rapidly to her lips. It was barely forestalled by a smile of blood-red lips and needle-like teeth.

"All in good time, my daughter."

The smug satisfaction on Brianag's face drew an angry flush to Sidheag's prominent cheekbones. It was then another issue surfaced. *How could I have overlooked that, even in the gloom? Did it just happen, and what does it mean? Was it a mistake to feed my blood to one whose veins were filled with the blood of A 'Bhanrìgh Fuil?* Never before had Sidheag's mind been so uncertain.

Brianag's Greek-style chiton was not white as Sidheag's or her Brood's. Its colour perfectly matched her green eyes. Sidheag watched as Brianag transformed into her wolf persona and, with a howl, bounded into the forest. Yet even the undulating yowl seemed to mock Sidheag. *What have I created?*

From the trees came another howl—or was it laughter?

✲✲✲

The atmosphere in the Great Hall swung from annoyance and rebellion to resigned acceptance that the Sidhe could kill them all in a breath. A score of chieftains, who commanded almost three thousand warriors, had gathered. They tugged great whiskers and polished the pommels of well-used and sharp-edged swords with calloused palms.

Mongfhionn slammed the gnarled head of her ancient staff on the oak table. As she was already standing, it proved an efficient method of silencing her audience. "I know your thoughts." The voice was imperious and compelling. It was also terrible. In turn, the Sidhe stared at each chieftain, and, to a man, none challenged her obsidian gaze.

"To the traitors and oath-breakers among you. Crawl on your belly from this place and seek refuge under a rock." The smile that lit on the Sidhe's full red lips sent chills up spines. "Although, I doubt you will get that far."

Cassán dipped his head to Eimhir's ear and whispered, "Why didn't you think of that approach?" A sharp kick to his ankle was her answer.

"Eimhir did better than most," retorted Mongfhionn. "Perhaps you would permit me to continue?" Cassán reddened at coming under the Sidhe's attention and muttered his apologies. His colour deepened at Eimhir's chortling beside him.

"The Baobhan Sith has risen." While a few had stubbornly refused to believe the claims from the north-eastern highlands, Mongfhionn's statement gave them no room for interpretation. "Drostan Ruadh is dead, along with over four thousand warriors." Anger and fear rippled through the assembly, but the Sidhe had not finished. "Blàr Mac Artair is also dead, along with over three thousand fighters. Cùil Daothail is little more than a smudge of ash." Silence descended on the chamber, along with a flurry of nervous glances.

"The Baobhan Sith, Sidheag, travels west to the stronghold of Dùn Brion accompanied by her Brood and an army of over ten thousand. She will enthral many more on the way." Before proceeding, Mongfhionn paused to allow the stir to settle down.

"Sidheag and her Brood have weaknesses, which we shall discuss as well as countermeasures. However, one shortcoming is a lack of battle-ready commanders and captains. She has a horde, but she needs an army." Mongfhionn paused for emphasis. "There is only one place that she can get that expertise and one rìgh who will be unable to resist her."

"The Hag's arse! Gormal!" snarled Brion. "Can anything be done to prevent this alliance?" Mongfhionn's silence was ominous.

✻✻✻

As the nobles and chieftains departed the chamber, Brion stood and placed a hand on Mongfhionn's forearm. "I will not kill my daughter."

"Neither will I kill my sister," said Cassán. More pragmatically, Eimhir and Cearbhall appeared less unwilling to consider the possibility.

"If need be, you will, or you will die," thundered Mongfhionn. Then in a more reasonable tone, she elaborated: "Like Sidheag's daughters, she may be a mere shadow, a husk of the Brianag you knew. Sidheag fed Brianag blood from her veins if only to keep her from freezing in the mountains. I have no idea whether Brianag remains aware of who she is, because she banished Neamhain and closed her mind to Gràinne and me."

Brion's eyebrow lifted, and he held Mongfhionn's gaze. "You say Brianag banished Neamhain, Gràinne, and you—a Sidhe." Brion's tone was incredulous. "Tell me, my Lady, does that sound like someone who has no will or is no more than a puppet?"

Irritated by Brion's astuteness, Mongfhionn side-stepped his observation. "The Aes Sidhe have never dealt with such a phenomenon. How Sidheag's blood has twisted Brianag, no one can know." Mongfhionn frowned. "And we have no idea what designs she may have formed." The Sidhe inhaled deeply, and those around the table braced for more unpleasant news. "She is still an adolescent, which may add to her instability and unpredictability."

⁎⁎⁎

Brianag awoke as the dawn light bathed the wildwood. On the edge of the ancient forest, her chosen location was more vulnerable than the depths of the woods. Yet, unlike Sidheag, she preferred sunlight over the perpetual gloom under the canopy of the tall oaks and pines. Sunlight gave Brianag freedom and advantage, but how to use it?

A tear meandered down her cheek, skirting the dried blood and fragments of flesh. *I should not have to think of such things.* Brianag's mind told her that she was fifteen summers, but her body disagreed. Seeking comfort, she nestled closer to her still-warm victim. The long belly slash allowed her to rub against the animal's exposed organs.

She did not mind the slush of gore and writhed to fully cover her body in the blood. "Better than a mud bath." She giggled. It seemed so long ago that she puked even at the thought of what now was no more than food and pleasure. She smiled as she remembered how Seirbhiseach had cleaned her messes in the crannag.

"Thanks," she whispered. "I hope the Goddess has given you respite." Then she howled. "It's more than she ever gave me. I was faithful in my sacrifices, but that was a waste." Brianag sobbed. "No one cares."

Then she snarled, and another feral howl escaped her lips. They did this to her. None, save Seirbhiseach and Neamhain, had helped her. Everyone who had professed their love for her and sworn to protect her had abandoned her to Sidheag. Even now, they were probably more focused on destroying Sidheag than rescuing her. *Can I be saved?* Adolescent petulance joined with rage, and she howled again. Then Brianag sobbed for just one embrace in her da's arms.

From Brianag's lips came three names. "Gràinne, Mongfhionn, and Sidheag." She would make them suffer. Even better, if there was any justice, her hand would send them to the Otherworld.

Brianag stood and stretched. There was no speck of blood on her milk-pale body or on the emerald-green léine that shrouded her curves. She grinned as she recalled that Sidheag and the Sidhe never had to deal with bloodstains. *That may be the only benefit of this curse.*

Sidheag would be wondering about her daughter's whereabouts. Brianag needed Sidheag hesitant but not actively hunting her. She took a pace away from the body and stopped. Then she reached down and ripped a piece of flesh from the corpse's belly. "A snack for the journey."

CHAPTER 30

Night frosts kept the surface of the snow solid until boots crunched through its icy veneer. The snowfall was knee-deep, but Madadh said that was no bad thing. "Apart from some pools of slush from increasingly frequent showers, it keeps the ground firm. Otherwise, we'd be marching and fighting in a bog." Gormal grunted at his shield-man's wisdom and shivered as a brisk wind sought to undo the warmth of his thick wolf fur.

He glared with undisguised animosity at Ealasaid, who stood nearby, basking in the admiration of a group of foolish captains. Their aspirations were straightforward: they vied for the privilege of rutting the striopach. It was highly likely that some, if not all, would be successful. Ealasaid's carnal appetite seemed bottomless.

That said, the unrestrained satisfaction of her natural desires angered Madadh's young kinsman. He saw Ealasaid as a future hand-fast partner. Stupid boy! She was more likely to rut him, tire of him, and cut his throat. Ealasaid's ambitions were much higher than a lowly captain in Gormal's army.

"She'll have to be killed," said Gormal.

Madadh nodded his agreement. Although undoubtedly pleasurable, access to Ealasaid's body and pit came at a high cost. Gormal's voice was soft, but few conversations remained secret in the crisp air of a Northern Albu dawn. As Gormal spoke, Ealasaid turned to face the two men and smiled. Her mien shouted, *Try it!*

As dawn broke, Gormal's army reached the limits of the forest cover. Another few paces and they would emerge from the treeline and enter the plain north of Dùn Brion. They would be visible, yet given the distance to Brion's stronghold, they would appear no more than tiny specks against the whiteness.

"Brion will have posted lookouts in the treelines, and some of those humps of snow are likely warriors covered with thick hides. He'll know we are here," said Madadh.

Gormal dipped his head in agreement. "Do you wonder at the wisdom of this?"

"It's too late for such thoughts now."

To Gormal, Madadh's retort was abrupt and disrespectful. It was also imprudent. "Send people to survey the landscape. Find a good place to pitch our camp, preferably on high ground." Madadh made to walk away, but Gormal's hand forestalled the act. "Have *her* watched. When the dùn is ours, kill her."

✷✷✷

Most times, the small room was used for intimate gatherings between friends and allies. However, as Brion glanced around the table, he wished he had organised the meeting in the Great Hall. The tension was palpable. Indeed, the only ones who looked relaxed were Amodocus and Cearbhall. That, however, was due to the volume of beer each had drunk.

According to Gràinne, who had entered Dùn Brion at sunrise, Seonag would arrive in six or seven sunsets. Brion let a soft moan escape his lips at that thought, causing curious glances and expressions. He shook his head irritably. Until he passed through the veil, his thoughts were his own. Yet the mocking smile on Mongfhionn's face suggested his logic was flawed.

"Where is my sister? And why have you not rescued her?"

Cassán's question to the Sidhe came out of nowhere. That he was ignorant of his father's recent conversation with Mongfhionn became quickly apparent. Eimhir murmured in agreement while Cearbhall gasped, knowing the path the conversation would take.

"Do not go down this path, son," said Brion, but Cassán brushed off the advice.

"It was, after all, what you rode to Cùil Daothail to do, wasn't it?" The sharpness of Cassán's tone caused Mongfhionn's cheeks to burn red—a remarkable, if imprudent, achievement.

"We misjudged Sidheag. When we got to her crannag, Brianag was already gone." The Sidhe's voice trembled. "I almost lost Neamhain, too."

"But you didn't." There was no compassion in Cassán's words. Gràinne choked at Cassán's words. *He has no idea.* She opened her mouth to defend her ma, but Cassán spoke first. "And for what? A Pyrrhic victory at Cùil Daothail? A bloody nose to Sidheag. Was it worth it?"

Amodocus looked apprehensively at Cassán and Cearbhall and then at Eimhir and Gràinne. He wanted to grasp the hilt of his sword, yet he knew that would be a grave error. So he resisted and prayed to his gods for a peaceful resolution. They had Gormal and Sidheag to fight, not each other. His hopes were quickly dashed.

Cassán looked at Eimhir and smiled. Yet his demeanour changed rapidly to displeasure, and he glowered at Mongfhionn. "A stranger rescued me from Gormal's dungeons. Yet Brianag could not count on her powerful grandmother, one of the Aes Sidhe, to save her?" Cassán turned his ire on Gràinne. "And *you* prevented me from going to her aid. Where is my sister?"

"She fights alongside Sidheag." Mongfhionn, growling like a wolf, rose, straightened her shoulders, and drew herself up to her full threatening height. The oak staff in her hand trembled in a white-knuckled grip. Only Gràinne's hand on her forearm stopped whatever the Sidhe had in mind.

The speed at which Gràinne moved shocked all in the room except Mongfhionn. In a room that had suddenly fallen silent, only the sound of Cassán's choking broke the silence. Eimhir rose to help, but the savage look from Gràinne made her fall back onto her seat. "For one who recently tried to kill my daughter and your sister with a spear in the back, your defence of Brianag lacks credibility," hissed Gràinne.

So close were their faces that flecks of spittle sprayed Cassán's increasingly purple face. Cassán's eyes widened until he thought they would burst, for he looked into the blood-red eyes and swirling sigils of A 'Bhanrìgh Fuil.

"Shite!" gasped Cearbhall.

Brion's hand went to his sword but stopped when Gràinne snarled, "Touch it, and I'll rip his throat out." Turning back to her victim, Gràinne's lips curled upwards. "This is what *I* had to become to rescue *my* daughter. Do you think I wanted or relished it? Without A 'Bhanrìgh Fuil, there could be no saving Brianag." Gràinne looked at the Sidhe. "Without this creature at her side, my mother could never defeat Sidheag."

With an effortless flick of Gràinne's wrist, Cassán was flung to the chamber's stone floor. Only the sound of his head hitting the wall and his descent into blackness stopped his struggles for breath. "We should go, Mother. Let these arseholes fight Gormal and Sidheag. Our duty is to Brianag."

The room's doors slammed shut behind Gràinne, Mongfhionn, and Amodocus, and Cearbhall exclaimed, "The Hag's tits, now we're in trouble."

✳✳✳

From the gloom of the deep woods to the east of the plain, Sidheag watched Gormal's army emerge from the treeline and choose a location for their encampment. She was impressed by their order and how the encampment was protected by traps and stockades. They would be useless against her but effective against humans.

Sidheag pondered her strategy. A cunning creature, like most predators, she relied on instinct, which had let her down at Cùil Daothail. Undoubtedly, she and her Brood could enthral Gormal's army or terrorise them into submission by selecting a sizeable sample to feed on. She chuckled. Was there a difference? Still, was that the best plan?

Brianag's right eyebrow lifted fleetingly, but Sidheag ignored her. The child was a problem to resolve, but not now. She had other more pressing priorities. The most immediate was her lack of experienced leaders. Thus, she ruled out enthralling Gormal's battle commander, captains, and chieftains. Her teeth ground against each other at having to admit she needed veterans with free will.

She chortled again. Yes, they would have free will, but only until she defeated her enemies and ruled Northern Albu. In the meantime, she would incentivise their cooperation by demonstrating how unwise it would be to refuse to command her army. That said, Sidheag judged the time was not right for her to intervene. She needed to observe how Gormal's army fought without her.

Cries of distress interrupted the Baobhan Sith's musings. She looked to a nearby pen into which dozens of men, women, and children had been herded. It was time for her and her daughters to feed. A frown fluttered on Sidheag's normally wrinkle-free brow, and she stared at Brianag. That Brianag knew of her attention and yet ignored her irked Sidheag. *How much does the bidse know of my thoughts?*

A turn of Brianag's head was followed by a knowing smile on plump, inviting, red lips. *All of them, Mother. Yet do you know mine?* Once again, Sidheag's teeth ground against each other. She had her unwelcome answer. The Baobhan Sith's cold eyes turned to the pen. None would die quickly or painlessly today.

* * *

Mongfhionn lay on the cot in her chamber and reflected that she was acquiring too many human traits. For there was little doubt that she was sulking.

"You must rise, Mother. Many are counting on you." The soft, chiding voice of Neamhain brought a smile to Mongfhionn's lips, and her eyes opened wide.

"I have failed Brianag and made her and Gràinne nightmares."

"No. Although many of the Aes Sidhe think they are omniscient,

257

neither they nor you know everything. That is the realm of the Goddess. You have not failed Brianag or Gràinne—yet. However, if you continue to lie on your back brooding, you may well fulfil that prophecy.

"Get up from your bed, Mother. Brianag needs you, Gràinne needs you, and your friends, who are many, need you, as do the people of Dùn Brion and the North. Sidheag needs to be destroyed, but without Gràinne and you, she cannot be defeated." Inhaling deeply and with determination, Neamhain said, "Either you rise and fight, or I will openly enter the battle. Do you wish to lose me? We both know I cannot best the Baobhan Sith, *but I will try.*"

Mongfhionn's chest heaved, and she sat upright abruptly. A deafening cry of "No!" resounded off the room's stone walls.

∗∗∗

The door to Gràinne's room burst open, startling her and Amodocus, who sprang to his feet, sword in hand. It was obvious that Gràinne had been crying. A long, slim finger plucked the tear rolling down Gràinne's cheek, and the Sidhe smiled. "I think we have had enough tears, daughter. Now it's time to fight."

∗∗∗

"Neither Gràinne nor I intend to apologise, but maybe your son should consider it." The whirlwind that was Mongfhionn appeared suddenly before Brion as he peered to the north at Gormal's growing encampment. In her wake trailed a much happier Gràinne and an unnerved Amodocus. Brion smiled crookedly and nodded to Cassán.

"I let anger overrule common sense and courtesy. I apologise. I should have chosen my words better and considered your feelings. For that, I am truly sorry." Cassán paused momentarily, wishing to weigh his words. "I will not hold my breath, but perhaps you should consider that the absence of contrition is a character flaw."

Mongfhionn's peal of belly laughs echoed off the walls of Dùn Brion. "A king in the making, but let's hope it's many summers away." Then she looked at Eimhir and said, "I see a queen before me, if I don't kill her first." Turning to Brion, the Sidhe said, "I expect you have a plan. Let us retire indoors and discuss how I might contribute. Hopefully, the discussion will not be as acrimonious as before."

Cassán dipped his head and brought his lips closer to Eimhir's ear. "I guess that's as much of an apology as we're likely to get."

CHAPTER 31

It was the moment Brion had dreaded, yet standing on the southern rampart, he sighed with relief. A deep *barrr ewww* announced the arrival of Seonag, together with a mix of Ravens and Forest People—the survivors of Cùil Daothail. *They look like shite.*

The battle and long trek from the settlement had taken a severe toll on the warriors. Many bore expressions that spoke of horrors yet to be experienced by Dùn Brion's garrison. Brion scratched at the long scar on his left cheek and frowned. The dùn was already overcrowded. How and where could he accommodate another two thousand warriors?

Once more, Brion scanned the landscape, hoping for tactical inspiration. To his east, the Abhainn Dubh river looped and meandered tortuously northwards, setting a border on his right flank. Beyond the river rose the Sleagh range. To the south-west, tall, forested mountains spread across the land. *Good for a retreat if the battle is lost.* Brion shook his head. Thoughts of defeat were not productive.

As he looked to the north-west, a smile opened Brion's lips, exposing teeth yellowed by age. Cearbhall and Cassán looked at him with quizzical expressions.

"You've thought of something, Father."

Brion nodded and exhaled, anxious at what he was about to ask of his son and Seonag. "Let's go and greet our allies."

***

Those present sat around a rectangular oak table, stained with beer and wine, and smoothed with age. However, Brion was discouraged by the placings chosen by the assembled individuals. It sent ominous signals to the few with a more neutral or open-minded disposition.

Seonag, her shield-woman, and Niall sat opposite Brion, Cassán, and Eimhir. Gràinne, supported by Amodocus, sat on Seonag's right, although noticeably, the two parties did not sit as one. Nervous glances were shared between the women. *Seonag knows about Gràinne*, thought Brion. Cearbhall, feeling awkward, chose to sit opposite Gràinne. Unsurprisingly, the Sidhe stood, imposing her presence on everyone.

"I am very sorry about your father's death," said Brion. "I counted Drostan as a close friend and ally. The loss of so many of the Forest People is also a tragedy. That you are Bhanrìgh of the Forest People is a great honour, and I wish you a long reign. I know you will serve your people well and be loved by them." Seonag's jaw clenched and unclenched. Eyes, full of pain and unfulfilled love, could only glare at Brion.

Brion then addressed Niall. "I was not well-acquainted with Blàr Mac Artair. That is a loss from which I cannot recover. His reputation as a courageous and fair king was well-known in Northern Albu. He will be deeply missed by the Ravens and your neighbours." Niall smiled, which was the only relief for a meeting that teetered on a crumbling edge of acrimony and violence.

"Look around this table," barked Mongfhionn. "Remember each face. Some you will not see again until you cross the veil and enter Mag Mell. How many will die is in your hands." The simple brutality of the Sidhe's statement drew troubled expressions from all seated. Each had already suffered greatly. That it was not finished was sobering.

"I cannot force you to be agreeable, but I demand that you work together and fight as one. Otherwise, everyone seated at this table will die, along with many thousands who look to you to lead." Mongfhionn looked at Seonag with an expression that asked, *Well?*

261

A chair scraped on the stone floor as Seonag stood and bowed stiffly to Brion. "Thank you for your kind words. They were timely—this time."

"You're a queen, not a resentful adolescent. Act like one!"

Seonag flinched. The sharpness of Mongfhionn's censure felt like a hard slap to the face. Not wanting to intrude, the others seated around the table suddenly became interested in their fingernails' state. Yet the awkwardness derived precisely from everyone knowing the history of Brion and Seonag.

"My apologies. I am new to this role and find it difficult to be both a woman and a queen." Seonag looked at Brion and smiled wistfully. "Perhaps it is equally hard to be both a man and king." Then she turned to Cearbhall. "It is good to see you again. I hope I can still count you as a friend."

Once seated, Seonag looked at Brion and said, "I see no good reason you should not continue to lead our strategy. Given your knowledge of the land, it makes perfect sense that you should. You have my full support." The relief around the table was unmistakable. "Where would you like us?"

Unsure of the reception his words would receive, Brion inhaled deeply and rose from his seat. "Gormal is our priority, if only because he is human. He will expect us to defend the walls. Yet Gormal is not stupid and knows Dùn Brion will be impossible to breach with his numbers. Even with the addition of the Na Mèadaidh traitors, his force will not number more than seven thousand. Between us, we can put five thousand on the ramparts of Dùn Brion.

"Gormal's only hope of victory is to draw us out of Dùn Brion and onto the northern plain. Once there, he can fight on more equal terms and let the Goddess choose the victor. We can use this against him, but to do this, we need bait." Brion looked uneasily at Cassán and received a wide-eyed glance. Eimhir shifted anxiously on the hard wooden seat smoothed with many arses; she was grateful to avoid splinters.

"Brianag?" queried Seonag.

"She is aligned with Sidheag and, for the moment, outside Gormal's grasp."

"I'm so sorry," choked Seonag, seeing the pain on Brion's face.

"There is a tree-covered hill a short march north-west of Dùn Brion and between Gormal's forces and us. The mound could hide two thousand warriors without much difficulty." Brion looked at Seonag. "I want the Ravens and the Forest People to take up position on it—along with the ballistae you brought."

Seonag's eyes opened wide, and anger flared in the deep blue orbs. *Am I to be sacrificed?* She made to stand, but Brion, in a quiet voice, said, "Please." Then he looked at Cassán. "You, and your caomhnóirí, will accompany the bhanrigh." Seonag's eyes flashed again, but this time in shock.

"No!" Seonag, Eimhir, and Gràinne gasped as one.

"It seems that we are the worm on the hook." Cassán smiled grimly at Seonag and looked at his missing hand. "At least, this time, I'll have a sword in my hand. I agree."

"Travel under cover of night and prepare good defences. With the Goddess's help, Gormal will do something rash." Brion then smiled at Gràinne. "Mongfhionn would prefer you to remain in Dùn Brion." Both women nodded. "However, I want you, Amodocus, and your riders and chariots to take up a position where you can strike quickly and fiercely. I need an edge." Gràinne bit her bottom lip until it bled; Amodocus laughed heartily.

A cough brought the room's attention back to the Sidhe. "I am unhappy with this strategy. Sidheag and Brianag are watching. I can feel them. Gràinne remains our single advantage against Sidheag." Mongfhionn held Amodocus' eyes. "Guard my daughter well, Thracian. Lose her, and we lose the land." Then she turned to Brion.

"Make sure the precautions I advised are put in place."

⋆ ⋆ ⋆

The chamber emptied quickly, leaving Brion, Cassán, and Eimhir.

"Kings often execute unpleasant strategies, hoping that good will come from them." Brion looked into Eimhir's clear, green eyes, and they

263

instantly took on a suspicious tone. "Do you have watchers observing Gormal's camp?" Eimhir simultaneously dipped her head and bit her lip. Where was the conversation going?

"Choose one of them to alert Gormal to Cassán and Seonag's location."

Eimhir had guessed what Brion might ask, but that he put it into words stunned her. She looked at Cassán, and his expression said everything. "You knew about this?" Cassán nodded but avoided Eimhir's gaze. "Why didn't you tell me?"

"Seonag couldn't know. She may have objected to being as much in jeopardy as me. We couldn't take the risk of the plan not going forward." Cassán's cheeks flushed in embarrassment.

Eimhir turned to the king. "This will mean a painful death for my informant. Gormal and Ealasaid will not simply take his or her word."

"It is a king's decision," said Brion.

"It will not be you who deceives and delivers the lamb to the butcher's block."

As Cassán and Eimhir exited the room, Brion murmured, "And yet, the Goddess will judge me, not you."

＊＊＊

The family—father, three sons, and daughter—were aged from eighteen to forty summers. As with previous generations, in battle, they fought together alongside kin and clann. Their trade was war, not farming. Only a newborn suckling on her breast prevented the mother from joining them, which was a pity. Among them, she was the fiercest warrior.

As they listened to Brion's orders, the family members smirked, but not at Brion's words. Brows wrinkled, causing cracks in the newly painted sigils. The Sidhe had commanded every warrior to wear them, and most— there are always those who ignore good advice—complied. Yet perhaps their reluctance was understandable. Curling designs were a highland tradition, and the Na Mèadaidh were a lowland people.

The father checked his sons' and daughters' armour, sgiathan, and weapons. He made sure sword and axe edges were honed sharp and that shields and boiled leather cuirasses had no weaknesses. After, he turned to the eldest. The young man knew what to do. He inspected his da's equipment and tightened leather belts, cuirass, and straps with a zeal that made the chieftain gasp… and then smile.

As the family took their places on Dùn Brion's ramparts, the girl turned to her da. He grunted at the sight and shook his head. She smiled, guessing his thoughts. Aided and abetted by her ma that morning, her long tresses of blonde hair had been cropped short, dyed blue, bright green, and yellow, and set into spikes with resin. It was a practical hairstyle for war, but his eyes misted at the loss. *Bloody hair will crack when she puts her helmet on, but she'll be easy to find in the battle.*

"Surely, they cannot seriously mean to attack us, Father. Why would Gormal throw brave men's and women's lives away senselessly? Our walls are strong, and we have the numbers to defend the stronghold."

The tall, burly chieftain stroked a full beard and tugged long braided whiskers. "There is a madness that overwhelms a tyrant's senses and drives him to arrogance and folly." He placed hands on her slender shoulders. "Do not place your faith in stone walls. With enough warriors and cunning, any defence can be breached. Our strength is in our family, clann, and the shield-wall."

Several blasts of horns sounded from the stronghold's courtyard. The young woman looked at her father. "I have to go." The chieftain nodded and hoped she did not see the pain in his eyes. Outside Dùn Brion, he could not protect his daughter. Yet she was one of Cassán's caomhnóirí, which said much about her qualities as a warrior. And so he kissed her forehead and prayed the Goddess would keep her safe.

✳✳✳

Teàrlag sat around a smoky campfire in the deep, northern woods with her closest advisors and chieftains. That she ripped apart the plump limbs of a freshly roasted hare mercilessly and with venom aptly summed up her mood. "Bloody Comhairle-Chatha and my bastard sons!" She snarled and

265

grunted as incisors ripped the meat apart, sending trails of pinkish drool down her chin. What she left out of her tirade was, "I will make them pay." Yet those with her knew the inevitability of what was unspoken.

It had been a half-cycle of the moon since Teàrlag departed the smoking ruins of Cùil Daothail for the main settlement of the Forest People. There she demanded that the High Council of the Forest People convened. Usually pragmatic and reasonable, although not when it came to her children or clann, Teàrlag had argued passionately for their support and an army to fight Sidheag.

In turn, she received prevarication from the politicians of the Comhairle-Chatha and sullenness from her sons. The latter seethed with jealousy at Seonag's elevation. The council members were weasels, not warriors, minded to preserve and protect what territory, power, and wealth they already held.

"The Forest People have no defence against the Baobhan Sith. Drostan tried, and he lost four thousand fighters in one sunset. We must ally with and fight alongside the other tribes," she railed at them.

When one of the members implied incompetence on Drostan's part, Teàrlag glared at him and demanded an apology. He chose not to, and before the council, Teàrlag plunged the dagger she used for spearing food into his ear. The bloodletting did not end there. Teàrlag's burly shield-man drove his sword into the belly of the dead chieftain's protector. Predictably, the meeting ended in uproar.

"Send messengers to my clann and *fine* chieftains," ordered Teàrlag. "I want our warriors assembled at the edge of the southern foothills in five sunsets. Others may join us, but if not, we will fight alone." The shield-man nodded his agreement. In a cold voice, Teàrlag added, "Pray to the Goddess that we arrive in time." The man grunted, for he well knew what lay beneath Teàrlag's words. Retribution to those who turned their backs on Seonag, including her sons, was inevitable.

✳✳✳

Ealasaid took a step backwards to admire her work and savoured the moans of her victim. The spy could no longer see her torturer, for her eyes had been plucked from their sockets and cast aside. However, not before Ealasaid had demonstrated her expertise. Her ears were untouched, for Ealasaid needed the young woman to hear her inquisitor's questions and, of course, her own screams. The tongue also was whole, for how else could she communicate her confession?

Starting at her breasts and nipples, Ealasaid had slowly and expertly flayed her victim. In a short time, she was no longer a person but a quivering body of raw, bloody flesh. Thin strips of skin lay scattered on the snow, awaiting the unkindness of ravens in the trees. Friend or foe had no meaning for predators—or Ealasaid. Ealasaid sighed. She had her information, and now her pleasure would end.

A deep cut and slash across and upwards on the girl's belly released the coils of her guts. Ealasaid stepped closer and cut across her throat, almost severing the head from the neck. That she deliberately stepped in front of the blood, which pumped from torn arteries, made Gormal and Madadh squirm. Ealasaid preferred to work naked as it avoided stains on her clothing. Still, that was not the entire reason. All heard her gasp in orgasmic delight as the warm blood splashed her body.

"Quite clever of my sister to choose a woman to sacrifice," said Ealasaid as she approached the two men. She twisted thick, hard nipples as she walked, adding horror to the tableau. "We can suffer deep pain longer than men," she said disdainfully.

"Well?" snapped Gormal.

Ealasaid pointed to the south. "Cassán and Seonag are hidden in the trees on that hill. It's a trap, of course, but an excellent one. How can you resist attempting to capture the new Bhanrìgh of the Forest People? Her tribe will pay a great ransom to get her back. And Cassán's the key to unlock Dùn Brion's gates." Ealasaid drew a finger through the thickening gore on her breasts.

"Well, I need something warm, hard, and penetrating between my legs, and neither of you deserves or could satisfy me." Ealasaid's voice was husky with lust as she turned about and walked towards her pavilion.

CHAPTER 32

Seonag turned to Cassán. "It appears Eimhir's informant has successfully betrayed our location." Cassán's sour mien and grunt were his only comments. His concern focused on Eimhir's state of mind at having sent the scout to her death. Dying in battle with a sword in your hand is one thing but being strung up, helpless, and tortured endlessly is an entirely different matter.

In the distance and north-east of the mound, the dark smudges against the snow-carpeted landscape steadily resolved into solid figures. Soon the faces of Gormal's warriors would be revealed. Veterans with miens of impassive stone marched alongside young men and women wide-eyed with fear and those too drunk to know where they were or on whose side they fought.

At two and four hundred paces, green ribbons fluttered in the breeze. Several paces back from the treeline, Seonag spotted Niall as he walked along the row of ballistae, checking the machines and stocks of bolts. She smiled as he offered advice or shared *craic* with the bolt-thrower teams.

A twig snapped behind Seonag, and she turned to see a smiling Gràinne. "My riders will stay on the hill until our arrows are exhausted before mounting our horses." Gràinne hoped to raise Seonag's spirits, but the mask of swirling crimson sigils made Seonag shiver. She remembered Gràinne's red eyes and the fires that burned in them, from the Battle of

Cùil Daothail. Who was stronger—her friend or A 'Bhanrìgh Fuil?

"Now," said Seonag to her shield-woman. Immediately, the war horns of the Forest People resonated across the battlefield in the chill of a brisk spring morning. *It's a mournful sound. Yet perhaps that is how it should be.* How many men and women would fall, turning the perfect whiteness of the snow into a slush of maroon gore? Seonag looked up at a sky filled with grey clouds and sighed. She inhaled sharply as her shield-woman tightened her cuirass and frigid air filled her lungs.

∗∗∗

With Madadh alongside, Gormal rode at the head of his army. In the vast plain, only their voices and the crunch of boots on frost-covered snow broke an almost reverential early-morning silence. The king laughed derisively, although not loudly, at his warriors' shouts of how they would slaughter, plunder, and violate their enemy. All men and women were brave until they stared into the eyes of the enemy and saw the glint of raised blades.

The king turned to Madadh, a look of concern on his face. Where were the voices and taunts of the enemy? The tall pines and oaks on the hill rose before them; undoubtedly, their foe could see them. Against the snow, his five thousand warriors could not be missed.

Was Ealasaid's information wrong? Had she been deceived? Yet Ealasaid could not be asked. She remained in the encampment with a reserve force comprised of Na Mèadaidh rebels. Gormal growled. It was no surprise. Ealasaid's battlefield was the shadows.

Madadh coughed, and Gormal nodded. They were close to the hill, and it was time to dismount. A green ribbon fluttered, catching the periphery of Gormal's vision. With a laugh, he pointed it out to his commander, who instantly scanned left and right. Madadh's instinct screamed alarm, and he shouted, "Sgiathan!" before brusquely knocking Gormal from his mount.

∗∗∗

Along the hill's treeline, the foliage used to conceal the ballistae was dropped forward, giving the machines a clear line of sight. The young female warrior winced as the skeins squealed as they were tightened. She knew what would come next, yet she still started when the bolts were loosed. The crack and rattle of twenty bolt throwers firing as one was deafening.

She heard a shriek of agony from a ballista team member when one of the great war machines recoiled and rolled over his foot. However, the fierce look of disapproval from Niall appeared to cause him more pain. He gritted his teeth and limped back into position.

The barrage was seamless and ridiculously fast. Having just loosed one volley, the skeins were tightened, and new bolts slapped into the firing groove. She looked closer at the stacks of bolts and shivered. Wooden shafts, twice the thickness of spears, ended in arm's-length iron blades.

Some were simple spikes, like the javelin she held, only shorter and heavier. Others had leaf-shaped heads, like the spears the Ravens preferred. She trembled as she visualized the trauma such a weapon would do to frail bodies of flesh and blood. As a pink mist hovered over the enemy, she prayed to the Goddess she would be spared from that fate.

***

Gormal howled in anger and despair as his army was ravaged by weapons from the Otherworld. Warriors were ploughed into the ground, and their limbs scattered like seeds. Gore splattered him from head to toe. A crimson deluge soaked his face and dribbled into his mouth, forcing him to spit in disgust. With the back of a bloody hand, he wiped his eyelids to regain sight and then wished he had not.

"Stand and die! March and live!" bellowed Madadh. Under the assault and trauma, Gormal's army had shuddered to an almost halt, leaving them easy targets. "March!" roared Madadh again. Soon, the call was taken up by the chieftains and captains, and the warriors inched forward once more.

"They cannot have an infinite supply of these missiles. The storm will pass," he hissed at Gormal. "Show leadership. Your army needs you."

"Bastard!" snarled Gormal. While many disliked, even hated, him, few could accuse Gormal of cowardice. Raising his sword, he shouted, *"Lean do rìgh!* —Follow your king!"* Lengthening his step, he strode several paces ahead of his force. The army followed, gathering momentum, and leaving a crimson trail of torn bodies and limbs in their wake.

***

"He has guts," said Seonag.

"Let's hope he leaves them in the snow," replied Gràinne. "He is a distraction who delays me from finding my daughter and killing Sidheag."

"I hope you will not see those who die here today as fighting against a 'distraction'." Seonag's tone was even and low as she pointed to the warriors who stood alongside her in two rows. Still, the bite in her words was unmistakable.

Gràinne blushed and muttered, "I misspoke. Sorry." Quickly changing the subject, Gràinne pointed to her riders stringing their recurve bows. "Gormal will pass the two hundred pace markers very soon. My warriors have two quivers of arrows—fifty shafts each. Once they are loosed, they, and my chariots, will mount up and take up our agreed positions."

Gràinne's eyes misted for a moment as she looked into Seonag's. "I fear for Brianag. Only the Goddess knows what Sidheag may have done to her. I may seem heartless, but the guilt of abandoning her is a heavy burden." Gràinne bowed her head and walked to stand with Amodocus. Seonag watched the mountain of a man swallow her in his arms and wished she had someone to embrace and comfort her.

Perhaps, after the war, Brion and I might have a new beginning.

Wiping tears from her eyes, Seonag turned to Cassán and smiled at his discomfort. "Women!" she exclaimed, and he laughed. "It will be your turn shortly. Speak with your warriors."

***

Madadh, ever watchful, cursed those on the hill as he spotted more ribbons fluttering in the light breeze. Yet, what choice did the army have other than to keep advancing towards the mound? Two hundred paces separated Gormal's force from what awaited them on the hill.

The bolt-throwers continued to hurl missiles at them, although he detected a slowing down of the frequency. But what next? Traps of some kind were a certainty. Yet the fine hairs on his nape foretold of something else. "Shields!" he thundered and was comforted by the resounding clash of rims.

He pondered the dark cloud that suddenly appeared in the sky. Like the never-ending flow of waves breaking on a sandy beach, it was followed by another… and another… and another. His warriors cried out as arrows fell on them. Most slammed into their wooden sgiathan, but there were enough that found exposed flesh and faces. Volley after volley arched high in the sky before descending on his fighters.

As they weathered the iron storm, Madadh detected a change in the flight of the black shafts. "The bastards!" His warriors had marched into the killing field, and the bowmen now picked out specific targets—the chieftains and captains. He heard a cry to his left and heard Gormal curse. The king stumbled, pulled an arrow from his arm, and got to his feet.

Arrowheads clanged against Madadh's helmet, and he felt the arrows pluck at his leather armour. Like many, only the gold, silver, and copper bands around his upper arms saved him from deeper scars. He cursed the whimsy of Fate, the Goddess, and Serendipity, who chose who fell and who walked onward. Warriors charged ahead of him and Gormal. They were the first to find the next line of defences.

There had been no time to excavate ditches or build berms around the hill, and Madadh thanked the Goddess. Yet there had been enough to dig arm-deep holes and fill them with sharpened stakes, and to sow the ground with iron thistles. The cries and curses of his warriors ascended into the meadhan-latha skies. Ankles and calf-bones snapped; sharp sticks and iron brambles punched through bare and booted feet.

"We underestimated the bastard," snarled Gormal, breathing harshly as he stood beside Madadh.

"No, we underestimated the Bhanrìgh of the Na Daoine Tùrsach. Who else could have brought knowledge of these weapons? She has seen these battle tactics used before."

Gormal glanced to his side and behind him. "How many have we lost?"

"At least one-quarter of our warriors, dead or injured," growled Madadh.

"We have more than enough to conquer whoever is on that hill. Sound the battle horns and gather the warriors together."

* * *

"Time to get bloody," said Seonag. "Are you sure you want to stay with the plan?"

There was a brief flicker of uncertainty on Cassán's face, but he nodded grimly. "My caomhnóirí are the best armoured and can take more punishment." He smiled and lifted his right arm. "But I would prefer not to find myself surrounded and cut off. Gormal's hospitality is not something I'd like to partake of again."

Seonag smiled. "Draw them into the woods. There are no better forest fighters than my people, and the Ravens have no rivals when fighting with spears." Turning to Niall, Seonag issued her first command of the battle.

"Sound the battle horns."

Two rows, each with one hundred warriors, men and women, marched out of the woods to meet Gormal's advancing army. All bore oblong, waisted shields that protected from neck to knee. As a tribute to Brion's origins, they were painted red and emblazoned with the swooping black raven of Clann Ui Flaithimh. For obvious reasons, Cassán's sgiath had to be strapped to his right arm.

Most wore boiled leather armour reinforced with iron scales. The rest wore sleeveless chainmail vests on soft lambskin and under red woollen tunics. A few—the brawlers—wore chainmail gloves. All wore red-and-black plaid triubhas tied at the waist with braided wool cords. Broad leather belts rested on slender and broad hips. Each carried a wide range of weapons in scabbards or hanging from thin strips of hide. Those favouring long-swords or battle-axes had them in simple loops of leather that secured the weapons to muscled backs.

Each head was crowned with an unembellished helmet of iron and bronze. A ribbon of chainmail protected the neck. From the acorn nubs of the helmets sprouted hands' lengths of horsehair, dyed red or black. Around the warriors' necks, thick torcs of twisted gold showed wealth and status. Yet, as with the bands of gold, silver, and copper on their upper arms, the jewellery served a practical purpose, often turning a blade strike from a killing blow to a scar.

To assert that Cassán's caomhnóirí looked impressive was an understatement. They comprised the best, hard-faced veterans from Clann Ui Flaithimh and the Na Mèadaidh. All knew war and would deliver death or die.

"Javelins!" roared Cassán and then yelled, "*Gun teàrnadh; cha gheill!*—no retreat; no surrender!" The refrain was immediately taken up by his warriors.

As Gormal's army approached within thirty paces, Cassán's shield-wall immediately relaxed and hefted throwing spears. They threw the first volley of two hundred missiles with a communal grunt. Each warrior carried four, three for throwing and one retained for stabbing. The young woman cursed her burning arm muscles as she launched her final javelin. Yet she also thanked Cearbhall for what she had considered very harsh training exercises.

A well-organised shield-wall is a voracious grinder of flesh and bone, stabbing high and low at the enemy. As he heard the ringing clash of rims, Cassán stood confident that his wall would not fail him and bellowed, "Forward!"

The young woman swore as the boss of her opponent's sgiath slammed against hers with a loud ring of iron. The force numbed her arm and partially lifted her booted feet from the slippery ground. She slid backwards and then gasped and snarled as another shield hit her. This time it was from behind, bruising her unprotected spine. It was accompanied by a gruff "Hold!" from the warrior at her back.

She felt a javelin brush her ear as the veteran thrust the weapon forward, over her shoulder, and into her opponent's face. The man's nose and cheek collapsed, and hot blood splattered her face. Cheeks flushed red from humiliation, she set her jaw, stepped into line, and thrust her javelin forward through the shield's waist. A grunt of agony was followed by a gush of blood over her hand.

"Much better." She smiled and thrust again.

The wall advanced steadily and inexorably, tramping and sometimes slithering over a gore-soaked melange of blood, guts, mud, and snow to reach the enemy. Cassán's chest heaved as he fought to inhale deep gulps of air. Blood and snot gushed from a broken nose, and he blinked away salty tears to restore his vision. Increasingly, the wall fought the dead as much as the living. Over the sound of battle cries, curses, and slashing blades, Cassán heard a bellow of frustration.

"Flank the bastards! Go round, not through them."

That was the moment Cassán chose to retreat. "Fall back to the forest—slowly. Hold the shield-wall. We leave no one behind."

On Cassán's right, the lass muttered, "Thank the Goddess and my armour." Her reserves of strength were almost spent, and blood flowed from many cuts. She grimaced as her opponent slashed and felt a stinging pain in her cheek. "Bidse! I better not have a scar," she snarled and thrust forward forcefully but wearily. The iron spike punched through the woman's throat, eliminating any prospect of her shouting the curse that formed on her lips. More gore spurted over the young warrior but made little difference. She already looked as if she had bathed in blood.

✳✳✳

Gormal turned to Madadh and stabbed a finger in Cassán's direction. "A one-handed runt is slaughtering my warriors. Instead of 'executing' him, I should have made him commander of my army." Madadh gritted his teeth and ignored Gormal's diatribe. The rígh was rightly frustrated as his army chose to confront rather than overwhelm Cassán's shield-wall.

"Flank the bastards!" Madadh roared his order once more, and this time, the call was taken up by his chieftains. He heaved a sigh of relief as his army widened its forward line. "Cut off their retreat. Don't let them reach the forest."

As he watched the steady withdrawal and observed the rear rank of the shield-wall turn about to face those who sought to cut them off, Madadh reluctantly admitted his admiration for Cassán. The manoeuvre was tricky in a training setting, let alone in a battle. "The fat arsehole had hidden depths," he muttered. Had his capture and stay in Gormal's dungeons been the fire that forged his steel? Gormal should have just tortured and killed him.

"Push!" Madadh bellowed.

The shield-wall edged nearer and nearer to the hill's treeline. Once inside the woods, who knew what they might face? Madadh rotated his neck to scan the battlefield. He did not like the thought that bubbled to the top of his head: where were the mounted warriors who had destroyed five hundred of his men in the frozen marshes around Dùn Brion?

∗ ∗ ∗

Seonag's knuckles blanched white as she gripped the hilt of her sword. Blood trickled from a bitten lip. *My relationship with Brion,* she snorted. *What relationship?* Yet whatever their bond, it would be sundered forever if Cassán fell before Gormal's army. If they could see through her eyes, Brion and Cearbhall would be proud of Cassán.

She watched the shield-wall, although it had become a ragged square with a third of its force severely wounded and protected by their comrades. Seonag heard a loud shriek and a string of vulgarities that no young woman should know. She watched the girl batter the enemy with her sgiath until it shattered and then tear off her helmet and beat her foe's face with it. Seonag grinned at the multi-coloured spikes of hair. A broad smile broke on her lips as she watched one of the wounded hand a shield and helmet to the young woman.

"Don't die on me," said Seonag, turning to her husky shield-woman. Then she pointed to the lass and added, "But if you do, I could do worse than choose her as your replacement." The laugh from her protector was loud and infectious.

"Please. A few more paces. Please." It was Seonag's plea to the Goddess. She cursed the plan all had agreed to and which she had to execute. She cursed the burden of being the bhanrigh. *I never sought or wanted it.* Then she took a deep, calming breath, looked over her shoulders, and smiled.

Behind her, Seonag saw the two rows of spear-wielding Ravens with their weapons held at waist height. She looked forward and saw nothing, and that made her happy. Her Forest People had melded with the trees. And so, Seonag held her position and prayed again. "A few paces."

Another slash, another screaming muscle, and more blood spilt by him and his opponent. Cassán mirrored Seonag's prayer and, in a voice thick with the grime of battle, shouted, "Only a few more steps!" Yet the distance seemed increasingly impossible for those who stumbled, protecting the injured and fighting the horde surrounding them.

"Please, Goddess. Haven't we done enough?" asked Cassán.

✳✳✳

Cassán's answer came from a furious Madadh, who roared, "Stop them! Kill them!" Still, Cassán's shrinking square of sgiathan refused to die or surrender. *What will it take to stop them?* Alongside him, Gormal seemed almost apoplectic that his former captive might escape his grasp again. Looking for a scapegoat, he railed at Madadh.

"What use are your warriors if they cannot overcome two hundred men, most of them injured?"

"We should retreat," was Madadh's answer.

"What?" asked Gormal in a voice charged with disbelief.

"We should retreat. Cassán and his caomhnóirí have fought well. By my reckoning, they will soon reach and enter the forest." Madadh breathed deeply. "We do not know what will face us on the hill. Yet it is plain that

Cassán is the bait for the trap. They want us to follow into the trees." The battle commander looked Gormal in the eye. "We would be foolish to accept their challenge. Who knows how many await us?"

"Coward!" shouted Gormal, spitting flecks of saliva. "I will replace you after this battle. Drive *my* army forward."

The firm hand on Gormal's forearm shocked the king for its impropriety. He tried to pull away, but Madadh's grip was unyielding. "I am no coward and will kill any man or rìgh who makes that assertion. You would do well to remember who commands the army."

✱✱✱

The timing was perfect. As Cassán's beleaguered caomhnóirí, followed by Gormal's army, crossed the treeline and into the forested hill, hunting horns blasted shrill notes into a grey, meadhan-latha sky. As if called to action, clouds laden with snow began to discharge their burden, perhaps in an attempt to cover up a landscape scarred red with blood and bodies.

Emerging from behind the hill, Gràinne's five chariots—she had reclaimed two from Brion's discarded inventory—bumped and clattered on the frost-hardened ground. Two hundred riders, led by Amodocus, raced along Gormal's left and right flanks. Javelins and heavy darts savaged the flanks as vehicles and riders sped to their target.

Men and women shrieked in pain and cursed an enemy they could not hope to confront—or catch. They recoiled from the spinning knives of the chariots. The unfortunates were those pushed into the path of the *carbaid* by others attempting to avoid injury. The belly of the army gave thanks when the riders and vehicles charged onwards—to the force's rear.

An army's discipline is weakest at its rear. While the forward ranks of Gormal's force were tightly packed and, under Madadh, held to their formation, the back resembled the debris in the tail of a shooting star. In that chaos and space, chariots and horses reign. Truthfully, Amodocus' main concern was not the enemy as he swung left and right, crushing skulls with his mace. Instead, it was that his riders avoided the spinning scythes of Gràinne's chariots.

The long-handled bludgeons and swords of the riders reaped a bloody harvest. The ululations of A 'Bhanrìgh Fuil, standing naked in her chariot, froze their hearts and her blood-red eyes grabbed their gazes. Curling crimson designs flowed like rivers over Gràinne's body and into the longsword gripped in her hands. Raised high, the sword chopped down on fleeing warriors.

***

Deep in the ancient forest to the east of the battlefield, Sidheag cursed the battle cry of A 'Bhanrìgh Fuil and felt Gràinne's growing powers. Sidheag had needed the Blood Queen to kneel before her. Must she now destroy her?

Across from Sidheag, Brianag finished her meal. Her blood-smeared face gave nothing away. *What is the bidse thinking?* Sidheag had snatched her as leverage to use against her pure-blood mother. But who was using who? As if reading her thoughts, Brianag lifted her dark gaze and smiled. Sidheag's growl rumbled from deep within.

***

Seonag looked to her left and smiled at the blood-splattered warrior at her side. She had tried to persuade Cassán to rest with his injured warriors further up the hill, but he shook his head and insisted on standing with her. In this, he was not alone. After a short rest and ensuring their injured comrades were safe, almost half his battered but defiant caomhnóirí joined Cassán, including the young woman with the colourful hairstyle.

There were fresh, raw wounds on Cassán's face and shaven skull. At least one would heal as an impressive scar. Yet it was evident from the constant touching and scratching that his main concern was a red, swollen nose. Some helpful comrade had pinched and snapped it back into some semblance of its original shape, but there was no disguising the break.

"The swelling will reduce, and your nose will heal—if not perfectly. I doubt very much that Eimhir loves you only for your looks." Seonag chuckled. Cassán's cheeks flushed, and he grinned sheepishly. Then he pointed to where the sound of warriors crashing through the trees and undergrowth revealed the enemy.

"They will be on us shortly."

The bhanrigh dipped her head and called out several final orders. Seonag's hedge of spears stood four hundred paces from the foot of the hill and before the mound climbed abruptly to its peak. Below them, the slope was steep, although not enough to discourage a moderately fit warrior.

Yet harsh breathing from those approaching suggested that many neared the limits of their endurance. The missile attacks, Cassán's stand, and the march to the knoll had taken their toll. Seonag ground her teeth. These were the young, foolish, and drunk. Largely untouched, Gormal's veterans walked at a measured pace behind them.

Seonag pointed to Gormal's warriors. "The trees are our allies and will break up Gormal's advance. My spears will make our stand on this spot. I would like you and your caomhnóirí to target the leaders, the chieftains. Cut the head of the beast." Cassán nodded.

"And your Forest People?"

Seonag chuckled. "They have their own way of fighting."

⋆ ⋆ ⋆

Madadh bellowed orders from the veterans' ranks: "*Ionnsaigh*—Attack! Kill the bastards!" Yet, to the chieftains around him, he nodded. The nobles had an understanding with Madadh. No chieftain, or his men, were to go forward unless and until Madadh gave the order. Those at the front were to be sacrificed. To the tribe's hierarchy, it made perfect, if callous, sense. Thus, accompanied by the war horns of both armies and by tribal and clann battle cries, Gormal's unseasoned warriors charged.

Held in the hands of a skilled warrior, the spear ceases to be a weapon scoffed at by sword- and axe-wielding warriors. It becomes a weapon of terrifying simplicity that wreaks horrendous damage on weak flesh. Seonag had one thousand sleaghan in two ranks. The front row planted the shaft's butt-end in the dirt and held the spearhead at waist height. The rear row

281

gripped the weapon, ready to thrust, twist, and withdraw.

"Horses have more sense than these," murmured Seonag as she watched hundreds hurl themselves at the fence. Worse, seeing their comrades hung up and dying on iron spearheads or their bellies opened and their guts slopping onto the forest floor did not deter the attackers. Caught in the fever of battle, like a river, they flowed only in one direction.

A frustrated Cassán muttered, "Madadh is holding back his chieftains, and Gormal is nowhere to be seen."

Seonag dipped her head in Niall's direction. He smiled and signalled the battle horns. Deep, loud *barrr-ewww*s reverberated and were soon overtaken by the war cries of the Forest People. Over a thousand warriors dropped from the trees and onto the rear ranks of Gormal's force. Seonag looked to Cassán and said, "I think Madadh may have to change his tactics."

With a gulder of "Ionnsaigh! Make them pay!" Seonag charged forward, followed by her spears. On the other flank, Cassán led his warriors down the hill and hoped he never had to meet a tactician like Seonag in battle.

∗∗∗

Battle or brawl? Whatever the description, finesse or swordsmanship was a luxury for the nobility, even in one-on-one duels. Often, a sly stab in the back marked the victor from the vanquished. The shock and ferocity of the attack astounded Madadh and his chieftains, forcing them to whirl around. Previously hidden in the trees and wearing little or no armour or clothes, the Forest People fell on Gormal's veterans.

A few wielded battle-axes, but most swung the tribe's traditional weapon—a club. Some were nothing more than shaped pieces of timber. Others were "improved" with iron spikes and studs. All inflicted crushing blows on their enemies' heads and upper bodies. For most, it was a very bloody, painful, and unpleasant way to die.

Attacked on three fronts and with diminishing numbers, Madadh's options became limited. The lie of the land was against him and favoured the enemy's momentum. Even the trees opposed him. He swore at the shrill blasts of hunting horns. If he retreated from the mound, the chariots and riders would harass his army with little pushback. Madadh hacked and shoved his way down the slope to Gormal.

"We have to retreat. Nothing helps us. The Goddess has turned her back on us."

"No!" snapped Gormal. "Commit the veterans."

In the midst of a chaotic battle, Madadh bellowed at Gormal and pointed to a wedge of Cassán's warriors, forcing a path towards them. "You may be a cunning rìgh, but unless you want your head hanging from Cassán's belt, the veterans you wish to sacrifice are your only salvation. My counsel is to sound the retreat."

Gormal ground his teeth. "We will need a scapegoat, or the chieftains will ensure neither of us will survive this debacle."

"Agreed."

* * *

Men and women stared at Ealasaid as she sashayed through the camp. She usually relished their adoration. Yet now, their gaze was harsh rather than lustful. It was accompanied by curses and shouts of "Witch!" and "Traitor!" which unsettled her. Those she had previously rutted or who had vied for her attention dropped their eyes and steadfastly ignored her presence.

Only the pressure of the blade strapped to her thigh and confidence in her skill to kill swiftly and without mercy gave Ealasaid comfort. *What is going on?* The camp was anxious and fractious, which was not unexpected after Gormal's humiliating retreat. She had warned him that it was a trap. Why did he not accept her counsel? She had no interest in losing the battle and every incentive in Gormal being victorious. A successful campaign would give her the throne of the Na Mèadaidh.

Yet Gormal had lost a third of his army, dead or injured, and Brion's army, ensconced within Dùn Brion's walls, taunted them. Did she need a new path to the throne of Na Mèadaidh? "Stupid question," she snorted. "Of course I do." But first, Ealasaid needed information. How boggy was the ground she stood on?

While it is challenging for someone of lower social status to camou-flage themselves as a member of the hierarchy, the reverse is not always true. The nobility and wealthy often stick their noses in the pig trough and wallow with commoners in shite. Indeed, many actively pursue such degradation.

Thus, it was not difficult for Ealasaid to change the colour of her hair to black and darken her skin tone with dyes. She stole clothing from a striopach and rubbed dirt and ash into her cheeks to simulate the bruising whores often received from brutal clients. Those of a cynical nature would say that being a slut was Ealasaid's natural environment. As for Ealasaid, being wanton without consequence made her curvaceous body tremble with anticipation—and could be profitable.

Striopachan were efficient and business-like in being rutted, getting paid, and moving on, which suited Ealasaid's tactics perfectly. The brutal rutting and absence of emotion matched Ealasaid's needs. After the first handful of clients, she had a pleasant throb between her legs that threat-ened to disrupt her requirement for pragmatic disinterest.

Yet Ealasaid became increasingly frustrated. It was ironic that few men, and even fewer women, wanted anything more than instant gratifi-cation. Hence, violence was expected, and conversation was either limit-ed or non-existent. Ealasaid needed information, so a change of tactics was required. She resigned herself to sampling a few more victims before changing her strategy.

A naive warrior gave Ealasaid what she desired. Likely this had been his first battle and an inauspicious start to a military career. Being young, he had not yet attained the callous detachment of his more experienced comrades. Thus, while appreciating the unfettered and undeniably pleasant access to Ealasaid's pit, he also needed an ear for his opinions on where Gormal had gone wrong.

"It's the witch's fault. She betrayed us and led us into a trap." He gasped sharply as her hand tightened on his manhood.

"The 'witch'," Ealasaid's throaty voice purred in his ear as she nibbled his earlobe.

"The whore—Ealasaid. She's a spy for Brion. Gormal and Madadh held a meeting of the chieftains and exposed her treachery. Many search for her. Gormal has promised gold for her capture and to give her to the army to violate before executing her." The young man chortled. "That's if she survives."

As he spoke, Ealasaid felt the loquacious warrior's manhood stiffen. Clearly, the thought of her rape proved stimulating. Of course, he had to die, but Ealasaid was never one to waste an admirable erection. Tossing her clothes aside, Ealasaid straddled him, displaying her luscious beauty. She rode him hard until he gasped in pain before exploding inside her.

The young warrior's eyes widened in clarity as he inspected Ealasaid in the light of the isolated campfire. Ealasaid chuckled malevolently and hissed in his ear. "Finally, you recognise your peril. I could give you sage counsel about not speaking when you rut a whore, but that would be pointless." The young man gasped and gurgled as the sharp blade was drawn across his Adam's apple. As his life ebbed, so did his erection.

Ealasaid disengaged from the still-warm corpse and grabbed her clothes. "I have business to attend to."

✶✶✶

Madadh pushed the young whore aside. His manner was brutal, and the bruises on her face, upper body, and between her thighs and arse cheeks told of his contempt for her profession and need to cause pain. Yet he appreciated the firmness of her breasts and buttocks and the flatness of her belly, which youth provided. Unlike his hand-fast partner, the striopach gave him pleasure, if one-sided—but who cares what whores think?

"I'm going for a piss. Don't move. I'll be back." She nodded and looked up at him with fearful eyes.

Madadh's tent was the obvious choice. Burning torches and fifty hard-faced warriors surrounded Gormal's pavilion. Ealasaid considered the risk of being discovered too great. *He can't hide from me forever. I will bide my time and strike.* Yet Madadh's hubris would not allow him to change his ways for any woman. Thus, only his usual quartet of burly protectors guarded the entrance. More than their physical presence, they were well-trained to ignore any brutality and cries for mercy within the shelter.

Ealasaid's knife cut through the tent's fabric noiselessly and with ease. She stood for a moment, adjusting her eyes to the gloom. Only a few rush-lights shed light in the pavilion, and they had almost reached the end of their utility. A young woman sat upright, naked and sobbing on a pile of hides. *Foolish girl. You should have made better choices.* Aided by the dirt floor, Ealasaid moved silently closer to the striopach.

Madadh pulled back the tent's flaps and entered the pavilion. He cursed that it was in complete darkness. "Useless bidse! Can you not light a torch? If I stub my toe or trip, you'll pay dearly." Gormal's commander retraced his steps to the entrance and shouted for a guard to bring him a brand from the campfire. By its fluttering light, he saw the outline of the striopach.

That she appeared to be sleeping enraged Madadh, and he strode over to the bed of furs and kicked the girl. She made no noise or movement, so he booted her much harder. This time the body rolled over noiselessly. Curious, Madadh knelt beside the whore and passed the brand across her.

"Shite!"

While the young whore's body had moved with his kick, her head had not. Madadh then sensed the wetness of his knee. When he placed a hand on the furs to steady himself, they were soaked, saturated in the girl's blood. Madadh's mouth opened to call for help, but no sound was heard beyond a sharp gasp of pain.

Striking from behind, Ealasaid's knife drove hard between Madadh's ribs, piercing his lungs. As a finishing touch, she twisted the blade. "You will die slowly and painfully, drowning in blood. No one will come to your aid because you ordered privacy, no matter what noises might occur."

Ealasaid's voice was colder than ice, and Madadh would have shiv-ered had shock not numbed him. "You lied about me to cover your and

Gormal's incompetence. You betrayed me and that I will never tolerate." Ealasaid's voice hissed like a viper in Madadh's ear. "Know this. You have condemned your hand-fast partner and sons and daughters. I will show them no mercy when I retrieve my daughters from Dùn Athad."

A "No" formed on Madadh's bloody lips. As he slumped over, Madadh fell across the torso of the young whore. His last memories were of Ealasaid's mocking laughter as she retreated from the pavilion. She had to escape the camp with haste. Ealasaid vehemently cursed Gormal for ruining her plan to be crowned queen of the Na Mèadaidh and swore retribution. Still, it consoled Ealasaid that when she killed Madadh's partner and his children, she would also take his wealth.

Always a practical woman, Ealasaid had one final task to complete before fleeing. Thus, she dashed to the river that flowed east of the encampment, stripped, and entered the frigid waters. Now was not the time for another baby, and certainly not from the arseholes she had rutted that night. And so she cleaned herself. When she got to Dùn Athad, she would consult with the old woman who had knowledge of herbs and plants. Better safe than sorry.

CHAPTER 33

When Gormal finally stopped raging about the death of Madadh and rep-rimanding those around him for allowing Ealasaid to escape, he turned to face his chieftains. He was not impressed. The squabbling nobles vied for attention, jockeyed for position, and accused each other of incompetence. Gormal swore loudly, which succeeded in gaining their attention—and silence. Still, Gormal had relied too much on Madadh and neglected to groom a successor.

A young slave walked past Gormal, and he recoiled. His orders were that no females were allowed within fifty paces of him. Ealasaid's talents were undeniable, and he would have been surprised if she had not trained others. Revenge probably sat atop the bidse's future priorities, and Gormal knew he would never sleep peacefully until he watched her die.

The king signalled to a hard-faced guard. The girl smiled as the guard approached her. Then her eyes opened wide as he unsheathed a blade and, with a smooth, backhanded stroke, slashed across her throat. Her neck was graceful and swan-like, and the dagger's force almost cut through it. Her owner's death would be much slower and much more painful.

An uproar outside the pavilion drew Gormal's attention. He exited the tent surrounded by a coterie of bear-like guards. Blinking several times, his eyes adjusted to the glare of the snowy landscape. Gormal's tent sat at the centre of the encampment, on its highest point. Thus, he had a perfect view of what had prompted the commotion.

Before two ranks of veteran warriors, fifty in total, stood nine young females wearing white, diaphanous léinte. They stood silent and motionless as if waiting—but for what? Their behaviour contrasted starkly with those around them, who leered and uttered obscenities. Yet, it was their faces that disturbed Gormal most. Carved stone exhibited more emotion. Where had they come from, and how had they got so close without discovery? For the second time that morning, Gormal shuddered.

Behind the Brood, ribbons of mist merged into a shimmering veil. Nervous chatter and whispers of "Baobhan Sith" rippled through the army. Many recalled rumours of the uprising in north-eastern Albu but few, including Gormal, believed the tales. How could they? She was a fiction to control unruly children. Indeed, who could be that monstrous?

Two figures moved, although the taller of the duo seemed to prance on tiptoes through the misty curtain. One was clothed similarly to the nine. The smaller one's gown was also gossamer-thin but coloured a vibrant green. *Why is she different? And why do I have some recognition of her?*

Gormal licked dry, cracked lips, and coughed to clear his throat. Some premonition made his heart race. Sweat soaked his shirt, and his breathing became shorter. *Why? What is my body warning me about?* His answers came all too soon.

"I am Sidheag, the Baobhan Sith, and these are my daughters." Gormal observed the momentary hesitation as Sidheag indicated the one in green.

"Why do you grace us with your presence?"

Sidheag laughed. It was not a pleasant sound, serving only to silence all around the small group. "I want your army." Sidheag's disdainful gaze swept over the camp. "Well, at least your captains and chieftains. The rest bear the brand of a miserable, defeated mob." Gormal bristled at the insult, and his guards' hands went to their swords. Sidheag's chuckle was ominous.

"I find it amusing that you think you have a choice or can resist me.

Perhaps a small demonstration."

The nod was imperceptible, but the howls emitted from the Brood's gaping maws were not. Frozen to the spot, Gormal and his chieftains watched as Sidheag's Brood fell on the fifty warriors. Fully aware of their fate, the victims watched flesh stripped from bones and spurting blood guzzled down. That the veterans made no sound and offered no resistance as they were consumed alive was, to Gormal, the more horrifying.

Gormal's nightmare continued as Sidheag's long, blood-red talons caressed his scrawny neck and her fetid breath filled his nostrils. Only abject terror prevented him from puking and shitting his triubhas. "Do we have an agreement?" Sidheag glanced at Brianag. "Or should I let my other daughter feed on you? She holds you responsible for removing her brother, Cassán's, hand. The lust for retribution appears to be deeply seated in your foolish culture."

"The Hag!" gasped Gormal.

"She cannot help you," cackled Sidheag. "Do we have an arrangement? I have an army of twenty thousand in the forests to the east. You and I have a common cause. You desire Dùn Brion taken and Brion dead. As for me, A 'Bhanrìgh Fuil is within the stronghold's walls, and she is mine by right."

Reluctantly and very slowly, Gormal dipped his head.

As Sidheag walked away, Brianag sidled up noiselessly and stood next to Gormal. "If you believe that you are not a dead man, no matter what happens at Dùn Brion, then you are a fool who deserves to die." Brianag's breath smelled of raw flesh, and once more, Gormal fought to quell his stomach.

"She will, most certainly, drink your blood and devour your flesh once she has her victory." Brianag smiled, revealing rows of needle-like teeth. "But I may kill you sooner for Cassán. It's all about the blood. Blood holds memories that are never washed away." Brianag watched Sidheag's retreating back. "That's what *she* doesn't understand."

"What are you?" asked Gormal.

"I would love to know the answer to that question."

⋆⋆⋆

The Forest People's Comhairle-Chatha called another meeting of the clann chieftains. Yet as politicians are wont to do, they deliberately stamped on any discussion regarding the threat of the Baobhan Sith. Instead, and to Teàrlag's fury, they pronounced that the Forest People would go deeper into the ancient woods and defend their territory.

"So, your strategy is to cover yourselves with the forest's debris and hope the Baobhan Sith will not see your cowardice." An angry rumble rippled through the members of the High Council. The insult was deliberate, and cheeks flared in embarrassment among the clann chieftains. Yet Teàrlag had not finished and rasped, "You intend to abandon your bhanrigh?"

"She has not been officially seated by the High Council."

The speaker was the eldest of Teàrlag's sons. Plainly incensed that he had been passed over, he saw a chance to wrench the throne from Seonag before her arse graced it. His words brought a flush of anger to Teàrlag's cheeks. Foolishly, he assumed his mother was embarrassed and that he was in a position of strength.

"The words of a weasel, unworthy to serve, or to have the loyalty of, the Forest People," spat Teàrlag and glared at the High Council. "Seonag was chosen by Drostan. It is the Forest People's tradition to follow that guidance, and it has served the tribe well."

"It's a tradition that has outlived its time," snapped the pretender.

"The Aes Sidhe have blessed Seonag's elevation. Are you also disputing their approval?" Teàrlag chuckled, but there was no humour in the sound. "Name a man or woman who defied the Aes Sidhe and lived a long or prosperous life. Would like to discuss it with Drostan in Mag Mell? *I* can arrange that."

A sobering silence fell on the gathering as the chieftains grappled with the implications of the High Council's decision. Yet Teàrlag could see that bribery and procrastination would win the day. There was nothing she could do, and so she stood.

"As I speak, my clann's warriors move through the forests towards Dùn Brion."

Shouts of "Outrageous!" and "Disloyal bidse!" rippled through the Comhairle-Chatha's members. Teàrlag ignored them.

"I welcome any true warriors who wish to join us."

"We will not join such foolishness," roared Teàrlag's eldest.

"That is of no consequence. Your actions proclaim that you are neither Drostan's nor my sons." Teàrlag paused as if savouring her next words, and her lips parted. "By my authority, you are no longer part of Drostan's and my clann. From this moment, I name you outcasts. Find another home or tribe." Teàrlag's lips twisted into a spiteful smile. "Try claiming the throne of the Forest People as an outcast." She gestured at the members of the Comhairle-Chatha. "Even these arseholes won't support that."

One final time, Teàrlag stabbed a finger at her sons. "Do not face me, or Seonag, on the battlefield, for we will show no mercy. You have brought dishonour on our clann, which will never be forgiven." Teàrlag swept the audience with fierce eyes, but none held her gaze. "And that goes for any who support these pariahs."

✳✳✳

"You could have been more diplomatic," said Teàrlag's shield-man as the pair walked away from the meeting. The tone was mildly chastising and caused her to smirk.

"They had already decided their path, and the time for diplomacy had passed." She inhaled deeply. "How many warriors do we have, and how many might join us?"

"We have five thousand, and they are the best of any clann." The burly warrior tugged his long whiskers. "Another two, maybe three thousand, might join us."

Teàrlag shrugged. "It will have to do."

"Your sons?"

"They are a danger to Seonag. Should we survive the battle with the Baobhan Sith, we will remove that threat and those on the Comhairle-Chatha who supported their sedition."

***

"I don't like the location of the ballistae, Cearbhall," said Brion. "Your position is not defensible, and I do not want to appoint another new battle commander."

The blustery wind and light flurries of snow that swept over the group standing on the northern rampart were not unusual. Still, the breeze made it challenging to keep furs and words from being snatched away. Brion looked across the battlefield and then at Seonag and added, with a sad smile, "I have already made a mistake in that area."

"It's the logical place for the bolt throwers," said Cearbhall. "Anywhere else would be an exercise in futility." As Brion opened his mouth to protest, Cearbhall shook his head and firmly said, "Cassán recovers from his wounds. If I ask the ballista teams to risk their lives, I will not do that from the safety of Dùn Brion's walls." The muscled warrior looked at Amodocus and grinned. "Besides, Amodocus and his riders will be there to spirit us away from danger."

Alongside her partner, Gràinne bit her lip in anxiety and frustration. Mongfhionn had made it clear that her place was within the stronghold, and the Sidhe would tolerate no dissension this time.

"How do we stand?" asked Brion of his battle commander.

Cearbhall pointed to the north and sighed. "I estimate we face over twenty, and possibly twenty-five thousand. Our spies report that Sidheag and her Brood linked up with Gormal at sunrise." The commander hesitated and wondered if he should keep one piece of information from Brion or Gràinne. "They saw Brianag. By all accounts, her physique has changed considerably.

"I'm sorry," Cearbhall added in a quiet voice at the looks of pain in Brion's, Gràinne's, and the Sidhe's eyes. Navigating the conversation into safer waters, he continued, "Within the fort, we have less than five thousand warriors. In a typical siege, that should be more than enough." Cearbhall looked to the grey skies. "But this will not be a typical defence. Will it?"

Brion looked to Seonag. "When do you expect Teàrlag to join us?"

She frowned. "Since she is not already with us, I suspect the High Council has been uncooperative. That is not good—for now or in the future. We should make our sacrifices to the Goddess and pray my mother does not arrive only to build our funeral pyres."

✳✳✳

"They're a plague."

Cearbhall spoke of the horde of dark smudges against the white landscape. During the night, Nature had sprinkled the land with a hand's depth of snow. Perhaps she wished to hide the splashes of red from the Battle of the Mound. Or was it simple perversity to observe whether the humans could outdo themselves in barbarity on a new sunrise?

Amodocus squinted and nodded. "They appear better organised than those we faced at Cùil Daothail. We will not have much time once they pass the outer markers before they reach your bolt-throwers and my bows." The burly Thracian inhaled, relishing the chilly morning air. "I have assigned a rider and a spare horse to each of your warriors. Each will have one chance to swing up and onto the mounts. Misjudgement will mean death. We cannot wait for anyone."

"Thank you, they know," said Cearbhall. "All had assumed they would die. If any escape, it will be a gift from the Goddess—or Ares." Cearbhall smirked, and Amodocus gave a great belly laugh, which spread infectiously among both sets of warriors.

"To your positions," bellowed Cearbhall. Only the squeal of skeins tightened, bolts slapped into firing grooves, and arrows applied to bowstrings disturbed the still air.

✳✳✳

"Have I sent them to their deaths?" asked Brion.

"It's a dangerous but good position," answered Seonag.

Dùn Brion sat, a glowering stone fortress, atop a rocky crag, but at the foot of the northern bluffs, the landscape sloped steeply downwards to meet the plain. While the upper incline of dirt and shingle was covered in gorse, thistles, and heather, the final twenty paces were an entanglement of wildwood and younger trees. Hence, it provided the perfect cover for the ballistae and archers.

"I wonder what *they* are cooking in the cauldrons of their minds?" said Seonag, dipping her head to the duo who stood further along the walkway.

Brion smiled. "No one ever knows what's in Mongfhionn's mind, and I'm not sure I want that insight." He nodded in the direction of Gràinne and sighed. "I once knew her as a simple, impulsive girl. She was free with her favours and a good sword to have at your side in a fight." Brion shook his head. "Now, I'm unsure whether anyone understood her or what demons drove her to this place." He rubbed his chin. "She reminds me of my sister, Mórrígan. She, too, had a darkness within her."

"From what I gather, Mórrígan conquered her nature," said Seonag.

"Did she subjugate it or make it a weapon to get what she wanted?"

"Does it matter? Mórrígan and Gràinne appear much like their mentor, the Sidhe."

"In that, we can agree." Brion turned to Cassán. "Bring the dùn to full alert. Have the braziers stoked and ready the cauldrons of oil, water, and pitch. Take command of the southern wall." Cassán nodded and barked orders, and the great war horns reverberated from the ramparts.

Further along the walkway, two women dropped their cloaks, reached up to the skies, and began to chant.

✳✳✳

Astride his horse, Gormal looked down on Sidheag as she walked alongside him. Impotence carved a troubled look on his face and stirred the stew of turmoil in his head. Many attributes had been applied to Gormal but being stupid was not one of them—although his acquiescence to the apparition cast doubt on that assumption.

He shrugged. *What choice did I have?* Brianag was right. *I can die horribly now or after we take Dùn Brion.* Gormal shuddered at the creature Brion's daughter had become. The likelihood of him stepping into Dùn Brion's courtyard was excellent. How long he would survive beyond that was subject to Sidheag's capricious whims. Between this moment and the capture of Dùn Brion, he needed an escape plan. Gormal grunted, taking comfort that at least his thoughts were his own, but an evil chuckle from Sidheag disabused him of his final place of solace.

Seeking a diversion, Gormal turned his attention to the army. Almost twenty-five thousand marched nominally under his banner. Not even Drostan could make such a claim. Yet his glow of pride was transient. Unlike him, most were under the fear or thrall of Sidheag and the Brood. Those allowed to keep their minds were his chieftains, veteran warriors, and Sidheag's priests. Gormal spat at the mere thought of the depraved zealots. "Bastards!"

He grumbled that the army seemed better organised than it had been under Madadh's command. The fear of being Sidheag's or her Brood's next meal had sharpened his captains' tactical minds. The force marched towards Dùn Brion in three columns. The right flank comprised his warriors and those they had identified as experienced fighters; the left were the priests and zealots. Gormal prayed that the latter would be slaughtered.

The central column was a diversion. It contained about fifteen thousand of the enthralled—farmers, young adventurers, drunks, and arseholes. They were disposable. Their only role and value were to keep the garrison occupied, exhaust the enemy, and put them at the mercy of the veterans.

Only the strains of the songs of Mongfhionn and Gràinne, drifting over their heads and the strengthening southerly wind that accompanied the chanting, suggested anything to the contrary.

As Gormal's army stepped forward, Brianag looked at Sidheag and smiled. It was not the look of a daughter's affection.

✳✳✳

Cearbhall's nose crinkled. The growing smell of Gormal's army, even in the cold of early spring, exposed their debatable hygiene. Worse, it was enhanced by mouths that spewed not just curses and taunts but also spittle laced with the stench of rotting teeth and diseased gums. "Thank the Goddess for the wind," he muttered and then as if chastising himself, he added, "And the Sidhe."

Taking advantage of the wind to start his barrage sooner, he bellowed, "Fire!" Twenty ballistae hurled the first of many volleys at the advancing column, tilling the horde as a plough would soft earth. Two hundred archers nocked arrows but would wait until the enemy came much closer.

The family in the front rank of Gormal's army—mother, father, two daughters, and three sons—were enthusiastic conscripts to Sidheag's cause. A failing farmstead in the highlands and no talent for crafts, metalworking, or weaving saw them embrace their proclivity for brutality and thieving. Thus, they preyed on their neighbours until they were eventually forced from the community.

They swore loyalty to Sidheag, perceiving that as a first step on the ladder to wealth. To the family, enthrallment was an escape. They happily joined in the depravities embraced by Sidheag's priests, desiring to be elevated to the Baobhan Sith's priesthood. Still, they felt nervous when they heard the refrains from Dùn Brion's ramparts as layers of Sidheag's control were peeled away as if scraping a parsnip.

Confused, they continued to rush forward. What else could they do? Thousands surrounded them. The army had become a beast with a single mind. As Cearbhall's first bolts struck the front ranks, the father and mother watched their sons and daughters turn into a ghastly mist of blood, bone, and severed limbs.

Their corruption was deep, and kinship shallow. Thus, they sighed in relief at having been spared, although that proved short-lived. Whimsically, a least to the Goddess, bolts from the second volley neatly removed their arms. As they fell to the ground, blood pumped from torn arteries. Inevitably, the couple died, but not before their heads and chests were crushed by the boots of those who took their place.

The efficiency of Cearbhall's bolt throwers and the mayhem and carnage wreaked on an army compelled to push forward stunned Amodocus. He started and then smiled at the nudge from his second-in-command. The Thracian nodded and roared, "Loose arrows!" One thousand arrows arched high into the grey sky before falling on Gormal's column. By the time Cearbhall's teams slapped the last bolts into the ballistae, ten thousand arrows had savaged the enemy.

Stunned at the storm released on them, Gormal's force no longer trampled through a field of calf-deep snow. Instead, they slid and slipped through a slush of blood and ice and stumbled over a blood-soaked berm of hundreds of corpses and limbs.

"Cut the skeins. Mount your horse. Retreat!" shouted Cearbhall. Then he looked at Amodocus and shrugged. "But where do we retreat to? The bastards have flanked us on all sides, except to the south."

"On horseback, we ride faster than they run. Keep to the wildwood along the hill's slope. If needed, we batter our way through and regroup on the mountain slopes to the south-west of Dùn Brion. I doubt our role in this battle is done."

CHAPTER 34

He was justifiably proud of his daughter. Yet being a father, he was also apprehensive. Among Cassán's warriors and the garrison, campfire tales were told of how she fought with everything she possessed. The fresh cuts and scars on her arms and face testified to the truth of the stories.

The father watched his daughter exit the armoury and chuckled. She looked displeased. Reluctantly, she had exchanged her leather armour for chainmail. It was not her first choice, and her da smiled as she remonstrated with comrades about the additional weight.

Yet what remained of her original protection lay in tatters on the steps to the barracks. Little more than a few strips of torn hide and iron scales clinging to the leather by threads. The father watched her cross the yard and walk stiffly to her quarters and winced. Her triubhas were so ripped she was almost naked below her waist. He grimaced at the long slashes and red welts that covered her legs.

She looked up and saw his pain and concern. That hurt her more than any blade slash. Pressing fingers against her lips, she blew him a kiss, smiled, and mouthed, "I'm fine, Da. Don't worry."

A smile creased his face, and he nodded, hoping he looked reassuring and accepting of her request. Yet how could he not be concerned? Her place was to stand on the southern wall, along with her family and Cassán's caomhnóirí. They would be the first to face the enemy charging up the long southern slope to Dùn Brion's gates.

* * *

"If rage could bring down stone fortresses, Dùn Brion would lie a mass of rubble," muttered Brion. Bolstered with stakes, straw, and pitch, the stronghold's defensive ditches burned, sending ribbons of acrid, black smoke upwards. They had taken a heavy toll on the horde. Yet the fort was surrounded on all sides by howling, slavering mobs of the enthralled and the witless. Inflamed by depravity and fanaticism, Sidheag's priesthood needed no mind control. For that, the Goddess doubly condemned them.

Dùn Brion's towering walls looked disdainfully at the tiny figures searching for hand- and footholds. They laughed at the sharp slaps of siege ladders against their stones and the clanging of iron hooks seeking purchase. The ramparts watched with cruel joy as waterfalls of boiling oil, pitch, steaming water cascaded over its lip. They observed, with delight, pitch-soaked bales of straw set alight and tipped over the edges.

Yet the walls were oblivious to the howls of pain and the agonised shrieking of the maimed. The crunch of bones as besiegers lost their grip, fell, and were broken on the rocks below meant nothing to them. Few were killed, but thousands were irredeemably maimed. They would cross the veil at a time of the Goddess's choosing.

Perhaps, unlike Dùn Brion's defenders, the stone was happy to be deaf. Blood flowed in the stronghold but, as yet, only from thousands of lips and cheeks bitten to distract from the awful screaming. Still, the self-in-flicted pain proved as useless as the scraps of cloth and wool stuffed into many ears.

Following Cùil Daothail, Mongfhionn had improved the design that offered protection from Sidheag's enthrallment and the Brood's Siren song. Now, many pleaded with Brion to prevail on the Sidhe to give another sigil to paint on their faces. Why would she not provide another to seal their ears against the wailing of their attackers?

Yet perhaps that was the point. Would men and women then ask for a sigil to protect their eyes from the horrors of what their blades did to their enemies? If war was not brutal and merciless, men might never pause to reconsider its use.

Two paces behind the parapets' edge, the shield-walls stood with Brion, Cassán, and Seonag. They knew their time to fight drew closer. No army fought with over twenty thousand warriors without reaching and overcoming the walls. Much greater numbers would always tell. At that time, only the garrison's fence of flesh and courage would save Dùn Brion.

* * *

Seonag breathed harshly, looked upwards briefly, and prayed for a sign that sunset might save them. Since meadhan-latha had passed only a short time ago, she was disappointed. Ignoring the protests of her muscles, she swung a battle-dulled blade and instantly grimaced. Her shoulder joint juddered as the weapon struck and shattered bone.

At her back, she felt the strength of her battle partner, Brion. Was it a cruel irony that they were a natural pair, if not as lovers, then as fighting companions? She pushed the moment of bleakness from her mind. *After the battle, it will be different.*

The fight on Dùn Brion's battlements was fierce if little more than a brawl fought thousands of times over and over. There was no finesse, no noble duels between enemies, and no displays of incredible swordsmanship. Survival meant killing your opponent swiftly, with no compassion, and with any weapon to hand. Swords became clubs, hands tore throats, fingers blinded eyes, teeth bit and tore ears and noses.

In the battle for life, breasts and manhoods were seized, twisted, and bruised. Not in erotic pleasure but for advantage before the delivery of a fatal thrust or the bundling of an enemy over the wall's edge. Not for the first time, Seonag grabbed an opponent's cock and wrung it like a chicken's neck. She heard the sharp intake of breath and knew it would be his last as her blade stabbed his throat. Pumped by a failing heart, blood surged from a torn artery, adding more gore to her torso.

A walkway awash with a slop of blood, gore, and guts no longer gave attackers or defenders an advantage. Instead, it added an element of serendipity or a levelling-up to outcomes. Wintry weather could not overcome the stench of piss and shite. Along the parapet, Brion, Cassán, Eimhir, and their captains shouted hoarse commands and encouragements to stand firm. They were met by an incoherent, amorphous growling from the beasts within and without the stronghold.

For a moment, Brion turned to Seonag. Anger and sorrow filled his eyes, and bloody tears trickled down cheeks stained with battle grime. Over half of his defenders lay dead or dying in the courtyard. He felt every death and wept in shame at the need to kick the heroes from the walkway. His warriors needed space to fight.

"I'm sorry." Seonag lips pursed, and she placed a fleeting kiss on Brion's lips before turning to block another opponent's blow with a cracked shield.

"I think we need a miracle," said Brion through gritted teeth. Then he gasped and cursed as an axe blade ripped through his chainmail, pushing its links deep into his flesh. "Focus," he chastised himself and slashed across the woman's throat. His reassuring smile to Seonag was welcomed… and false.

✳✳✳

Sidheag screeched as she watched her grand design begin to crumble. The strain on her face was apparent, for she had not fed since the battle commenced. Maintaining her grip on her horde's mind challenged and depleted her strength like the slow drip of a thawing icicle. Additionally, she also fought against the songs of the Sidhe and the Blood Queen.

Strategically, Sidheag had always relied on control, brutality, and speed. She had learned much from Cùil Daothail. Dùn Brion did not have a wealth of iron like Cùil Daothail, yet its rock defied her. Once more, she screamed in frustration, unable to comprehend why the humans continued to resist her.

"Humans have a saying that 'Pride goes before destruction.' It is a lesson that you should heed." Brianag's body bore the fullness of a young woman, but her mind retained the snarkiness of an adolescent. Her accompanying smirk lasted as long as it took Sidheag to backhand her across the face. The force of the blow launched Brianag high into the air. Yet, like a lince, Brianag landed on all fours and grinned as she wiped away the blood from her lip. *We will meet again, Mother. But I have work to do.*

The Baobhan Sith growled as she watched Brianag scamper away. That the young bidse purposefully left a trail of bleeding and dead leaders in her wake creased the Baobhan Sith's normally marble-smooth brow. *What is her plan?* Sidheag had no answer to her question, which made her angrier. *Why am I unable to dominate and control her? How can she read my thoughts, but I cannot hers?* Sidheag's skills were in destruction and chaos. She had never created anything until Brianag. Hence the mystery she could not fathom remained: *What is she?*

"Enough!" Sidheag shouted. "I have work to accomplish." Her prize was within Dùn Brion, and she would sacrifice every warrior in her army to possess A 'Bhanrìgh Fuil. No sooner had Sidheag reaffirmed her plan than she heard her prey's voice reach a crescendo as she sang the long-forgotten verses of the Na Daoine Tùrsach's Death Song.

Sidheag sensed her grip on the horde weakening. The strength in Gràinne's voice reminded Sidheag of the original 'Bhanrìgh Fuil. She cursed the cunning of the Ancient One and the arrangement that bound her. Then Sidheag's maw opened in a garish smile. Soon Gràinne would be in her grasp, and the balance of power would be restored in her favour as it always should have been.

Sidheag's momentary expression of regret at what she intended to do was an affectation, yet it was strangely comforting. In a blur of movement, she fed on those closest to her. Blood restored her strength; Sidheag gathered her thoughts and increased her grip on the enthralled. One more push and the fortress would fall. She nodded to her Brood, and they opened teeth-filled maws. Yet before her daughters could sing, another voice and a different song came from the walls of Dùn Brion.

Mongfhionn called out, and Sidheag imagined her sister's long fingers reaching upwards. The skies became a darker grey, blocking out the sun and for that Sidheag said, "Thanks, Sister." Propelled by unnatural winds, clouds raced across the firmaments, and ragged branches of lightning struck the land.

Freezing rain and hail as big as fists fell, and Sidheag's army shrieked as one. Thousands cried out as hands and feet were frozen and became useless wax limbs. Scores fell from the fort's walls, leaving bloody fingernails embedded in the ice. Frustrated and rapidly losing patience, Sidheag screamed a final command.

She overrode the free will of her commanders and veterans and launched them at Dùn Brion's southern wall and gates. "I will prevail!" she bellowed. Then, from the forests to the north-east, Sidheag heard the great war horns of the Forest People challenge her.

"No!"

***

On a mountain slope south-west of Dùn Brion, Amodocus heard the battle horns, grinned at Cearbhall, and slapped Brion's battle commander's broad back.

"It looks like we're back in the battle."

***

Gormal shivered at the ice-covered fort's terrible beauty rather than the brutal bone-numbing cold. He flinched at the ear-splitting booms of thunder and was blinded by the violent fists of lightning pounding the land around the stronghold.

His nostrils were overwhelmed by a sweet, pungent fragrance that reminded him of rainy days in the highlands. Gormal sneezed. From inside Dùn Brion, he heard the witches' songs and wondered which one was responsible for the abrupt change in the weather. Maybe it was both women. That made him shiver more, and Gormal reflected that he had made terrible choices.

Had he stopped to think why he was not throwing himself at Dùn Brion's glistening southern wall and gates like the horde, Gormal might have taken umbrage at being so blatantly disregarded. Instead, he smiled, spat in the direction of a visibly irate Sidheag, and took to his heels. Any route was good enough, but Fate chose north-west for Gormal. In a very unkingly manner, he scrambled, slipped, and crunched over bodies, hail, and ice.

"What made you think you could escape me?"

Startled, Gormal's heart pounded. Sword in hand, he whirled around in circles. Expecting to see Sidheag, he saw nothing in the steel-grey curtain of rain and hail. Mocking laughter stung his ears, and he looked in its direction. At first, it was a shimmering shadow, then Gormal saw its colour change to green as the shape came closer. "No!"

Gormal tried to run, but his legs would not respond. What had ensnared him? The bidse or his fear? The apparition moved smoothly and steadily towards him through the deluge that soaked his clothes and pommelled his skin. Soon her awful visage was no more than an arm's length from his, and obsidian eyes gripped his own.

He saw her cavernous mouth and the rows of needle-like teeth. He noticed the strings of meat and wondered how many she had slaughtered. Then Gormal heard the click of long, crimson-red talons and felt them trace the pulsating artery in his neck. He gulped and fought for a few more seconds of life. "What happened to you? How did you know?"

"The first question is complicated, and you do not have enough time remaining to hear my story. As to the second, your mind is not difficult to read—even in the absence of Sidheag's gifts bestowed upon me."

"Why do you care? Everyone knows there was no love lost between Cassán and you."

"Times change. People change. Even monsters change. Cassán's rage was honest and understandable if wrongly founded." Brianag's mouth formed into an awful grin, and she cocked her head slightly as if recalling a memory. "Besides, I was a bitseach to him." Gormal watched Brianag's face and thought it softened. Hope soared, only to be swiftly dashed to the ground.

"It's all about the blood." Brianag shook her head. "Humans, even gods, don't realise the simplicity of that. In the end, Cassán shares my blood and, as his sister, I must and will deliver retribution."

Gormal felt talons slice effortlessly through his tunic and armour. They caressed his belly, and he flinched at the sting of the long, thin cut. Steeling himself for worse, he snarled, "Stop playing with me, bidse. I deserve that, at least."

"You deserve nothing but pain." Gormal gasped as the talons pierced deeper.

Two great, snorting shapes thundered from the curtain of rain, scattering Brianag and Gormal in opposite directions. Armour and tackle glittered, and ice shards fell to the ground as the horses reared up on their hind legs. Gormal felt his spine crunch as he hit the frozen ground and his breath violently expelled. Relief flooded his senses; he rose and began to run… anywhere. The boot to his head curtailed any thoughts of escape, and he blacked out.

"You will die. Just not today," scoffed Cearbhall.

Brianag landed on all fours and, like a wolf thwarted, howled at having her prey taken from her. She bounded back to search for Gormal but instead heard a horse snort and stamp its hoofs as she approached.

"He is mine," she spat at the tall shadow emerging from the rain.

"No. Gormal is Cassán's to judge," said Amodocus. "If you want him, you will have to kill me. Choose, Brianag, for you know I will not retreat."

For a moment, Brianag's eyes misted over. The sadness in Amodocus' voice reminded her of Neamhain, and she shook her head.

"It is not your time, Amodocus." Brianag turned and howled, and the great wolf she became bounded eastward towards Dùn Brion.

∗∗∗

Gods and demi-gods of great power often underestimate or fail to recognise their limitations. The more astute, and hence longer-lived, learn to operate within these constraints. Thus, the Goddess had become reconciled to the reality that her influence derived from the worship and love of her people.

As she soared in the stormy skies, watching Sidheag rage at the gates and walls of Dùn Brion, the Goddess deeply regretted not destroying the Baobhan Sith when asked to intervene. Had the Aes Sidhe even understood the lesson she had sought to teach them? The Goddess looked down on Brianag and Gràinne, two horrors that, by her negligence, she had helped create. The Goddess wept, adding to the deluge sweeping the land.

* * *

Streams of blood flowed down the ice-covered walls of Dùn Brion before finally slowing to a stop and freezing. The screams of hundreds of men and women thrown from the ramparts and broken on the crag's rocks prompted no emotion from Sidheag. Neither did the cries of those torn apart by the murderous crossfire from the ballistae on the southern wall.

With some justification, Sidheag claimed she was more powerful than her sister, Mongfhionn, or indeed any of the Aes Sidhe. Didn't they need to call on the Goddess to subdue her? So, why had her forces not overwhelmed Dùn Brion's defenders? How many could be left inside the stronghold? Sunset approached, yet the unceasing lightning lit up the terrain garishly.

The strain continued to show on Sidheag's face. Tasks that were once instinctive and came easily troubled her. Holding her horde's mind for so long was a great effort. Maintaining the Brood's collective power together sapped her strength like blood seeping from numerous cuts.

Red, spidery lines of strain spread across Sidheag's normally unblemished appearance, and she swore at those on the ramparts who continued to resist. Mongfhionn would likely concede she was ill-matched against her. However, Sidheag reluctantly acknowledged that the Sidhe was nimbler and more imaginative in her thinking. *We should be on the same side, Sister.*

She had underestimated A 'Bhanrìgh Fuil and the Ancient One. The strength of Gràinne's cursed chanting of the Tuireadh had grown since Cùil Daothail and the embrace of her destiny. Gràinne's power also flowed through the Sidhe, lessening the strain on her sister.

"Where is Brianag—the duplicitous bidse?" Sidheag snarled, for she knew it had been a mistake to feed rather than enslave Brianag. She had tried to be too clever, too subtle. That would never happen again. Sidheag growled as she recalled the scene in the crannag and the looks shared between Brianag and Seirbhiseach.

What had Brianag whispered to the priest before killing him? A sudden realisation widened Sidheag's eyes, and she ground pointed teeth. It had been a sacrifice, not a slaughter, and both had played their parts well. "*Bidse!*" Sidheag screamed. "Where are you?"

I am close and will have my retribution on all who turned me into a monster. A mocking cackle, of which the Hag would be proud, rippled through the charged air.

Sidheag shivered and then taunted, "Come to me, daughter. You are no match for me." Then Sidheag did something out of character. She stilled her mind and listened to the ebb and flow of Mongfhionn's and Gràinne's songs. After a moment, she smiled and called her Brood to her.

✳✳✳

It was the tiniest crack in Mongfhionn's and Gràinne's defence. A mere breath as they simultaneously replenished their lungs. Hitherto, the duo had synchronised their songs with their need, but not this time. In the gap, Sidheag and the Brood appeared out of the mist on the northern wall. Although quick to react, the defenders were no match for the Brood or Sidheag. Their only consolation was that Sidheag and her daughters had no time to feed.

Defenders on the eastern and western walls ran to avenge their comrades. Still, they were ill-matched, and only the narrowness of the walkway slowed the killing. The apparition and her Brood moved forward: a ghastly inhuman shield-wall. Talons slashed and teeth tore flesh.

"We need to join the fight," shouted Gràinne to Mongfhionn. "Our friends are dying."

"You *are* fighting. Your song restrains Sidheag and the Brood from conquering Dùn Brion. Many more will die if you cease."

Gràinne shook her head. "That fight is over. *Look!* Sidheag has breached the walls. Brion and Seonag need our blades now."

∗∗∗

On the southern wall, Brion looked at Seonag and Cassán with resignation and regret. He pointed to Gràinne and Mongfhionn. "Those two are not entirely of this world. If Dùn Brion falls, they will survive and fight other battles. Our fight is here and now. Organise your warriors. If I fail, you will be Dùn Brion's only hope." Ignoring their protests, Brion strode to a small group of warriors. "I need a guard."

The father looked at his daughter and shook his head. "You will stay and fight alongside Cassán. That is your responsibility. Your brothers and I must protect the king." Protest perched on the young woman's lips, but the determined look on her father's face gave her no hope.

Instead, she put her head on his shoulder and whispered, "I love you, Da."

The eastern ramparts were awash in blood and gore as Brion and his protectors locked sgiathan and blocked Sidheag's path. The mocking laughter only increased Brion's determination. "Your army is defeated. Your cause is lost. Surrender and serve me," hissed Sidheag.

"I am neither dead nor ready to yield," said Brion and advanced.

"*No!*"

The young woman's scream echoed off the stronghold's walls as she watched the Brood fall on her father and brothers. Only the strong arms of her comrades prevented her from running to join and die with them. She cursed the Goddess and the hands of those who grasped her before collapsing to her knees. Yet they forgave her. In a small settlement on the Sleagh, the daughter's mother rocked a newborn in her arms and sobbed.

Brion showed no fear, set his jaw, and firmly grasped the sword in his right arm. Several paces away, Sidheag laughed and inspected Brion as a farmer would a cow about to be slaughtered. "Too foolish to run. You should have spent a few moments in your lover's arms. Yet how will you miss what you never seized? You will die here, very painfully."

"A brave boy gave you that scar on your cheek, bitseach. Perhaps I can give you its match." Brion circled his sword as he watched Sidheag's movement and the Brood who hovered behind her. "As for me, I have no fear of death. The Goddess has a place for me in Mag Mell. You have no place in this world or the next, not even the Otherworld."

Sword raised; Brion attacked. "Let's fight, bitseach."

＊

"*No!*" shrieked Brianag.

Everyone stopped, even the Brood and Sidheag, at Brianag's heart-rending cry of pain and loss. Startled, all wondered from where she had appeared. Those who knew or had known her stared, hoping their vision of a creature who seemed more terrible than Sidheag deceived them. Brianag rushed barefoot to where Brion and his guards lay, ignoring attackers and defenders. The path of ice and gore to the fallen king was uncontested.

Seonag had only moments to see Brianag through grieving eyes. Instinctively, her hand went to the sword by her side. "*My father, bitseach!*" snarled Brianag. Razor-sharp talons grasped and punched holes in Seonag's shoulder. Lifted up, she was tossed aside as if she were little more than a straw doll. The Bhanrìgh of the Forest People landed with a thump and an "Ooof!" of expelled air, sliding to a halt at the feet of the newly arrived Gràinne and Mongfhionn. Blackness came as Seonag cracked her head on the icy walkway.

Brianag fell across her father's still-warm body and wept. She had barely known her father, but, in her young mind, he and Neamhain were the only ones who had not forsaken her. Blood soaked her delicate, green robe, moulding it to her figure. Yet on this occasion, the stains showed every sign of permanence. Brianag looked up with eyes darker than charcoal and screamed.

"*Look at me!* I wanted to be a girl, and you made me a monster."

Brianag's heartrending cry accused Gràinne, Mongfhionn, and Sidheag, although none were named. As Gràinne stood before Brianag, her eyes and curling designs were blood red. "*Who are you to accuse me?* Do you think you're the only one to feast on human flesh? Do you think I wanted this?" she challenged, indicating her body. "*I did this for you.*"

Sidheag laughed, relishing the havoc she had created. Yet as Brianag turned her gaze on her, Sidheag's face showed uncertainty… and concern. Had she made a grave mistake? How strong was the bidse? With a thought, she gathered her Brood and placed them as a fence before her.

"They cannot protect you, bitseach. Even now, I feel them hesitant and conflicted. Who do you think controls them? Me… you… or A 'Bhanrìgh Fuil?"

"What hubris makes you think that a mere girl, with some abilities *I* gave you, can stop me?" Sidheag mocked Brianag. "Not even the Goddess could bind me forever, and she has long flown from this place." In the air, a great eagle screeched, and Sidheag flinched.

"It seems the Goddess has not fled far," taunted Brianag.

The speed of Brianag's movement drew gasps of admiration from the garrison's survivors. The long, red talons, cavernous maw filled with needle-like teeth, and stench of the Otherworld prompted prayers to the Goddess for safety or a quick death. Amid the slaughter and gore on the parapet, Brianag faced Sidheag. The young apparition smiled and said, "I am more powerful than you, bitseach, and my blood is stronger."

Sidheag ignored her Brood and filled with wrath, surged forward, slashing with long, crimson talons. She swore as her claws only disturbed air. Brianag had gone. Then Sidheag screeched. The sound echoed off Dùn Brion's walls, bursting defenders' eardrums with its pitch. That it was a cry of genuine pain made it more unbelievable.

The Baobhan Sith rose unsteadily and faced Brianag. Those standing close by gasped in disbelief. From her shoulders to her arse, the apparition's back had ten deep slashes, and each bled freely. Across the back of her thighs were cuts deep enough to slash tendons. That Sidheag could still move seemed incredible and testified to her strength. Whispers of "No" rippled through the crowd as they witnessed the wounds begin to knit together.

Brianag crouched, ready to pounce, as Sidheag advanced on her. She heard the clicking of talons, stronger than steel, and replied with her own and a roar of defiance. "Your time is over, mongrel," shouted Sidheag. The abomination's burst of speed stunned Brianag. Lifted off the ground, Brianag felt long fingers tighten around her throat, and sharp claws pierce her skin.

Sensing revenge about to be snatched from her, Brianag refused to panic or yield. Ten talons stabbed deep into Sidheag's breasts. The Baobhan Sith screamed, dropping Brianag to the rampart with a force that made her tailbones crunch.

"Ma!" shrieked Brianag.

"Enough!"

Gràinne's voice boomed across the stronghold, and all watched her step towards Sidheag's Brood, longsword in hand. Blood-red sigils flowed over her body as if gathering power. "There is no hope for you. Pray the Goddess will have mercy, for I will not."

The sword was raised and slashed parallel to the walkway. Nine heads fell with sickening thuds to the stone. Yet perhaps the worst part for those watching was the total silence from the Brood… and the absence of blood. Pointing to a defiant Sidheag, Gràinne held black eyes with blood-red ones and thundered, *"I am A 'Bhanrìgh Fuil,* and you will surrender to me. You live only to serve me, not I, you. *Kneel!"*

With every fibre of her being, Sidheag fought the compulsion to obey. Step by ungainly step, she dragged herself closer to Gràinne and, with each, vowed to kill A 'Bhanrìgh Fuil. Close enough to share a breath, two pairs of dark eyes stared unrelentingly at each other. Their bodies quivered, straining for dominance. Then from Sidheag's maw came a long wail of humiliation. Carried on a gust of wind, an awful stench soured the air. The apparition collapsed to Dùn Brion's stone.

"Shackle and chain her," roared Mongfhionn.

✶✶✶

"You think one act washes away your guilt at abandoning me to *her?*" screeched Brianag, struggling to understand conflicting emotions.

Gràinne flinched, shook her head, and softly said, "No." Her daughter's words lashed like a multi-tailed scourge. Still, she stood resolute, weaponless, and arms wide as a shrieking Brianag hurtled towards her. She would accept what the Goddess had decided was her fate.

What Gràinne had not expected was to be pushed aside and, losing her foothold on the icy walkway, to fall on her arse. Mongfhionn's oak staff was as ancient as the Sidhe and had survived countless battles with man, beast, and demi-god. As Brianag leapt at Gràinne, the rod struck her on the forehead with a resounding crack and shattered into a thousand splinters. Brianag hung in the air like a bird of prey before collapsing to lie next to her mother.

"I'm sorry, so sorry," Gràinne sobbed raggedly as she smoothed Brianag's long tresses.

"Shackle her," commanded a sorrowful Mongfhionn.

✶✶✶

Released from Sidheag's enthrallment, her horde scattered to the north-east, hoping to find sanctuary in the ancient forests. They found only the spears and clubs of Teàrlag's Forest People, and none of those were in any mood to be merciful. So fierce was the slaughter that the ground, quickly satiated, refused to accept the blood sacrificed to it.

Those who fled to the north-west heard only thunderous hoofs and snorting horses before their skulls were crushed by maces and their bodies pounded into the icy terrain.

CHAPTER 35

Gormal scratched his arse and plucked a splinter of wood from his left buttock. He pulled the threadbare *brat* closer. It did little to keep him warm in the cold, dank cell but at least hid his nakedness. He chuckled at his sudden preoccupation with modesty.

Following his escape from Brianag and capture by Amodocus and Cearbhall, Gormal was quickly bundled through the gates of Dùn Brion. There he was stripped and thrown into the dungeon. Sharp pains in his chest reminded Gormal of the kicks and punches he had suffered before his imprisonment. His broken ribs were a testament to their brutality. He was not surprised. Everyone was distraught at Brion's death, although that could hardly be laid at his feet.

He looked up as the cell door opened, and in stepped Cassán and Eimhir. What would be his fate? By their faces, Gormal knew that freedom was an unlikely outcome. Besides, where would he go? If his guards were truthful, Dùn Athad was under siege by the combined forces of the Forest People and the Na Mèadaidh. Without a king, the stronghold would fall by negotiation or starvation. The latter was highly possible. He had been a poor steward. Then there was Ealasaid. The bidse would never let him live.

"Well, what is your judgment?" asked Gormal.

Cassán looked at Eimhir and shook his head, more in sadness and resignation. The fires of revenge had cooled but had not departed. "You could have been a friend to my father and me. A good neighbour to share feasts and festivals. A buttress against the Forest People. But you chose to be his enemy and mine. In a half-cycle of the moon, Dùn Athad and your clann will be ruled by Eimhir and me. In several cycles of the moon, you will be forgotten, or, at best, a cursed memory of your tribe."

A roll of his eyes was Gormal's response. "Spare me the sermon. We fought. I lost. Now tell me my fate or piss off."

Cassán's jaw set, and he nodded to the cell door. Two burly men entered, dragging a brazier and a few iron bars. Gormal looked at Cassán's missing hand and shook his head. "I expected more imagination from you." Cassán's hand went to his sword, but Eimhir stopped him.

"Stay with the plan."

Pulled from his tree log, Gormal cursed as he was made to kneel and his arms stretched across the rough bole. He heard the crunch of iron forced into the depths of hot embers and felt the sudden release of warmth. It was the first time he had felt warm in many sunsets, and he enjoyed it.

The soft hiss of a sword drawn from its sheepskin-lined scabbard came next and was quickly followed by the worst pain of his life as Cassán's blade cleaved his right arm just below the elbow. He screamed as red-hot irons seared his raw flesh, and choked on the smell of charred meat.

His eyes widened in shock as once more, the blade rose and fell. This time, his left arm was sundered. Again, Gormal felt the glowing metal seal his wound. "No!" Gormal screamed. "You cannot leave me like this."

Cassán spoke to the guards. "Take him to the gates and cast him out. Send messengers across our land. No man or woman is to give him succour." One final time, Cassán addressed Gormal.

"The Goddess will judge if you are to live or die."

CHAPTER 36

On the Sleagh, Sidheag, shackled with iron chains, knelt before her judges. There was no breeze on the mountain. Thus only the soft fizzle and scent of her flesh branded by the iron links broke the sombre atmosphere. Yet the pain of her confinement did little to stop Sidheag's cackling. She was a powerful demi-goddess, and in time she would escape and retaliate.

"End her—now!" said Cassán, glaring at Mongfhionn.

The Sidhe shook her head. "*You* do not give commands to a member of the Aes Sidhe. Learn this lesson, Cassán, or you will have a short reign." Mongfhionn looked at Sidheag, and in the Sidhe's eyes were sadness, anger, and resignation. She shrugged and said, "I cannot end a sister, no matter how evil. The Aes Sidhe will not allow it, and I have already broken too many of our rules."

Sidheag smiled and lifted up her hands. "Thank you, *Sister*. I acknowledge your victory. You have defeated me. Now, please remove these shackles. I promise to leave these lands forever and live elsewhere."

"That is my problem, *Sister*. Letting you go free does not resolve the problem. It is equivocation. As to your oath, what value does it have?"

The sound of a drawn sword focused the group's attention on Cassán. "Then I will kill her. Iron will cleave her head from her shoulders." Cassán glowered at Mongfhionn. "As it will *any* Sidhe."

"Drostan made the same threat, and he is in Mag Mell," snarled the

Sidhe before pointing to Sidheag. "If you insist, however, I will not stop you. It will be amusing to see how long she lets you live. She is bound. Yet, like a cornered bear, she is not helpless. If I were to let my concentration lapse momentarily, Brion's heir would die."

Mongfhionn turned to Eimhir. "Curb your lover's temper lest he becomes an arsehole again." Eimhir bristled at the insult but kept a firm grip on Cassán's hand. The Sidhe turned to face Gràinne, who stood watch over Brianag. "I cannot execute Sidheag, but you can."

Sidheag shouted, "No!" Then, looking at the shackled Brianag, she crowed, "*She* is still mine. Kill me, and you kill her." The hoofed apparition's words taunted Mongfhionn; Sidheag revelled in the horror on Gràinne's face.

Gràinne stared at Mongfhionn, and her sigils throbbed. "My daughter has suffered enough, Ma. I will not allow her to endure any more hurt." A triumphant hissing spewed from Sidheag at Gràinne's words, for she sensed division and opportunity.

The Sidhe looked at Gràinne and, in a gentle voice, said, "Sidheag lies. Yet we do not know the limits of Brianag's power. Certainly, her abilities are too dangerous for an adolescent girl to wield." Mongfhionn grasped Gràinne's shoulders, barely controlling the shudders at her daughter's appearance.

"Brianag's powers cannot be taken from her and will grow. Thus, she must learn control, and that cannot be done in this world. Neamhain promised Brianag to be with her, always. You must trust Neamhain and me on this. There is hope for Brianag among the Aes Sidhe. I only see death here."

"Do not fail me, Mother," said Gràinne to Mongfhionn.

Gràinne faced Sidheag and stared into Sidheag's black eyes with enough venom to cower the abomination. She pleaded, "No!" as Gràinne's longsword rose and flashed red in the sunrise. Tales were told of Sidheag screeching long after her head rolled down the slope of the Sleagh and how it could be heard across Northern Albu.

✳✳✳

"Is it ended?" asked Cassán.

"Sidheag, yes. Yet evil comes in many forms. Like a moth to the flame, humans are attracted to its promises of wealth and power," answered Mongfhionn. As the Sidhe sighed, another sound was heard in the Great Hall: a baby demanding food. "Yet, there is hope… and there is Brianag."

CHAPTER 37

393 B.C—Before Lugnasad

The door creaked open, and two pairs of tiny feet padded across the room to the cot where Ealasaid slept. The young girls looked long and hard at their mother and wondered if they would be as beautiful when older.

One sighed. She, and her twin, did not mind living in the small round-house in the community on the northern side of the Sleagh. However, their ma constantly complained about the unfairness and injustice of their situation. That being the daughter of Finnean Mac Sèitheach, she was of noble birth and deserved better. Yet the twins did not think that being the granddaughters of the mad and murderous rìgh of Dùn Na Mèadaidh was a good thing.

They stood at their mother's head, and a look of sadness and pity alighted on their faces. Yet something sinister also lurked behind the pale, blue eyes. Two blades flashed in the torchlight. As they bent over the cot, long black hair fell forward, brushing their mother's nose. Ealasaid sneezed, and her eyes opened. She felt the sharp point of the knives prick her throat and the thin lines of blood trickle down. For the first time in her life, Ealasaid froze.

"This is for our da."

The blades sliced through Ealasaid's neck like a knife through summer butter. As the young girls stepped back, they listened to the horrific gurgling as Ealasaid fought for life. "You should have killed us, too, Mother.

That was a mistake."

"I know, yet I had hopes for you," Ealasaid choked out in her last moments before drowning in her blood.

CHAPTER 38

393 B.C.—Samhain

Gràinne Ni Fearghal, A 'Bhanrìgh Fuil and Bhanrìgh of the Na Daoine Tùrsach sat on the ornately carved throne and listened to the waters lapping against the great piles of the crannag. Winter had come, and soon the loch would freeze. Only the songs of the wind would break the silence of the high mountains. Thoughts of deep winter made her shiver, and she pulled the thick wolf fur closer.

To Gràinne's west, her closest neighbour, Seonag, Bhanrìgh of the Forest People, battled to forge unity in her tribe. Turmoil and bloodshed reigned as Seonag and Teàrlag fought to defeat the rebellion and secure the throne. If successful, Seonag would be the most powerful of the northern rulers. Would she be content to stay in the forests?

Gràinne knew that many of the Forest People, including Seonag's mother, Teàrlag, mistrusted Gràinne. Could she blame them? They argued for one last battle to rid Northern Albu of the curse of the Blood Queen and the Na Daoine Tùrsach. Gràinne sacrificed daily to the Goddess and prayed that her friendship with Seonag would forestall war.

Before sunset, Niall, who remained the Battle Commander of the significantly depleted Ravens, and his men would join Amodocus and her to celebrate Samhain. So far, the Ravens had not selected a king. Gràinne hoped to convince Niall that the Na Daoine Tùrsach, the Ravens, and the handful of minor, north-eastern tribes, should merge. Would they accept her as bhanrigh, or would she have to conquer them?

Further west, Cassán and Eimhir, now rìgh and bhanrigh, ruled their expanded kingdom from the fortresses of Dùn Brion and Dùn Athad. Seonag had not been happy at ceding Dùn Athad to Cassán, which did not bode well. Yet Seonag had more immediate priorities. Also, while Gràinne mourned the loss of Brion, as did Cassán and Eimhir, Seonag had been inconsolable and stricken with grief.

Cassán saw Gràinne as a curse on his family. He blamed her for his father's death and Brianag's exile to the Aes Sidhe. Yet how could she be held responsible for the Baobhan Sith? Without A 'Bhanrigh Fuil, Sidheag would be the ruler of Northern Albu. Gràinne frowned. She also worried that Cassán and Eimhir had adopted Ealasaid's daughters. The act of charity was lauded by the Na Mèadaidh, but could mother-killers ever be trusted?

Gràinne sighed deeply. The burden of her throne rested heavily on her slender shoulders. What had happened to the carefree young woman who rutted whomever she wanted? A kick in her belly made her smile, and she caressed the growing swell. *Maybe not all is bad.*

Sadness furrowed her brow as she thought of Brianag. She ached for the touch of her daughter. Both had heightened powers, which meant they could "talk." But Brianag had shunned any contact since being taken away by Mongfhionn. Only frequent updates from Neamhain lifted Gràinne's mood.

She exhaled another great sigh and smiled as she watched the cloud of crystals dissipate. Then she inhaled deeply. There would be no more Blood Queens. The bloodline from the dawn of the Na Daoine Tùrsach had been broken. All her daughters were *bastardaí* and impure. She was the last of the pure-born queens. Gràinne laughed loudly and listened as the sound echoed pleasantly off the crannag's wooden walls.

Maybe being a wanton slut had its advantages.

The End

BACKGROUND

Modern-day Scotland is, undoubtedly, a beautiful country. However, the Scotland of 400 B.C. must have been truly breathtaking. Coast-to-coast, much of the land was covered by vast swathes of ancient pine forests: the Caledonian Forest. Today, less than one per cent of the immense forests of Scotland remain. The woods contained not just pine but also birch, rowan, oak, and juniper. The forest ecosystem would have been abundant in ferns, mosses, lichens, and wildlife. Wolves, lynxes, deer, aurochs (giant wild cattle), elk, boar and bears hunted or grazed. Many species of birds were present, including ravens, eagles, hawks, and buzzards.

Dùn Athad (Dunadd): Situated in western Scotland, Dunadd is a rocky crag that may once have been an island. It now lies inland near the River Add. The surrounding land was boggy and known as the Mòine Mhòr ("Great Moor") in Scottish Gaelic, which, no doubt, increased the defensive potential of the site. Detailed analysis of sea-level changes in the region argues that the dùn was an island or promontory into historical times.

Dùn Brion (Stirling Castle): The location of Stirling Castle, at the divide between the highlands and the lowlands of Scotland, has to be one of the most strategic strongholds in Scotland and the United Kingdom. It sits imperiously atop a rocky crag. The Romans bypassed Stirling, building a fort at Doune instead. The rock may have been occupied by the Maeatae: a confederation of tribes, and the inspiration for the Na Mèadaidh in the story, at this time.

Cùil Daothail (Culduthel): Situated two miles south-west of Inverness, the Iron Age settlement at Culduthel is one of the most significant later prehistoric sites identified in mainland Scotland. Archaeological excavations have revealed a craftworking centre which specialised in producing iron, bronze and glass objects between the late 1st Millennium BC and early 1st Millennium AD. (*An Iron Age Craftworking Centre in North-East Scotland, Candy Hatherley & Ross Murray*).

***

Modern man (or woman) thinks in terms of days, minutes, and hours or in miles, feet, and inches (kilometres, metres, and centimetres), which is quite boring. The Gaels were much more imaginative. In the novel, as far as possible, I have measured time and distance by referring to natural or physical attributes and traditional festivals.

Specifically, regarding time, I have used the sun and moon cycles, with a heavier emphasis on the moon. The ancient Gaels counted time by nights rather than days, hence the use of "sunsets" rather than days. Distance is a more straightforward concept to convey than time. Using metrics such as hand, arms-length or pace is readily understood. The challenge is describing long distances, but this can be overcome by indicating how long the journey would take a person to walk, jog, march, canter, or gallop.

I have read that some Ancient Celts measured long distances by how far away they could still hear a bell clang. One measurement of area was based on how many cows could graze sustainably on the land. As I said, much less boring than the metric or imperial systems.

***

Baobhan Sith: According to Scottish Mythology, the Baobhan Sith (*baa'van see*), also known as the White Women, were thought to be fairies. Not all fairies are like Tinkerbell in Peter Pan! They usually appeared as beautiful young women. Legend has it they had hoofs, which they kept hidden under long dresses, instead of feet.

Similar to vampires, the Baobhan Sith drank the blood of human victims and avoided exposure to sunlight. Unlike vampires, the Baobhan Sith used their long, sharp fingernails to slit their victims' necks to drink blood. The Baobhan Sith favoured a wolf form and had only two known weaknesses: fear of horses and vulnerability to iron.

* * *

The Hag (Cailleach): Many Celtic goddesses are beautiful young women with flowing red hair—but not all. Some of the most powerful goddesses in Scottish and Irish lore are "hags." Among the more powerful deities in Celtic mythology, hags can command the elements—earth, wind, water, and fire—and control the weather.

Most myths claim the Hag was the mother of all the other gods and goddesses. Despite being a creator, the Hag was a harsh and brutal figure. She was a goddess of storms, high winds, and bitter cold. She was a healer but also a terrible destroyer of life.

The Hag has appeared in *The Conall Series* since the first book and in subsequent spin-offs: *The Dog Roses* and *The Blood Queen*. She is seen as the alter ego of Mongfhionn, who is already a fearsome Sidhe. The Hag strives for dominance over Mongfhionn and appears increasingly aggressive in her desire. I often wonder what will happen to Mongfhionn if the Hag succeeds!

GLOSSARY

<u>**IRISH GAELIC**</u>

Aes Sidhe (Race of demi-goddesses)
An Fiagaí Dorcha (The Dark Huntress)
Bean-sidhe/mná-sidhe (Banshee/s)
Bitseach/bitseacha (Bitch/s)
Bròg-éille (Boots)
Caomhnóirí (Personal guard)
Ceannairí céad (Leader of one hundred)
Chomhairle (Council)
Craic (Good conversation)
Cret /creta (Chariot box/s)
Dillat (Thick horse blanket)
Léine/léinte (Dress/s)
Póg mo thoin (Kiss my arse)
Prionnsa (Prince)
Seanchaí (Storyteller)
Sgiath/sgiatha (Spear/s)
Sidhe (Demi-goddess)
Striapach/striapacha (Whore/s)
Rí/Ríthe (King/s)
Triubhas (Pants/trousers)
Tuilí (Bastard)

A 'Bhanrìgh Fuil (The Blood Queen)
A ghlaoic (Idiot)
Baobhan Sith (Female fairy/succubus/vampire-spirit)
Bastardaí (Illegitimate)
Bàta/bàtaichean (Boat/s)
Bean-shìdh/mnathan-shìdh (Banshee/s)
Bidse/bidsean (Bitch/s)
Bradáin (Salmon)
Brat/bratan (Blanket/s)
Brògan (Shoes)
Caisearbhan (Dandelion)
Caolas (Straits)
Carbaid (Chariots)
Ceannard-ceud (Leader of one hundred)
Ceann-sleagha (Spearhead)
Clamhan (Buzzard)
Comhairle-Chatha (High Council)
Crannag (Fort on water)
Dùn/dùin (Fort/s)
Fear-bàta (Boatman)
Fine (A subset of a clan)
Fuath (Malevolent spirits)
Gruth (Oatmeal/gruel)
Gun teàrnadh; cha gheill (No retreat; no surrender)
Ionnsaigh (Forward)
Lean do rìgh (Follow your king)
Lince (Lynx)
Meadhan-oidhche (Midnight)
Maighdeanas (Virginity)
Meadhan-latha (Midday)
Pit (Vulva)

Prionnsa (Prince)
Seanchaidhean (Storytellers)
Sgiath/Sgiathan (Shield/s)
Sleagh/sleaghan (Spear/s)
Rìgh/rìghrean (King/s)
Strìopach/strìopachan (Whore/s)
Tha thu a' bruidhinn tro d'asal (You talk through your arse)
Tuireadh (Death Song)

<u>TRIBES</u>

Aos na Coille (Scottish)
Clann Ui Flaithimh (Irish)
Gaiscedach (Gaul/France)
Na Daoine Tùrsach (Scottish)
Na Mèadaidh (Scottish)

DRAMATIS PERSONNÆ

<u>**IRISH**</u>

Áine Ni Dedad

Beacán Ó Cathasaigh

Brianag Ni Brion

Brighid Ni Conall

Brion Ó Cathasaigh

Cassán Mac Brion

Conall Mac Gabhann

Cearbhall Ó Domhnaill

Danu Ni Conall

Fearghal Ruadh

Gormal Mac Eachdonn

Gràinne Ni Fearghal

Íar Mac Dedad

Iasg

Mongfhionn

Mórrígan Ni Cathasaigh

Neamhain Ni Fearghal

Nuadha Ó Dubhghaill

Sorchae Ni Íar

Torcán Ó Dubhghaill

Uallachán Ó Dubhghaill

<u>**SCOTTISH**</u>
Blàr Mac Artair
Brandubh Mac Artair
Carmag Mac an t-Sionnaich
Ceana Nic Sèitheach
Crum Dubh
Diadhaidh
Drostan Ruadh
Dùghlas
Eachdonn Breac
Ealasaid Nic Finnean
Eimhir Nic Finnean
Failbhe
Finnean Mac Sèitheach
Gòrdan
Madadh
Malmhìn
Mòrag Nic Artair
Ròidh Mac Eachdonn
Seirbhiseach na Fala
Seonag Nic Drostan
Sidheag
Sionn
Teàrlag Nic an t-Sionnaich

<u>**OTHER**</u>
Amodocus (Thracian)
Ares (God)
Kartimandu
Heilasa (Thracian)
Pytheas (Greek)

LOCATIONS

<u>SCOTLAND</u>

Abhainn Dubh (River)

Abhainn Nis (River)

Cùil Daothail (Culduthel nr. Inverness, Scotland)

Dùn Brion (Hillfort, Scotland)

Dùn Athad (Hillfort, Scotland)

Mòine Mhòr (Marshes)

Northern Albu (Scotland)

Otherworld (Gael Hell)

The Sleagh (Mountain range)

<u>OTHER</u>

Aremorio (North-west France)

Albu (England)

Curraghatoor (Hillfort, Ireland)

Ériu (Ireland)

Gaul (France)

Great Sea (Mediterranean)

Lugudunon (Fortress, France)

Mag Mell (Warrior afterlife)

Mai Dún (Hillfort, England)

Massalia (Marseille)

Southern Albu (England)

Thracia (South-east Balkans)

ABOUT THE AUTHOR

Born in Belfast, Northern Ireland, internationally published and award-winning author David H. Millar is the founder, owner, and author-in-residence of A Wee Publishing Company. This business seeks to promote Celtic literature, authors, and art.

Millar moved from wet Northern Ireland to Nova Scotia, Canada, in the late 1990s. After ten years of shovelling snow, he relocated to warmer climates and settled in Houston, Texas. Quite a contrast!

An avid reader, armchair sportsman, and Liverpool Football Club fan, Millar lives with his family and Bailey, a Manx cat of questionable disposition known to his friends as "the small angry one"!

Millar is the author of the five-volume, ancient Celtic-based Conall series and *The Dog Roses* spin-off. *The Blood Queen* is a second spin-off from the Conall series.

KEEP IN TOUCH

Comments and feedback will be greatly appreciated. You can find me at any of the following:

FACEBOOK
https://www.facebook.com/aweepublishingco

GOODREADS AUTHOR PAGE
https://www.goodreads.com/DavidHMillar

INSTAGRAM
Author.DavidHMillar

TWITTER
@DavidHMillar

WEBSITE/BLOG
http://www.aweepublishingco.com/